The Graelian Chronicles Book One

THE TALE OF TIERNAN

James Colson

To request permissions, contact the publisher at info@jamescolsonbooks.com.

ISBN:979-8-9901227-2-7 (Hardback)
ISBN: 979-8-9901227-0-3 (Paperback)
ISBN: 979-8-9901227-1-0 (eBook)

First edition printing 2024

Cover art by Renee Colson
Book design by James Colson
Map design by John Flanagan II & James Colson

James Colson
PO Box 64
Dunkirk, OH 45836
www.JamesColsonBooks.com

To my loving wife who has supported me through many edits and revisions, not to mention her tireless dedication to our family. Also, to both of our children who are without a doubt, the best kids a father could ask for.

To God be the Glory for helping me complete this work.

CONTENTS

Rosewood Forest
Mystic Mornings
Fabled Wonders
Oakshadow
Farna
Castle Abria
Abrian Plateau
Cave of Tera
Lakedon
Lake Conchobar
Milston
Northwick
Great Sea
Lorelei
Valley Woods
Lily of the Valley
Valley Mountains
Whispersong
Clericsfold
Alwyn Point
Alwyn
Kingscrown Rock
Lorelei River
Windale Mountains
Kingscrown Bay
Great Sea
Idlewind
Windale Desert
Abria

Prologue

Inititium

Tiernan didn't want to think about the last time he was here. Standing at the entrance of The Drunken Alligator, his heart was heavy. Full of regret. Sadness. Loss.

The cool, twilight air blowing throughout this once sizable village seemed to remind him of the coldness permeating throughout his soul, of a world come and gone.

As he reached for the door handle in front of him, a twinge of pain surged through his body. The metalwork bore a distinctive trademark design he knew all too well: Borun. Tiernan slowly retracted his hand, letting his arm fall to his side. He froze in place for a moment. He didn't *expect* to feel this reaction, yet probably *should* have. Tiernan came here, to the village known as Lily of the Valley, hoping to find some closure.

Maybe even an answer.

How is it a piece of metal could remind me of my failures? Finding the strength somehow, Tiernan turned away from the door. Instead, he walked around to the Alligator's western wall in the direction of an abandoned lumber mill a few hundred meters away. Standing proud — or at least, it used to — was Borun Mill.

One last look. Slowly, he walked toward the outer wall of the mill. Already, the giant water wheel that sat along the banks of the Lorelei River was gone — sold by the new owners to cover their personal debts. Its impressive visage had been a symbol of hope and prosperity for this community, not to mention all who passed through its boundaries. Now, however, the absence of the water wheel felt wrong. Which, so far, was all Tiernan had been feeling on this journey.

Step by step, he made his way to his intended destination. He figured the doors would be locked, but maybe he could peer through a window? Alas, it was not meant to be. The flowers in the field *between* the Alligator and the mill betrayed his emotions greater than he could handle. Their fragrance made his sorrow flare up even more than it already was. The aroma of the Valley Rose brought about a rapid outpouring of an emotional flood, overwhelming all his senses.

Every scent from each rose reminded him of her. Her joy. Her passion for life.

Her sacrifice.

Tiernan fell to his knees, sobbing. He pounded his fist into the ground, crushing a few other flowers in his anger. In a moment of fiery warrior fierceness, Tiernan yelled with all of his might as he grabbed the handle of his sword with both hands and thrust it into the ground in front of him. He drove the blade deeper than expected, which was fine by him.

He was powerless, and didn't need that worthless piece of metal anyway. *Let it stay here and rust, for all I care. I'm done with it all.* Using the sword's hilt, Tiernan stood up and wiped the tears from his cheeks. He stared at the mill for a moment until he couldn't take it anymore and turned away.

Borun Mill, the flowers, the smells, and all these things represented were too much. Maybe one day he could come back here. Take a tour of the mill and see what it had become. Rumors had spread in recent months that Tammith and Dagnall planned to turn it into some kind of wedding venue, like one for couples to get married in.

Like the one Eislyn and I were married in. He shook his head as he slowly walked back to the entrance of the Drunken Alligator. *How the mighty have fallen.*

This time, he closed his eyes as he reached for the door handle. Perhaps this time if he didn't *see* its Borun-designed metalwork, he wouldn't know it was there. Quickly pushing the door open, he took one final breath before walking inside.

Maybe no one will notice me.

The Drunken Alligator smelled exactly as he remembered: a curious mix of wood, mead, and whatever bottom-of-the-barrel cheap paint they used for the walls. A person could walk into one of these blindfolded and know exactly where they were. The floor was slick with condensation from the Valley and yet sticky every so often. It was warmer in here than outside, probably because of the burning fireplace on the eastern wall.

Its flickering glow exuded warmth, and was some of the only light in the entire room. It looked like there may be a candle or two at the back of the bar, and perhaps a fire from an oven somewhere out of sight. Otherwise, the inside of the Alligator gave off a brooding, dim atmosphere. Two other patrons were huddled over their respective drinks, using a set of chairs nearest the fireplace, not saying a word to each other.

Tiernan scanned the rest of the establishment, and thankfully, no one looked up to meet his gaze. Better yet, there was a single, unoccupied table in the corner. Each Drunken Alligator across the Kingdom was unique. Some were large; others, like this one, were much more standard-sized. Rumor had it there was even a smaller Drunken Alligator hidden somewhere at Fabled Wonders, one of the few places you could still go in the Kingdom to forget about the war.

In the back of the room, another man was already passed out. The bartender behind the counter seemed too focused on counting money to pay attention to the drunken man she had in her establishment. *Funny. In my day I wouldn't have allowed that.*

He heard a voice chastising him. It was the voice of his sister telling him to get off of his self-righteous soapbox. Or, as she used to put it in not so pleasant words, 'his almighty, all-knowing, all-arrogant, ignorant, feeble-minded soapbox.' The memory of his sister's words made him smile, even if briefly. It was a fleeting moment though, as his sadness quickly resurfaced and his self-loathing took over.

Tiernan considered purchasing a famous Lorelian Mead. He hadn't had one since the night before his wedding. That day felt like a millennium ago. *So much has happened since then.*

On the eve before, he and his best friend Wayland had celebrated, as most men do. The next day, Tiernan and Eislyn exchanged their eternal vows. Their joy was short-lived, however, as not long thereafter they witnessed the futility of the threat facing them with the arrival of the great and imposing Leviathan.

Wayland, my friend. How I need you by my side once again. Tiernan's internal monologue continued to remind him of the events that followed, though they were just as painful to recall as any other. Tiernan remembered how he had promised everyone present he wouldn't touch mead again until they won the war facing them.

Unfortunately, victory never came. *So, what right do I have to celebrate now?* Instead, Tiernan walked over to the unoccupied table and laid his shield on the ground next to one of its legs. Taking a long, slow breath, he sat and immediately closed his eyes to rest.

It was a moment all too short, as he sensed the presence of another person. Did he hear their footfalls? Or was it the subtle change in the surrounding air announcing the arrival of whoever was about to disrupt his respite? Either way, his attempt at rest was over almost before it even began.

Time to face the music.

Tiernan opened his eyes. Standing before him was the bartender from before. She was a tough, rugged woman with long, flowing locks of hair. The shadows from the fire's flame behind her partially obscured her ebony complexion in an almost sinister-like glow. Her face was firm, chiseled, and confident even if somewhat hidden by the light.

Still, he recognized her. Her confidence alone revealed her identity.

"Nice to see you again, Tammith. How is Dagnall?" His friendliness betrayed reality. Tiernan was only vaguely aware of the couple, instead letting an associate handle most of the process of selling the mill.

But, while Tiernan himself had only met Tammith and Dagnall once — he was too busy with the war by that point — he also had an uncanny ability to remember everyone he met. You could almost call it a curse. *Perhaps the Dark Elf did something to me after all.*

To her credit, Tammith kept a serious, businesslike demeanor, which now appeared more intense with the flame from the fireplace encompassing her head. Instead of acknowledging his question, she moved on. Coldly so, perhaps ready for matters to move along to more important decisions: his order.

"What will you have?"

Not Lorelian Mead. No matter what, he would not break his oath. Tiernan leaned around Tammith, trying to see what else she had behind the bar. Maybe someone from Oakshadow had delivered some Dorian Ale, the drink his father preferred? Sure, it was called "ale", but this was only to increase sales to adults during theatrical performances.

Noticing his movement, Tammith stopped him. "No, we don't have any Dorian Ale. Only the real stuff here."

Tiernan sighed. *Maybe she'd be happy if I ordered food? Time for some of that famous Tiernan charm Eislyn fell in love with.* He looked at her and smiled before talking. "Could I get a loaf of your famous bread? People from Northwick to Alwyn have told me about it. And, if it's not too much trouble, a water?" If she was annoyed he wasn't ordering Lorelian Mead, Tiernan could not tell. Tammith nodded her head and headed back to the bar without saying a word.

As she left, Tiernan leaned forward on the table, resting his head in his hands. *It's going to be like this everywhere, isn't it?* King Rhys had offered him a quiet place in Lorelei to stay out of sight, and Tiernan was beginning to wonder if he should have accepted the offer.

After a few moments of silence, Tiernan began to smell something different than the usual odors of the Alligator.

Tammith's bread. Tasty, or so he had heard. Soft, warm, and fluffy, rumor had it one taste of her bread could make you forget any heartache.

Truth be told, the Lorelian Mead she often served with it was the more likely culprit of erasing one's memory.

"You've been through a lot, haven't you?" Tiernan raised his head toward the sound of the voice. One of the men near the fireplace had approached him. A tall, frail man, one who appeared to be near the end of his life.

Did he used to work at the mill?

"That's one way of putting it. Can I help you?" *With any luck, he doesn't recognize me.*

"Your shield. I know its design. That means you're *old*." He chuckled. "Like me." It took everything Tiernan had not to laugh out loud.

Old! Sure, people in our Kingdom live a long time. But have you looked in the mirror? Tiernan realized he hadn't looked in a mirror for a while, not to mention, the years hadn't been kind to him. Do *I look as bad as this old guy too?*

"Abria is gone. Zoran made sure of that." This was a half-truth, Tiernan admitted to himself. *It's my fault too. All of this is my fault.* Before he could say anything else, the old man placed his hand on Tiernan's shoulder.

Immediately, things changed. He felt something different inside of him. His sister used to describe the surge of magic through her veins as a powerful, unbelievable sensation. Truth be told, Tiernan had never entirely understood her Dragonborn connection.

Until this moment, anyway. The man spoke again. "My name is Zachary. I served in the Abrian Royal Guard long before you were born.

"Those alive today need to know what happened. The *full* story. Not part of it. Too many have already forgotten how things were before Zoran, let alone before Kane. But you remember. You were there for all of it." The old man smiled. "Well, most of it. Look." Tiernan shook his head in confusion at first, but followed the old man's gaze. His focus was on the table where a quill and large stack of paper now rested.

"How did…" In the blink of an eye, the man was gone. Tiernan felt the hand leave his shoulder and turned his head to look for him. It was to no avail, as there was no evidence of the man whatsoever.

Tammith reappeared with his water and bread. She didn't act as if she had seen anything, nor did the man still sitting by the fire seem aware his partner was now gone.

"Your bread. *And water.*" Tammith put an emphasis on the last part. Was she mocking him? Was she annoyed? Either way, she placed his food and drink on the table. "Going to do some writing?"

Tiernan didn't know what to say, and instead just bobbed his head up and down. Tammith gave him a slight nod, turned around, and headed back to the bar.

The bread felt warm to the touch as Tiernan tore off a small section of the loaf. He could smell the aroma even more powerfully now, and there was something in it he didn't recognize — a taste of the Valley, perhaps? Something she learned during the heyday of the Market?

Either way, it was good. Almost as good as everyone claimed it to be. Unfortunately, he hadn't forgotten anything yet. *Definitely the mead.*

Tiernan realized that even more odd than the appearance of the quill and paper, his pain seemed to intensify. *Probably just me thinking about the old market.* Tiernan took a drink of water and remembered the first meal he had enjoyed from a now-famous culinary artist named Kellag after the latter opened his restaurant in the Market.

This thought brought his attention back to the quill and paper. He picked it up, and an overwhelming urge to write filled his soul. *A magic quill?*

"Snap out of it, Tiernan. You're not drunk." Still full of doubt, the urge to write refused to leave.

Where would he start? *The beginning, obviously.* But what was the beginning?

The old man's words and smile flashed through his mind: "You were there for all of it. Well, most of it."

Tiernan frowned. "What good is this going to do? We're in a war, and so few people even have access to the Alwyn Böchord." He chided himself. *Who am I even talking to? I'm alone at this table!*

Tiernan looked down at the blank paper once again. *Here goes nothing.* In large, bold, artistic script, he wrote the first thing that came to his mind.

The Tale of Tiernan

Chapter 1

899NE

The 16th day of Florin began like any other day. As usual, the sun rose in the east, first peeking its head over the Windale Desert coastline followed by the Valley Mountains before eventually illuminating the rest of the land. As its rays spread westward across the Kingdom of Abria, the cities and towns within the realm slowly began to wake up and start their morning routine.

First, the shops of Idlewind opened their doors and pulled back their curtains, signifying they were ready for business. Meanwhile, the stable hands at Whispersong began their assigned daily duties, some tending to the animals while others prepared a caravan of horses for a northbound trek to Lorelei.

There — the home of the original Drunken Alligator — community leaders were discussing plans for expansion. Lorelian Mead was catching on throughout the rest of the Kingdom, and local brewers were looking for ways to grow their customer base.

Further to the north, both Milston and Northwick were alive with activity. Sister cities within the Kingdom, they often shared resources and leadership. Residents from one community would often work in the other and vice versa. Northwick had plans to one day open a shipping port, though there were the usual uncertainties — especially since it had the potential to overhaul the entire economy of Northeastern Abria. Not to mention, this act might even necessitate the two communities declare independence from each other. No one knew how this would play out exactly which had delayed the rollout of this new endeavor.

In the far west, playwrights in Oakshadow were busy looking for cast members for an upcoming theatrical production. In the southwest, those in the community of Alwyn were looking for ways to grow tourism along the beaches lining the Abrian coastline.

Central Abria was no different with the Clericsfold Council looking for ways to transition their economy into the new millennium. While a little over one hundred years away, it would be here before anyone knew it. Meanwhile, further north in Lakedon, leadership had begun the process of capitalizing on the extensive opportunities Lake Conchobar presented.

Simply put, across the rest of the Kingdom, city by city and village by village, it was the same happening: trade negotiations, recreational activities, commerce, couples preparing to take the next stage of their relationship, families planning trips to the famed Mystic Mornings, and so on. Throughout the land, *nothing* would prepare the residents of Abria for what was about to happen.

By all measurable standards, 16 Florin 899NE was a relatively unremarkable day when it began.

Farna was the Kingdom's westernmost fortification, sitting proudly atop the Abrian Plateau as the capital of the Kingdom. The royal residence, a structure known as Castle Abria, occupied a large portion of the northwestern section of the town.

Beyond the Abrian acropolis was a vast wilderness that began with a mountainous barrier. This kept Abria relatively isolated from many other parts of the world. Once in a while, travelers would make their way through the treacherous wilds on the other side and scale the mountains, making landfall near Oakshadow. Far more commonly, if infrequently, visitors arrived via the docks at Alwyn.

Within Farna itself, skies were clear. As usual, birds told their stories through song while animals roamed free, unafraid and at ease. Smells of Abrian Flake Pie — made popular by the local Drunken Alligator — filled the air with their sweet yet somewhat savory aroma. Overhead, the mid-morning sun shone brightly, illuminating the land with its piercing glow. Townsfolk moved throughout the streets, laughing and talking with each other. Children played with their friends in a friendly game of Smithblitz, a sport with formal rules, though no one seemed to ever follow them to the letter. After all, why worry about unimportant details like rules when things were so pleasant and joyful?

The city walls themselves helped keep things moving smoothly. Made of a rare mineral extracted from the mountains near Milston, they had a permanent — if subtle — golden glow.

Some have said it was impossible to have a bad day in Farna, even if the skies were overcast. The city itself exuded joy, which made all who visited her embrace life.

Around the third hour of the morning, vendors began opening their doors for business. Shop owners in Idlewind often mocked their counterparts within the walls of Farna for their perceived lack of urgency. According to the residents of Idlewind, if the sun was up, you were already running late. While nothing more than a friendly rivalry, it did highlight the different ways of life across the Kingdom.

After all, in Idlewind they had made their home in the harshness of the Windale Desert; yet in Farna, they had the perpetual luxury of relatively comfortable weather all year long. Whether in the middle of the year during Flametide or the cool of Darkember, the ambient air temperature remained pleasant all twelve months of the year within the Abrian Plateau.

Indeed, the month of Florin wasn't known for its warm temperatures throughout the *rest* of the Kingdom. In the northernmost regions such as Milston, Northwick, and Lakedon, snow was continuing to fall. Lake Conchobar was still frozen over, though further south near Kingscrown Rock, the Darkember and Begynde snow had mostly melted.

This past season, Farna only had a few days where temperatures cooled enough for snow to fall, though it didn't stick and was mostly warm by midday. Some questioned this weather pattern. After all, even as far south as the beaches near Alwyn, temperatures during the season of Frost could drop below freezing. While the warmer waters of the Great Sea kept the city of Alwyn itself comfortable, more than a few times in recent years there was enough precipitation on the northern beaches for children to build snow forts.

Granted, the snow never lasted long enough, often gone in a day or two. Nevertheless, even when this particular weather phenomenon hit Alwyn, Farna stayed comfortable. Rumors spread, as they do, that there was some kind of magic protecting the Abrian Plateau from the change in the seasons.

Others claimed there was an underground river or ever-persistent flow of lava that somehow made the difference. Expeditions below ground to confirm either theory were few and far between. The Cave of Tera — the primary entrance to what lay beneath the surface — was too treacherous to risk exploring. Therefore, the residents of Farna simply accepted reality rather than try to understand it.

Regardless, none of this made 16 Florin 899NE any *different* than the day before, a week ago, or even the same day from the previous year. It was warm and sunny with relatively low humidity. The grasses of the fields were as green as they could be. Even the insects seemed to be content. This was in sharp contrast to more humid areas of the Kingdom, such as the Rosewood Forest where a small Elven population lived.

Not long after the vendors and shops opened their doors within Farna, a worried man began frantically walking from shop to shop. His countenance was a stark contrast to the rest of those in his community.

This individual, a woodworking craftsman named Davien, was a simple man — and one who worked hard to support his beloved wife, Kyrie. Despite the joy around him, on his face today was a look of sickly worry and concern, one focused on the love of his life and the ailment she was experiencing.

For a moment, he allowed himself to reminisce. Their wedding had been simple. Her father hadn't necessarily liked him, as Davien had no recorded biological family. They had died when he was a newborn in a random accident which left Davien orphaned. He was raised in the community of Clericsfold, living in the orphanage there for many years. Davien made friends with ease and even befriended one of the town elders at a young age.

Davien would grow to think of this man as his father. This became a reality on his fifteenth birthday when the elder formally adopted him. Later in their life, they moved to the Valley until Davien set out on his own.

Kyrie's father held the lack of *biological* parents against Davien for whatever reason. When he had asked for her hand in marriage, Kyrie's father only begrudgingly said yes. Davien could tell his soon-to-be father-in-law did so because he was forced to. Davien assumed it was because of his now mother-in-law, who adored him. Not long after, Davien and Kyrie tied the knot at the reception hall within Alwyn.

As time went on, Davien had some difficulty finding his place in the world, despite his friendliness and ability to be well-liked. He had taken a few random jobs since they married twenty-some odd years ago. They moved to Farna not long after exchanging their vows. And while jobs were plentiful, Davien struggled to keep one. The formative years of their marriage found them living in a single room home. However, the cramped conditions did not mean they were unhappy.

After all, the peace, joy, and happiness surrounding all who lived in Farna flowed through Kyrie and Davien's home as well.

One year, he worked the docks in Alwyn. This meant he was gone for weeks at a time, often staying in the local inn where they had taken their honeymoon. After that adventure, Davien tended the fields within the Abrian Plateau, acting as a farmhand for whomever would hire him.

Finally, he found a passion for woodworking. He opened a small shop in his home, which allowed him and Kyrie time to be together more than they had at any prior point in their marriage. Eventually, this grew into a substantial business. Davien's reputation as a craftsman preceded him. One of his favorite pieces was a desk he had made for the leader of Idlewind. More well-known was the throne he made for the current King of Abria some time ago.

Davien smiled to himself, reflecting on the path his life had taken. "And then there were three." His words snapped him out of his trance, and he remembered where he was standing: inside the local apothecary. In his hand was a bottle of pills. A voice behind him spoke.

"Those won't fix morning sickness. Trust me." Davien turned to the voice behind him. "My wife tried them too, back when we were expecting our son. How far along is she?" The shop owner smiled in welcome. Whether he overheard Davien's comment or recognized the look of a man desperately trying to help his wife, Davien couldn't tell. He put the small bottle back on the shelf and walked up to the counter.

"Believe it or not, she's due in about three weeks. What's your name?" Davien asked as he offered his hand to the shop owner.

Grabbing Davien's outstretched hand and shaking it firmly, the shop owner responded, "Arnon. So, she's been sick all this time?" Davien nodded in frustration.

"It's been maddening. We've seen her doctor weekly for the past few months. Most women told her she'd be feeling better by Origlow, Moonshadow at the latest. It hasn't gotten any better, and seems to be getting worse by the day as we get closer to the due date." Davien raised his head to meet Arnon's gaze before he continued. "She's been feeling the baby move more, and he or she has taken a special interest in kicking her stomach. I don't think she's kept anything down this week."

Arnon bent down behind the counter. He returned holding a small brown box. Not much more than a handful of centimeters square, it had the mark of a dragon's head on its top. Arnon pulled out a key from his pocket to unlock it. Next, he opened the box, inside of which sat a single red jewel.

"About sixty years ago, my wife found this on a...what did they call it? Ah yes, an 'Escaping the ball-and-chain ladies' trip.'" He shook his head as he smiled. "She and a bunch of her friends visited Oakshadow to the north and on the way home, she found this lying on the path. Unguarded, no one in sight for miles. We took it to Clericsfold and the scholars there scoured the Archives for weeks. Eventually, all they could tell us was, 'One day you will know when this is needed.' Cryptic, right? I dunno, maybe they were right. I feel like this is for you."

Davien picked up the jewel and carefully eyed it. There wasn't anything special about it. The jewel was no bigger than his thumb, distinctly oval. Where it had rested on a bed of purple satin was now a perfectly shaped indent. He returned the jewel, to its bed. *He's had this since I was ten...wait, was that a glow?* Confused, Davien closed the lid. "How much? I only have a couple silver din with me..."

Arnon shook his head. "It's on the house." Davien looked down and admired the dragon head carving on the top of the box. Arnon noticed his gaze and spoke again. "Don't ask me what it means. Last I knew, dragons were mythical. Or at the least, had gone extinct long before the New Era began."

Suddenly, Davien remembered the reason for his visit. "And my wife, with her morning sickness. Do you have anything?" Arnon shook his head as he pointed at the box. Still confused, Davien asked, "Are you serious? This jewel...?"

"I can't explain it. It's a strong impression I can't shake. Listen, just take it. If she still feels bad tomorrow, come back. I'll give you anything you want, on the house. Do we have a deal?" Arnon extended his hand. Davien eyed it for a moment, looked at the box, and turned his gaze back to Arnon's hand. He grabbed the outstretched hand, gave it a solid, single shake, and turned for the exit.

Davien knew he was in trouble. Kyrie had sent him out for several items: Abrian Darkloaf Bread (the only food she could keep down), water (he was to refill their jars at the central well, which he also forgot to take with him), and something for her sickness. Instead, he brought back a box with a jewel inside. Davien stood motionless at his home's doorstep for a few moments, trying to decide what to do.

He couldn't do anything about the forgotten jars. For that, he would have to go back out. It's possible he could still find bread to buy from the Full Moon Bakery, though it was more likely her favorite would be sold out.

And what about this jewel? What is she supposed to do, hold it? Look at it, gaze into its shiny reflection? That's sure to fix her stomach problems.

Maybe her father wasn't such an idiot after all?

Davien reached for the door. Their home, a small and simplistic cottage near one of the town's outer walls, betrayed the wealth they had accumulated in recent years. Nevertheless, they had one (if not random) exterior sign of luxury.

Their door had the most elaborate metal handle in the entire region. More elegant than those gracing the doors throughout Castle Abria, complete with intricate details and a pull perfectly fitted for Davien's hand. It seemed out of place compared to the frugality of their home. In addition, this piece of art stood out compared to the rest of the row of houses near his home and was the one thing Davien was known for.

Besides, of course, his expert carpentry skills.

Indeed, it was this unique piece of metallurgy that drew the attention of the King of Abria. After seeing it one day, the King sent a runner to discover who owned the estate. While Davien himself did not sculpt it, this encounter led to increased awareness of Davien's woodworking capabilities, and the order for the throne came in through this same messenger not long thereafter.

The King ordered two thrones, though no one understood why. After all, he did not have a queen, nor did he have an heir. In fact, if there was one cause for concern throughout the realm, it was that no one knew who would inherit the throne upon the King's death.

"Just act casual. She loves you. Remember, she loves you." Davien pushed open the door and walked into their living area. They had ample seating, a small table in the corner near Kyrie's stove, a fireplace along the eastern wall, and a bedroom separate from the main living area.

That in of itself was a rarity, a testament to Davien's woodworking skills as he custom modified many areas of their home as a gift to his wife. Detailed scrollwork adorned the mantle, matching the intricate designs he etched into the various crossbeams along their ceiling.

"If only it hadn't taken me almost two decades to figure this out," he would often say to Kyrie. They moved here from their first home, a one-room, small space on the opposite end of the city. However, they promised themselves to maintain a humble existence, saving money for whatever came next.

"Kyrie, I'm back." His voice cracked, though she was nowhere to be seen. "Kyrie?" he asked again, this time louder. Less worried about how she would react to his mistakes and now concerned she hadn't responded, he walked into their bedroom.

On the floor, his wife was lying motionless, a small pool of water near her abdomen on the ground. Davien rushed to her, dropping the box on their bed. Frantic, he began calling her name.

Inside of the box, the jewel began glowing.

Castle Abria was often a lonely place for Tiernan. He had made it what he could, but he frequently regretted not finding a wife or having children. Somewhere across the Kingdom, he had family. His brother had a son, though he hadn't heard from his sibling in years. Decades even. He had never even met his nephew. Tiernan had dispatched his best scouts on several missions, and none of them had found either his brother or his son.

It was almost as if they had disappeared. Tiernan had been considering what to do for years. Now an older man, time had replaced his once vibrant looks with wrinkles. His sandy blonde hair was now gray. Tiernan had never liked facial hair, always preferring to shave it off as often as he could. Yet, even in his later years he had given up on that. Now, he had a full beard extending just to the edge of his neck, colored as white as the hair on his head.

The passage of time had taken a toll on his body. He walked with a slight limp, though he hadn't sustained any injury. The doctor said an unknown disease was taking away his mobility. His hands shook at times, often when sitting at his desk or on his beautiful throne. What was the name of the man who made it for him? Daniel? Darius?

That was another problem. His memory and ability to think straight were fading. Memories from long ago were solid. The more recent ones, he struggled to recall. Tiernan knew the end was fast approaching, and the dilemma he had ignored for far too long was now staring him in the face.

Each morning, he sat in Castle Abria's tallest tower. Overlooking the fields of Farna, the window faced the east. From there, he could just make out the Valley Mountains in the far distance. As the sun rose over them today, he contemplated life. More importantly, he wondered who should take his place as King of Abria.

Should he step down and let the people decide?

Perhaps he should name a successor from the denizens of Farna?

Or what if he left it to fate? Would one of the other cities rise up and become the new hub of the Kingdom?

Could he convince one of the other city leaders to succeed him?

So many questions, and never answers. His family had ruled the Kingdom since the beginning of the New Era. Now, with just a little over 100 years to go until the first millennium concluded, he had accepted he was unlikely to live that long. After all, he had felt — more than once — the chest pains that took his father from him centuries ago. They often followed major episodes, either uncontrollable tremors or time slips, almost as if he closed his eyes and a few hours had passed.

Likewise, his grandfather had died in the same way. Doctors assumed the condition was hereditary, and all the signs pointed to him also passing away in a similar fashion as his two predecessors.

"At least they had an heir to take over," Tiernan lamented. Usually, one of the other members of the royal court would have been nearby. But not today. Earlier, he had asked for solitude, so his words faded into oblivion, no one to hear them or offer comfort.

Tiernan's habit was to sit here at least until he knew Idlewind began their morning. Under no circumstance would he start his daily routine until they were engaged in their activities.

It let him hold one over on his best friend, Midir. Both men were raised in Farna, though they didn't meet until both were nearing adulthood. After becoming as close as brothers, Midir's family moved to Idlewind not long after both boys finished their collegiate education. Midir's father was a powerful orator and had worked his way up in the political leadership here in Farna. After a while, he desired a new challenge and relocated his family to Idlewind.

Midir considered staying, but the rest of his family talked him into joining them. Not long thereafter, the people of Idlewind elected his father to the title of Manus, a label only used in Idlewind. In simple terms, it meant mayor, but to those who didn't know, it sounded deep, dark, and mysterious.

After a few decades of service, the title of Manus was made into a permanent position for Midir's father, not too dissimilar to that of a king. This meant the mantle would be passed to his next of kin. So, upon his father's death, Midir became the new Manus. Manus Midir.

It did not have a nice ring to it, a fact Tiernan made sure to point out to Midir every time they saw each other.

Nevertheless, the friendship and relatively friendly rivalry between the two regions grew as a direct result of Tiernan's connection with Midir. Still loyal to Abria, Idlewind often acted as a mini-kingdom-within-the-Kingdom. They had their own trade deals with Lorelei, for example, and had even sent a few expeditions deep within the Windale Desert. It was those explorers who had first mapped the outer edges of Abria. They openly shared the knowledge they amassed in exchange for building supplies. Idlewind had, under Midir's leadership, built a much more extensive fortress around the town. It helped to protect them from the rigors of the Windale Desert.

Tiernan watched as the sun's shadow over the Valley Mountains disappeared, which meant all the shops were open in Idlewind. It would be another few hours before anyone dared open their doors in Farna. It also meant his time of gloating was over. Tiernan was up and active before Idlewind, and therefore, he had once again "won" this rivalry. However, deep down Tiernan knew Midir was probably staring back at him from across the land with a smirk on his face. Whether from his desk or from a morning run, Midir was probably already up and moving about.

But Tiernan couldn't confirm this, and used the sun as his guide. As long as he was up before the sun, it meant he was up before his friend. And yet, more than anything he wished he could see Midir one last time. Before he stood, Tiernan took a final look toward Idlewind.

"King Midir. If there was one person in the world my father would approve of, one family my father would be willing to hand the Kingdom over to, it's Midir's." Of course, no one heard this statement either. King Tiernan stood up and walked away from the window and toward the stairs leading to his study.

High above in the sky, far out of sight, a winged form silently hovered. Waiting.

Chapter 2
Escalation

Midir approached his desk, unsettled. Something about the day hadn't felt right since the moment he observed the sun beginning its ascent across the eastern horizon. Its piercing light often brought a sense of determination and excitement.

Today, its normally invigorating rays conveyed dread. Midir couldn't explain why. Nothing about this moment differed from any of the previous days. Each day began with joy and anticipation. Indeed, since assuming the role of Manus, Idlewind had grown beyond its borders twice. His father had focused on internal growth, such as opening a Drunken Alligator and establishing the community market. Upon his passing, Midir was automatically in line to become the next Manus, a position he graciously accepted. As his first act, he established a committee consisting of some of the community leaders to begin plans for expansion.

To say this initiative brought new trade to Idlewind would be an understatement. Idlewind became a kingdom within *the* Kingdom. This, in turn, helped build the rivalry between Farna and Idlewind.

A friendly rivalry, of course, but one nonetheless. Each day became a competition between the two towns, with residents of each town claiming their way of life was superior over the others. Amongst the residents of both towns had been discussions about running a friendly economic competition to see which lifestyle could generate more growth and revenue. But no one took this idea seriously. Once Midir's second expansion entered the planning stage, the royalty in Farna never brought it up again.

Of course, this was because King Tiernan always gave his friend a wide berth to run the southeastern portion of the Kingdom however he saw fit. Likewise, Midir returned that respect and loyally served his best friend. King Tiernan always showed both honor and deference to Manus Midir's requests.

Needless to say, all was well. Happy. Prosperous. Midir woke up every day before the sun rose and ran laps along the stronghold's inner walls before most of the community had even thought about awakening. He presumed this meant he was up and going about his business long before.

Afterward, he would sit at his desk: an ornately designed piece of furniture he purchased from a craftsman in Farna. It was adorned with intricate scrollwork, evoking a sense of harmony and discord at the same time. Its finish featured a rich, deep mahogany color as well as built-in storage customized for Midir's preferences. Whenever the Manus sat at it, he felt like he himself was the King of Abria.

That's what made this day feel even more confusing. Anxiety overwhelmed him while sitting at his desk. Midir couldn't remember feeling like this before, which caused an even greater sense of unsettledness. He considered consulting his advisors to see if there was anything in the historical records on 16 Florin jogging a long-buried memory. Perhaps a battle from the history classes of his youth or an omen passed down from the Elves living in the Rosewood Forest?

Midir tried to sit once again, but couldn't. A hint of uncertainty hung in the air, and he knew he had to figure it out. By now, the sun had risen over the Valley Mountains to the North. This meant he would have a council meeting soon. Then, he had a consultation with a few builders for a possible third expansion, followed by a lunch with representatives from Lorelei, and so on.

Instead, Midir looked to the west toward Farna. He smiled, knowing his friend was staring back. Tiernan described it as a smirk, and that by sitting in his chair and gazing this way, Tiernan somehow "won." Midir didn't know what Tiernan thought he had won, but it didn't matter.

Between friends, sometimes, you don't need an explanation. Midir's smile turned to a frown. He suddenly understood his unsettled nature. He stood from his desk and resolutely turned away from the window. He sprinted toward the door to leave his study. Outside, one of his servants was waiting.

"Cancel everything." Midir made a beeline for the building exit. "Tell the stable hand I'll be leaving soon."

To his credit, the servant seemed to take in stride the task he was just assigned. No one had cancelled a council meeting in years, and the incoming delegation from Lorelei wouldn't be pleased. "Manus, will you be traveling alone, or should I ask some of the guards to accompany you?"

Midir stopped to consider the question. The Idlewind Guard didn't like to let Midir travel alone, though he often did. It would be safer if they came, yes. However, traveling across the kingdom would be faster if he did so solo.

His wife might also like an explanation. And what would he tell her? He woke up with a weird feeling telling him to travel to Farna *alone*? Or, he planned to undertake a normally two-to-three-day journey in less than one, based solely on a hunch? Neither answer would ease her concerns.

What if I'm right? He turned to the servant. "I'll be traveling alone. Let my wife know it was urgent. Tell the Lorelei delegation I'll make it up to them. And the council…" His voice drifted off. He thought for a moment before he spoke. "Tell the council I'll explain when I return."

Midir turned to leave. Right or wrong, he had committed to his course. *No turning back now.*

Fear gripped Davien's heart. Kyrie was breathing, but unconscious. He couldn't tell if her water had broken and then she fell, or if the fall had caused her water to break. Nevertheless, he knew what came next.

The baby would be here soon. Ready or not, Davien and Kyrie were about to welcome their first child into Grael.

A cold realization washed over Davien: the baby may be coming, but he had no idea why Kyrie was unconscious. He had heard frightening stories of mothers not surviving childbirth, and there were always varying reasons why.

This was something he could not fathom. His love for his wife ran deep, a core piece of who he was. He couldn't imagine a life without her.

Frantic, he rushed to their kitchen area, dampening a washcloth in one of the nearby water buckets. He ran back to their bedroom and laid it carefully on her forehead.

"Kyrie?" he implored, as he tried to wake her with a gentle shake.

No response.

"Kyrie, honey. Love. Ky…" And he stopped. Nervously, he placed his hand on her torso. He felt it rise ever so slowly, then lower. She was breathing, even if shallow. This meant Davien had time. Or so he hoped.

He leaned over to kiss her cheek and stood to turn toward the door. He couldn't quite remember where the doctor lived, but he was sure someone could direct him to the right house. However, as he began to take his first step, a hand grabbed his ankle. Davien's head turned back toward his wife, who had started to stir.

"Kyrie! Oh Kyrie, my love, are you okay?" As Davien kneeled back down, Kyrie turned her head toward the sound of his voice, and slowly opened her eyes.

"Help me up." Davien put one hand under her arm and the other behind her back. She was unsteady on her feet, so Davien braced her with each step.

"It's too soon. The baby can't come yet. We have to get you to the doctor." Kyrie closed her eyes in pain, tried to laugh, and took another step.

"I don't think…" A coughing fit caused her to pause mid-sentence. "I don't think we have a say. What's that?" Kyrie noticed the box on the bed. Once she sat down, she picked up the curious object and placed it on her lap, patiently waiting for her husband's answer.

Great. Do I have to explain that now? Rather than saying anything, he smiled. Kyrie shook her head as she opened the box. Inside, the jewel was now glowing a bright, vibrant red.

"You forgot everything, didn't you?" Kyrie tilted her head to one side, then grinned. "If there's one thing about you, Davien, you're consistent. And that's why I love you." She leaned over to give him a kiss, to which he reciprocated. Immediately, his guilt overwhelmed him.

"I'm sorry, the man at the store, Archer. No, Arnon. Yeah, Arnon. He said he thought you would need it, and if it didn't help to come back tomorrow. I, uh, I forgot everything else." As he tried to explain his faux pas, Kyrie continued to inspect the glowing jewel.

"How much dinage did it cost?"

"None. He said it was on the house."

"Free is good. Was it glowing when you bought it?"

Davien nodded. "Yeah, I think so."

"And it does what?" Davien shook his head in uncertainty. His wife smirked. She then touched the jewel and marveled at its curious warmth. *Not too hot, more like lukewarm bath water.* Kyrie shrugged and picked it up.

Faster than either of them could react, the jewel absorbed into her palm. "Kyrie!" Davien exclaimed, as the glow moved from her hand up her arm. Helpless, Kyrie looked at her husband for what they both feared might be one last time before they returned their mutual gazes back to the glow now making its way across her body.

"I don't know what's..." as she shook her head. She had no idea what was going on. All she could say were the words she meant more than anything else. "Davien, I love you," she said with trepidation as the glow made its way to her stomach. It glowed an even brighter red as Kyrie grabbed her husband's hands.

Without warning, a pain pulsated throughout her abdomen. A sensation she had heard her mom describe but never understood until now, a contraction followed by a strong, overwhelming need to push overtook her. This was unlike anything Kyrie had ever felt before. The pain rocked her body as she fell backward on the bed. Davien tried to help her get positioned as she let out a blood-curdling scream.

Far above Farna, the winged form began its slow descent.

Borun opened his front door. Newly fallen snow had decided to make its uninvited yet welcomed appearance overnight. Borun smiled, because while others were ready for the season of Flame, he loved this time of year and the crispness it brought to the air. During early Bloom (and the tail end of Frost), it was cool enough snow could still accumulate, yet warm enough he could walk to the field he had purchased without a heavy coat.

All the seasons had their pros, of course. During Flame, the sun shone overhead longer. Falling leaves dominated Ember. The peak months of Frost meant Borun could spend more time inside focusing on his business without feeling guilty for not being outdoors.

None of them were quite as magical to Borun as Bloom, the season of crisp mornings and the beginning of new life. Only 13 short days away, Borun was more than ready for his favorite time of year to kick off.

Today was 16 Florin. Borun walked out without donning his tunic because, well, why not? The cool Valley breeze felt invigorating as it blew over his exposed chest and through its grayed hair. It tickled his skin in a way that would make most people throw on a jacket.

Not Borun. With all his heart, he loved it here. He had made his home on the eastern edge of this small village forty years ago this month.

Borun hadn't been home to see his family since then. He had kept a low profile after leaving Clericsfold, and an even lower one since his son moved out, which wasn't easy. Borun wasn't a small guy by any means. He had a distinguishable face and stature, a stocky build with well-defined and enormously strong arms. His beard was unkempt, though Borun didn't care how he looked — only that he had the strength to do what needed to be done.

His hands bore the scars of his metalworking trade. He sold his goods throughout Abria under a pseudonym, trying to stay off of the proverbial radar. This practice allowed Borun's son to establish a life of his own without his father's reputation hanging over the young man's head. Last he had heard, his son was living somewhere in Farna. Borun smiled, remembering the small boy playing in the snow around Clericsfold.

That was years ago. Today, with the sun high above the Valley Mountains behind his home, Borun felt more alive than ever. His advanced years were of no consequence to him, and his health betrayed his true age. Borun expected to live for many, many years to come and exuded a youth-like appreciation for life.

The warm light invigorated him as it touched his exposed skin, which had grown physically cold from the wind. Borun himself didn't mind the sensation. He loved life, and could not be happier.

"You're going to die of hypothermia, old man!" Borun heard the voice behind him and turned to see who it was. To Borun's delight, it was Tolith, an Elf who had left the Rosewood Forest and made his own home high in the Valley Mountains.

"Tolith, you no good, thieving Elf! What are you doing here, my old friend?" Borun grabbed a tunic from just inside of his door, a blue, tattered one he had worn for decades. He closed the door and walked toward Tolith, who was just coming down the final hill and into the Valley itself.

Tolith was no thief, obviously. Instead, he was one of the most honest, trustworthy individuals Borun had ever known. Those uninformed, and especially with a racial bias against Elves, had presumed assumptions about their race. This included a predisposition to thievery. Borun made it a point to discredit it whenever he could, though in moments like these the two friends used it as a term of endearment.

With every step, Borun heard the crunch of the snow below his boots. It made him walk faster, more excited, as he and Tolith approached each other. This morning, in the crisp Florin air, Tolith's pale skin seemed to blend in with the sun's bright rays bouncing off the fresh powder.

The moment they finally reached within arm's length, Borun and Tolith embraced each other. Friendship between a Graelan and an Elf was rare, mostly because the Elves kept to themselves after Telford welcomed them into Abria centuries ago. This contributed to a few of the rumors about their race, most of which were false.

"You still making devilish potions in the mountains?" Borun knew this also wasn't true. It was a rumor started by the Elves themselves. Everyone in Abria knew health and restorative potions came from Clericsfold.

"You still planning a mill or wedding hall or whatever with that land you bought?" As the friends finished their hug, they turned back toward the center of the village. Borun began pointing at various spots around the town.

"One day, Tolith, there's going to be a Drunken Alligator here and a mill way out there. Just wait. Lily of the Valley will be known throughout Abria as the place to be. Just wait." Tolith smiled as he grabbed his friend's hand.

"When is the last time you saw your son?" Borun stopped dead in his tracks. Such a weird question, especially since just moments earlier Borun had been thinking about Davien.

"Why do you ask?" Borun continued his walk with Tolith, and pointed toward the center of town. "Right there, Tolith. I've already spoken with the Drunken Alligator in Lorelei. They're interested in that exact location."

Borun excelled at answering a question with another question, or redirecting the question toward what he was focused on. Tolith knew this. He grabbed his friend's hand again.

"Borun, stop. Look." He pointed at their footsteps. "Suddenly, there were two. Do you know what that means?" Borun laughed. Tolith had a knack for talking in riddles or saying things that made sense to him, though no one else around him understood their meaning.

Borun liked this about Tolith, among other things.

"Footprints. Yeah, we all know how they work Tolith. I take a step, that's one. You take a step, that's two. Did you fail your math classes too?" He laughed, the sound echoing throughout the empty fields and bouncing off distant trees. "Here, let's go look at where the mill is. Will be. Whatever. Forget it." Borun laughed again as he continued. "Actually, I have a surprise to show you."

Step by step, the two walked toward Borun's destination. In the distance, Tolith could see a small building under construction. From Tolith's admittedly limited knowledge of Graelan structures, it looked like…

"A blacksmith shop!" Borun smiled at Tolith. "I finished building it a few weeks ago. Now, I can do all of my work here and keep my home clean. Maybe you'll visit more often?"

"It will still smell like you, Graelan."

"Ha! Well, in any case, I'm going to repurpose it as part of the mill once it's complete, but for now, look." Borun pointed at the door handle. It was exquisite, formed with intricate detail. "Watch." Borun put his hand on the handle. "Fitted perfect to *my* hand. I think I'm going to make this my signature design. Enough of the generic pieces I've made. This design will be the mark of Borun."

Tolith patiently waited for the other man to finish speaking. He would let Borun have this moment. Reaching forward, he grabbed the door handle. "Big for me." His small Elven hand barely grasped it. "But perfect for a Graelan. Does this mean the great Borun will be discriminatory against my brethren? Will you, too, accuse us of thievery and casting horrible spells on the poor townsfolk?"

For the third time, Borun laughed.

Correction, Borun boisterously laughed, loud enough a neighbor on the north end of the Village peeked their head out to hear the commotion. She motioned something, then made a *shhhh* motion with her fingers.

Borun waved her off, and she rolled her eyes as he continued talking. "I'll make a *special* product line for your homes in the Forest. Same design, just smaller." Borun eyed his friend. "Maybe less fancy, of course." He sighed as he turned to face

Tolith. "Why are you here? I know you well enough, my friend. You've given me this moment. Now here is yours. Explain the riddle. 'Suddenly, there were two' or something, right? You're not talking about footprints."

"Ah ha! Yes, you're pretty sharp for an old Graelan, if I do say so myself."

"I'll have you know I'm only 416 years old. I have plenty of years ahead of me!"

"Then you would do well to respect your elders, Graelan."

"You're *only* 82 years older than me. That's nothing! Thinking you're so much older and wiser than me."

Tolith smiled but ignored his friend's jab. "Come, I have someone I want you to meet." Tolith stopped and turned to the empty field. "Actually, what if I bring them here?"

"More of your Elven magic?" Borun quipped to his friend. From time to time, Tolith liked to show off his magic abilities. As far as anyone knew, no Graelan in Abria had any whatsoever.

Tolith raised his hand and, with a yell, fired a blast of blue magic out of his outstretched palm. It traveled high into the sky and flashed like a lightning bolt. Whether this was Frost Magic or something else, Borun wasn't sure. But, even in the midst of the sun's bright light, the flash was distinguishable and spread across the sky.

"Nice light show," Borun mumbled. Tolith laughed in response. He began pointing to the sky.

"If that impressed you, my Graelan friend, wait until you see what comes next." From high in the Valley Mountains, a winged form appeared. Borun's lips parted with a hint of continued disbelief at the gravity of what he was witnessing.

"They're…they're *not* extinct?" Those were the only words Borun could get out before a giant white dragon blocked out the sun's light. Tolith, in his excitement, stomped his feet while moving in circles, laughing and chortling. When he stopped, he tugged on Borun's tunic.

"Ready to go for a ride?"

Within a few hours of leaving Idlewind, Midir had made his way out of the Windale Desert. He had taken the most direct westward route, entering the plains near Kingscrown Rock. Even from the opposite side of the Lorelei River, he could see the light from the sizable rock formation. Midir wished he had a few moments to stop and admire the beautiful, natural structure after he crossed the river, but he wouldn't have time if he hoped to make it to Farna today.

Kingscrown Rock glowed with an eerie, golden hue. Whether it be day or night, warm or cold, in the middle of Frost or the height of Flame, Kingscrown Rock burned bright. And not from the fires rumored to reside deep inside of the caves. The outer rocks *themselves* were full of light, enough that stargazers often had to travel far into the desert or closer to Clericsfold to get a clear view of the night sky.

Rumor had it a fabled flower made of metal grew at the top, though no one had figured out the paths within the caves to reach the top.

To the south was Kingscrown Beach, split into two segments by the Lorelian River. No one claimed the east beach. However, the orphanage and other residents of Clericsfold often used the western beach. After crossing the great waterway, it would normally take Midir another day to reach the city.

As he approached the Lorelian River, Midir would have to take a chance at fording it. Depending on the time of day, the waters could be rough. And unfortunately, there were no bridges this close to Kingscrown Bay, which meant he would *have* to traverse its waters.

His steed, a horse named Shadow, earned her name after winning several competitions at Whispersong. Shadow held the Abrian Records in speed, Barrel Racing, and Show Jumping. Midir had won both events before he became Manus, and thankfully so. Otherwise, Midir wouldn't have been able to compete as town leader.

"Good girl," Midir said as he patted Shadow on the neck. "You'll get me there on time. I just don't know what for…" Before he could say another word, however, he noticed a looming shadow overhead. One that blocked out the sun. One that materialized with a tremendous presence. It caused Shadow to recoil in a slight shock. Midir himself noticed the sudden shift in both the air and aura across the land.

"Whoa there, girl. Easy." Midir said as he slowed Shadow. In the far northern distance, a few deer drinking from the Lorelian River stopped. They raised their heads, looking in the same direction as the shadow. Midir brought Shadow to a complete stop before dismounting. He looked up and froze in place.

"Impossible. They're extinct. This isn't…" But before he could finish his sentence, he saw something else even more unimaginable: two people riding on the dragon's back. No, one was Graelan, and the other…an Elf?

Shadow, after her initial recoil and shock, seemed at peace once she saw the beast. It was almost as if there were some kind of mesmerizing awareness and connection between the two creatures.

This spooked Midir even more, as Shadow's lack of concern felt uncharacteristically out of place after the dragon jolted the horse out of a steady gallop. And it was even more unsettling as the winged beast finished its descent and landed on the beach.

Or rather, halfway on the beach. Its enormous feet meant it landed on the beach and the Bay both. It lowered its neck, allowing its two passengers to disembark. As both motioned to Midir to come closer, Shadow began walking toward the white dragon, almost as if she was being drawn to its side.

"Hey there girl, wait for me." Midir grabbed Shadow's reins and followed his horse's lead.

Chapter 3
The Day of Tiernan

A gust of icy wind blew past Midir and sent a shiver down his spine. It came out of nowhere, different from the perpetual breeze flowing from the dragon's wings. He nudged his companion on the side.

"Are you sure this is safe?" Midir said to Borun, who sat on the front seat — if it could be called as such — of the majestic beast. Midir looked over the edge of the dragon, which was now flying westward. And flying fast enough they would make it to Farna within a few hours — far, far faster than Shadow could even on her best day. Curiously, at this height Midir could see most of Abria, and the peninsula that made up the Kingdom was completely visible.

In the far northwest, he spotted the Rosewood Forest. He could see the spires of Mystic Mornings, the Kingdom's acclaimed theater, breaking through the treetops. Outside of the Forest sat the artistic haven named Oakshadow. As Midir followed the path to the east, he could see the Northern Plateau, an unexplored portion of Abria. Rumor had it a settlement once existed there, but there was no evidence to confirm the speculation.

Between the edge of the Forest and the Plateau sat Fabled Wonders, a family establishment Midir was now wishing he had taken his son to when he was younger. *No time for regret,* Midir thought. *Live in the moment today.*

Beyond the plateau were the Milston Mountains, with the city of Milston itself nestled in the corner of two of the western and southern ranges. At the northeastern-most edge was Northwick, Milston's sister town. Further south was Lorelei, a booming community. Not far to the west was Lakedon, a town with residents who made their living through the tourism trade.

South of Lorelei, Midir could just barely see Lily of the Valley and Whispersong, as both communities were small compared to other localities. Of course, even further south stood Idlewind with the Windale Desert. Separated from the rest of the kingdom by the Windale Mountains, Midir smiled as a sense of pride for his community washed over his face.

Midir's gaze followed the coastline of the Windale Desert along to Kingscrown Bay, then to the beaches of Clericsfold, finally stopping at the Port of Alwyn. As his eyes traveled north, he could see Farna situated between Alwyn and Oakshadow.

So, this is Abria. Separated from the rest of the world by the unexplored wilderness to the west and the ocean in every other direction, it became even more apparent to Midir that Abria would need to expand its ports and shipping system if it wanted to grow. Once, about five hundred years ago, visitors landed on the coastline near Alwyn from a distant land known as The Isles. This was the Kingdom's first exposure to the rest of Grael and prompted the Kingdom to build its first ports. Visitors had been rare since.

Borun answered, snapping Midir out of his thoughts. "Tolith said it would be, and I trust him. So yes, it's safe." Midir was glad Borun had added that last sentence, as in his observations he had forgotten what he had said.

"And you think he'll take care of Shadow? She can be challenging to ride. It took us years and years of riding to build our bond…" Borun cut Midir off mid-sentence.

"Shadow will be fine. Don't worry. I'd trust that Elf with anything, including my own life. Hey, look!" Borun pointed toward Central Abria where Clericsfold stood tall. "There's Clericsfold. I helped run the orphanage there for many years."

"Doesn't Kane run that now?" Borun shook his head. His countenance changed as he closed his eyes.

"Run isn't quite the right word. He's a part of the city leadership, yes, but Eskil is the mayor. Kane just serves on the Clericsfold Council." Midir raised his eyes in surprise, as that wasn't what he had heard. His father had tried to develop trade deals with Clericsfold, only to fail time and time again. Midir continued those efforts, only to be met with resistance at every step. Each time, a single name kept coming up.

Kane. Kane said no. Kane wants to go in another direction. Kane has other ideas. Kane thinks it's best to wait.

"So, who are you?" Midir asked. "I figure we should get to know each other, considering we're in such close quarters." Midir tried to make light of the situation, since he was leaning his full body into Borun's back. To be in such close proximity to an unknown person was uncomfortable, to say the least. Borun was holding on to one of the dragon's spikes, and Midir couldn't tell if he was relaxed and used to doing this or it was a case of beginner's luck.

"My name is Borun. I'm the King's brother." Midir did not expect this answer, as he had never met Borun before. Considering how close he was to Tiernan, all he knew about the King's family was that, well, they were "long lost." His friend would never elaborate, as it appeared to be a painful topic. Midir, out of respect for Tiernan, never pushed the issue.

"Right. I'm Midir. The King's best friend." Borun smiled. He knew who Midir was, since Lily of the Valley and Idlewind were geographically nearby. Borun had simply never needed to reach out to Midir.

"I know who you are. Well, except that you're my brother's friend. That's new information. I live in the Valley. I'm the one building the mill." Midir didn't react, but instead internalized the info. He was always on the lookout for business deals and ways to grow the economy of Idlewind. This detail could be helpful.

If Borun is trying to ignite the economy of the Valley, it could be a way to expand Idlewind too. Midir would have to mention this at the next council meeting.

"So, you're the King's brother and I'm his friend, and the Elf gathered both of us on a mythical, long-extinct creature..." At those words, the dragon emitted a long, deep roar.

Did I just offend it? "Sorry, a large and *majestic* creature. Is that better?" The dragon angled its head backward to the men, making eye contact with Midir. "Got it. So, on a majestic creature like this, Tolith sent us to see our mutual acquaintance. Doesn't that seem...?" Midir didn't finish. He didn't have to.

Borun felt no such qualms. "Worrisome is the word you're looking for, Manus. I may not have seen my brother for years, but I've heard the rumors. I know they say he's dying." This was new information to Midir, and Borun felt his companion stiffen behind him. "I'm sorry. I thought you knew. Maybe I have too many connections."

Borun cleared his throat. He had connections, yes, but they helped him stay hidden. The more people he knew, the more people he could avoid. Through those acquaintances, he learned his brother was dying.

"I wanted nothing to do with the crown, Manus. None. Our father passed it on to Tiernan since he was the eldest by a year. But even as a child, I saw the same health problems in Tiernan that plagued our father. I took after our mother's side, I think.

"I knew I would one day outlive my brother and the crown would make its way to me if I stuck around." Borun shrugged. "So, around age fifteen, I left home and apprenticed with a master blacksmith in Milston."

Midir realized this was why he had never met Borun. He didn't befriend the King until two years later. He shook his head. "Wait, Tiernan doesn't have a son. Or a daughter even. There is no heir. If you don't take the crown, who will?" In response to the question, Borun smiled.

"My son."

King Tiernan's chest tightened with each passing breath. It had been building for several moments before he mentally acknowledged its existence. *Not again.*

Since the moment he walked away from his favorite window, he knew something was different. Wrong. Almost as if it were a final farewell to his friend from across the land. Tiernan didn't realize it at first, but with each step he took, his body weakened.

Not long after he left his chambers, he encountered one of his servants. She had said nothing, though she noticed the king's paler complexion and his slower movements. As he made his way through Castle Abria, Tiernan's mind shifted, almost as if he was seeing each face from across a vast chasm.

It was a few hours past high noon when the finality of his condition sunk in. He held his favorite goblet, a family heirloom given to his grandfather by someone who had been important back then. Tiernan couldn't remember who. All he knew was the hand holding the goblet couldn't stop shaking. And yet, his arm had never felt more rigid, unmovable.

"King Tiernan. King Tiernan." Though right next to him, the voice might as well have been coming from a faraway tunnel. It took a few moments for it to come into clarity. Tiernan blinked as he looked at the face of the woman standing before him. "Can you hear me, my liege?" Tiernan slowly nodded his head before looking around at the rest of the room.

"Is everyone in the Kingdom here right now?" he asked. Indeed, most of those in the castle had gathered in the dining room where Tiernan had sat. To his left stood a doctor from the community, though Tiernan couldn't remember his name. The doctor spoke.

"What is the last thing you remember?" Tiernan raised his head in the doctor's direction.

Dr. Aldous, Tiernan thought. *His name is Dr. Aldous.* "I p-p-picked up that cup I always use. I n-n-noticed my hand was s-s-shaking, and then you were all here." In response to this statement, the doctor made a few notes in his book.

"Sir, that was *two* hours ago." The words didn't register at first as Tiernan tried to understand what the doctor said. *Another time slip. Another hand tremor. What other symptoms had they all just witnessed?* Tiernan tried to blink, but couldn't. He wet his lips as he looked at the doctor.

"How long do I have?" To his credit, the doctor gave Tiernan the privacy worthy of his title. He leaned over to whisper his opinion into the King's ear.

Tiernan took the news in stride with dispassionate acknowledgement. At the same time, a runner entered the room and whispered to one of the nearby attendants. The young guard wedged his way through the crowd to get as close as he could to Tiernan.

Once he was close enough to the King, he spoke. "My liege, you have a visitor. Two visitors, actually. It's Manus Midir, from Idlewind. And someone who claims to be your brother."

Midir and Borun had spoken little in the last half hour. Together, they were standing in a room near the primary dining room. They had arrived together, walking side by side not long after the dragon landed on the outskirts of the Abrian Plateau.

There, the beast left them near the Royal Cemetery, a tranquil, vibrant place just outside of the peninsula. Each day, volunteers from the Castle tended to the flowers and grasslands that made up the cemetery. Nearby, birds sung a peaceful song, blissfully unaware of the tone they were setting for visitors.

The grass was soft underfoot, and Borun kneeled down to feel it. The effect of the Abrian Plateau — with its perpetually warm climate — had a secondary effect here in the cemetery. It was cooler, yes, but warm enough the place resembled paradise.

A perfect moment of reflective respite for whatever he faced next. Borun was only vaguely aware of the dragon's departure as he marveled at the surrounding beauty of the landscape. Meanwhile, without making a sound, the magnificent beast rose high in the sky before heading westward toward the wilderness barrier separating Abria from the rest of Grael. As Midir watched it disappear in the distance, he also thought he could see another similar shadow high in the sky above Castle Abria itself.

Meanwhile, Borun had taken a bit of time to visit the graves of both his parents and grandparents. His mother, Maeve, had died first, a full two decades before his father Keelan passed. Borun hadn't been here when Keelan died, as he was too far away learning his trade to make it back in time. That was a detail Borun often tried to forget.

Next, he moved to his grandparents. King Telford and Queen Netta had died within a year of each other. His grandfather passed first while his grandmother joined him not long after Keelan ascended to the throne. His parents were already of advanced age when they became rulers of Abria, having the shortest recorded reign in Abrian history thus far.

Borun knew he only had a few moments here. He didn't linger, as Midir was impatiently but politely waiting at the cemetery's edge. Borun walked by his parents' grave one last time, mouthing *I Love You* before heading toward the exit. He nodded to Midir as he met back up with the Manus, and together they walked the rest of the way to Farna.

Once they neared the entrance to Farna, an unexpected sensation of awkwardness hit Borun square in the gut. After all, if he wanted, he could easily ascend to the throne today.

He wanted no such thing.

Meanwhile, Midir was eager to return to his childhood home. He couldn't remember how long it had been since he had last stepped foot on this hallowed ground. Unexpectedly, a man greeted them at the doors. The attending guard was an old friend who welcomed Midir with open arms. Borun did not know the man, but that didn't surprise him. He didn't develop his knack for social connection until much later in life. For all Borun knew, he may have even attended primary school with this guy.

Neither man mentioned the dragon to anyone in Farna. To explain such a miraculous, yet believed-to-be-mythical, experience would take too much time. By now, both men heard rumblings something was amiss within Castle Abria. The story of the dragon could wait.

As they entered the fortress, they heard a woman yelling, "Call the doctor! King Tiernan is dying!" Both men exchanged a look, and their escort brought them to one of the nearby rooms.

They had been there for a long time. At least, it felt like it. In reality, two hours had passed between their arrival and now.

In addition, things were slowly beginning to make sense to both men. Details such as how the dragon knew to bring them here, why the beast used Tolith as an intermediary, and the significance of these events now seemed more clear.

Unknown to either man, across Farna, a much different scenario played out.

Davien held his beloved wife's hand as she reclined on the bed. It had been difficult to find a doctor as, based on the increased commotion, there was something going on within Castle Abria as well. Kyrie had been crying out in pain for several hours. After much searching, one of their neighbors — a kind, wise woman named Gudrun — had found a doctor who could help.

The doctor was not on Kyrie's good side. Constant sniffing, random "hmmm" noises, and a general sense of naivety made the experience less than ideal. Not long after beginning his evaluation, he said something she would later call the most ignorant thing she'd ever heard.

"Ah yes, you're ready to push. You may give birth now." Kyrie's head shot up in a fit of rage. At the same time, she began squeezing Davien's hand tighter. Davien winced, but kept his cool. Noticing her barely contained rage, Gudrun tried to distract Kyrie next.

"Do you have a name for the baby?" Kyrie took a deep breath, laid her head back on the pillow, and first counted to eight as she exhaled before answering.

"Saoirse if it's a girl. Edward if it's a boy." Davien smiled. These names were how they knew they were destined to be together.

Lost in his thoughts, Davien began thinking about that moment. Though in practical terms, the memory helped him forget about the loss of blood flow within his right hand.

It was during the first year of their courtship. Davien had already fallen madly in love with Kyrie. They met when he was between jobs, though Davien couldn't quite remember which two jobs it had been. He and Kyrie were walking along the shores near Alwyn, admiring the new home construction at the edge of town.

There, they had talked at length about the future. What job would make Davien happy? Where would they live? Who would perform the wedding?

Davien suggested returning to Clericsfold to tend the gardens near the orphanage where he grew up. It was then Kyrie revealed the names she wanted for their children.

"I don't know. I'd rather Saoirse or Edward grew up somewhere near Farna. Don't get me wrong, I know you had an incredible life in Clericsfold. It's just…busier here. Plus, who could ever leave such a nice, warm…" By this point, Davien stopped listening. He was in a daze, internalizing that the love of his life wanted the same names for their firstborn daughter and son as he did.

A sudden, hard squeeze brought Davien back to reality. The daydreaming worked temporarily, but out of the blue, Kyrie began squeezing with more intensity than before. Davien did not know a woman of her stature could possess such strength.

Kyrie yelled, though Davien thought the word might be an understatement. Pain shook her body, and the volume of her exclamation was louder than anything he had heard in his life. It was then the doctor said something that made Davien's skin grow cold.

"The baby has not turned. He's coming out feet first." Simultaneously, both Davien and Kyrie felt anger and excitement. Anger that the doctor was just now revealing the detail of a breech birth.

At the same time, excitement washed over them as the doctor revealed a long-awaited secret: Davien and Kyrie were having a boy. Edward was on his way!

My firstborn child is a son! Davien immediately began thinking of the various activities they would do together. *Maybe Edward will be a carpenter like me!*

"You're just now letting us know he's breech?" Kyrie retorted. Then she looked at her husband. "But, a boy. Edward. Davien, *a boy!* He'll be here soon." Davien kissed her head and gave her a gentle hug.

Then an extraordinary yet unexpected thing happened. Gudrun nudged Davien. It took a moment for him to realize, but he followed her glance to where her hand was pointing. Davien's eyes widened as he saw a foot pressing against the right side of Kyrie's stomach.

"How can that be? The baby's foot is already..." Mid-sentence, Kyrie noticed it too. Both fear and astonishment enveloped her face. In a single word, Kyrie stated what everyone else had just realized.

"Twins."

✣ ✣ ✣ ✣ ✣ ✣ ✣ ✣ ✣

Far above Farna, a winged form began to descend with purposeful urgency...

✣ ✣ ✣ ✣ ✣ ✣ ✣ ✣ ✣

Borun and Midir followed the servant into the room where they had taken King Tiernan. Borun hadn't been in this room since the throne belonged to their father. Back then, this area was merely a spare room. A small space, enough for a large bed and a few dressers. Far smaller than the room that had been his parent's bedroom.

Borun assumed, and would later confirm, Tiernan did not desire to sleep alone in such a large area. Not having a wife, Tiernan hated the traditional royal bedroom. It was too big. Too foreboding.

Too lonely. Borun always wanted to ask his brother why he never married, though now was not the time for such a conversation. He remembered a few maidens his brother had shown interest in when they were young adults. "We never hit it off," is how Tiernan would often explain it. Borun couldn't help but think in the decades since he had left Farna that surely the King would have found someone.

Borun's thoughts returned to the present as he and Midir walked into his brother's bedroom. By now, there were only a handful of other individuals surrounding him. Midir pushed past the servant and ran to Tiernan's side. Borun kept his distance, allowing the two friends a moment.

Tiernan turned his head toward Midir. He smiled, then shook his head back and forth. "The d-d-doctor thinks it'll be soon. Midir..." Before Tiernan could finish, he began coughing. Once it subsided, he continued. "I know Idlewind is your home. Yet I can think of no one better, more suited to become King than you." Tiernan smiled. "Of course, you'll need to give up that ridiculous t-t-title."

Midir laughed. "One last insult, eh, my dear friend? How long did you stare across the countryside today? Did you know I ran this morning before the sun had even thought about rising? What did you do?"

Tiernan smiled. It wasn't Midir's best comeback. "I started dying." He then remembered the distance between the two towns. "Midir, how did you make it here so fast? Even on Shadow..."

Midir raised a hand. "That's a story you wouldn't believe if *I* told you. Perhaps you should hear it from him instead," he said as he pointed at Borun. Borun moved into the room. Tiernan tried to sit up at the sight of his brother, though it was more than his failing body could handle.

"Hello, Tiernan." Borun walked around to the other side of Tiernan's bed and took a seat. The King looked at everyone else in the room, and raised his hand toward the door, finger extended. Once the room was empty, Tiernan grabbed the nearest hand of both men. Borun spoke again. "What if I told you a giant, white dragon picked me up from the Valley, flew southward toward Kingscrown Rock to find Midir, and brought us both here faster than anything you've ever seen before?" Tiernan's eyes grew wide, despite his failing strength.

"I'd say you're lying. Besides, dragons are m-m-mythical. They've been extinct for years."

Midir spoke next. "We assumed so too. Apparently, they're out there. Somewhere else in Grael waiting for us." As if on cue, a shadow enveloped Tiernan's bedroom window. A hulking, incredible shadow. All three men noticed as a winged form lowered past Tiernan's chambers. First, they saw the bright red skin of its hind legs. Next, its expansive yellow and orange abdomen came into view.

In unified disbelief, they watched as it shifted its face, filling the portal. One by one, the dragon's eyes made contact with each man.

Borun noticed that, unlike the white dragon, this red one seemed to be glowing. Its skin seemed to be full of fire, yet it was producing no light. It was the most unusual thing he had ever seen. The dragon hovered for a moment. *Was that a smile?* Borun couldn't tell. It closed its eyes, nodded in what appeared to be a sign of respect toward Tiernan, and then reopened them, gazing once again into the room.

"I guess you weren't lying, Brother. I should have known better. You always were known for telling the truth." He reached his hand toward Borun to sit up. "This d-d-dragon is red. The dragon that brought you here was w-w-white. This one, and the other, must have known I was dying." Tiernan thought for a moment about the implication. "But why? Why bring you here today?"

Tiernan looked at his brother in a lucid moment of clarity. "Borun, why are you here? I tried to find you for years and…"

Borun put his other hand on his brother, clasping both around the dying man's right hand. "I needed to build my own destiny. This life was not for me."

"But the throne…" Outside the window, the dragon made a sound. Tiernan stopped mid-sentence as it did so. It was looking at Borun and moving its head in a peculiar way. Borun let go of Tiernan's hand and walked over to the window. The dragon extended its head closer to the window, and Borun put his hand through. He touched its nose, and both man and beast closed their eyes. In the moment of silence, Borun realized it was talking to him.

It wasn't an audible sound. No words were exchanged. Borun simply knew what it wanted him to know. While standing at the window, he said, "It's telling us there is no need to worry. All is as it should be." He released his hand from the dragon, and both opened their eyes. He nodded to the dragon, which blinked in acknowledgement. It resumed its descent once again.

Borun walked back to his brother's bedside, grabbing his hand again as he continued. "My son lives *here*, in Farna. His name is Davien." At the mention of the name, Tiernan finally remembered who had made his glorious, beautiful throne. It wasn't Daniel. It wasn't Darius.

His name was Davien, and as it turned out, his own nephew. A person he had longed to meet, and thought he never would. Instead, he had been right here the whole time. Tiernan smiled.

"Then let what is destined to be, be." And with those words, Tiernan relaxed. The pressure lifted, not only from his chest or proverbial shoulders. The tension in his soul disappeared. Everything felt softer. Lighter. The single thing holding him here — the worry of an heir — was no longer a concern. Borun wouldn't ascend to the throne. Nor would Midir.

King Davien would succeed him. Tiernan smiled. He grabbed the hands of both men, Borun to his right, Midir to his left. He took one final look at both — Midir first, then Borun — and then laid his head back on his pillow. With a relieved, peaceful smile on his face, Tiernan closed his eyes. He breathed in through his nose, parted his lips, and exhaled a long breath.

Midir spoke, "It's okay. You can let go, my friend. Abria will be in good hands." Midir looked at Borun, a single tear moving down his cheek. The Manus smiled, let out a small, somber sound full of emotion, nodded at Borun, and then looked back to Tiernan.

Borun looked back to the dragon, still barely occupying the window, with only the top of its deep, fire-red wings still visible. He watched as it continued its descent. Then he looked back at his brother. Watched his chest rise and fall. Then a gap. A shallow breath in. An even more shallow breath out. Then, a longer gap. One final breath, and a long, drawn-out exhale.

Tiernan's grip on Borun and Midir's hands loosened. His chest remained still. After 272 years of rule and at the age of 417, King Tiernan was dead.

Legend has often said that when one life enters the world, another must leave it. As King Tiernan was taking his last breath, another was taking his first. Davien and Kyrie had but a moment of joy to embrace their newborn son as, within minutes of his birth, Kyrie began pushing once again. This time, the pain was beyond anything she had experienced just moments before. Gudrun held their son as labor continued forcefully and with a fiery intensity.

Kyrie had lost a lot of blood, but unknown to everyone else, this was the least of their problems.

Their unborn child was in far worse condition than anyone knew. Anyone, that is, except for the dragon that had just landed outside their door.

Borun walked out of Castle Abria and into the inner courtyard in solemn reflection. While he had come here with a sense of composed sensibility, the passing of his brother awoke many emotions he hadn't realized he had. It also made him determined to track down his son within the city. After wandering for a bit, he snapped out of his shock and began asking various people if they knew where Davien the carpenter lived.

A few pointed in the general direction of Davien's cottage. However, it didn't take long to realize which house belonged to his adopted son. The red dragon who had stared at him from Tiernan's window was now sitting in front of his son's home. Peaceful. And waiting.

Surprisingly, most people seemed more inquisitive toward the dragon than afraid. As far as Borun knew, today was the first time in over a thousand years anyone knew dragons still existed. And yet, within the past few hours, he had met two. Rode on one, and telepathically communicated with another.

Near Davien's home, a few guards were approaching the giant beast with a sense of caution. Though they, too, seemed less afraid and more intrigued. As Borun approached it himself, he understood why.

The air near the red dragon had a curious quality. Blissful. Peaceful. Euphoric. Despite its similar size, this one differed from the white dragon that flew him here.

If Borun didn't know better, it was almost as if the beast was in control of the situation. As others slowly crept out of their homes and shops to see it, their initial fear transformed into a serene acceptance and sense of connection with the creature.

Borun observed all of this from a distance, then — as if drawn to the dragon himself — walked up to the crowd standing around it. Unlike the others, Borun remained in control of his body, almost as if he had to *willfully* join it.

As he did, the people nearby created a path for him to pass through, almost as if acting on instinct and unaware of what they were doing. The dragon turned its head toward him, and even took a step back from the door to let him approach. It lowered its head to him once again, extending it toward the man's smaller body.

It's as if the dragon is showing me some kind of respect.

Borun put his hand on the dragon's head. Both man and beast closed their eyes. The dragon spoke to Borun again, though just like in his brother's bedroom, in a way he didn't understand. Within his mind, it somehow told him all he needed to know.

Borun's eyes shot open. If he didn't know better, he would have thought time was standing still. The dragon did the same, opening its eyes and staring directly into Borun's. There was no other movement anywhere else in Farna, if not the world, at least as far as man and beast could tell.

The white dragon destined me to be here.

Go now. There is no time to waste. They need you.

Borun moved his hand once again, breaking the connection. He wasted no time in doing as he had been told. Borun walked up to the door in determined confidence, despite this unusual aura surrounding the day's events. He grabbed the door handle, looked down, and smiled. His son had used one of his earliest pieces of metalwork for his home. It brought Borun a sense of satisfaction as he opened the door.

His joy turned to sorrow in an instant. Inside, the home was a sharp contrast to what was going on outside, devoid of any sense of peace or bliss. He could see into his son's bedroom where a woman was laying, having just given birth. The blood-soaked bedsheets alone attested to this detail. In the living room, a woman held a crying baby boy, trying to calm him. As Borun walked up to the entryway of the bedroom, he saw his daughter-in-law holding another child.

A child that was not breathing. Davien was standing next to her, his face full of tears. He didn't notice Borun at first, at least not until the doctor felt the older man's presence standing behind him and turned to see who was there.

"Son," Borun finally said. Davien looked up and saw his father, but couldn't say anything. Kyrie took her eyes off of her child for only a moment to acknowledge Borun and returned her tearful gaze to the baby. The doctor stood, put his hand on Borun's shoulder, and motioned for him to leave the bedroom.

Once they were outside the couple's earshot, he spoke. "They did not know they were having twins. Suddenly, there were two." Borun's head tilted in acknowledgement as the doctor repeated the exact words Tolith had said just a few hours earlier.

The doctor continued, "The delivery of the boy was difficult. The twisting during his delivery caused the umbilical cord of the girl to prolapse. By the time Kyrie delivered her, she wasn't breathing." He glanced back at Borun with sadness as he moved to the woman holding the other baby.

Borun scratched his beard with his left hand as he turned to go back into the bedroom. This time, things were different. The child glowed red. A fiery red, though it cast no shadow nor did it illuminate its surroundings. It was now Borun realized the shadow of the red dragon, discernible through one of the living room windows, had shrunk.

Davien finally noticed the commotion through the cracks in the shutters on their bedroom window. Kyrie's gaze remained fixated on her daughter, unaware of what was happening anywhere else.

Realizing there was more going on here than he or anyone else understood, Borun walked over and opened the shutters. The dragon, now closer in size to a standard horse, walked up to the window. It gave Borun one last look before looking at the couple.

This broke Kyrie's attention as she noticed the red dragon for the first time. The beast tilted its head back and roared, a small burst of fire rising high into the air and exploding in a stunning show of power and control. At the same time, Kyrie's newborn daughter glowed brighter — far more luminous than the dragon had earlier.

Everyone's eyes shifted toward the baby. No one noticed what the dragon did next. It transformed, bit by bit, dissolving into a small stream of energy. This power flowed and twisted like a river, yet had the magnificence of the nighttime sky. It touched the girl's body and enveloped her from head to toe.

Kyrie and Davien watched in silent amazement and gratitude as their daughter took in a deep breath for the first time.

Chapter 4
New Beginnings

Most parents get a few moments to spend with their newborn child. Davien and Kyrie would have no such luxury. The events following the birth of the twins were a whirlwind of decisions and actions neither parent could have ever expected.

As soon as their daughter began breathing, Davien and Borun embraced. It was a deep, powerful hug that only a father and son could truly understand.

"I'm happy for you, boy." Borun's comment was a sincere one, expressing parental tenderness, relief, and fatherly pride all wrapped up into one expression.

"I had a good example. The best, really." Davien let go of his father and returned to his wife's side. He sat on the edge of the bed as Gudrun returned to the bedroom with the newborn boy.

"Do you have a name for them?" she asked. Kyrie and Davien exchanged knowing smiles.

"Edward," said Davien.

"And Saoirse," continued Kyrie.

After hearing both, Borun smiled. His reaction was one of approval, yet one marred by hidden sadness, as he knew one of those names could not be used. *It's not fair to them. I should tell him now.*

Borun began to speak, but stopped. The death and rebirth of his granddaughter was emotionally overwhelming. Besides not knowing what had happened with the dragon, Borun did not have the courage or strength to break his son's heart.

It didn't take long for someone else to do so. After only spending a few moments with their twins, now both breathing peacefully, a contingent from Castle Abria arrived. Without so much as knocking, they opened the doors and burst into the couple's home.

Borun turned around to face them. Three guards stood at attention, none sure of how to proceed. Borun nodded, knowing what was about to happen.

"Son. You're needed in the living room." Borun kept his back to the bedroom door. It took Davien a minute to walk into the room. Once he did, he took a step back. The presence of the Abrian Royal Guard was not what he expected to see in his home.

"What's going on?"

"Son, there's something about me you didn't know. The King of Abria was my brother."

Davien froze in place. In his head, a hundred different scenarios played out. Everyone knew King Tiernan lacked an heir. But no one knew he had a long-lost brother.

"You're to become King one day?" Davien asked. Borun closed his eyes.

"No." He turned to his son, who had begun to tremble. "Many years ago, long before I began working at the orphanage in Clericsfold, I abdicated my rights to the throne. Since my brother had no heir, it was assumed Tiernan would pass the kingship to a man of his choosing."

"Dad…"

Borun continued. "However, there is someone else who can become king."

"No…" Davien pulled his father aside into the far end of his home. He began whispering. "You know I'm not a blood heir…"

"That doesn't matter. My brother gave me his blessing before he passed away just now."

"The King is *dead*?" Davien swallowed hard. Of all the scenarios he had played out in his mind, this was not among them.

"My King." Across the room, one of the guards spoke. Davien and Borun ignored them.

"Why aren't you to become King?" Borun looked for the answer within himself. He smiled.

"Do you remember the day I adopted you?"

"Of course."

"And I told you that your humble, gentle nature meant you were destined for greatness?"

"This? You adopted me for this?" Borun shook his head. "Then what, father?"

"Abria needs someone greater than I to lead her. That's you, my son."

The guard spoke again. "My liege, where is Tiernan?" Davien gave his father a confused look. Instead of answering, Borun lowered his head.

"If you're referring to the King, I guess his body would be in the castle?" Davien didn't know how to answer, and instead said the only thing that came to mind.

"No, sir. I'm looking for the newborn Prince." Davien whipped his head around to look at his father. Borun was resting his arm against the fireplace mantle while rubbing his forehead with his hand. Davien turned back to the guards.

"My son, Edward, is with his mother in the bedroom."

On the way to Castle Abria, Davien learned of an obscure royal edict carried over from centuries ago. It was one signed into law by the first King of Abria, Farris, though few understood his reasoning.

Davien stopped dead in his tracks. "Wait a minute. Back up. You're telling me we can't name our son Edward?"

"That's correct, my liege."

"And that we have to name him Tiernan? Why?"

"The law states the first male child born after the passing of a king — no matter where they lived or the family they came from — must carry the name of said royal figure."

"And you *know* my son is the firstborn child? How?"

Another guard answered instead. "Word travels fast. And everyone in Farna saw the dragon. All eyes were on your home."

Davien protested. "But I'm the *King*. You're telling me my hands are tied?" It was a moot point, as Davien would learn. The Abrian Royal Guard continued to escort him to the throne room. There, a group of attendants and legal scholars were waiting. Upon his arrival, they ushered him to the exact throne he had carved all those years ago. Someone looking proper and official handed him a quill. Another stood by with what Davien assumed was the crown his predecessor had been wearing not too long ago.

The first paper he had to sign was his acceptance of the throne. Next came the induction ceremony. After that, stacks of papers issuing orders and commands.

Buried deeply in one of those piles was the formal naming of his son, continuing the law put in place by rulers long dead. Borun stood near the doorway, watching all of this unfold with curiosity and a hint of sadness.

Davien was not prepared to be thrust into the spotlight, let alone leadership of the Kingdom. His wife stayed behind in their home to recover, though a group of midwives and guards now stood by, ready to assist.

After what felt like a tireless — and thankless — series of tasks, Davien sat on his throne. Borun finally walked into the room.

"You're welcome to yell at me."

Davien smiled. "You know I couldn't do that, but…" He chuckled. "I'll admit, more than once today I've thought 'Thanks, Dad' while signing paperwork. Please tell me I'll have time for carpentry?"

"You always did a great job in those classes back in the day. Top of the class! Your friend, though, spent his time on other pursuits, didn't he? Where was he when you were busy with woodworking?"

Davien lowered his head. "Kane? History. He believed the key to power was buried in books written centuries ago." Borun noticed Davien's diminished expression.

"Sorry, son. I always blamed myself for the way things ended between you two. I shouldn't have brought it up today."

"Well. Let's forget about him. Am I allowed to leave Castle Abria, Dad, or am I stuck here? I'd like to go home and see Kyrie and the twins. Tiernan and…"

Davien paused. Tiernan's name change had been forced on them. But now, their chosen name for their daughter sounded uncomfortably ironic.

Saoirse loosely translated to freedom, a luxury Davien and Kyrie now lacked.

"Of course you can. Though, it might be helpful to think of this as home. Come on, let's go see your babies."

Kyrie held her twins tightly in her arms. She kissed her son, who seemed content to sleep the evening away.

Her daughter, on the other hand, was wide awake. She wasn't doing much besides staring at her mother.

"You. You gave us quite a scare, little one." At the same time, Gudrun walked in. Kyrie smiled. "You can go home any time you want. The midwives have really taken over things."

"I know. It just didn't feel right with your husband and his father leaving so suddenly earlier." She walked over and admired the newborns. "Besides, I heard one of the guards say he was on his way back from the Castle. I'm going to get going before they return. Tell Dav…tell the *King* I said congratulations."

Kyrie watched as Gudrun left, looking through her bedroom window as the woman walked across the fields of Farna.

She caught a glimpse of one of the guards as he approached with an arriving contingent. *That must be Davien!* Kyrie looked at the twins. "Your Daddy is coming to see you," she said with a loving smile.

Suddenly, it hit her. *This is how it's going to be from now on. Guards. Formality.* Her eyes widened and the next realization sunk in.

If Davien is the King, then that means I'm the…

She couldn't finish the thought. Instead, she watched as the group walked closer until finally she caught a glimpse of the face of the man she loved most.

He saw her face through the window. Instead of entering through the door, walked over to the windowsill. He smiled as he placed both arms on its ledge.

"Did you leave this open all day?"

"Well, not all day. The midwives helped me organize the place, to 'make it presentable', they said."

"Uh huh. So that all of Farna can gaze upon its new Prince and Princess." With the last word, he broke down in tears. He tried to reach out to touch his twins, but the bed was too far away.

"Oh, Davien. Come inside, my love." He left the window. Once inside, he reached for Tiernan. Love flowed through his eyes as well as sadness. Kyrie noticed.

"What's wrong?" Davien breathed deeply, then sat next to his wife on the bed.

"We need to talk about their names."

To put it in basic terms, the dragon changed things. Whatever the beast had done to itself gave their princess a new life, rejuvenating her stillborn body into one full of vivacity, energy, and spirit.

If there was one thing the castle staff noticed about Davien and Kyrie right away, it was their bond. They could often complete each other's thoughts and sentences. Their feelings often mirrored each other, whether through some strong mystical power or through the love they shared.

In the same way they were not *allowed* to name their son what they wanted, they equally decided it was inappropriate to do so for their newborn daughter. Instead, they chose a name honoring her changed — and reborn — nature.

After two days of deliberations, they landed on one with an appropriate meaning: Enid. The name roughly translated to spirit, which she, at just a few days old, possessed in full.

To celebrate, Davien signed a law doing away with the archaic requirement that forced his son's name change. While nothing could be done for Tiernan, at least no other family would be subjected to this unfair edict.

And thus the twins, Tiernan and Enid — two relatively insignificant newborn children born on 16 Florin 899NE — became the Prince and Princess of Abria almost immediately after their births. Their parents, Davien and Kyrie, were likewise suddenly the King and Queen of a land they only partially knew.

Not long after Kyrie moved from their home to Castle Abria, Borun announced his decision to return to the Valley.

"You can't leave, father. I don't even know what I'm doing. I'm a craftsman, like you. You were born into this, and at least can help me navigate what I'm doing and how I need to act."

Davien's words struck a chord with Borun, who, after a short period of deliberation, agreed to stick around for the foreseeable future. For as much as he didn't want to be a part of the royalty, he couldn't just up and leave.

After all, he *was* raised in it.

Though it had been many decades since he had been a part of the daily operations of the Kingdom, he equally knew his son would need help adapting to things in his transition from carpentry to leadership.

Not that it didn't take some convincing. Borun preferred the freedom he had in the Valley, or in the case of his younger years, serving at the orphanage in Clericsfold. Royalty was not for him. Nevertheless, his experience as a member of the Royal Family — though years removed — would give his son the needed insight and guidance that would help Davien and Kyrie acclimate to their new life.

After the funeral for Tiernan the First, Midir returned to Idlewind. Duties as Manus would prevent a prolonged stay in Farna, though Midir sent a messenger to explain his sudden absence and when he planned to return to the Idlewind Council.

In fact, one of King Davien's first acts was to send similar messengers across the land to each of the major cities and settlements in Abria so that all denizens of the land knew of the King's passing. By the end of the month, the entire Kingdom knew 16 Florin would be known as the Day of Tiernan. It gave Davien a small sense of satisfaction to know the birth of his son — a child whose name was marred due to ancient customs put in place by his adoptive great-great-grandfather — would be forever marked on the calendar of the Kingdom.

Some communities sent supplies and gifts of condolences. Davien questioned these kinds of decisions, as — from what he could tell — the Royal Family did not need anything. After every shipment, Davien had each gift's value calculated and kept in a ledger. "One day," he vowed, "I will return their kindness tenfold." Kyrie approved of the decision, though she left many of these types of decisions to her husband.

One day, she would be required to take her rightful place as the Captain of the Abrian Royal Guard. Until that day, however, she left many of the day-to-day decisions to her husband's wisdom — guided by his father, of course.

For example, the funeral for the former King itself was simple. Upon Davien's arrival in Castle Abria, one of the many documents the castle attendants presented him with was a sealed letter. In it, his predecessor explained his desire for a nondescript funeral. Though his reasoning was partially self-loathing for the lack of an heir, Tiernan the First did not want to draw undue attention away from whomever the new king may be.

Tiernan's friend, Midir, opposed such an idea, wishing to give the King a proper sendoff. However, in the end, he acquiesced to Tiernan's final wishes.

They buried the King in the Royal Cemetery near his parents. As Davien and Kyrie left the cemetery, it independently dawned on both of them that they, too, would be buried here someday.

Davien brought it up first. "Kyrie, did you realize..."

She put her finger to his mouth. "Stop. I know what you're thinking. Not everything needs to be said, my love."

After a brief period of mourning, life returned to normal in Farna. The bakers made their Abrian Pies; blacksmiths crafted tools; shop owners sold their wares again. Throughout the land, teachers updated their texts to include the now-known continued existence of dragons and the ethereal peace everyone felt surrounding them.

Indeed, it was a topic that seemed to be on the top of everyone's minds for a while. Some advocated sending expeditions beyond Abria to see if other dragons still lived elsewhere in Grael. Others tried scaling the mountains surrounding the Northern Plateau in search of them, only to perish in the attempt.

One small group of explorers tried to cross the western mountains separating Abria from the rest of the land, though they found the rocks impassable.

And like all things, the continued existence of dragons became part of the accepted way of the world. The red dragon was gone and the white one had flown off. It was likely other dragons existed somewhere else in Grael, far from Abria, but out there.

Mysteriously waiting.

Settling in to royalty was a challenge for Davien and Kyrie. The new King insisted one of the spare rooms be turned into a workshop so he could — hopefully — continue his carpentry trade on the side. It wasn't for money, obviously, but rather as a hobby. "My way of escaping from the newfound pressures of Kingship," he explained to his wife.

Meanwhile, Kyrie found little time for the immediate duties of a queen. Her responsibilities to her newborn twins, in her words, "superseded any imposed-on-me queenly duties." To most of those living in Farna, Kyrie was essentially absent from public view until the twins were old enough to walk, a fact she didn't mind one bit. Being thrust into the spotlight was hard enough for her, and Kyrie found solace in her children.

Davien, meanwhile, formed a new council of advisors who could help him decide actions that would best serve the people. His predecessor had no such team, despite Tiernan's generally successful rule. Davien invited his adoptive father to be a part of the Abrian Council. Borun accepted under the implicit understanding that his son realized this was a temporary measure.

It lasted about six months before Borun decided he was ready to return to the Valley. Borun wanted to get home by the middle of Flametide so he could enjoy the end of the season of Flame in his home.

As a parting gift, Davien used some of his pre-royalty personal funds to buy all the necessary building supplies from Milston, Northwick, and Oakshadow. He had them shipped — along with a contingent of workers — to Borun's field. Borun Mill was up and running in less than a year, with the owners of the Drunken Alligator in Lorelei opening their second location in the Valley not far from the new establishment.

Indeed, the opening of Borun Mill was one of Abria's first celebrations of the new year. On 12 Daisymoon 900NE, Davien held a party in the Valley. Delegations came from everywhere in Abria. Performers came from Oakshadow along with the shop owners who had profited from selling their supplies. Miners from Milston brought their families to enjoy the fruits of their labor.

Idlewind, being relatively close to the Valley, contributed the most to the celebration. Midir wanted to showcase to the rest of Abria that his community could thrive and provide for the Kingdom despite the harsh conditions of Windale. Everyone who attended left with some kind of souvenir from Idlewind, regardless of their status or class. In the case of Borun, Midir gifted him with a stone carving of the white dragon.

One notable absence was Clericsfold. Though it was Davien's 'hometown', no one attended, no one acknowledged the event, and travel through the region was often greeted with an uncomfortable coldness.

Near the end of the celebrations, Davien and Midir sat down in the newly built Drunken Alligator to have a private conversation.

"It's been a whirlwind," Davien stated plainly as he took a sip of Dorian Ale. Midir took a larger gulp of his Lorelian Mead before responding.

"How can you drink that stuff?"

Davien smiled. "Dorian Ale? It grew on me as a kid. Besides, I'm not a fan of mead in general." Satisfied, Midir raised his glass. The men clinked their glasses together. Midir took another drink.

"I barely know you, but I feel a kinship with you. Your uncle was a fine man," explained the Manus.

"I barely knew *him*. We never even met before he died. He ordered a set of thrones from me through one of the castle attendants." Midir about spit out his drink.

"Wait. Are you *the* carpenter from Farna?" Davien raised his glass as if to say yes. "My prized desk came from you! The King himself! I had heard about the Abrian-famous carpenter in Farna..."

"...and ordered through a..."

"...castle messenger," they finished together. Midir laughed.

"How did I not make that connection?"

"Maybe you've been having one too many of these things?"

"Nah." Midir took another gulp, and Davien followed suit. After both men swallowed their drink, the King got down to business.

"I need a favor."

"Of course. Idlewind served your predecessor faithfully, and we will continue to do so now and in the future."

"You know I'm adopted."

"Of course."

"My father served the orphanage faithfully for many years, long before I was born even. I'm sure you noticed no one from Clericsfold was here for the celebrations."

"An oversight?" Midir took another drink.

"I don't think so. You see, when I was there, I had a friend. Someone who, last I knew, had risen in the political ranks in Clericsfold.

"We haven't talked in years. Actually, once Dad announced he was adopting me, I never saw him again." Davien took a drink and cleared his throat. "Manus, I need someone to investigate and find out what's going on, and whoever does so needs to come from someplace else besides Farna.

"After all, they haven't responded to *anything* I've sent and have even refused our most recent messengers."

"Consider it done. I'll send my best scouts. Undercover, of course. They can pretend to be from Lorelei or something. After we find out what's going on, I'll send a messenger to you with our findings." Davien took one last drink and stood. He reached out his hand to thank the Manus.

Instead, Midir pulled him in for a hug. Davien reciprocated the gesture, and the men shook hands to seal the partnership.

"If you'll excuse me, Manus, I'm going to go visit my father at his mill. Please let me know what you find as soon as possible."

Two weeks later, Midir's messenger arrived in Farna. What the scouts found didn't surprise Davien. Their investigation revealed someone other than their mayor seemed to be calling all the shots in Clericsfold.

This person's name came up time and time again. In basic conversation. In hushed whispers between the city guards. When spending dinage in the shops. Everywhere they went, someone would mention his name.

The scouts never encountered him, and eventually someone described a recent trip he had taken with a group of orphans. But, even when out of town, his presence seemed to be near. Ominous. Ever-present.

Controlling.

His name: Kane.

Chapter 5

Intermissio 1st

Tiernan put down the quill. Somehow, despite all the writing he had finished so far, he never once needed to dip it into an ink well. He stared at the words he had written while tearing off a piece of Tammith's bread. It was still warm to the touch, oddly so.

No one had ever figured out how she kept the bread warm even after it sat on your table for a while.

Tiernan remembered the words from Zachary. "You were there for all of it. Well, most of it." Tiernan assumed this was the "most" the old man referred to. He didn't physically witness any of these events, though he had heard the story of his birth from Borun, Davien, Kyrie, and everyone else for years. Large portions of the story he had yet to write would also come from other people over the years.

Tiernan threw his head back and took a drink of water. He finished what was in his cup and raised his hand toward Tammith, indicating he would like another. From across the Drunken Alligator's common area, she saw his motion.

She also shook her head in disapproval. Tiernan wondered how long Tammith would allow him to continue ordering water before kicking him out or forcing him to order something else.

Knowing her, it would be the former. Tammith wasn't known for her tolerance. This was her place, and when you walked in, you were expected to treat it as such.

Royalty or not, Tiernan would have to up his game if he planned to finish writing his *Tale* from these hallowed grounds.

"Hallowed grounds," he said out loud, looking around. No one paid any attention to him, as they were too busy with their own drinks and misery to hear the words of another. Tiernan raised his hand to the wall next to him and dared to touch it.

Sticky, as one would expect. He couldn't believe that, in all the years these places had been open, no one had come up with a better source of paint for the inside of these taverns.

"Wait a minute." Tiernan picked up his quill and pulled out a sheet of paper from the back of the pile. On it, he wrote a simple phrase.

Family is Strength

He put that sheet toward the middle of the stack, intending to come back to it later. He didn't want to forget, and the paint of the Alligator had unlocked a memory fragment buried deep in his mind.

Meanwhile, Tammith had brought him another cup. He didn't notice her at first until she cleared her throat. This made him look up as she put the drink in his face.

"You get one more after this. After that, you're on your own." Her eyes noticed the stack of papers he had written. "Since when were you so eloquent with words? I thought you were a warrior." Tiernan said nothing. Instead, he nodded at her in gratitude. Tammith harrumphed, turned away, and let Tiernan resume his work.

Chapter 6

Clericsfold: Then and Now

The region known as Clericsfold was more than the city itself. Situated in the southwest corner of Central Abria, over the centuries 'Clericsfold' had come to include the Cave of Tera and the southern beaches, as well as the surrounding plains — not to mention the city itself.

The homes of the denizens were surrounded by tall castle-like walls not too dissimilar to Farna. Many visitors to the region thought the walls betrayed the nature of the populace. For those who lived further away, such as in Oakshadow or Northwick, it appeared to be a foreboding place. The city walls were black, made using stone mined from the nearby cave.

Inside, however, it was generally a peaceful, welcoming, and pleasant place to live.

The town was split into two: the northern section was where most of the community was located. The southern portion primarily housed the only orphanage throughout all of Abria. Children who had no family often ended up living in the dorms until they reached an appropriate age to take up a trade or join the Abrian Royal Guard.

"Our town was named after one of its founders, a knowledgeable man named Cleris who developed the skills to craft — fold, as he liked to call it — various potions and other elixirs from nearby foliage." Borun turned around to the class he was teaching in Abrian history. Some of them had been taking light notes; others had fallen asleep.

One teenage boy paid close attention, jotting down every word Borun said.

He continued. "Since magic itself is uncommon in the Kingdom, these concoctions are primarily used for medicinal purposes. Occasionally, an Elf from the Rosewood Forest will request an ether. This is a specific recipe, and it helps them sustain their magical abilities in stressful situations."

Borun watched as the teen taking notes pulled another notepad from his carry bag. He began flipping through the pages, and Borun could see it was full of markings from top to bottom.

The teen finally raised his hand. "Yes, Kane."

"Why is it only Elves can use magic?" Borun chuckled.

"That's a great question, but not one I can answer. You'd have to ask them." Kane raised his hand again. "Yes, Kane?"

"But Graelans can't use magic? Even if we absorb an ether?"

"No, we can't. Only Elves can use magic." He turned to the rest of the class. "I think that's enough for today." The students began packing up. A smaller boy, barely past ten years of age, suddenly dropped his book. It landed next to Kane's feet.

Who deviously laughed as he kicked it across the room. It slid, bouncing off a couple of desk legs. Another teenage student bent over to pick it up. He left his own books at his desk and brought it to the boy.

The younger boy smiled. "Thanks, Davien."

"You're welcome." He slightly punched Kane on the shoulder. "Why'd you do that?"

Kane only responded with a fake smile and a half-hearted apology to the smaller boy. "Sorry."

Beyond the importance of the orphanage, Clericsfold contained the historical Abrian Archives. Many of these documents dated back to the beginning of the New Era, though records began in earnest halfway through the rule of the second King of Abria, Telford. Much of the first King's rule was lost to history, save for a handful of documents.

Few used the Archives outside of historians. One man in particular, however, took a special interest in studying these ancient manuscripts. A man whose love of history led to him spending many days here, often studying for hours.

Today, that same man carried extensive weight within the Clericsfold Council, often dictating policy and swaying opinions with a single look. A man who was head first into his studies at this very moment.

Kane.

Lennart, one of the city managers, was unsure if he wanted to enter the Archives and disrupt its only occupant.

However, it was necessary. Earlier this week, a celebration had kicked off in the Valley to commemorate the opening of something called Borun Mill. Any time a member of the Council mentioned the name Borun, the Royal Family, or travelers from Farna, Kane stiffened up. His countenance would shift and his gaze would grow colder than it already was to most. No one knew what caused this reaction exactly, but that didn't matter. Kane had made it clear: he was to be kept apprised of all activity in the Valley.

Lennart knew this would be an uncomfortable conversation. There was no way around it, however, so he had to move forward with his assigned task. Nervously, he opened the door.

A foreboding figure sat at one of the tables in the far corner. As one of the senior members of the Clericsfold Council, Kane had served longer than the current mayor. The last election had been a landslide in favor of a man named Eskil, though Kane's endorsement helped secure the mayor's victory.

Lennart approached the door to the main hall containing the historical archives. Kane's visage was partially obscured by the light coming through a nearby window.

Most of the scrolls and books in here were covered in a thick layer of dust. The walls themself were a rich cherry wood color, though just as unattended to as the manuscripts. Shelving lined every wall with a deep vermillion brick fireplace occupying most of the northernmost side.

Lennart cleared his throat in a futile effort to alert Kane to his presence. Futile, of course, was the operative word, as the latter was too absorbed in the current manuscript to be disturbed by a minor sound.

To get Kane's attention, Lennart would have to be more direct: he would have to say the other man's name.

"Kane."

Nothing. No reaction, and Kane seemed just as lost in his reading as he had been a few moments ago. Lennart cleared his throat again, and raised his voice as he said the man's name again.

"Kane."

Kane blinked, suddenly brought back from the past and acutely aware he was no longer alone.

"You have news." It was less of a question and more of a statement. An acknowledgement. Kane's eyes narrowed as he closed the book. Lennart caught a glimpse of a name on the spine that meant nothing to him.

Zoran, 432NE.

Kane stood. Lennart knew Kane was a tall, muscular man. Today, he was downright foreboding. On days like this, when Kane would throw himself into studying the archives, he preferred wearing a sleeveless tunic. Whether intentional or not — though most presumed it was on purpose — these types of shirts revealed his broad, well-defined shoulders and immense biceps.

Today, his garments of choice were a mix of black and brown, wearing the darkest sleeveless tunic and trousers he could find. Kane paired the ensemble with a dark brown belt and a pair of boots of the same tone. A purple cape was laying over the edge of one table, the only semblance of color he ever seemed to embrace.

Furthermore, Kane preferred to shave his head. Naturally, he had blonde hair. He hated that about himself, feeling it exuded weakness for whatever reason.

Instead, he used a specially created blade to remove all the hair from his head each morning. It highlighted his chiseled jaw and ocean blue eyes. Kane turned to face Lennart, who wasn't sure what would happen next as the imposing man stood up.

"I said you have news. Enlighten me." Kane wasn't in a mood for niceties this morning, and Lennart stiffened as he spoke next.

"King Davien and his family are at Lily of the Valley. Our scouts observed them arriving early this morning. There is a celebration going on this week. Borun Mill is now open." Lennart was unprepared for what came next.

Kane growled, exuding a guttural, primal sound full of rage. At the same time, and in one smooth motion, he picked up his sword laying on the table and threw it across the Archives, blade first. It penetrated the wood and split one of the pillars in half near Lennart's head.

A sword weighing several kilos, thrown as if it were the dagger of a mere paladin, thought Lennart. Most knew Kane was strong, but this had an almost unnatural quality.

"That man," Kane raged. "That *name*. Never say it in front of me again. Do you understand? Only *I* am allowed to speak his accursed name."

"Borun!"

A younger voice cried from behind the older man's back. Borun turned around to see who had yelled for him.

"Hello, Kane."

"Back in class, when you said Graelans don't have magic. Why don't we?" Borun continued walking with Kane following behind.

"I think a better question is, 'Why are you interested in magic?' Planning to do something with it?" Kane ran in front of Borun and handed him his tablet.

"Haven't you read about all the things magic can do? There are Frost Rings and invisibility and, and…" Kane's voice rose as he got even more excited. "There's something called Ultimus magic rumored to pull power from one of the stars. Just think about what that means!"

Borun opened his mouth to speak but stopped. Kane's excitement was palpable, though the underlying tone was concerning and his obsession seemed misplaced. "How old are you, Kane?"

"Fourteen."

"It's about time for you to choose your trade, isn't it? What are you thinking of choosing?"

"History. I want to be an archivist."

Borun nodded his head. *Sounds about right.*

"There is a concert downtown tonight. Have you thought about going? Davien is planning to be there." Borun smiled. Mentioning Davien's name caused Kane to stop and think.

"I might. Will you be there?" Kane asked.

Borun shook his head to the affirmative. And with that, Kane ran off.

Lennart stood in place, still frozen in shock over what had just happened. The only way he could snap out of it was by letting his curiosity get the best of him. He pointed at the book.

"Zoran. Who or what is Zoran?" Kane raised his eyebrows. Rather, he raised the space where his eyebrows would have been. For the first time, Lennart realized Kane had shaved them off too. *Something is wrong with Kane today.*

"Zoran is a name lost to history. The King at the time, Telford, defeated him after a long, bitter, and drawn-out war. The records call it the Dark War."

Lennart was confused. "So, why study it now? It sounds like a page out of ancient history to me.

"And I'm curious. What is your opposition to the opening of Bo…I mean the Mill in the Valley?" Kane's eyes grew cold, which Lennart didn't think was possible. Already icy, they somehow lost every drop of Graelanity with the question.

"Because, Lennart, Zoran is still out there. He's here, somewhere in Abria. And the key to unlocking him is buried deep within Farna." Lennart shook his head and slightly shrugged his shoulders, not following Kane's logic.

"You don't get it, do you? No matter." *He's such an inferior being.* Kane walked over to the sword. With little effort, pulled it out of the wood. With one swift motion, he flipped it up, resting its metal blade on his shoulder. Kane smiled at Lennart, and with his free hand, politely motioned to the door. Lennart followed without saying a word.

That was another thing about Kane. In one moment, he could be full of rage and hate. In the next, his cordiality would make you feel at ease. Lennart had witnessed this switch in personality time and time again, often during Clericsfold Council meetings.

Without saying another word, they walked down the hall of the Archives toward the exit. When they stepped outside, Lennart squinted until his eyes adjusted to the bright Graelian sun shining overhead.

Kane paid it no attention. Instead, he issued a simple command.

"Take me to the orphanage."

"Kane!" Davien yelled for his friend who, at present, was walking toward the seating area. In the middle of town, volunteers had assembled a large stage. Davien patted the empty spot on the bench next to him. He handed his friend an apple. "Hungry?"

"No." Davien shrugged and put the apple back into his bag as Kane sat.

"What's wrong?" Davien inquired. "You seem, I dunno, distracted."

"It's nothing, Davien. It's Borun. He just…" Kane's voice drifted off.

"What? Come on, we've been friends forever."

Kane opened his mouth to speak, but instead began following the movement of a fly. He waited until it was just within arm's length. In a lightning-fast move, he grabbed it.

"Hey, that was quick," Davien commented. "Are you…" He stopped talking as he watched Kane gradually open his hand, just enough that the fly could move a tiny bit.

"Worthless bug." Kane squeezed his hand, ending the small creature's life.

"Was that necessary?" Kane shrugged. "I'm serious, Kane. What did the fly do to deserve that?"

Kane turned to his friend. "It was an inferior being. It didn't deserve to live."

Davien stared into Kane's eyes. *Is he joking?* The comment seemed cruel, even for Kane.

Before Davien could say anything else, a young woman walked on stage and whistled for attention. It broke the tension between the two.

"Thank you so much for coming out tonight!" The crowd was still talkative, and she was having a hard time getting control of them. Davien stood up.

"The young lady is talking! Everyone, be quiet!" Another man in the crowd echoed the sentiment, and two others followed. Their combined efforts quieted everyone down. Satisfied, Davien sat back in his seat.

"Thank you, whoever you were. As I was saying, thank you for coming tonight. My name is Teska, and we hope you enjoy the festivities. Remember, all profits tonight from any purchase at my parent's store will benefit the orphanage." She turned around to the group behind her.

"Ready, fellas?" The four teens — a lute player, a frame drum player, one young man playing the clavichord, and a flute player — gave her a thumbs up.

She cleared her voice and began singing. "The sun shone brightly in the sky. Tears flowed down her face. The love of her life…"

While she sang, Davien elbowed Kane. "What did she say her name was?" Kane seemed disinterested, instead following the flight of another fly nearby. "Hey, snap out of it." Davien shook his friend's shoulder.

Kane blinked, and stuttered. "Uhh, Teska. I think? Yeah. Teska."

Two rows behind, a silent Borun watched all of this unfold.

Teska smiled as the students she was teaching worked on their assignment. The Clericsfold orphanage, originally founded merely as a place to house Abrian children without parents, had grown to include a full school complete with a rigorous academic program.

From the ages of 5 to 15, students attended classes learning traditional subjects: Abrian History, Language Skills, Mathematics, Art, and so on. For their last two years in the orphanage, teens would focus on a trade to prepare themselves for what came next in life.

Each room was made of the same type of stone as the city walls. The classroom layouts were all rectangular, with the teacher's desk along one of the longer sides. Four windows adorned each wall, allowing natural light to spread throughout the room.

The windows were a later addition once the orphanage expanded to include the education focus. It was a pet project of Borun before he left for the Valley. He believed natural light would be more conducive to the teaching process and spent many months helping with the window installation. Now, instead of illuminating the classrooms with a bunch of candles, the Graelian sun lit up the faces of each child.

The typical day consisted of subjects one would come to expect of a school. Today, however, was different: the focus was *exclusively* on Science. Yesterday, each child had selected their favorite type of science. The assignment today was simple: students were to put together both a report and an overall outline for a larger subject-specific project down the road.

Several students were studying the stars. They planned to chart a group of the ones that moved across the night sky over the month of Lysere. Another handful of students were studying Biology with a third group focused on the process of creating potions. Teska was proud of their creativity. With the dedication they were showing, she was seriously considering making this the *only* focus for the next several weeks.

Teska moved from one student to the next, observing their work. She was oblivious to Gwenda's arrival. Her colleague taught another group of students at the school. Gwenda tapped on the door. "Teska." Teska looked in her direction and noticed the expression on Gwenda's face. She quickly walked to the door. "Kane is coming. He just left the Archives."

Teska smiled. While others, such as Gwenda, feared Kane, Teska did not. She had known him since Kane himself was an orphan here. Her father owned a shop in town, and when they were younger, she had frequently met up with Kane to eat lunch with him.

There was never an attraction between the two of them. Their relationship was akin to that of a cousin. She understood Kane had his odd tendencies, though to her they were nothing more than a form of self-expression.

✣ ✣ ✣ ✣ ✣ ✣ ✣ ✣ ✣

"Here, take it," Teska said. Kane shook his head. "I said take it. What's wrong with you? It's an Abrian Spiced Muffin. Isn't that your favorite?"

"It is, Teska. I'm just not hungry." The two were sitting on a bench near one of the city walls. "I turn fifteen tomorrow. I'm nervous."

"I don't know why you're nervous. You're just picking a trade. It's a rite of passage."

Kane stood up, angry. "See, that's one thing you city people don't understand. You're free to pursue whatever you want, whenever you want, and however you want. For orphans like us, we get one shot. I don't know why Borun made things so…rigid."

Teska stood. Kane had begun pacing. He walked over to a nearby tree and kicked it with his foot. He didn't acknowledge whether or not it hurt. Teska walked over to her friend.

"It's okay. I'm sorry, I didn't mean…" Kane turned around. He had a smile on his face.

"I know you didn't." He leaned in to hug her. His anger seemed to have disappeared almost as fast as it had reared its ugly head. "There's something else bothering me, I guess."

"I know." She didn't want to say it, but it was obvious. Many of the orphans didn't know when they had been born. Often, their birthdate became whatever day they first arrived at the orphanage.

"I…" Kane slumped back against the tree and slid to the ground. "I was young when my parents died. I don't remember them. At all."

Teska sat down next to Kane and leaned her head. "It's going to be okay." She sat up. "Hey, I saw Davien the other day. He mentioned you had been talking with one of the Kearney Sisters. The older one. What's her name again?"

Kane's face flushed. "I can't believe he told you that! It was nothing. I helped her tie up a horse. That's all."

"Liar!" Teska teased, as she playfully hit Kane on the shoulder. "Davien said you talked to her until sunset."

Kane, to his credit, didn't try to hide it. He smiled as he sheepishly lowered his head. "Thanks for letting me know. Sounds like I owe Davien a visit."

"Thanks for letting me know," Teska said to her colleague. "Could you cover my class for a moment? I'll be right back."

Gwenda graciously agreed to do so. With that, Teska left the room and headed in the direction Kane would be walking.

It did not take long to find him. He walked with a sense of urgency she hadn't seen from him before. *Something's not right today.* She smiled and pushed the thought from her mind as she met up with him, near the outskirts of the path between the two sections of Clericsfold.

"Kane! Welcome! Oh, hi, you are…?" she asked. Lennart shook his head. Kane was on a mission, and pleasantries would have to wait. Teska shrugged. "Kane, is something wrong?" Kane walked past her toward the orphanage, saying nothing in return. She trailed behind, never out of sight but giving her friend a wide berth. *Something is definitely off with him.*

When Kane entered the gates of the orphanage side of Clericsfold, everything changed. It confirmed to Teska something today was different. Kane walked into the first classroom, a group of boys nearly aging out of the program. Most of them had chosen a trade instead of military service, with woodworking and metallurgy being the two most popular choices. Kane surveyed the room and pointed to the nearest seven boys. With that, he motioned toward the door for them to follow.

Their instructor, Dolan, stood up. "Kane, can I help you?" Kane shot him a look, but surprisingly, Dolan did not back down. "You cannot take my students without a reason." Kane walked over to Dolan, standing almost nose to nose. Rather, Dolan's nose reached Kane's chin, as the latter stood a respectable head taller than the instructor.

"These men are needed. We're going to the Rosewood Forest on a mission that's vitally important to the city." A cold chill entered the room. While there was no reason to be afraid of the Forest — the Elves who lived there were friendly — the way Kane said it carried an ominous note. Plus, why wouldn't Kane recruit town guards?

Each of the boys processed this differently. One stiffened in his seat, sitting up from a typical teenage slumped over position.

Another looked back and forth at the two boys on each side of him. A third narrowed his eyes, both in a state of rebellion and curiosity. Most of the others reacted similarly.

Meanwhile, Kane walked up to the boy nearest to him. On his bench was an orange carving of a deer. Most people would have been impressed with his ability to evoke the different layers of fur within such a small piece of wood.

Kane, however, was not. He picked it up as if he was inspecting it. "What is your name?" he asked, while flipping the deer around in his hand.

"Lucerne," he responded. Upon hearing his response, Kane regarded his face for a moment. He smirked, shook his head, and proceeded to smash the deer against the wall.

"Pathetic. Woodworking. As if *this* is a viable career path."

"Woodworking!"

"You're kidding. What made you choose that?" Kane's question caused Davien to become even more excited.

"I've been spending time with Borun. He has amazing hands-on skills, and has been helping me learn the different techniques I'll need to know to become a certified tradesman."

Kane's brow furrowed. "You've been spending time with Borun? *Outside of class*?"

Davien was oblivious to Kane's implication. "Yeah, he does a lot of metallurgy in his free time. I started going over after class, but metallurgy wasn't quite right for me. When he mentioned woodworking, everything just clicked."

"And you think this is a viable career path?"

Davien nodded his head again in excitement. "I do. Who knows, maybe one day I'll become a famous carpenter. Maybe I'll make new bookshelves for your Archives."

"They're not my Archives," Kane said with a slight chuckle.

"Yet, anyway! Come on, let's go celebrate my Selection Day!"

Kane turned to walk toward the door. Teska had been observing all of this from her position in the doorway. Her opinion of Kane had never wavered until this moment. Even some of his more barbarous tendencies, such as intentionally crushing insects whenever he saw them, never came across as heartless as this interaction with Lucerne. Kane met her gaze for a moment before turning to face the classroom again.

"One hour. We leave then. Meet me at the city gates." He looked down at the broken deer carving. Lucerne had picked up the pieces, whether to fix them or to reflect on what had just happened. The boy's face reminded Kane of someone he once considered a brother.

That was ages ago. *Time to set things on the proper path*, he thought as he walked out of the room. This time, he made no attempt to acknowledge Teska, brushing past her without a second glance.

At the designated time, all eight boys showed up at the city gates. Waiting for them were Kane and Lennart, along with four city guards. Kane motioned to the guards, who began removing their armor. Next, Kane pointed at four of the boys and back to the discarded armor.

The men stood in silence for a moment until a glance from Kane said it all.

Leave now.

The four guards exchanged a series of looks, but knew better than to question a senior member of the Council. They studied the boys who were, in all four cases, struggling to put on the relatively oversized armor. They didn't know what Kane planned to do with these kids, and the plan itself seemed to make no sense.

After all, men across Abria were required to train for months before donning armor such as this. While lightweight compared to that of a long-ago fabled knight, it still took some getting used to. It wasn't as easy as changing a tunic or pair of trousers.

After the guards disappeared back into the city, Kane finally spoke to the boys not wearing armor. "Which of you can ride a horse?" No one raised their hands. Frustrated, he turned to the four wearing armor. "Which of you?" One boy — Lucerne, the carver from earlier — raised his hand. Kane laughed.

This is going to be fun.

Chapter 7

The Tall Elf

It took Kane's group a day and a half to reach the Rosewood Forest. By the time they arrived, the celebrations in the Valley had concluded. Crossing the northern path meant there was a small chance Kane's group would meet up with the Abrian Royal Contingent, depending on which way they chose to go home.

It was a risk he was willing to take.

Fortunately, at least from Kane's perspective, they had an uneventful journey from Clericsfold to the Forest with no random encounters of any kind — Royal Family or otherwise. On their way there, Lucerne rode the horse pulling a cart full of supplies: swords, a couple of shields, rations, and a handful of potions.

The group arrived several hours westward of the popular recreational facility called Fabled Wonders. This positioned them directly south — as far as Kane knew, anyway — of the Elven population. Elves and Graelans had infrequent interactions, with both races traditionally keeping to themselves.

"Only Elves can use magic." Kane had meditated on Borun's words time and time again since that day in class.

Time to find out why.

Through his studies in the Archives, he had found a few references to a leader known as the Tall Elf. Unlike many of his other brethren, this particular member of their species had shown an innate sense of curiosity. The manuscripts also described him as outspoken and discontented.

The Rosewood Forest was the largest wooded area in Abria. Five times the size of the Valley Woods, black bears comprised most of the animal population here. This was in stark contrast to the more docile creatures, such as deer and horse families, living in and around the woods near Lily of the Valley. As Kane's group approached the outer edge of the Forest, he could see a mama bear with her cub. Known for their general aversion of other species, no bear had attacked a Graelan in recorded Abrian history. Instead of a confrontation, bears throughout the land ran away.

Today, this would change. Lennart watched in silence as Kane walked over to one of the boys not wearing armor. Kane handed the youth his sword, and gestured to the bear family.

"Bring me its hide." The boy looked terrified. Not just at the sight of the bear, but at the *mere thought* of taking another life. He reached out to hold the sword, shaking.

At the same time, the mama bear realized the Graelans were at the edge of the forest. Immediately on guard, she stood up. In a split second, she would decide what to do.

Kane saw the commotion from the corner of his eye. Faster than most other people would react, he did a full 180 and launched his sword at the cub a good thirty meters away. The blow was on point, and the lethally fast weapon struck the cub on its side before the mama bear could even react. The blade drove itself deep into the cub's torso, and it let out a painful, sad cry before falling on its other side.

Deep within the Rosewood Forest, the Elves heard the commotion. One of the outspoken leaders of their community, an unusually Tall Elf named Folas, took special attention to the sound. It made him curious, and he turned to one of the nearby Elves to speak.

"Let the Elders know I'm going to go investigate."

The Elf he had spoken to tried to shake off his fear. "Y…yes, Folas." He ran off as Folas dropped his tools and started walking toward the sound. A few moments later, Folas' curiosity increased as he heard a more intense, ferocious sound, followed by a similar — if louder — cry of pain.

Then silence.

At the edge of the Forest, Kane stood over the fallen mama bear. He pulled his sword out of the mother's side and wiped its blood off of his sword and onto the bear's fur.

Two of the boys had thrown up. Another began crying at the senseless loss of life. Meanwhile, the group heard the sound of another bear nearby, and Kane motioned for them to enter the Forest.

Frightened, two from the group ran away: one wearing armor, the other without. Lucerne, still on top of the horse, sat in shock. The other five boys and Lennart stood motionless, which irritated Kane to no end. He decided to change up his plan. He pushed Lennart from behind into the Forest and handed him the sword.

"Stop. Kane. What is the purpose...no, stop." Lennart's protests fell on deaf ears as he shook his head in confusion. He struggled long enough that he was able to turn around and face Kane.

"Take charge of the situation, Mister Manager," Kane said, shoving Lennart in the chest. When the man didn't budge, Kane began pushing him deeper into the forest, in the direction of the bear sounds.

Lennart was no match for Kane's strength, tiring after a short struggle. After stumbling over some foliage and broken branches, Kane turned to face the boys. He grabbed his sword out of Lennart's hand and raised it in their direction, a signal they knew meant one thing.

Come with me now or pay the price. Lucerne dismounted and tied the horse to a nearby smaller tree. A few boys each grabbed a sword, while a few others picked up the shields on the cart.

Lucerne and another boy tried to gather as many potions as they could.

Slowly, full of fear and trepidation, they made their way into the Forest just as another bear family came into sight. Kane rushed over to one of the armored boys and grabbed the sword from his hand. He performed the same dagger-like throw as before, hitting one of the older bears in the group square in the side. As the bear let out a howl and fell over, the rest of the pack turned and began charging toward the group of boys.

Within moments, the normal collective fear within the Abrian Black Bear transformed into rage as the pack of four bears rushed toward the group. In fear, everyone began preparing for the oncoming onslaught.

Except for Kane, who step by step backed up as the battle began.

After all, inferior beings do not deserve to live.

When Folas arrived, only Kane remained standing. In the ensuing chaos, one boy without armor ran deeper into the woods, hoping to escape. This left five Graelan defenders against a pack of four angry bears.

As expected, the Graelans stood no chance against the animals. Lennart was lying face down in the mud, trampled on, motionless, and bloodied. Two of the armored boys were lying slumped against nearby trees, one face down as if he had been thrown into a tree and never stood up again. The third had been tossed across the floor of the Forest and crushed by the pack's paws. The armor was worthless against the bears' might.

The remaining boy without protection lay motionless on his back, facing the sky, a deep set of slashes across his chest and a shocked, final, painful yell etched into his frozen face. The bears had retreated, since Kane had remained out of sight during the ensuing encounter.

Kane kept a stoic face as he heard the footfalls of an approaching Elf. *My plan worked. A curious Elf can only mean one thing. It's the Tall Elf!*

Kane feigned surprise, startled by Folas' presence. "It's alright. I ran them off. This one," he said, pointing to Lennart, "did not accomplish what he set out to do." Folas looked around, inspecting the scene before saying anything. He stopped at the top of a small hill, which gave him a relative bird's-eye view of the situation.

"What happened?" he finally asked. Kane waved open-handedly first toward Lennart, then the rest of the fallen.

"This one brought a group of guards here to cause problems. My students," he said, as he pointed in the direction of the armor-less boy on the ground, "and I were on a field trip. We were on our way home from Lakedon. We heard the commotion, and saw one of them kill a defenseless cub. By the time we made it here, we tried to stop them. One of my students ran that way," he said, pointing toward the direction of the youth's escape. He kneeled down to the fallen armor-less boy, coming up with a name for him on the spot. "Diron didn't make it. He wanted to be a bricklayer. He died fearlessly trying to protect the cub, but got caught between one of the guards and the mama. It's so tragic…"

Folas walked down the hill, still curious. "What was the purpose behind the attack? What did this one," he said, pointing to Lennart, "hope to accomplish?" Kane shook his head in anger.

"These men wear the crest of Abria," he said, pointing to the fallen armored youths. "All I can assume is they hoped to send the bears into a frenzy, perhaps even angering them enough to attack your brethren."

Whether Folas fell for the lie was unclear. Elves and Graelans had a harmonious partnership. They had for centuries, ever since King Telford had welcomed them from faraway lands. *It might take more to get them to mistrust the Royal Family,* Kane admitted to himself. Still, this was the first seed. He stretched out his hand.

"I'm Kane. I am a part of the leadership at Clericsfold and a teacher at the orphanage. Or rather, I was until today." Folas accepted the gesture, grabbing Kane's extended hand. Upon grasping it, the latter could feel the magic radiating throughout the Elf's body. *Exactly what I will need.*

"Folas. Otherwise known as the Tall Elf." Kane nodded, noting the disdain in which Folas used the description. Traditionally, elves were noticeably short. Instead, Folas was almost as tall as Kane, which meant he was a rarity among his people.

"It's good to meet you, though I wish it were under better circumstances." Kane paused for a moment. "Tell me your story."

"Sixty-two thousand five hundred and eighty-two: that was all that remained of our once proud population. There used to be several hundreds of thousands of us. Not long after the New Era, we found ourselves facing extinction.

"Day in and day out, barbarians chased, hunted, and summarily executed us. My brethren had been on the run since 112NE, and had slowly made their way across a vast, unknown continent during our exile.

"I don't know much about where we came from, other than its sacred name: Lyra. It was somewhere in the far western part of this continent, destroyed by those same barbarians from the north.

"I was born during the exile. My mother once told me it was around the year 373NE, but that didn't matter at the time. I spent most of my childhood on the run. By the time I entered adulthood, only sixty-two thousand five hundred and eighty-two of us were left.

"No matter how hard I try, I can't remember all of their names. So many of my friends and family were killed before I reached maturity.

"One particularly painful memory is the day my beloved mother died. I was six. We had to cross a turbulent river. Its intensity swept many of them away, including her. We never saw any of them again.

"Weeks later, many others were ambushed and executed on the spot during *another* barbarian raid. We think they followed us across the river, but the details are too blurry. There is just too much loss to remember it all.

"We've been ruled, loosely, by a group of elders who had been there during the initial attack in 112NE. As much as we tried to get them to talk about it, few would. And those that did often spoke in distant thoughts and broken emotions.

"We had heard rumors of a sacred land in the east. Eventually, the Elders decided the only hope was to try to venture to it through a forbidden wilderness. Forbidden, because no one knew how to navigate the vast, densely wooded area that preceded it. Forbidden, because no one knew how to survive the harsh desert that followed. And forbidden still, because from what we knew, once we crossed both, there were still treacherous mountains to climb.

"And worse yet, Orcs were known to live throughout this wilderness. We fear them most of all, and few have ever lived to tell the tale of their encounter with one.

"Nevertheless, there were no other options. If we stayed in the region near Lyra, we would soon be extinct. The northern barbarians were vicious, cruel, and determined.

"The journey to the wilderness was as excruciating as it was long; the challenges awaiting us during the journey were unimaginable. Thousands died along the way. Hundreds more had unfortunate encounters with Orcs, never to be heard from again. And, once we reached the desert, an untold number died of heat exhaustion.

"By the time we reached the mountains, less than 600 of us had survived. By this point, I was one of the oldest of the group despite my relative youth.

"And I was also the tallest Elf. Abnormally tall, if I'm honest with myself. This naturally made me a leader, if not slightly feared. I helped to guide the remnants of my family and friends up the path of those incredibly high, not to mention rocky, mountains in the region west of here.

"When we descended from those heights, we found ourselves in a foreign, yet peaceful land. We made landfall in 479NE near a town the residents called Oakshadow.

"As it so happened, the King of the land at the time, Telford, welcomed us. He just happened to be in Oakshadow during our arrival and explained how Abria was isolated from the rest of Grael, save for rare visitors via boat. It was the first time we had heard anyone tell us the name of the world.

"The other 531 Elves who arrived with me were the first large group of travelers since the dawn of the New Era. Telford welcomed us with open arms. He gave us a portion of the Rosewood Forest as our own, and granted our leadership autonomy to make their own decisions as we rebuilt our numbers.

"It was all one broken promise, though, as Telford never carried through on his word."

Kane sat and absorbed every triviality from the Elf's story. He was thankful his love of history had given him an ability to remember stories and events in such extensive detail.

"Independence. A chance to rebuild. A chance to regroup. *Freedom*." Folas and Kane had moved to a group of rocks within the forest, sitting a few dozen meters from the fallen youths.

Kane couldn't believe his luck. Not only did he plant a seed of discord within Folas, but the Elf himself was already frustrated with Abria.

"Continue, my friend." Kane egged him on, hoping Folas might reveal some hidden nugget that would create an ally. Perhaps a revelation that would uncover a magical means to explore the catacombs of the castle. A way to unlock the power he craved.

The Soul Sword.

It was one of three mythical, magical relics within Abria. The other two, the Mind Shield and the Power Ring, were powerful in their own right. However, the Soul Sword itself was, according to the Archives, how the King locked away Zoran. With its power, King Telford sealed his nemesis within a supposed hidden cave somewhere in Abria, though the Archives made no mention of where.

Folas continued, "King Telford promised Abria would welcome us. That we would have the means to develop magic and powers that would eventually enable us to leave this forsaken land and return to our home.

"To overthrow the Barbarians that killed so many of us."

"So, what happened next? The Elves are barely mentioned in the Archives." *A lie*, Kane thought. The Archives talked fondly of the Elves after their arrival. Yes, they did mention their desire to return home. They were also referred to as a peaceful, aloof group.

"He trapped us. Boxed us in. Not long after our arrival, Oakshadow began building that accursed hall, Mystic something or the other.

"A few years later, someone else built that amusement place on the *other* side of the Forest. The Kingdom of Abria began using our *home* as a supply for lumber, shipping the trees we loved elsewhere. Tearing them down."

A beat. "Tearing down our home. Can you even begin to fathom what that was like for us? We were, what did Telford call it? Ah, yes, refugees. And instead of fulfilling his promises, he almost immediately began a process that has trapped us here for centuries."

Kane spoke up. "In other words, Abria is not your home. The Kingdom treats you as squatters, foreigners." Folas nodded as Kane continued. "Then, acts like today. The Abrian Royal Guards themselves, stirring up the local anima…" Folas raised his hand. Kane stopped speaking, suddenly wondering if his words went too far.

"I may not have any love for the Kingdom or the Royal Family, but I can smell a lie. Kane, isn't it?" Kane nodded his head. "I could tell from a quick glance those were not Royal Guards. Your story was weak, which is of no consequence to me. Tell me why you're here. The truth, Kane. No more lies." He smiled. "After all, that's not a way to treat a potential ally."

Kane smirked, raised his eyebrows — or rather, the skin where eyebrows would have been — and nodded to himself. "It must be fate that brought us together, after all. You want to know why I'm here? It's because I need help." He pointed south-westward, toward Farna. "Somewhere in there is an item called the Soul Sword. I need it."

"But why? And why come here?" It was a valid question, Kane concluded. *Time to come clean.*

"Maybe you can relate to a decision made in haste?" Folas made no indication of yes or no, leaving Kane with no other choice but to continue. "In my case, I let my anger consume me." He sighed. "Simply put, I thought he could stir up some dissension with the bears and your group. At the least, I could get your attention.

"Which I did, but it sounds like the easiest path forward may have very well been to ask for your help." Kane sighed again as he prepared to reveal it all.

"You want to know why I'm here? Because I *need* to kill King Davien. That man, someone I once thought of as a brother, is an imposter to the throne. He's not even of royal blood, but that's beside the point. If Borun, that foul-mouthed, ignorant, arrogant teacher was going to adopt someone, it should have been me. Someone *fit* to lead this country.

"Instead, he chose a woodworking nobody to call his own." Anger welled up. "And now that imposter sits in power on the throne of Abria." He stood, determined, staring toward the castle. "I must right that wrong. And to do so, *I need help.*

"This plan," he motioned back toward the fallen orphans, "may have been done in anger. Borun opened a mill over in the Valley." He nodded, understanding something about himself for the first time. "I rushed in. I let my hate of him get the best of me. I won't do that again.

"I made a mistake today, but at least something good came from it, for my error brought me to you."

Folas' eyes narrowed as he contemplated Kane's words. A moment later, he spoke, "There is one part I still don't understand. Killing Davien? That's something I would have willingly helped with. You didn't need to go through this trickery. The Royal Family lied to us. Trapped us here and boxed us in. They made us second class residents of this accursed land. Davien's death will be my revenge on them for those transgressions."

Folas rose to his feet. "But I feel like there's more to this than you're letting on. There's something you're not telling me. What is it?"

Kane laughed at the Tall Elf's forwardness. But it wasn't a chuckle or normal laugh, rather a deep, foreboding, sinister sound. "That one, my newfound friend, is a little more complicated. But no matter. I need the Soul Sword, along with the magic keeping Farna perpetually a paradise.

"And that will take more work than you or I can pull off. We'll need more of your brethren to accomplish this task."

"I see. I don't know what the 'Soul Sword' is or if there is any special underground magic, but I digress. Killing the King will be easy enough.

"A far more complex task will be getting the rest of the Elves on your side, especially since you're asking them to betray our hosts for a purported myth.

"You're right, Kane. The two of us can't defeat Abria alone. But convincing the others? That might take some time. Most of them are content. They *like* it here. Few see it the way I do, though there are some dissenters." Folas visibly recoiled as he continued to elaborate. "One *traitor* even lives over near the Valley, but he can be dealt with." Kane could almost taste the disgust in Folas' words.

"I may be able to help, Folas. But beyond dealing with traitors, I'll need the Sword to unseal the power keeping our ultimate ally, Zoran, locked away.

"And, I'll need that hidden magic deep below the castle to restore Zoran's power. With Zoran, we can destroy Farna once and for all. After it's gone, I'll set up my seat of power from where it rightfully belongs: Clericsfold."

Chapter 8

Intermissio 2nd

Tiernan put down the quill. He reread the words he had just written. His knowledge of the initial meeting between Kane and Folas was from ages ago. And like so much of this portion of his life, he was relying on what he heard from others.

In this case, Lucerne had *not* perished in the bear attack. After being knocked backward by one of the pack, he struggled to stand up in the oversized armor. Once he finally did so, another bear threw him across the forest field where he landed chest first into a tree. After wrapping around the large trunk, his body fell face down, motionless. The pain that enveloped Lucerne's body was more excruciating than anything he had ever experienced in his relatively short life.

However, his will to survive was far stronger than the agony raging through his body. From that moment onward, Lucerne pretended to be dead. During the conversation between the two conspirators, Lucerne knew he had to be quiet. Still.

Completely and unreservedly silent. Everything they said, he tried to remember as best as he could. It ached to breathe, which made focusing on their words difficult.

Nevertheless, he had an innate realization this information would one day come in useful.

Years later, Lucerne would describe to Tiernan the struggle he experienced here as he waited for Folas and Kane to leave the area. The two conspired and planned forever, or so Lucerne thought. Time seemed to have lost all meaning as his body ached more with each passing moment. During their meeting, the boy who had run off into the woods had wandered back by.

Lucerne breathed as silently as he could as Kane painfully ended the boy's life. *Another senseless death,* he lamented while trying to stay quiet.

Next to Lucerne was his dear friend Vincent, though the poor orphan was now dead. One of the attacking bears had viciously crushed Vincent's chest. Lucerne had already been thrown into the tree by this point, and inside his mind, he cried out in anguish as his friend perished.

As the battle waged on, Lucerne refused to cry despite the pain, despite the overwhelming emotions, despite the uncomfortableness and abject horror surrounding him.

Once the other boys, along with Lennart, were dead, Lucerne breathed as shallow as he could to avoid making any type of sound. Even when Kane walked over to him, he stayed motionless. Kane picked up Vincent's arm and checked for a pulse. He was about to do the same to Lucerne when Folas arrived.

Most of the plans Folas and Kane discussed made no sense to Lucerne. There was something about a person who was 'sealed away' — whatever that meant — and a plan to exact revenge against Abria for perceived wrongs.

Eventually, the two conspirators left. Once Lucerne believed enough time had passed, that Kane and Folas were far enough away and out of sight, the wounded youth began to move. He took his time standing up, removing his armor as quiet as possible.

Despite the presumed distance of Kane and Folas, Lucerne knew he couldn't afford to make any sound. Once he was down to his basic tunic and trousers, Lucerne checked each of the fallen, from his fellow orphans to Lennart.

Proving his worst fears, Lucerne discovered he was the only survivor. Later in the day, Lucerne came across the bodies of the two boys who ran away near the plains outside of Oakshadow. As best as Lucerne could gather, Kane and Folas had tracked them down.

He assumed it was so they could eliminate any witnesses. This confirmed what Lucerne was most afraid of: in his heart, he couldn't return to Clericsfold ever again. If he did, Kane would know he survived and finish the job.

So instead, Lucerne went to Farna. He wasn't sure how many people would believe him, especially regarding the actions of Folas and Kane. So once there, he lied and stated he was from Milston looking for work, explaining the stains and tears on his clothing came from an injury sustained while crossing the plains.

And most of all, he avoided any mention of the word orphan or Clericsfold, claiming he decided to look for work in Farna as a way to start a new life for himself.

"Enough reflection," Tiernan said to himself. He picked up the quill to begin writing again. Lucerne would disappear for a long time, serving within the Abrian Royal Guard as best as he could as a faceless, nameless sentinel.

Later, he would play a role in the story, but Tiernan didn't want to get ahead of himself.

Though, much to his frustration, once again he was out of water. However, he dared not ask Tammith for any more. *Maybe I'll have to go elsewhere to continue my writing.*

A moment of remembrance flashed across Tiernan's face. "Ah yes." His memories between the opening of Borun Mill and *that day* were scattered.

"Poor Enid," he said, slightly chuckling to himself. Laughter felt good. *Maybe that's what this is all about,* he wondered. *The old man wanted me to remember joy before I died of self-loathing.* He flipped over a blank page and resumed writing.

Chapter 9

The Investigation

The 2nd day of Windbloom in the year 903NE was unusually warm for that time of year. Some leftover snow, remnants of an intense season of Frost, had fallen a few days earlier, though the high temperatures meant none of it had stuck. While it gave the residents reason to get out for a bit of fresh air, it also meant Lily of the Valley was open and ripe for business.

The recently completed Drunken Alligator had brought an influx of travelers from Lorelei and Idlewind alike. Many of those decided to make the Valley their home, building homes along the town's eastern border.

Along with that came an escalation in business. Borun Mill expanded twice during its second year of operation, hiring more and more people from around the region who often chose to become residents of the Valley.

Borun walked out of his home just as the sun was beginning to rise. Today felt like a good day, and that was saying something.

After all, to Borun, *every day* was a good day. He stepped out of his door and surveyed the growth. A picturesque well now stood proudly in the center of town. To the north, the Drunken Alligator was already open, with the smell of freshly baked bread permeating throughout the warm air.

To the east of the Alligator was a newly opened shop. They sold wares and weapons forged in Northwick. On both sides of that vendor were multiple market businesses: food, fabrics, building supplies, and home goods. Borun, as the town's de facto leader, wanted to create some kind of name for this emerging hub of commerce.

"The Eastern Market!" he kept telling Tolith. His Elven friend would laugh, before pushing back with a friendly yet not untrue remark.

"Silly Graelan. Is that the best you can come up with? You need it to be catchy, memorable. Something like," as Tolith would often reply, smiling wide as he dropped the dramatic reveal each time, "The Tolith Market. Named in honor of your best friend!"

Borun smiled as he remembered the last time they had this same conversation. "Let's go to the *Tolith Market,* my friend," he said to the Elf, putting emphasis on the name with a sense of defiance. Today, Borun walked north along the same path, passing the homes of couples and families who had recently moved in.

First, he passed by the home of Gudrun and her sister Moselle, elderly residents from Farna who had visited and never left. Behind their home was a large complex where several families had set up communal housing.

With each and every step, he passed new friends, new residents, and new opportunities to turn the Valley into one of the most powerful regions within Abria. After several moments of walking, he finally reached the market.

"The North Market?" he asked himself. True, the collective groups of shops *were* in the northernmost section of the Valley. But they were also situated along the eastern path within the town — not the exact northern tip of Lily of the Valley. Instead, construction was underway for a lush flower garden.

"You're still trying to think of a name for this place?" asked a woman. Borun turned around to see who had spoken. Through an open window, he could see that it was Morta, owner of a new shop named Bakes and Cakes, selling — naturally — baked goods and specialty cakes. A tall, red-haired woman, she and her husband had moved in a few months earlier, and it was an immediate hit with the residents.

At least her baked goods were. Her husband hadn't quite found his place in the Valley yet.

A warm breeze blew through the air. Borun breathed in deeply, taking in all the sensations before answering. "Ah, Morta! How are you today? Smells like you're preparing something divine!" Remembering another question, he moved closer. "How do you like the metal framing I dropped off last week?"

Morta smiled. One of Borun's *Welcome to the Town* gifts for each new resident was some kind of metalwork. He tried to make it custom-tailored for the personality of each person.

Some, such as the Drunken Alligator, received exquisite door handles and knobs. Others, such as Morta, received metal accent pieces for the walls of their business. In Morta's case, she was going for a distinctive look within the bakery: a blend of ornate dragon-inspired carvings across the top half of the walls, complete with metal framing along each beam. At the bottom, carpenters had been working on a design that included hints of intricately detailed flowers. Borun loved the concept and was excited to see the finalized product.

"My husband hasn't had a chance to attach all of them just yet. When it's completed, I'll let you know. You ignored my question."

Borun laughed. That was one thing about Morta: when she asked a question, such as what a customer wanted, she wanted an answer. No hem-hawing about it.

"Yes, yes, I have yet to come up with a name for this collection of vendors. My friend Tolith wants it to be named after him for some bizarre reason. What do you recommend?" Morta paused, raised her eyebrows, and half frowned. Clearly, she didn't have an answer herself. Finally, her eyes lit up.

"The Dagnall Market, after my son." Borun laughed again, as he remembered his first encounter with the small boy. Dagnall was born around the same time as his grand-twins. During the opening of Borun Mill, one of the celebrations included a dance. For whatever reason, Borun had picked up the boy and carried him around while enjoying the music.

To no one's surprise, Dagnall had spit up on one of Borun's favorite tunics. Everyone had a good laugh, and Borun proceeded to spend the rest of the dance shirtless.

While most found the spectacle hilarious, Borun's daughter-in-law was less than impressed.

"Perhaps. It's open for discussion at any rate. How is your husband?" Morta smiled through the window and resumed whatever pastry work she had been engrossed in before the conversation began.

"You know him. He's thrown out several ideas about new business ventures. First, he said he wanted to convince your son to move the Archives here. Then he would become, what did he call it? Ah yes, the 'Grael-famous archivist.'"

She shook her head as she began measuring flour. "That lasted about a week. Then he spent a day with one of his friends working in your Mill. Literally, a day! I told him it was okay. He could be a full-time, stay-at-home father. The money we make from Bakes and Cakes more than supports us. What do you think?"

Borun thought about the question, but before he could answer, he heard a commotion from behind. A crowd was gathering at the far western end of town.

Near Borun Mill.

He gave Morta a quick glance back, a courtesy nod which she returned, and took off toward the increasingly louder and louder noises emanating from the direction of his beloved mill.

It didn't take him long to arrive. Borun may have been old, complete with a body composed of one too many ales over its life, but he was fast. As he ran across town, he saw a small crowd near the central well.

Curious, he thought as he passed by them. One of them was pointing downward in the well, with another holding an empty water bucket.

At the Mill itself, it was unclear what was going on from a distance. As Borun approached, a few in the crowd noticed him. One man tapped the shoulder of the person in front of him who turned and saw Borun. The two cleared other residents out of the way as Borun walked in the general direction they were all facing.

Borun built the mill in an open field along the shores of the great Lorelei River. There, the massive water wheel used the river's flow to power the mill's operation, giving the workers a helping hand of automation as they produced lumber harvested from the Valley Woods.

For the first time, Borun noticed the water wheel itself wasn't moving. "Impossible..." The Lorelei River was the most formidable, naturally occurring phenomena in Abria.

Nothing should be able to slow it. The wheel moved even when workers had gone home for the day, purely because of the river's momentum.

Today, the Lorelei River was at a virtual standstill. The source of the river started in the mountains near Milston and Northwick. It flowed southward past the city of Lorelei, from which the river got its name.

It continued southbound through this region, acting as a separation between the town of Lily of the Valley and the Valley Woods on the other side. Further south, it twisted and turned, banking west slightly as it went around the Windale Mountains and emptied into the ocean at Kingscrown Bay.

This flow could not be stopped. Even on a day with low winds, it was extremely difficult to cross the river, which is why several bridges in key areas had been built over the centuries.

Now, one could take a swim in the river without fear of being washed out to sea. A few Valley residents carefully approached the river. Two dared to put their feet into it, with one of them venturing waist deep.

"Stop…never mind," said Borun, initially fearful for their safety but quickly catching himself. For all intents and purposes, the Lorelei River was dead.

And for all intents and purposes, Borun Mill would be dead too, unless they could find out what stopped the river's flow.

Bright and early the next day, Borun dropped a saddle onto the back of a borrowed horse. It had taken him most of the previous day on foot to arrive in Whispersong, the community south on the path out of Lily of the Valley.

Borun planned to head south to Kingscrown Bay and back again northward so he could explore every nook and cranny of the Lorelei River. He reasoned it would be more efficient to head south anyway, beginning at Kingscrown Bay and following the river northbound, since he would need a horse first.

Whispersong primarily housed horse stables and the homes of those that tended to them. With the majority of the horses in Abria living in and around this region, it only made sense this would be the equestrian hub of the Kingdom.

Farm hands from Whispersong both raised horses and captured wild ones, domesticating them and training them for various tasks. The owner of Whispersong Stables, a man named Ahern, had owned them for a long time. A few months earlier, he and his wife had welcomed a newborn son into the world, an heir named Steve who would one day inherit the homestead.

"Such an unusual name," Borun said as he paid the going rate for a horse rental. Ahern didn't acknowledge the comment. He had other matters to attend to, and what an old man thought of his son's name was of no consequence to him.

Borun finished brushing the horse's hair before placing a pad and saddle on its back. Finally, he patted his borrowed steed on the side. Ahern said the horse had no name yet, which Borun decided needed to be rectified. He committed that, on this journey, the horse would come back to its owners with one.

Borun made it to Kingscrown Bay by nightfall. Here, he set up camp on the east side of the Lorelei River near the Bay itself. The brightness of Kingscrown Rock shone across the bay and in nearby fields.

"No stargazing tonight." He wondered if he would sleep at all, considering how the rock's glow permeated throughout the night sky.

Borun's eyes snapped open. Apparently, he *did* sleep. By the height of the sun's rise, he estimated it was somewhere near mid-morning. He couldn't remember the last time he slept this late, and began packing up his supplies. Nothing here, as far as he could tell, would dam up the river. Based on everything he saw at this end, the Lorelei River should be raging as usual.

Several hours further north, he ran into a herd of deer drinking water from the now still river. Usually, deer and horses drank from the outlying tributaries of the river. Instead, today they had full access to the Lorelei River itself. This group, a buck, doe, and two fawns, paid him no mind. Their smooth fur reflected some of the sun's light, and he only paused for a moment to admire their beauty before continuing his journey.

As he trekked further northbound, he approached the town he called home. Even from a faraway distance, he could see the giant water wheel of his mill remained motionless. Still a distance from town, Borun approached the southern edge of the Valley Woods.

On the side Borun had been riding was an immense grassland populated by the Valley Rose. On the opposite side of the Lorelei River, trees of varying heights and sizes began to take shape. He could see empty spots where workers from the mill had cut down trees and brought them across via one of the nearby bridges.

His employees had begun creating an alternative path, unintentionally of course, as they hauled the wood up to the mill. This was one of the reasons for the flower garden at the north end of town: preservation.

The Valley Rose was a delicate flower. It also only grew here, and collectively, the townspeople wanted to preserve it. As Lily of the Valley grew, they didn't want to cause this magnificent flower to go extinct.

For the first time, Borun questioned the name of his home. "Why didn't we call it Rose of the Valley?" he said, though no one heard him. His eyes lit up. "The Rose Market."

This new name for the collection of shops carried a sense of weight and appropriateness, continuing the floral naming convention of this part of Abria. The remaining roses in this region gave the fields an intoxicating smell, and Borun was tempted to stay and enjoy it for a few moments. However, he was on a mission, one he needed to complete sooner rather than later.

By nightfall, Borun arrived at the bridge near the northern path. He set up camp here, and upon unpacking his tent, laid on a cot he brought to admire the stars.

Stars that, tonight, were mostly obscured by cloud cover. Borun grumbled, moved the cot inside of the tent, and called it a night.

The next morning, he woke up early to the sound of rain on his tent. *Great. A soggy day ahead. Better get going.* It took him less time than usual to pack up, and off he went. He passed through the fields of Lorelei, noting the growth of the town since the last time he visited.

Borun passed another deer family, though this group noticed him without moving. They watched quietly as he continued northward toward the Milston Mountains.

"What in Grael?" From the distance, Borun could see *something* at the head of the river. He pushed his dripping hair out of his eyes to get a better view. Where the water normally flowed out of the Milston Mountains was a small encampment.

Small, he realized, was more than an appropriate word. Three Elves stood at the base of the mountain. Two of them had wands pointed at the river's source. Another was sitting in a chair eating something resembling soup or porridge.

Not long after spotting them, the sitting Elf saw him in return. The diminutive being yelled to the other two, who momentarily dropped their wands. The river began flowing again with intense agony, almost as if the blockage had physically hurt it.

The three Elves said something to each other, raised their three wands in unison, and fired a blast of blue magic toward the river's source. This time, deep in the cave where the Lorelei River began, it froze behind a thick wall of ice. The Elves turned to face the approaching Borun, snapped their fingers, and disappeared.

Borun didn't have a chance to say a word before any of this happened. Instead, he was powerless to do anything as all of this transpired before him.

A few moments after the Elves disappeared, Borun arrived at the edge of the cave. The rain continued to pour, so he dismounted from his still nameless horse just inside of the entrance.

As he walked inside, he noticed how wet and damp the walls were. They glistened with moisture, and moss lined the base of the cave all around. He could instantly feel the chill in the air as he grew closer to the giant mass of ice preventing the water from flowing.

Combined with the lessening of light as he moved deeper into the cave, the atmosphere shifted. The air carried a sinister note, making his skin crawl. Everything around him evoked hate and disdain.

For the first time since Borun left Whispersong, he heard another voice. "Shut down the mill." It came from the depths of the cave. Borun frozen in place as the person came into view.

It was another Elf, but this time a much taller one. In his estimation, this new Elf was taller than the average Graelan. Borun didn't know Elves could grow to this height.

As this new figure came into view, though still obscured by the shadows within the cave, Borun could see the Elf carried a wooden staff. Step by step, this 'Tall Elf' approached him until the latter could finally start to make out a few features.

"Who are you?" he retorted. "And why should I shut down the mill? It's brought nothing but good things to the Valley." The Elf responded by flipping his staff around and firing a blast of magic toward Borun. It knocked the old man backward, causing him to land on his back near the base of the cave.

"It's not your place to know, Graelan. It's only your place to submit. This will be your only warning." The Elf snapped his fingers like the others and disappeared into the darkness.

Borun stood up, his backside muddy from skidding along the damp grass. There was no sign of his opponent, and the blast didn't necessarily hurt.

It was just forceful. He continued walking into the cave until he could see the ice face to face.

"A frozen river. A Tall Elf. What will this afternoon bring?" Borun put his hand on the ice before he kneeled down to inspect it closer. A small, almost indiscernible trickle of water was beginning to flow once again at the base of the ice. "Hopefully it brings better luck."

He returned to his horse, now deciding it should be named Lucky for two reasons. One, it *felt* like luck the Elf's attack hadn't hurt him more. And two, he found the answer to his problem in such a short time.

The ice melted after a few days. Once it was gone, the great Lorelei River flowed once again. As the intensity of the river's force made its way southbound, it restored power to Borun Mill and the water wheel.

Likewise, the central well, dry once the underground tributaries from the river stopped flowing, resumed its duty of providing water to the residents of Lily of the Valley.

Contrary to his instructions, Borun did *not* shut down the mill, though someone started blocking shipments between the east and west sides of Abria. No one from Lily of the Valley was allowed to pass through Clericsfold. Posted guards prevented any travel. Borun Mill could produce all the lumber it wanted, but it had no direct means of shipping its goods.

Instead, any shipments would have to take the long trip: northbound to Lorelei, across the northern path, south along the western most path, and finally to Castle Abria and Alwyn. There were rumblings in Northwick about opening a shipping dock, but those were too far down the road to help right now.

Production at the mill had gradually slowed down when one day, workers from the mill made their trek southbound to the connecting bridge to harvest lumber for a special order for Milston. Upon their arrival, they found the bridge was completely destroyed.

Rather, the bridge was missing, almost as if it had never existed.

Borun Mill may have been up and running, but it was now a moot point. A bridge could be rebuilt, but with a limited customer base, it was impractical. One by one, families began leaving the Valley to rebuild a life elsewhere in Abria.

A few weeks after the bridge went missing, Borun was sitting alone near the fireplace in the Drunken Alligator. He heard a creak as the door to the tavern opened, but paid it no attention. With the owner's permission, Borun had brought in a large chair and put it near the fireplace. There, it stayed as a place for those who wished to use it.

Though open to all, Borun was its primary user. Night or day, Borun would sit in the chair, contemplating his next move while trying to understand why the Tall Elf threatened him in the first place.

It was in that same chair Borun sat as the door to the Alligator opened. Next to him, a slowly warming — and virtually untouched — Lorelian Mead languished on the table beside the fireplace.

Borun wasn't depressed, though outwardly it appeared to many he was. Instead, he was merely thinking. Contemplating. Planning.

Trying to decide what course of action would be best. Try as he might, Borun didn't know why he had to shut down the mill or why the Elves he encountered were so adamant he did so.

What did it matter? Who would care so much about a lumber mill? Why was it wrong to bring joy and happiness and economic prosperity to the Valley?

Borun's trail of thoughts was interrupted by the voice of the person who had just walked in. "Borun," they said. Borun blinked a few times, snapping out of his trance while sitting up and turning to face the voice.

"Tolith!" It was his Elven friend who had been missing for quite some time. Now, just a few weeks from Midfest, he had reappeared. Borun pointed to a nearby bench, and Tolith sat down.

"Wouldn't this be better with two chairs?" asked Tolith. Borun realized his friend was right, and mentally noted he should find another chair for the fireplace. "I think I know what happened."

With these words, Borun's eyes grew wide. Tolith had left town the moment Borun himself returned on Lucky — the same horse he now owned.

Borun didn't know why Tolith had left town, or — and he hated he even thought it — if his friend was somehow connected. His disappearance was perplexing, though seeing his friend again assuaged many of those fears. Borun didn't know how he would react upon seeing Tolith again; now had his answer: joyfully, as if nothing had ever gone wrong in the first place.

"Tell me. What's going on? Why is someone targeting the Valley?" Tolith jumped down off of the bench and came closer to his friend. He grabbed Borun's hand.

"Do you remember what Manus Midir discovered during his scouting expedition to Clericsfold?" Borun nodded. He closed his eyes in resignation as he made the connection.

"So, it's Kane." Borun pulled his hand back from Tolith and made a fist. He punched his other hand, angry he didn't see what was so obvious. "Kane is blocking the passageway between the two sides of Abria, isn't he? I mean, I guess that makes sense, considering my connection to Clericsfold from back in the day. No one else there would harbor resentment toward me but him. "But I don't understand, Tolith. What's the connection with the Elves?"

Tolith returned to the bench. "That's why I left. For one, I knew my presence here, in the Valley," he said, motioning around, "might create some friction. No one knew why those Elves had blocked the river, both with their Stop Magic and with their frost powers. I had to find out. So I went home." Tolith sighed.

"It's someone I once knew, someone from long before we came to Abria. Like him, I was born during our people's exile. I never knew our homeland. I later learned it was called Lyra, or at least the region was called that. Doesn't it have a nice ring to it? Lyra, almost like a flower. Maybe that's why I love it here."

Tolith sighed again. Like the others of his clan, he had an innate desire to return home. It was present in all Elves. Tolith often wondered if his homeland was like the Valley, which would explain why he felt at home here.

Then again, everyone else from his clan stayed in the Rosewood Forest and seemed just as content. So, maybe he was the odd one of his brethren.

Tolith continued. "When we came to Abria, there was one Elf who — like you, my friend — naturally became the leader."

Borun protested. "I'm not the lead…" Tolith raised his hand to stop Borun's objection.

"Whether you admit it or not, Borun, people here see you as the one in charge. The sooner you accept that, the happier you'll be."

"I'm already quite happy, thank you very much. Think of all I've built here and the…"

"Anyway, back to *my* story," Tolith said, interrupting Borun. "As I was saying, that person, an unusually Tall Elf named Folas, along with the other elders, helped bring us here. When we arrived, we made a deal with your grandfather."

"Telford?" Borun had been born fifty years before the end of Telford's rule. "I remember hearing about when your group arrived, but I've never heard anything but good things between our peoples."

"Well, it's a deal Folas feels your side did not uphold."

Borun shrugged. *If Folas had a grievance with the Royal Family, he needed to address it with them, not by messing with my mill.*

"So what's the connection, Tolith?"

Tolith then dropped the big one. "Folas has aligned with Kane." The words hit Borun hard, wincing at the mention of his former student and the path he had taken.

"I should have seen this coming." Tolith cocked his head to one side. "Many years ago, Kane was a student at the orphanage in Clericsfold. He loved history, which was one of the classes I taught. He chose the career path of an Archivist, which meant most of his latter teenaged years were spent with scribes, studying the ancient manuscripts of our Kingdom's history.

"Today, Kane is a powerful figure in Clericsfold. He embraced politics a decade or so into adulthood, though magic fascinated him as a teen. I assume he's the reason no one from Clericsfold came to the celebrations here a few years back." Borun clasped his hands together and brought them up to his face.

"What are you planning to do? I know that look. You wear your emotions on your sleeve, my friend." Borun lowered his hands and used them to push himself up off of the seat.

"I'm going to Farna."

"Mind if I tag along? I've never been to the castle before." Borun smiled and motioned toward the door.

"Got any dragon friends nearby to help get us there faster?" Tolith cackled with amusement as the two walked out of the bar.

"No, my lazy friend, I don't."

Most siblings have a bond only those with a brother or sister themself tend to understand. An only child will often look at a sibling pair with a sense of bewilderment and, depending on the relationship, a little bit of fear.

Twins are even more special, sharing a deep connection from the womb and beyond.

When Tiernan and Enid were five, they were a picture-perfect example of this type of family bond.

"...and according to Tibor, the Port of Alwyn recently had visitors from a region known as Lonlin. They have many delicacies there," Kyrie said as the King and Queen walked into their throne room.

"A large kingdom of farmers. I wonder if the ocean currents help keep it temperate there, like here in Farna?"

The first five years of Davien and Kyrie's rule had aged the King more than he had expected. Already, despite his relatively young age of seventy-two, he was beginning to gray. Streaks of salt and pepper ran along his sideburns. His wavy brown head of hair had only begun to thin on top, a fact Kyrie loved to tease her husband over.

The stresses of running Abria had led to a slight weight gain too, mostly because of the sedentary life he now lived. To complete the look of the wizened leader, Davien chose to grow a goatee. Kyrie hated it, and secretly vowed to figure out a way to convince him to shave it off.

Despite his physical changes, in those few short years, Davien had grown into his position. To outsiders, he always carried himself with a sense of power and honor. For those within his household, he was just an ordinary husband and father.

Queen Kyrie was every bit his outward match with eyes showing both authority as well as empathy. Four years younger than Davien, there was no sense of aging within her. Her golden red hair, often tied in a bun, exuded vibrancy. She spent large portions of her day tending to their children, which kept her physically active. This had an unintended side effect as well: many in Farna were exceedingly aware of the Queen's beauty. She hadn't lost any of her youthful appearance, and now in the public eye, her toned physique was difficult not to notice.

Together, they walked to their seats. Kyrie took off her crown and began removing the pins holding her hair in place. It was only when she was alone with her husband that she would take them out, letting her hair flow down naturally to her waist. After she finished, the King leaned in his chair toward his wife.

"What about timber? Could those farmers use timber from Borun Mill as a part of a trade deal?"

Kyrie smiled. "Davien, let it go. I know that your father's mill is eager to resume business. Just have patience. We can build a port not far from Lorelei, which would be faster than shipping it across the entire country." Her playful side emerged momentarily. "We could give this new port a *catchy* name. Northwick or something," she said sarcastically.

This made Davien laugh. "You know, I've always wondered why they went with such a simplistic name. They're in the north. There are trees nearby. You put wicks in a candle, and wicks come from wood. Let's call ourselves *Northwick*!" Together, they shared a chuckle and Kyrie placed her hand on her husband's.

"You know it's going to infuriate Tibor," Kyrie echoed. As usual, Davien had been thinking the same thing as his wife. After all, since assuming the throne, Northwick had been a curious situation for the Royal Family.

For years, there had been rumblings about opening a northern port. These talks escalated after Northwick harvested many of the trees from around the country side for lumber. The cleared land reinforced the idea the economy of Northwick was about to change, and the growth in the Valley had presumably been the boost they would need to expedite this process.

Leadership from the Port of Alwyn was opposed to this, as they had also recently completed the process of expanding their docks and shipping capabilities along their coastline. They advocated, via a series of meetings with Davien, that a second port was unnecessary.

They even tried to use the recent arrival of a few boats from the Isles once again as proof of their superior shipping access. These traders arrived during Begynde when the snow would make a Northwick arrival impractical.

During the debates, there was an underlying, if unspoken, threat: Northwick could not be allowed to disrupt the economic prosperity within the Alwyn community.

However, throughout those talks, Davien assured them shipping lanes would remain open for both cities, perhaps with a tailored focus. After all, if his plans for growth were to happen, they would need the power of both ports working together — not against each other.

Kyrie sighed. "What am I saying? Country? Kingdom? Trade deals? I'm not sure I'll ever get used to this." She stood up and walked to the same window where King Tiernan the First would often stand. Davien walked up behind her and placed his hands around her waist. He kissed her cheek before speaking.

"You're right, you know?"

"About what, my dear husband?" Kyrie's playful tone meant she knew what he was about to say, but wanted him to say it. Davien turned his wife around to face him while keeping his arms wrapped around her body.

"You know."

"Say it."

Davien sighed. "Yes, ok? I admit I'm trying to do what I can to help Dad's business thrive and grow. It's the least I can do for all he's done for me."

Her playful tone returned. "Such as leaving us with the responsibility of the entire Kingdom?"

"Well, except that one." He gently kissed her as he ran his hand along her cheek. "You know, everyone else is right, too."

For the first time in a while, Kyrie was confused. "About what?"

"About how beautiful you are. And how lucky I am to have you by my side."

"Ah. Well, I think I got the better part of that deal." She kissed him again, though the act was interrupted by a loud noise.

Outside in the hallway, the sound of footsteps was fast approaching. A pair. Running. Faster, lighter. These sounds were accompanied by the echo of kids laughing and yelling.

They quickly entered the King's chambers. First, a boy followed by a girl. The boy had flowing red hair and blue eyes like his mother, while the girl had short, bright, golden hair. Both children rushed into the throne room playing a simple game of tag.

"You're it!" the girl yelled.

"Besides," Kyrie said with a grin. "Who has time for shipping disputes when we have these two to deal with…Tiernan!"

For most children, to play tag meant a series of back-and-forth gentle taps. Instead, Tiernan took it to the next level and had just pushed the girl in an attempt to make her 'it'.

However, his action was too forceful, causing her to lose her footing and fall backward. She landed on her wrist, scraping up one of her exposed elbows.

Davien reacted with a typical overprotective, fatherly response. "Tiernan! Be careful with your sister!" The King rushed to their daughter, the Queen to their son. Davien kneeled down to pick Enid up who was, for the most part, unshaken. She looked at him confused, almost as if to say, 'I've got this, Daddy.'

Davien smiled. "You're a tough one, aren't you little Princess?" Davien tussled his hand through her hair, and Enid smiled back before giving her father a hug. After the moment passed, the King stood up, and turned to Tiernan and Kyrie. "She's fine. Just a few scratches."

"Good," said Kyrie. She looked at Tiernan, who stood there motionless. Kyrie couldn't tell if he was afraid or ready for round two. "I don't understand you two. Go. Play." Enid raised her head to the sky and roared like a ferocious beast, and Tiernan shrieked in anticipation.

Together, with Enid's arms in the air and Tiernan's out to his side, the twins ran out of the hall and disappeared elsewhere in the castle. Kyrie smiled and walked back over to Davien. Together, they returned to the same window.

"What are we going to do with those two?" Kyrie asked. "But also, she's tough. She'll forget that ever happened in a few moments.

"And besides, she has you wrapped around her finger. You know that, right?"

"She's daddy's girl, what can I say? But it's not like Tiernan isn't a mama's boy." Davien took his wife's hand in his own.

"Oh hey, before I forget, Talcot asked if Tiernan could join their family for a trip to Fabled Wonders. Apparently, it's an overdue birthday trip for Wayland."

Kyrie nodded. "Hoydan mentioned it to me as well. She said Talcot had finally returned from his trip and was eager to take the boys up there for a weekend away. Are you okay with that? It's so far away."

"Well, it's not *that* far. Maybe a couple days' journey. And besides, I trust Talcot. He's a good man."

"It's just it'll be his first time away from us." Davien sighed in contemplation. His wife's true concern finally broke through: her boy wouldn't be nearby.

"Told you he was a mama's boy. Listen, my dear, Wayland and Tiernan are inseparable. You see how often Way comes around. I'm surprised he isn't here today.

"And besides, you know it would break T's heart if he missed the party. Let's allow him to go."

"What will Enid think about her brother being gone?"

"What will Enid think, or what will Kyrie think?"

"Stop it." She smiled. "Either way, that's a tough question, isn't it?" Davien squeezed his wife's hand again and laughed. He pulled her into his arms as he kissed her again.

"All in a day's work, right, my dear? First, we have to keep the Council happy, though as King I *could* disband it, you know? But besides that, we have to stop Tiernan and Enid from killing each other 26/7. What will this afternoon bring?"

Davien barely had time to finish his sentence before there was a knock behind them. Both the King and Queen turned to see who it had interrupted them. Standing in the doorway was one of the Abrian Royal Guards. Next to him was Borun, with Tolith just barely visible behind the larger man. Kyrie looked at her husband.

"This can't be good." Davien raised an eyebrow. Once again, he agreed with his wife without needing to say anything. He motioned for his father to enter. Borun waited for the guard to leave before speaking.

"Son, Tolith and I need to speak with you."

Chapter 10

Collaborators

Manus Midir lowered his soup spoon into the bowl sitting on the table before him. Never in his life had he tasted a dish so *perfect*. The aroma alone would make the strongest man hungry; however, the blend of spices and vegetables was unlike anything he had had the pleasure of eating.

His first spoonful had been as enjoyable as the last, and while he normally talked throughout a meal, today his focus had been 100% on one thing and one thing alone: enjoying this unforgettable lunch.

After sipping his last spoonful, Midir raised his hand, signaling to a nearby worker he needed assistance. He caught the attention of a male, relatively young, and eager to please. Quickly, he made his way over to the Manus' table.

"Can I help you sir?" Upon closer inspection, Midir realized this server couldn't be more than 18 or 19 years old.

"Tell me, young man," he said, as he pointed to the empty soup bowl, "how the chef could prepare something this divine." The server beamed.

"Well, actually, I did."

"You did?!" Midir's reaction was less about the man's position and more his age. No one he had ever met could have prepared something so exquisite, let alone a man barely into early adulthood.

"That's right. I brought the recipe with me. At the orphanage in Clericsfold, I spent the last few years of my education perfecting the art of, well, cooking. I was the first 'Master Culinary Artist' according to my teachers there.

"When I aged out of the program, I had heard rumors of a rapidly growing market here in the Valley. So I brought what few personal belongings I owned and moved here, hoping to find a job."

Midir was surprised, and he did not hesitate to show it. For starters, the man's age betrayed his skills. But more importantly, it was the first he had heard of anyone leaving Clericsfold in recent years.

Midir decided to push the issue. "And your name is..."

"Kellag," the server responded.

"Kellag. They hired you to wait tables? To act as their sous chef while waiting tables on the side?" Kellag nodded enthusiastically, though Midir's countenance stiffened. "And I have to ask, how exactly did you get away from Clericsfold? Last we heard in Idlewind, no one from the orphanage was allowed to leave. All able-bodied men had been drafted into serving as guards for Clericsfold itself." As he said these things, Midir noticed the subtle yet immediate shift in Kellag's demeanor.

A moment ago, he seemed happy. Now he seemed...distraught?

"I snuck away. A friend covered for me. Since the rest of Abria stopped sending orphans to Clericsfold, things have been much different there.

"The Clericsfold Council began randomly drafting us into the army, like you mentioned. While at the orphanage, you were allowed to study whatever you wanted, but it was entirely by chance whether it would do you any good or not."

A beat. "I was drafted, and did not want to serve. This is my passion: cooking. So, a friend helped me escape. He took my place in my bed the night before they were to come and get me while I escaped through the countryside.

"I don't know what happened to him."

Midir regarded the server for a moment. It was true: since Borun and Tolith discovered Kane had aligned himself with some taller-than-normal Elf, and since passage through Central Abria had become increasingly difficult, Abria had opened up two different orphanages. The first was within Farna itself, in the west. The other was in Northwick. They were less equipped than the centrally located Clericsfold, each serving one half of the Kingdom with less than a tenth of the resources.

With those changes, the lay of the land had changed considerably. Effectively, there were two kingdoms within the realm now: Clericsfold and Abria.

Clericsfold claimed all land south of the Cave of Tera to the ocean, including both Kingscrown Bay and the mysterious Kingscrown Rock. The Lorelei River acted as an eastern border between the two nations while the western path acted as the other border. Things had been peaceful for the most part, with no skirmishes or confrontations between the two territories.

Midir had a hunch that was about to change. He extended his hand to the server. "Whatever you do in life, you have an impressive talent in the kitchen. Learn all you can here. Maybe one day, you'll have your own restaurant in The Tolith Market." The server grabbed it, shook it firmly, and left to take care of other patrons.

Midir stood up and headed toward the exit. As he passed through it, he turned around to take a final look at the restaurant.

"The Millstone Landing. Oddly close to Milston, dontcha think?" he said, smirking as he said so. "I'll have to come back here." Outside, patiently waiting, were two of his city guards. Midir noticed them and chuckled. "Fellas, did you actually stand here the entire time? Please tell me you at least got something to eat?"

The first nodded his head. "We didn't leave our post, Manus. But we paid one of the passing residents to get us something."

The other spoke. "So yes, we did eat. Where are you going next, Manus?" Midir didn't answer, but motioned for them to follow. Together, the trio walked through The Tolith Market.

In the four years since Borun Mill had stopped operating as a lumber mill, things had changed. At first, residents feared the town would become a proverbial ghost town.

Borun put a stop to those concerns, and committed wholeheartedly to growing the market. Secretly, he planned to reopen the mill at some point, but for now, his focus was on the community who had followed him here. Using funds he had earned from his metalworking business, along with a grant from the Royal Family, Borun began building more shops and restaurants. At first, these facilities sat empty.

Eventually, the community rallied around the project. To spur growth, King Davien agreed to forgo any type of tax for those who opened a business *and kept it open* within the market for at least three years. This encouraged local residents to hop on board the initiative. Others from outside of the Valley began relocating to the town once again, including many who had left after the closure of the mill.

The Tolith Market itself was in the shape of a crescent, with each business in a side-by-side continuous row. The outermost circle was the largest, with subsequent smaller crescent-shaped rows gradually getting smaller and smaller until they reached the center.

There, the statue dedicated to Tolith himself stood proudly. The crescent faced eastward, loosely in the direction of the Valley

Mountains on the easternmost coast of Abria. Borun did so to honor the place where Tolith chose to build a home for himself.

As Midir and his entourage walked, they passed Ofund's Roastery, a place serving various styles of smoked and roasted dishes. The reputation of this particular vendor had made its way across Abria, with the restaurant acting as one of the main attractions and draws for tourists to the Valley.

Next to Ofund's was Draydog's Emporium, known throughout Abria for its underground cooking techniques. In addition, Draydog's included one dish from each of the cities and villages across Abria, meant to make any visitor feel right at home as soon as they arrived.

Across the street were Haldred's Swine Brine and Frandlea's Famous Favorites, both nestled between Clashing Lanes and Waclaw's Revenge. The latter two shops were competing vendors of armor, swords, and other fighting equipment.

Row after row, store after store, there were signs of life. Joyfulness. Activity. Commerce.

Fun.

Oakshadow leadership, home to the famous Mystic Mornings, caught on quickly that this model was more than sustainable. It was highly lucrative and fostered economic growth faster than anything in recorded Abrian history.

Those same city planners had approached Borun recently, wanting to see if he would consider helping them open a similar shop within their borders. It seemed like a natural fit: with Mystic Mornings preparing for another season of performances, a market exactly like this one would help spur their economy ahead as well.

Borun agreed, under one condition: they had to keep the name. He made it clear any market he helped in this manner must follow this naming convention.

Midir recalled this nugget of info as his entourage walked up to the statue dedicated to Borun's Elven friend who mysteriously passed away in his sleep three years ago. The statue was life-sized, standing on top of a trapezoid base. Tolith's wand was raised high in the air, possibly in homage to the moment when he summoned the famous, yet mostly forgotten, white dragon.

The statue was made of the same rare mineral as the walls of Farna; Borun paid extra for the miners in Milston to harvest it for him. Artisans from Idlewind had spent tireless weeks sculpting each detail. Midir paused for a moment to read the inscription.

"For my friend. A guardian until the end."

Not long after, Borun formally renamed this hub: The Tolith Market. He had previously referred to it as The Rose Market, but decided this was a better way to honor his memory after the Elf's passing.

And, if Oakshadow wanted his help, Borun would gladly provide it. They simply had to keep the name. A few months ago, the first ten vendors opened, two of which were branches of existing businesses here in the Valley.

After giving respects to the memorial, Midir and his guards turned to leave. They walked westbound for a while before exiting through the Market's outer ring of shops. The group found themselves not far from the Drunken Alligator.

Midir stopped and turned to face his guards. "Fellas, this is where we part ways. Thanks for accompanying me, but where I'm going, you cannot follow.

"Stay here. Open a tab with the Alligator. I'll be back soon." When the first guard began to protest, Midir snapped to attention. He rarely acted this way, but when he did, it was his way of embracing his title of Manus.

"I need to make this clear. These orders are not up for negotiation. I have business to attend to that is *private*. You will stay here. Is that understood?" Both men nodded their heads, and

Midir headed south through town. He continued walking far enough to ensure he was out of sight and watched for the guards to give up and go inside. After waiting a bit longer, Midir turned west toward Borun Mill.

King Davien was in a pensive mood. This trip to the Valley had come after much deliberation. His wife was not convinced the plan could work, or if it was worth pursuing. Still, he had to try.

He paced back and forth. None of the others had arrived yet, so he was alone inside of the great hall within his father's mill. Outside, he could hear the water wheel spinning. Inside, the gears it powered spun, belts turned, and a sound he couldn't quite make out ticked in the back end of the mill.

Davien knew the others may be late because of distance, but that didn't matter to him. He had chosen to arrive early and had been here for most of the day.

Finally, the rear door opened. In walked Ulrich of Milston. With him was Kettil from Northwick. Trailing behind was Fenwick of Lakedon. The three, he gathered, had come together.

"Gentlemen! Welcome. I'd offer you a seat, but…" he motioned around the mill. There were no chairs to be seen, but perhaps his father would be bringing some or knew of a storage closet containing them.

"Thank you for hosting us, my liege…" began Fenwick. Davien cut him off mid-sentence.

"My name is Davien. In here, we are equals. No titles. No pretense." The others nodded in agreement as Davien extended his hand to each. "What I'm proposing is too important, and what you're about to learn is too personal. I need allies, not subjects." As he said that, the door opened again.

In walked another pair, though Davien later learned this was a coincidence. Tibor from Alwyn and Boswell from Lorelei entered together, sharing a quiet laugh over something inconsequential. Kettil cautiously eyed Tibor, a behavior Davien picked up on.

"Stop. Kettil, listen. Alwyn, Northwick, this 'rivalry' is built on suspicion and mistrust. It has to end. I need both of your ports open and fully operational, and Abria is committed to the prosperity of *both* of your towns. Am I clear?" Kettil lowered his face in shame, before raising it again quickly in renewed commitment.

"You got it," he said as he walked over to Tibor with an extended hand. The latter nodded, and gripped Kettil's hand in return. As they were doing so, the door opened again. In walked Manus Midir. Immediately, Davien walked over and gave him a hug. The two had developed a friendship over the years, though not as close as Davien's predecessor had been with Midir.

However, the shared bond of King Tiernan the First had opened the doors of an alliance, one backed by Idlewild's continual support — and eventual protection — of the Valley.

Next from the Valley itself, Borun walked in. Davien was in a hugging mood, and rushed over to embrace him. "Father," he said, as the men shared a familial moment. "Where are the chairs?"

Enough pleasantries, Davien thought. His father was one who appreciated directness, and Davien did not want to stand for the rest of the evening. Borun, without saying a word, motioned for Boswell to follow him. Midir looked at the others, shrugged, and tagged along.

Finally, Penrod from Oakshadow walked in. About the same time, Borun and the others returned with a set of chairs. They sat them in a circle, and Davien gestured for everyone to sit.

"Friends, I cannot thank you enough for coming tonight. I chose this venue, despite its distance for some of us," he said, looking at Penrod and Tibor, "because this is where things began. The division in the Kingdom stems from the opening of this mill, no offense, father." Borun acknowledged the statement with a nod, but without saying a word. "As I told a few of you when you got here, I am not 'King' Davien in this hall. It's simply Davien: nothing more. I cannot, under any circumstance, allow pomp and tradition to slow this down. Abria is in danger, and titles are less important to me than unity."

The men exchanged looks. Midir spoke up. "Does this mean I can't be Manus anymore?" He laughed as he said it, embracing the fact everyone else held the title of Mayor.

Davien smiled in return before he continued. "No formal titles, my friend. Though I believe my father is the only one here without one."

Borun interrupted. "Troublemaker?" Next to him, Boswell put his hand on Borun's shoulder.

"None of us hold you, or your family, accountable for what has happened."

"You might after this meeting is over," Davien said dryly.

"Isn't Kane to blame?" asked Ulrich.

"Yeah, who is Kane? He's not even the mayor of Clericsfold. That's Eskil, or at least it used to be." The question and statement came from Fenwick. His voice carried with it a sense of fear, and rightfully so. Of the other towns, Lakedon was the most exposed to the expansion of Clericsfold.

Davien took a deep breath, exhaling it slowly before speaking. "Have any of you ever had a friend that, despite no biological connection, was as close to you as a brother?" Without hesitation, Midir's hand shot up. Davien nodded in agreement, remembering the bond between Midir and Tiernan the First.

He continued, "As far as I know, I have no siblings. No brother, no sister. My parents were killed in an accident when I was young. Young enough I have no memory of them. I was dropped off at the orphanage in Clericsfold, where I was raised. At least, until Borun adopted me as his own."

"Borun!"

A younger voice cried from behind the older man's back. Borun turned around to see who had yelled for him.

"Hello, Davien. Where are you off to today?" The question was redundant. Borun knew Davien was meeting with the headmaster at the orphanage. Still, he didn't want to burst the teen's bubble and let him answer.

"It's my Selection Day."

"Which also means I owe you a happy birthday. Here." Borun began shuffling around in his pocket. He pulled out a small tool.

"Is that what I think it is?" Borun handed it to Davien, who began inspecting it. It was a short, flat measuring stick roughly thirty centimeters long.

"It is. It's now yours."

"But you've had this since…"

"Since I was your age, yes. That means it's old, Davien. Protect it." He smiled. "But don't forget to bring it with you tomorrow."

A look of confusion washed over Davien's face. "What's tomorrow?"

The meeting with the orphanage headmaster was short and to the point. Davien sat in a nondescript chair in front of the headmaster's desk as he announced his chosen career path with humble excitement.

"Carpentry!"

Behind him stood several of the teachers in the orphanage, including Borun.

The headmaster made some notes. "Well. It's a profession with lots of potential. What do you want to do with these skills when you're older?"

Davien answered with a grin. "I want to make things people *need*. Furniture. Dressers. Maybe one day, I'll even be able to carve a giant, decorative archway for a couple to be married under."

"Uh huh. And where will you be learning these skills?"

Borun raised his hand. "Through me. Davien will learn in my metallurgy shop."

The headmaster was less convinced by this suggestion. "There are other carpenters he can learn under, ones who may even be more effective than what you can offer. Your proposal doesn't make sense, Borun."

The older man took a breath. "And that's the other thing I wanted to talk about." He walked forward and placed his hand on Davien's shoulder. "If Davien is on board with it, I would like to take him in as my own."

The room fell silent. Davien turned his head around faster than anything the headmaster had ever seen.

"As your own...?" the teen asked.

"Yes. As my son."

Tears quickly welled up in the youth's eyes. Davien's body started to tremble. He tried to speak, but found his voice didn't want to cooperate. Sensing this, Borun kneeled down.

"That is, of course, if you want me to." Davien couldn't hold his tears back any longer.

A family. A father. Someone who will always be there.

"Yes!" He leaped toward Borun, hugging the older man's neck as he began sobbing.

Borun closed his eyes and placed his hand on the back of Davien's neck. "Happy birthday, son."

The next day, Davien moved into Borun's home. The others in the circle nodded in agreement as Davien told the story. None of this was necessarily new information, just more details than they had from before. One of Davien's first acts as King was sending messengers throughout the Kingdom. Those couriers spread the news of his ascension, including a brief explanation of why he was now the King of Abria.

In fact, no one even knew Borun was Tiernan's brother until that day, but neither did anyone object to Borun's adopted son ascending to the throne. It kept the Royal Family on the throne, even if it wasn't a *biological* bloodline.

"When I was 4 or 5, I don't remember exactly, I befriended another orphan. His name was Kane. He was as close as I had to a sibling. As the years waned on, he and I grew closer."

Borun interrupted. "But the two of you could not have been more dissimilar. Don't gloss over that part." Davien shook his head as he sighed again.

"Kane had tendencies. He could switch from being the nicest, kindest person to the cruelest, most cold-hearted monster in a blink of an eye. He seemed to take a perverse delight in hurting others.

"I say others loosely, because it began with simple things." He looked around at each. "I mean, who here likes a spider, right? Kane, if he saw one, wouldn't bat it away or let it be. I've stomped on my fair share of them, especially once I became a husband." He smiled at that last statement, and the others responded similarly.

Davien continued. "But, rather than just kill the spider, Kane would capture it. He would use whatever tool he had at his disposal, a pair of tweezers, a small tong, whatever he found to remove the spider's legs. One by one. No mercy killing, no swift 'stomp and go' like many of us do. He *enjoyed* torturing it."

Davien closed his eyes, remembering another story.

"He adopted you?" The look on Kane's face was one of hurt and betrayal. It was an emotion he wasn't used to feeling.

Deep down, Kane had been hoping Borun might consider adopting him, too.

"I can't believe it either. A family. I mean, I still won't have a mother, but a dad." Until this moment, Kane had been sitting on a fallen tree just outside of Clericsfold, staring at the distant ocean. However, he couldn't take it anymore. Kane stood and began running away from Davien toward the Great Sea. Confused, Davien started to follow.

"Hey, Kane, wait up!"

"Leave me alone, Davien. You got what you wanted. Go. Be with your *father*." Kane refused to turn around or stop. Finally, Davien caught up. He jumped in front of his friend.

"Kane. Stop, please. I thought you'd be happy for me." Kane allowed his shoulder to brush past Davien, pushing him out of the way.

"I said leave." Davien grabbed Kane from behind.

"Please, stop. Why are you so…" But, before Davien could finish the sentence, Kane punched Davien across the cheek. It caused him to fall backward onto his rear, which began to ache as much as his cheek.

"I said *go*." Kane bent over to address the fallen Davien. "We're done." He turned back toward the coastline. Davien sat up and watched his friend leave as giant tears rolled down his face.

"I don't want to share with you all the details. Because, honestly, they only get worse. I never spoke to Kane again after that. He kept a close friendship with a girl named Teska. She still talked to me and would keep me up to date with Kane and how he was doing.

"I had always hoped we might reconcile."

Davien thought for a moment about what to say next. "Kane's cruelty continued to grow. I heard stories how, when he captured anything, no matter how docile the creature was, he would hurt it. As a young boy, I didn't want to take part in anything like that, but I found Kane to be a good friend. Before Borun adopted me, we used to share stories of our dreams, of the path we wanted to take in life, of who we thought we would marry."

Borun noticed Davien's voice was shaking, so he cut in. "It was always my goal that, hopefully, through the teachers' efforts in their earlier years, the displaced orphans could find a passion for something. We encouraged them to pursue those dreams, no matter how obscure. Poetry. Woodworking. Culinary."

Midir's eyes grew wide. He spoke up. "Today, I had the privilege of meeting one of the boys who got to pursue their dream. His name is Kellag, and he works at The Millstone Landing at The Tolith Market. I have never, anywhere in Abria, tasted soup as wonderful as what this boy made. He's working there as a server, but apparently is able to get involved in the kitchen?"

"Ah yes, Klay is a wonderful person. He believes in helping the youth of Abria achieve their dreams. He often lets the wait staff create their own dishes. I'll let him know you were impressed."

Mentally, Borun made a note to find a place for Kellag to open his own shop.

Davien continued. "My father mentioned woodworking. Clearly, carpentry was my passion. Kane enjoyed history. Many of the boys didn't know what to do, and would naturally fall into the role of a palace guard. But for some, this was an opportunity unlike anything we thought we would have in our lives.

"Kane wanted to be an archivist, so once he turned fourteen, he began studying off campus in the Archives. Borun, as you may have guessed," he said as he motioned all around, "likes working with his hands. How many of the shops did you build by hand in the Market?"

"It's not important," he said, chuckling. "But if you must know, 13 of the 32 shops I built entirely myself." The other mayors were clearly impressed, nodding and making a few comments between each other.

Davien continued, "So naturally, he and I bonded." Borun raised his hand, and Davien's face flushed.

"You're downplaying it, son. I saw in you your goodness, your kindness, your compassion. I identified in you someone who saw the inherent goodness in *everyone.* At the same time, I knew my brother had no heir. And, one day Abria might need someone who could be both a leader and a friend. A King who could serve humbly and do what was right, no matter what he faced."

Tibor's eyes narrowed at the mention of the word 'leader.' "Is that why you adopted him, Borun? To be King?"

"Not necessarily. I knew my brother did not have an heir. I also knew it was possible, if I was able to remain hidden, Tiernan would choose to pass the throne to someone else." He looked to Midir. "Sorry. You were the most likely candidate of anyone. But, the white dragon apparently had other ideas."

Borun cleared his throat. "I did not adopt Davien *because* I wanted him to be King. I adopted him because he became like a son to me.

"I admit, I had a feeling Kingship might be on Davien's horizon. But at the time, I did what was right for Davien, not Abria."

"Here is where it gets tricky," Borun admitted. "Kane was the opposite of Davien in almost every way. And despite the bond he shared with my son, I could not adopt both boys."

"Why, exactly?" asked Penrod.

"It's a case of practicality. Kane is older than Davien, at least by our best guess. He was at the orphanage when the newborn Davien arrived. I'd estimate Kane is six to seven months older. If I adopted him, and Tiernan passed the throne to my heir instead of Midir, the title of King would go to my oldest."

"And Kane would be leader," realized Kettil. A wave of understanding washed over the men's faces.

"I couldn't take that risk," Borun stated.

Kettil raised his hand. "I hate to be the one to say it this way. Davien, it's been great to get to know you and your story. But why are we here in the first place? Surely this wasn't all for a history lesson. Clericsfold has been a growing problem for Abria since you became King. Why bring us all here *today*?"

Davien appreciated the question. "There's one last piece I need to say, and then I'll answer your question, Kettil. It's important for everyone to realize Kane *wanted* my father to adopt him, too. He grew to resent both of us after it became official. For as close as Kane and I had been in my early years, once I moved out of the dorms and into my father's home, he shut me out. Kane was stuck in the orphanage until he aged out of the program."

Davien lowered his head. "What I did not know is, from that point forward, he threw himself into the Archives. His cruelty grew as he became obsessed with history. I once heard someone mention the name Zoran in the context of Kane's studies, but, well, by that point, I was more interested in other things."

Borun roared with laughter. A loud, typical, Borun laugh that echoed throughout the halls of the empty mill. "Say it plainly, son! You caught the attention of a couple of maidens in Clericsfold. I barely saw you home." The other mayors each smiled to themselves, remembering that phase of their lives.

"Nothing more than puppy love, father. But, let's not bring that up in front of the Queen, shall we?" The use of her title stood out to the others, and was a subtle signal. *We may be friends, but my wife will be given the respect due to her.*

"As you say, son. But he's right. Davien spent his time courting…what were their names? OH! The Kearney Sisters. Yes, and eventually both of them rejected you for who? The sons of the town crier!" Borun laughed again, and Davien decided he needed to regain control of the conversation from his father.

"Have any of you ever heard the name Zoran before?" The other mayors either shook their head or said so. Davien continued. "I'm not surprised. Zoran is a name few people in Farna know of either, but a few in Castle Abria have heard of in passing. I don't know what Kane's obsession is exactly, but that's beside the point.

"The other problem is Kane has aligned himself with Elf separatists. Rather, it may be fair to say he has created an alliance with an unusually Tall Elf named Folas. And they have coerced or convinced some of the Elven population in the Rosewood Forest to align with their goals."

At the name of the Rosewood Forest, Penrod's eyes made the connection. "That explains why we've taken in several Elf families within Oakshadow. They won't talk about it, but they all seemed more scared than I've ever seen someone."

Davien nodded. "I don't know how many Elves live there exactly. Based on what I know of my great-grandfather, he welcomed in 532 Elves and gave them a home in the Forest. I don't know how their numbers have grown since then, though I haven't heard of or seen many Elven children in my years. About how many do you have living there, Penrod?"

Penrod thought for a moment, counting. "I think around 134? And no children."

"So it may be safe to assume the other 400 or so are aligned with Folas and Kane?" asked Boswell.

Borun nodded. "Tolith chose to live in the Valley. He never said where directly, but implied other Elves had also chosen to live outside of the Forest. Not that I've ever seen any myself, but then again, no one has explored the Northern Plateau."

"Climbing the rocks that surround the Northern Plateau is virtually impossible. Trust me, we've lost several expert mountain climbers trying to scale them," said Ulrich. "The Milston Mountains are treacherous to climb, but we've adapted and developed the tools to make it work. But the Northern Plateau? Not happening."

"For all we know, some of the Elves have moved there," suggested Tibor.

Davien continued. "Regardless, we know *some* of the Elves have aligned with Kane. What I want to do is offer a hand of friendship to *both*."

Around the room, the murmuring of disbelief made it obvious that this suggestion seemed far-fetched. Finally, Tibor spoke up again. "No offense, Davien, but friendship? With the person who once called you a brother, who has now isolated the vast majority of Central Abria from the rest of the Kingdom, and has aligned himself with disgruntled Elves? You want to offer him a hand of friendship? How? Why?"

Davien smiled. "Kane wants respect. I'll give it to him. The Kingdom of Abria cannot stand divided. I want to offer Clericsfold a place back in the Kingdom, similar to how Idlewind functions. But Kane won't take the offer without another concession.

"So, Kettil, to answer your question from a few moments ago as to why I brought you here, it's because I want to organize a Statuo."

"A *what*, exactly?" asked Fenwick.

"A Statuo," echoed Davien. "This will be a Kingdom-wide gaming event. It's going to take a lot of planning. It could probably even take us a few years to pull off the right way. We'll train our best athletes and create a fair scoring system."

"What, what's a Statuo?" asked Boswell.

"It's a word from ancient Abria," responded Borun. "I believe it means 'Decision.'"

Davien nodded. He noticed the faces of those gathered still seemed unconvinced, so he continued. "Listen, the name Statuo is intentional. This decides what happens next.

"If Abria wins, Clericsfold comes back into the fold. If Clericsfold wins, we'll give them freedom along with concessions. Water rights down the Lorelei River. We'll recognize their claim on Kingscrown Bay. We'll even open trade deals between Abria and Clericsfold."

The others began considering the implications of the plan. Finally, Borun spoke up. "In other words, son, you're saying the outcome of the games decides the *fate* of the Kingdom?"

Davien nodded, so Borun finished explaining. "So, Kane wants to rule. If he wins, we'll *formally* concede Abria's claim over the central region. Clericsfold will become an independent nation, with Kane at the forefront of his new Kingdom." Borun shook his head in disbelief. "It's a bold plan, son. We would need each of the towns here to be in agreement."

Davien said what the others were thinking. "If we don't do something, it's civil war. I know it. Everyone here knows it. The New Era could end with a fracturing of the Kingdom." He looked to the mayors of the eastern communities. "If Clericsfold advances further north and claims the Northern Plateau, you'll be cut off from us. But in the west, we'll also be boxed in between an enemy to the east, water barriers to both the north and south, not to mention the uncharted wilderness beyond the mountains to the west."

Davien stood. "Friends, this has to be a unanimous decision. I cannot pull this off without you, and we all have to agree on the terms. Do I have your support?"

One by one, each of the mayors stood up. Borun was last, and after a moment, he spoke. "So, when do we get started?"

Chapter 11

Statuo

Shadow came to a complete stop a few dozen yards from the outskirts of the Clericsfold gate. Midir dismounted from his horse, grabbed her by the bridle, and handed her off to one of his attendants. Together, the entourage stood on the outskirts of Clericsfold. Midir insisted no weapons be brought, a decision none of his attendants or the Council supported.

From the outside, Clericsfold was a unique structure. The walls surrounding the town had a dark feeling to them. The southern Abrian path cut through the heart of the city, creating a natural separation between the town to the north and the orphanage to the south. Outside, trees grew tall, lining the walls on all sides.

There were two primary sets of gates: the exterior bronze gates keeping travelers from entering Clericsfold while traveling along the path, and the internal smaller gates separating the two halves of the city.

Guards stood on the outside gates, and Midir thought that through the helmet he could see youth-like faces. *Probably orphans who had been drafted into service.* They stood motionless, waiting for something to happen.

Midir wasn't going to let anything happen.

He turned to his entourage and motioned east. At first, several hesitated. Finally, Midir's impenetrable gaze told them to leave, and they all walked further away than they would like, but still within actionable distance.

Midir turned again to face the guards. He raised his hands to show he had no weapon, pulling back his royal cloak to reiterate he didn't have anything on him. The guards, for the first time, exchanged a look and returned their gaze toward Midir.

"My name is Manus Midir. I come empty-handed. I come bearing no ill will. All I ask is an audience with the Council. To speak to Kane and the others." Another exchanged look between the guards. One allowed his eyes to widen, almost to ask what they should do. The other returned the expression of confusion.

Both youths had clear instructions to divert *any* travelers away from the city. Until this moment, no one had asked to enter the gates, but rather would obediently turn around. Midir's arrival and actions surprised them, and the inexperienced guards truly had no idea what to do. Finally, the one on the right spoke.

"Where are you from?" Midir lowered his hands in response to the question, and walked closer to them. He noticed the hands of both twitched, almost as if they were going to grab their swords. Midir stopped in response to their nervousness.

"I am the Manus, the mayor if you will, of Idlewind. I come as a representative of the rest of the Kingdom, as a neutral party. Please, a short dialogue is all I need." The guard on the left bit his lip as he turned to the city gates. He pounded on them, and to Midir's surprise, they creaked open. *There must be posted guards on the insides too.* The guard talked through the crack, which then closed.

The guard turned to face Midir. "Wait here." Midir lowered his head in acknowledgement and waited.

And waited.

And waited some more.

He had no idea how much time had passed, though based on the sun's movement, he guessed an hour or two. No one said anything. Neither guard moved from their position.

Finally, the gates opened. This time, it was more than a mere crack, but wide enough to let several people pass through side by side.

Through the gates walked five men. One in the center, who he assumed to be the mayor, had a nervous look on his face. To his left, a man carried a quill and paper. Behind him, another dressed similarly exuded a stoic expression. On the other side of the presumed mayor was a woman, one Midir assumed might be a shop owner based on her clothing.

Next to her was a tall, imposing man. One wearing a sleeveless tunic that showcased his musculature build and commanding nature. He had a square jaw, wore a purple cape, and had no hair on his head or eyebrows. His countenance was different from the others.

Without ever having met him before, Midir knew beyond a shadow of a doubt the name of the man: Kane.

Midir followed behind what he would later learn was a group known as the Clericsfold Council. The one in the middle, Eskil, was indeed the mayor. The woman was named Teska, and as it turned out, she was a schoolteacher at the orphanage. The other two, Vadim and Adair, were local shop owners turned politicians.

They allowed a few from Midir's entourage to follow him, though Midir insisted it not be any guard. Instead, he brought two of his advisors from the Idlewind Council. Midir realized, as he followed the group, this was the first he had ever been to Clericsfold.

They walked through the town center, passing a weapons shop followed by a blacksmith hut. Next to those were an apothecary and what looked like a food vendor. *Clearly not a Drunken Alligator,* Midir thought. This was surprising, since the fallout between the Kingdom and Clericsfold was recent enough that an Alligator tavern should have had time to get a foothold in this community.

After a short walk, they approached a house. It was a plain, two-story construction. There were two windows on the top floor, darkened out. A wooden porch stretched across the front where a single guard stood not far from the door. The building itself was made of a mix of brick, wood, and another type of stone. There were three steps leading from the ground up to the porch. The Council walked up these, one at a time beginning with the mayor, then Vadim followed by Adair, Teska, and Kane. The guard motioned for Midir's group to follow.

Inside was a relatively large circular table with 10 chairs around it. Midir noticed Kane sat first, though he couldn't tell if this was intentional or insignificant. The others followed suit, including Midir and the other two. Once everyone was seated, Eskil spoke.

"Manus, our guards tell us that you desired an audience with this council. I'll be honest, we were almost disinclined to give it to you. We know of your connection, excuse me, your *friendship* with the previous King." Midir couldn't tell why the mayor put the emphasis on friendship.

Eskil continued. "Your party arrived unarmed. Our scouts in the eastern fields saw you coming, and your lack of any weapons intrigued us. It's rare for a city leader to travel without at least some means of defense." He cleared his throat. "This means you either are stupid, genuine, or are planning something. I lean toward the second opinion, though that is not a unanimous opinion of this council."

Midir wondered who believed what, and against his better judgement, decided to push the issue. "Mayor, I can assure you the latter is not true. Though I am curious who believed I came here under false pretenses." A moment of silence followed. Teska raised her hand. "And stupid?" Vadim and Adair raised their hands. Midir looked at Kane. "What did you believe?"

Kane did not answer. Instead, he smirked and shook his head. Eskil spoke again. "You claim to be genuine. Don't waste our time. Why are you here?"

Midir took a breath. This was it. If he failed here, it was civil war. "The King of Abria has a proposal." At the mention of the phrase, Kane's entire face flushed. It was a rare outward sign of his disdain for Davien.

No one dared acknowledge it.

Midir continued explaining. "If you accept, it will help solve this *problem* we have between your city and the rest of the Kingdom." The Council exchanged a look, then Eskil motioned to the guard standing across the room.

"Bring us something to eat. That is, if you're hungry, Manus." Midir nodded, and the guard bolted to the door. The mayor leaned over toward Teska.

"What was his name, the guard?" Teska shook her head as if she didn't know. "No matter. That should occupy him for a moment." He looked back to Midir. "What is this proposal?"

Midir explained the concept to the Council. He watched each person closely, trying to gauge their reaction. After Midir finished going over the details, the Council asked for privacy. Jothan, the guard who had brought their food — a spread of roasted vegetables and various types of bread — escorted Midir to another nearby building: The Abrian Archives.

Midir sat at one of the tables, waiting without speaking. The other two in his group seemed agitated, rotating between standing and sitting. After a while, Midir himself stood, walked to one of the shelves and thumbed through various books.

Conquest of the Plateau, 104NE. Midir didn't know much about that era, though apparently it meant something worth recording. Next to it was *Colonization, 12NE.* These didn't appear to be in any order, as far as he could tell. *Ascension of Tiernan, 627NE*: now this he knew about. It happened not long after his family moved to Idlewind.

Then, another one stood out to him: *Zoran, 432NE.* Unlike the others, which were covered in a thick layer of dust, this one was clean and showed evidence of having been read recently. He pulled it off the shelf and carried it over to the table to flip through. The opening paragraph on the first page made him uncomfortable. He motioned for his companions to come over, and he read it out loud to them.

"'This is a historical record of the battle between the forces of Zoran, the Destroyer, and the Kingdom of Abria. Known as the Dark War, King Telford eventually triumphed over Zoran's minions, including the Leviathan and the Gamelyon, by sealing them all away with the Soul Sword.'" He looked at each man. "What is the Soul Sword?"

"A powerful, magical artifact that has been lost to time." A deep, icy, baritone voice provided the answer, and all three men turned to it. Without seeing who, Midir recognized it as Kane before even standing and turning around.

During Midir's presentation, Kane was the only one who had not spoken. Here, his voice carried a sense of command that created the impression this, somehow, was *his* abode. Kane elaborated. "I've read the one you're reading forward and back. Have you heard that name before?"

Midir nodded, but guarded his words carefully. "Only a handful of times. Mostly in passing, wives' tales, rumors of a time long ago. Who or what is Zoran?"

Kane walked the rest of the way into the room and unfastened his cape. He laid it on a table as he pulled out one of the chairs. He sat, resting his left arm on the table in a semi flexed position with the rest of his body slightly slumped in the chair.

Midir had to wonder if this was intentional, as it seemed this move was meant to highlight his physique. It also annoyed the Manus, as he felt this was nothing more than a bully tactic.

Still, he kept his composure as Kane spoke. "Who or what Zoran is doesn't matter. What does matter is your proposal. The carpenter signed off on it?" He extended his hand toward the chair across from him, and Midir accepted the invitation to sit.

"It was his idea," he said, ignoring the disrespect Kane showed toward the King. Midir pulled out the chair. "Kane, whatever you think of Davien, he does not want a war. He wants a way to end this…" Midir struggled for the word. It wasn't an open conflict. It was a…

"…disagreement. If Clericsfold is to break away from the rest of the Kingdom, he wants a way to do it *amicably*.

"And yet, he doesn't *want* that to happen if it doesn't *need* to." He sat forward, clasping his hands and leaning on his forearms.

"Abria needs Clericsfold. This," he said, motioning around him, "is more Abrian History than I even knew existed. There are small details to be worked out, obviously. Like this room. If Clericsfold leaves the Kingdom, I'd like to preserve this in another library. But those are terms we need to work out. Together."

Kane shifted his arm, resting his hand on his chin in a sign of contemplation. He blinked, lowered his hand, and sat up. "The Council is on board with your proposal. And, as a sign of goodwill,

I'd like to help relocate the Archives elsewhere, whether we win or lose."

Midir couldn't hide his surprise at this answer, though he was also greatly relieved. He didn't know what the outcome of the Statuo would be, only that he had a strange feeling there was more going on behind the scenes than Kane was letting on. Nevertheless, he extended his hand. Kane stared at it for a moment before giving in. The men exchanged a firm handshake, and with that, Kane turned to leave the room.

After the Idlewind contingent had left the city, Kane returned to the Archives. Midir had left the book on Zoran laying on the table, and Kane began flipping through it. Behind him, the room shifted. It was subtle. An almost imperceptible sound, a minor flash, and movement in the air.

"Must you always appear like that?" Kane didn't turn to look at his visitor, though he knew who it was: Folas, who had just appeared out of thin air. Kane continued to turn the pages, finally landing on one near the end of the book.

"Do you have any idea how much it takes to maintain a cloak of invisibility for that length of time? Why did you bring them here?" Folas knew Midir finding the book on Zoran was intentional, but he couldn't figure out why.

"Come here." Folas grunted in displeasure, but floated over to the nearby table to where Kane was standing. "Look." He pointed toward a passage on the page. Folas read the sentence out loud.

"'After sealing away the Dark Emperor, King Telford stated that the Soul Sword was destroyed in the battle.'" Folas spun his hand in a small circular motion. The nearby chair flipped around, and Folas sat on it while resting his hands on its back. He continued, "You don't believe it. I'm not sure whether to believe it, but what does it matter?

"Kane, speak plainly. The past few hours have been exhausting and I need an ether."

Kane closed the book and reached into his satchel. He pulled out a small round sphere and tossed it to Folas. "I thought you might," he said as the Tall Elf absorbed it into his hand. "Now to your question, I had the guard bring him here today to plant a seed of distrust between Midir and the Kingdom. A small one. Look around you."

Folas scanned the room. Kane continued. "Look at the dust. No one comes here. No one but me. This book would stick out like a sore thumb." He closed the book. "Midir was only vaguely aware of Zoran before today. The greatest threat the Kingdom has ever known and ever experienced…"

Folas interrupted. "Until you," he said with a bit of mistrust.

Kane smiled. "Yes, until me. No one in this backwater Kingdom has any clue what Zoran can do. Midir didn't know anything about him, and he likely had never heard of the Soul Sword until just now."

His intensity increased. "Think, Folas! Think! How will Midir feel once he realizes there is a high-powered object resting in the castle, one with power beyond anything he's ever heard, one that could level Idlewind with just a single act?"

"You're being dramatic. You don't know what the Soul Sword can do. Though, you are rather fond of planting seeds of distrust. How did that work out for you the last time?"

Kane ignored the question. "Midir is now aware of the Soul Sword, a secret his 'friend' is keeping hidden from him. It's there, Folas, I know it, and now Midir knows it. Wouldn't that make you suspicious of Davien's intentions?"

Folas threw his head back. "Your plan is flawed once again, Kane. Midir is loyal to the throne. How can you not see that?" In response, Kane reopened the book halfway.

"Here. Have you heard of the Leviathan? What about the Gamelyon? The Shapeshifters? These were all a part of Zoran's forces, and they're sealed away with him. Look."

Folas sat up to read the passage Kane highlighted. He skimmed the page, reviewing the stories about the Leviathan rumored to terrorize the Alwyn waters. He turned the page, reading about the myth of the Gamelyon said to have plagued the desert.

He continued reading where the text told the story of how Shapeshifters ruled the plains. He slowed down and analyzed the page more in greater detail.

"The Soul Sword can control others, destroy objects, and create sealing barriers. King Telford used the Soul Sword to tame both beasts and enslave the Shapeshifter population. Only one escaped." Folas thought for a moment. "Only one? As in one of the giant beasts or an errant Shapeshifter escaped?"

"It doesn't say, though I would lay money on there being a Shapeshifter out there somewhere."

"You know, Kane, there are Elves who *refuse* to join us. Throughout the Kingdom, there are untamed, docile animals. The Soul Sword might be able to change both situations.

"And these two," he said, pointing his fingers toward the names of Leviathan and Gamelyon, "could be used to subdue places like Alwyn and Idlewind once again. The Shapeshifters could act as spies."

"Now you're seeing things with a clear mind, my tall friend. That's the power of the Soul Sword. Once the rest of the Kingdom knows that Farna hides such an unfathomable power, it'll break trust. Destroy the alliance between Farna and the rest of the Kingdom." He put his hand on Folas' shoulder.

"All we have to do is show the Soul Sword still exists. And the Statuo will be our opportunity."

Folas removed Kane's hand from his shoulder. Instead, he stared deep into his compatriot's eyes. "I think the more important question is this: are you willing to play the long game, Kane?"

Just outside the doorway, an out-of-sight guard named Jothan stood in complete silence. He internalized every word he heard and, when it appeared the other two men were about done, snuck down the hall and into the open fields of the city.

Chapter 12
Four Levels Below

The first Abrian Games, formally known as The Statuo, took more planning than expected. King Davien's original goal was to hold them within two to three years after meeting with the mayors.

Eight years later, things were finally happening. They were organized into several major event categories: water sports, archery, horseback, a Smithblitz tournament, and running events. The entire day itself would conclude with a forty-five-kilometer race across the Abrian and Clericsfold country sides.

The race would begin in Farna in front of Castle Abria. It would continue out of the city and into the heart of the Abrian Plateau itself, down the rocky, natural steps into the open plains.

Next, it would loop near the beginnings of the Alwyn beaches, eastbound toward the main road that connected to Clericsfold, and circle back to the Peninsula before finishing at the starting point.

The exact course had been a back-and-forth negotiation between Abria and Clericsfold. Finally, Kane agreed to the original route as first proposed by the Abrian Council, an odd decision that confused leadership on both sides.

"Do you think he's up to something?" Kyrie asked. Davien was sitting at a desk in the throne room, reading over rules and various plans for the Statuo. He had been engrossed in his work, so much so that he was completely unaware his wife had walked into the Kings's Domain.

"Kyrie. Hi." He stood to greet his wife, giving her a kiss before sitting back down. Davien noticed how radiant she looked today. Her beautiful red hair was pulled back into a bun, the way she wore it when wearing her crown and in public.

Today, she had no crown. Likewise, Davien's crown was sitting on his throne, discarded.

"Since when do you wear your hair like that in here?" In this moment, they were not King or Queen. Just a husband and wife, two madly in love individuals, parents to Tiernan and Enid, and slowly growing older.

"I felt like a change. *Everything* seems to be changing around here. You have to admit, Davien, it's been quiet in the plains. Clericsfold hasn't shown any of the hostility they did after we first started doing..." she motioned around her, "...all of this planning. Once Midir suggested the games would be a way to settle the trade dispute, Clericsfold stopped blocking passage through the region. How long has your father's mill been up and running at full capacity again?

"It's almost as if none of the problems that led to the Statuo were ever there in the first place."

Davien put down the quill he had in his hand, leaning back into his chair. He had been thinking many of the same things, not wanting to admit it to himself.

Everything she had said was true. Clericsfold had been downright hospitable for the past eight years, almost as if the dispute that preceded the planning for the Statuo never happened.

"Do you think he's up to something?" she asked.

Davien began to speak before stopping to think about the way Midir described the first meeting in Clericsfold. He dropped the quill on his desk and leaned back in his chair. He began mentally recounting all he had heard from Midir, as well as his first encounter with the Soul Sword.

The day he returned from Clericsfold, Midir asked a pointed question: "What is the Soul Sword?"

"If I knew, I would tell you." It was only a partial lie. At the time, the King himself was barely aware of it. Like Zoran, his knowledge came from old wives' tales and drunken rumors spoken by old men at the Alligator. However, there was a man who might know more: Borun. Davien summoned a horseback runner to bring his father to Farna as quickly as possible.

Five days later, the older man returned once again to his boyhood home. When Borun walked into the King's chambers, Davien was alone.

"Hello, Father."

"It's good to see you, son. The runner said it was urgent. What's going on?"

"I must know. What is the Soul Sword?"

Borun sighed. *I always knew this day would come.* "Follow me, son."

Four levels below the throne room, about a dozen meters underground, a locked room waited, unguarded and forgotten.

"Where are we?" the King asked.

Borun mysteriously pulled a key from the pocket of his trousers and handed it to Davien.

"My grandfather, Telford, gave me this near the end of his life. He told me to keep it from my father and brother at all costs." Borun motioned for his son to open the door. As Davien did so, Borun ignited the torch he had been carrying to light up the darkened room.

Davien peered through the passageway, using the light of the torch to look around. Inside of the room were abandoned items: a painting of King Farris, neglected weapons, discarded armor, and a random round table in one corner, among other things. Standing on the far side of the room, opposite of the doorway, was a nondescript armoire barely visible in the light. Borun motioned for Davien to walk inside, and pointed to it.

Nervously, Davien did as instructed. He opened the double doors of the wardrobe simultaneously, curiously moving his head to one side.

A ring sat on a shelf to the left. To the right hung a shield. Both flanked a sword in the middle.

"My grandfather brought me here exactly once," Borun said. "He didn't tell me why these were locked away, only that these items must stay here, to be kept hidden until the Protectors of Abria emerged."

Borun smiled. "I have *no idea* what that means. I also don't know why he only told me, other than perhaps as a way of protecting the Royal Family."

"From who?" Borun shrugged and shook his head. "Okay, fine. I guess I should say thanks? I'm not sure whether to be grateful or upset."

Borun put both of his hands on Davien's shoulders and looked his son directly in the eyes. "No one else can know these are here. Not even Kyrie."

"That's going too far."

"I'm serious, son. Grandfather wasn't clear as to what was so special about these items, only that they could not leave this room under any circumstance. The fewer who know about them, the better."

Davien sighed as he looked closer. Each item shared a similar design. Gold, whether the mineral or simply the color, dominated all three items. Accents of navy and a striking, bright fuchsia flowed through each in varying capacities.

"So what do they do?"

"The ring is known as the Power Ring and can only be wielded by those who possessed the power of magic. As we know, no Graelan in Abria can use the Power Ring. Only an Elf.

"The shield is called the Mind Shield. Grandfather believed it could block evil's sight. On the back there is an inscription, but it's confusing."

"What does it say?"

"Animo clipeo uti soli qui in pace sunt."

"And that means what?"

"Only those who are at peace with their past can use the Mind Shield. In the middle is what he called the Soul Sword." Davien noticed it had several glowing orbs along its blade. These were the only source of light in the room, save for the torch Borun carried.

Davien reached to grab it off of the wall and watched in surprise as his hand seemed to pass through some kind of barrier. Immediately, its immense power radiated throughout his body. The weapon itself began to glow brighter as Davien held it.

"What is this, Father?"

"It's the Soul Sword, but beyond that, I don't have any idea."

"And the barrier?" Davien asked while seeming enraptured by its power, staring deep into the orbs along the blade. Borun placed his hand over his son's, the one holding the handle of the Soul Sword.

"Son." Davien blinked, snapping out of his trance. He placed it back in the armoire. "The barrier is a gift from a friend."

Realizing its power was immense, Davien posted a rotating contingent of Abrian Royal Guards at the door 26/7. While locked, he didn't want to take any chances. Eventually, Davien convinced

Borun they should loop in Kyrie on the mere existence of these items. This was so she would understand the sentry rotations, since Kyrie oversaw the Abrian Royal Guard's activities as a part of her Queenly duties.

Unfortunately, Midir was not to be among this inner circle. Davien decided the Manus was in too precarious of a position and knowing about the items might be dangerous.

Davien brought Kyrie to the room one time. He emphasized the importance and power of the three items. This revelation clarified why her husband had been posting guards deep in the catacombs, though it only made her more uneasy knowing they existed in the first place.

Davien kept the door to this room locked at all times. His father retained possession of the only key.

Kyrie's question echoed in Davien's mind again and again: *Do you think he's up to something?* Kane's willingness to abide by the terms of the game's proposal was odd, and — at the commencement of the games — would be the first time Kane had been in Farna since Davien learned of the existence of the ancient artifacts.

After much reflection, he finally answered his wife's question. "If Kane is planning something, I wouldn't know what that would be. As a precaution, we should double down on rotations and the presence of the Abrian Royal Guard, especially you know where."

Kyrie nodded. "If it's all the same to you, Davien, I think I would rest easier if we presume he isn't planning something and his intentions are genuine. Otherwise, if we doubt him, he can doubt us."

"And the whole thing could fall apart. That cannot happen, my love." He smiled. "How is our champion proceeding with her training?"

Kyrie was waiting for him to ask. Whatever concern she had over Kane faded with the question. "That's actually why I came here. I just left them. You would be so proud, Davien." She walked over to her husband, putting her hand on his shoulder first.

She gave him a hug, followed by a long kiss. "She's going to kick their Clericsfold butts."

Chapter 13
Training

The Graelian sun beat down upon the training field just outside of Farna. Throughout the area, trainers were coaching their athletes. A little way further in the fields, another group of trainers led a small gathering of female athletes on a run through the open fields. Closer to Farna, other athletes performed a variety of practice activities: archery, formalized games of Smithblitz, horseback riding, and so on.

In a group consisting of four male athletes, seventeen-year-old Tiernan completed his last set of push-ups. Today, he broke his all-time personal record: 225. He started at a mere 10 per day, gradually working his upper body in different ways until he — after months upon months of training — could do 100 in a row without a rest break.

After all, if Sis is going to be the runner, the least I can do is to be the strong one. Since breaking his goal of 100, and performing them consistently day after day, he began increasing his reps in sets of ten. His fellow athletes knew he wanted to hit 250; privately, Tiernan wanted to blow past that number.

In the open area next to him was his best friend, Wayland, who had been holding a plank. Beside Wayland, a trainer hovered over him, verbally counting. Time keeping was an informal process as, though they might try, no one could perfect a method of mechanized tracking.

Today, the wind stood still. It was the hottest day of the year so far, or at least that was the consensus among the athletes in training. Tiernan wiped his brow, eager to return to the Abrian Plateau. There, as usual, the weather was far more temperate and comfortable than in the training fields north of Farna.

"Fifty-three, fifty-four, fifty-five, almost there, fifty-seven, fifty-eight, *fifty-nine, seven minutes*!" The trainer raised his voice as the count continued, getting louder with each passing second as he tapped the passing time on his wrist.

"Alright, Wayland!" Tiernan exclaimed. He rushed over to his friend who, after spending all of his energy holding the pose, was now drenched in sweat from head to toe. After the trainer finished the count, Wayland collapsed face down into the dirt and grass. He raised his left hand above his head, giving Tiernan a thumbs up. The trainer, Dermund, leaned down and patted Wayland on the back.

"Solid effort. Again." Wayland groaned as Tiernan laughed at his friend's training misfortune. Both of them had been taking part in a grueling regimen, each for various (personal, though private) reasons. Wayland used every ounce of his strength to push himself back up, resting on his knees and forearms for a moment. He closed his eyes and raised his head to the sky.

"One moment. *Please*."

"No. Prepare." Dermund stood back up. "There is no break. On my mark." Wayland groaned, then got back into position. "Ready. Begin!" Wayland stretched out his knees on command as he began holding the plank pose for one more, painful time.

Meanwhile, Tiernan stood by his friend, watching him struggle to break through his first minute. "Come on, Way, you got this." Wayland began struggling. His abdominal muscles quivered. Tiernan noticed and encouraged his friend. "Way, you've got this. Don't stop! One more minute."

Wayland let out a yell, pushing through the pain. He lost count in his mind of the passing seconds. The world felt distant, dizzying. He noticed his triceps burning, the buildup of lactic acid which would lead to his next headache.

His quads began to shake. Wayland yelled again, and Tiernan looked at Dermund, who was standing by, counting. Tiernan gave him a look, raised his eyebrows, widened his eyes, and parted his mouth as if to ask how long it had been. After a few moments, Dermund raised his hand with two fingers raised.

Tiernan looked down at his friend. If he didn't already know better, he would have assumed Wayland had just gotten out of the lake. *One more minute.* "Don't give up, Brother," he said as Wayland began yelling even louder.

Except this time it wasn't a yell of pain, but of determination. "Don't tell me how long! I'm going for five!" Tiernan's eyes widened again as he smiled.

"This is it! Hold on, just a bit longer. Come on! Don't stop!" Tiernan's words of encouragement helped more than Wayland expected, and he flexed his core muscles in deeper determination. Dermund raised his eyebrows and raised his hand yet again to Tiernan.

Four fingers. Wayland had just broken his personal record. At the same time, he yelled again. His face turned beet red. His arms began shaking almost uncontrollably. His abs began their final descent into a jelly-like state, much like his mind from earlier. His quads lost all feeling.

And just like that, Wayland collapsed on the ground. Tiernan began clapping and cheering for his friend as Dermund spoke. "Excellent. You held it for four minutes and thirty-four seconds." He smiled. "After holding your first plank for a full seven minutes. Good job, Wayland. *Now* you may rest. We'll continue your training shortly." Dermund nodded to Tiernan and walked away from the area toward the city. Tiernan kneeled down to his friend.

"You in there?" He put his hand on Wayland's back, patting him as he asked. Wayland shook his head from left to right with his face still buried in the grass.

Tiernan continued with his praise. "Amazing! I don't know how this will help you in the Statuo, but who cares? That was impressive." Wayland began to stir, pushing himself up, flat-palmed, then coming to a sitting rest on his calves with his eyes closed as before.

"Strength is victory, or something," Wayland said as he opened his eyes to look at his friend. Wayland's curly blonde hair was soaked, glistening in the sun. His generally pale and freckled complexion was now a deep red, with sweat pouring down his temples. Tiernan put his hand out to help Wayland stand, who cleared his throat and accepted assistance to rise to his feet.

Or so he tried, anyway. Wayland almost lost his footing, and Tiernan grabbed his friend from the side to steady him. Wayland put his arms around Tiernan's neck and laughed.

"Too young to drink, so this will have to do," he joked. Tiernan chuckled as he helped Wayland walk toward a nearby bench, where the exhausted athlete promptly sat down and closed his eyes. Tiernan sat beside him.

"By the way, you smell."

"You don't smell so hot yourself, T."

Tiernan smiled, ready to share his news. "So, hey, I broke a record today, too. 225 push-ups." Wayland opened his eyes and put his hand out to give Tiernan a fist tap. Tiernan returned the gesture, then continued. "Not as impressive as what you just did, obviously. I know that, but I'm proud of it."

"You're too hard on yourself, T. Most people would be lucky to eke out twenty-five push-ups. You blew way past that."

Wayland coughed, trying to clear his throat. He leaned over to rest his arms on his legs.

Tiernan sat back and looked up at the sky. A sudden, forceful burst of air blew in, flowing through his shoulder-length, wavy red hair. His blue eyes glowed with joy, thinking about what he and Wayland had just accomplished.

The breeze cooled Wayland's sweat-soaked clothing and skin. Without opening his eyes, spoke. "You need to cut your hair. I can smell it over here."

In response, Tiernan punched his friend in the side and laughed, momentarily forgetting about the intensity of Wayland's planks. Tiernan ran his hands through his hair to pull it back into a ponytail as Wayland doubled over in pain, half laughing and half crying.

"I deserved that, I know." Wayland shifted to lean over and spit on the ground. "Remind me, why are we out here?"

Tiernan shrugged. "Dad wanted to host a gaming competition or something. That's all I know. We're training, but like I just said, I don't know how those planks are going to help you in the games. The Statue-thing. What are you even competing in?" Wayland shot his friend a look.

"What are *you* competing in?" Tiernan opened his mouth to answer, but realized he didn't know what he was going to try out for. He was here because Enid was fast, so he figured he needed to be strong. "Thought so," answered Wayland for Tiernan. "I have some ideas, but we'll see if they play out."

"So what?" Tiernan interjected. "You're telling me we're out here punishing ourselves to...look handsome on the benches?" Wayland shrugged.

"We'll think of something." He stood, struggling at first, but found his footing. "Come on. Dermund won't be back for a bit. Let's go watch some of the other groups." He gave Tiernan his hand, who grabbed it to stand. Together, the two friends walked past the others in their group: one doing some kind of core move, the other lifting a wheel back and forth off of the ground. Tiernan and Wayland raised a hand to say goodbye to them, though neither of the other two acknowledged the gesture.

The two self-proclaimed brothers headed east toward the group of female runners, who were now doing sprints between two sets of trees.

"Run, ladies! You're not going to win this thing by going slow. Remember, the other cities have some blistering fast runners. Is this the best you've got?" Maeli, a tall trainer who had been running for as long as she could remember, tried her best to push her group of six athletes. Two of them, she admitted, were fast.

Exceptionally fast, if she was honest with herself. One of them was Aoife, the daughter of Eldar and Freya who owned the Drunken Alligator.

The other was the Princess herself. Enid was the most determined of them all, unwilling to accept any type of personal failure. She pushed harder and ran longer, going out every morning before training commenced. She refused to acknowledge any type of pain. Enid heard Maeli's comment and shot her an angry look.

Good. Let's see what you're really made of, your highness. The distance between the two sets of trees was right around 400 meters. Enid stopped about a third of the way between the two landmarks and jogged back to the beginning. She put her hands on her hips.

Enid, like her brother, was a tall athlete. Unlike Tiernan, however, Enid kept her straight blonde hair shorter, barely touching her chin. She was dressed in a training outfit, a cutoff tunic highlighting her defined arms. She bent over for a moment, catching her breath, and stood back up.

Enid turned to look back and raised an eyebrow, annoyed at Maeli who responded with a question: "You ready?" Enid said nothing but positioned herself in a running stance.

Maeli smiled. "Good. Now go!" She began counting as Enid took off with a determination belying her frame. She watched as Enid defied expectations, and counted out loud as the runner approached the end. "Forty-five, forty-six, forty-seven, forty-eight, forty-nine, fifty, you're almost there, fifty-two, fifty-three!" she exclaimed as Enid passed the mark. Across the field, another voice was cheering just as much.

"Way to go, Sis!" Enid had her hands once again on her hips, raising her legs and trying to shake off the building sensation of lactic acid in them. She turned in the direction of the approaching voice.

"Of course," she mumbled to herself. It was Tiernan and Wayland, with the latter clapping as her brother was cheering. Enid grabbed a towel from her pack by the tree, and walked over to her brother. They met a few dozen yards from the finish line and gave each other a hug.

"They let you out *early* today?" she asked as they separated. She smiled at Wayland, who gave her a small nod in return. "Or are you slacking off again?"

Tiernan turned defensive. "Hey, I'll have you know I broke a record today. 225 push-ups. After, I might add, doing some other strength training and calisthenics exercises. So back off, will ya?" He smiled, pointing his thumb at Wayland. "Besides, it's this guy who really has some good news."

Enid doubted Wayland could impress her, but gave him an open door. "Is that so? What'd you do today, Wayland? Get out of bed *before* noon?" Enid knew Wayland well. He had been friends with Tiernan since they were little kids, and Wayland — when staying at Castle Abria with her brother — was often the last one to wake up.

Wayland cleared his throat and looked sheepishly to the ground. "Oh nothing. Besides hold a plank for seven minutes!" He raised his head as he dropped the bomb. And, try as she might to hide it, Enid was visibly impressed.

Then he continued. "Oh, and I might have held another one right after for over four and a half minutes."

Tiernan watched his sister as Wayland revealed the news. He caught a subtle shift in her facial muscles. He knew she was trying to hide it, but Enid was no stranger to physical activity.

Even if his friend thoroughly annoyed his sister, Tiernan knew her small reaction meant one thing.

Wayland had surprised her. His friend had practically grown up in Tiernan's home, but as a kid had packed on a few pounds. Nothing excessive, but nor did he show an interest in being active, unlike the twins who reveled in it.

Tiernan enjoyed a solid physical competition. Not as much as Enid, of course, but enough he had stayed fit throughout childhood and his early teenage years.

Once the date of the Statuo drew closer, and athletes began training, everything changed. Wayland made significant changes to his diet. He made a concerted effort to get in shape, rising most days before the sun. And though Tiernan would never admit it, his friend was now much stronger than him.

With her own training taking top priority, Enid hadn't noticed the change in Wayland until this moment. Nevertheless, despite her reaction, Enid chose to continue teasing Wayland much like she used to when the three of them were younger.

"Well, next time, do better," she retorted playfully. She punched Wayland in the abs, causing him to double over in pain. "Oh, come on, you, you…bunny!" She laughed out loud, and Tiernan couldn't help but follow suit. Comparing his friend to a soft, fluffy, timid creature was too perfect after an accomplishment such as this.

"Toughen up, Wayland." She turned away as a subtle, red glow not unlike that of a flickering flame became visible in her eyes.

Wayland stood back up straight and continued rubbing his stomach, before taking two steps back from the twins. "Hey, I don't know what it is with you two today, but this right here?" Enid blinked, her eyes once again normal and turned around to see what Wayland was referring to. He pointed to his midsection, circling around it. "No more punching or jabbing me here. Got it?

"Anyway, come on, T. We have to get back to Dermund." Tiernan realized Wayland was right, so he turned to his sister one last time.

"You doing good here?" She nodded. "Beating records?"

"You know it." She pushed Tiernan, who wasn't quite prepared for a physical altercation. "Go!" Enid said as Tiernan fell slightly backward, though he hopped back up right away. "Quit wasting time. Get back to whatever it is you boys do over there. The games are gonna be here by the time you make your way back. Get out of here."

Tiernan smiled. "Is that payback for the time Dad always reminds me of, when we were playing tag and I pushed you over and you landed on your *pretty face*?" He put a mocking emphasis on the last few words, and Enid just rolled her eyes. Tiernan proceeded to mock cry, rubbing his eyes with his hands. "Poor little thing got hurt that day, didn't she?"

"As if you could hurt me." She motioned. "Get out of here, Brother. Take your stinky, sweaty friend with you." Enid smiled as she said it, and Tiernan pulled her in for another quick hug.

"Show them why you're the best," he said into her ear. He let go and met up with Wayland, who had already begun walking back toward their training area.

As Enid warned, the Statuo showed up faster than anyone could imagine. By the time everything was finalized, there would be a total of twenty-two events. Tiernan tried out for six — and won a spot — on one: the Abrian rowing team. Wayland would compete in two: horseback show jumping and jousting. His dedication to core-based training, combined with a surprising knack for riding horses, made him a highly rated contender in both events.

To no one's surprise, Enid would compete in every racing event: relay, sprints, hurdles, and, of course, distance running. She was expected to win at least two of those: sprints and the final race.

The rules for the Statuo were straightforward: two groups or individuals from both sides would compete in each event. Five points would be awarded for a first-place victory, three points for second place, and one for third place. Zero points would be awarded for fourth place.

If Abria had more points at the end of the day, the Kingdom would reabsorb Clericsfold, though with one minor concession: a member of the Clericsfold Council would join the Farna Council of Advisors.

In reality, in this scenario, the entire Abrian Council itself would be reformed to include a member from each major settlement. This was an idea proposed first by Kane and expanded upon by Midir, who insisted this arrangement would better reflect the idea of a unified Kingdom.

If Clericsfold won, they would become an independent Kingdom. The two nations would each share rights of the western and northern paths along with the included portions of the Lorelei River. All three landmarks would act as a sort of neutral zone.

Within these boundaries, all land would belong to Clericsfold; anything outside, to Abria. This gave Clericsfold an official waterway and ability to create a shipping port near Kingscrown Rock.

The agreement also significantly raised the stakes, as the agreed upon terms meant Lakedon would also leave Abria and become a part of the new Clericsfold Kingdom. The mayor, Fenwick, opposed this concession, so much so it almost caused negotiations to collapse. This didn't help matters between the King and his in-laws who owned several cottages along Lake Conchobar.

Eventually, Fenwick agreed to it once the Kingdom made substantial investments into the tourism trade within his community in the intervening years. Also included in the agreement was the willingness of Clericsfold to relocate any Lakedon resident to the community of their choosing, fully paid for by Clericsfold, if the family wished to remain a part of Abria. Fenwick himself had even visited Oakshadow twice in recent months, rumored to be scouting a location in one of the nearby fields to start a new life.

This did not instill confidence in those living in Lakedon. Though only a rumor — and everyone knew how fast those spread, often with no basis in reality — it had led to several prominent families putting their homes up for sale. A few preemptively sold their properties, with the vast majority of them relocating to the Valley. Thankfully, the tourism business itself did not suffer, as Lake Conchobar was still a popular excursion activity for Abrian and Clericsfold residents alike.

On the morning of the Statuo, King Davien woke early, far earlier than usual. He sat in his predecessor's chair, though not looking directly at Idlewind as Tiernan the First often did. Instead, he stared for hours at the morning stars.

Never before had he noticed the Ailan Huntress. He had read about this constellation in his studies at the orphanage, but for the first time today had the opportunity to admire its beauty. Composed of nine bright and seven dimmer stars, it filled the southern portion of the sky with its majestic glory.

To the north, he followed along until he came across the most recognizable constellation in the Abrian sky: the Abriacholae. It was rumored the first King of Abria took the nation's name from this stellar grouping, as both the name of the land as well as the constellation itself meant strength and power.

"Strength is victory," he said to an empty room. It was an unofficial motto of the Abrian competitors, and one of the shops in Farna was even selling tunics with this saying embroidered on them. Davien didn't like this idea, as he feared the words had a confrontational connotation. Kyrie had even talked him down one day after hearing Tiernan saying it between each rep of push- ups.

After a short period of reflection, Davien noticed a few household lights across Farna turning on. Some of these hosted athletes from other towns. Davien went out of his way to ensure any host in Farna gave prioritized housing to competitors from Clericsfold instead of the other towns from Abria. He did not want there to be any sense of favoritism.

Behind him, he heard footsteps approaching. He turned around, expecting Kyrie. To his surprise, he saw Tiernan.

"Hey, Dad." Tiernan looked bright and awake, and it was clear he had been up for a while. His hair was pulled back into a knot of sorts, a style Davien hated. The King motioned to the back of his own head, and Tiernan laughed. "You like it?"

"You know I don't." It was especially prominent with Tiernan's red hair, but Davien chose to let the issue drop. He motioned to a nearby smaller chair, which Tiernan grabbed and pulled up next to his father. The sound of the wooden legs against the stone flooring echoed against the wall as the teen dragged it. Davien winced at the noise, wondering why his son didn't just pick the chair up to move it.

"Now that the whole castle is up, are you ready for today?" Davien wasn't sure what answer to expect, and the question was a genuine one.

Tiernan slid down in his seat, putting his arms up on its back, and letting his forearms hang down behind it. "Yeah. I wish I had been able to compete in another event or two, though. Wayland is in two. Sis is in, how many? Ten?"

"Four."

"It might as well be ten. I thought I would at least make it into another strongman event. Shot Put or something. Did you know Gareth made it into that one? He and I arm wrestled a while back and I beat him easily."

Tiernan sighed. "Even a place on the Smithblitz team would have felt fair." Davien smiled, looking back toward the window. He had refused to give either of his children any preferential treatment. If either Tiernan or Enid appeared to be unfairly favored, it could break the integrity of the games. Preventing a civil war mattered more, a decision that hurt Davien to make but was necessary to protect the Kingdom.

"You'll do fine. What time do you compete?" Davien realized, in this moment, he *didn't* know when Tiernan competed. An unpleasant realization hit the King in the gut, as his duties meant he might not be able to watch his son participate in his only activity.

The events were happening all over today, with the water-based activities kicking off along the northern Alwyn waterway. This river began not far from the edge of the Abrian Plateau, looping southwest around Alwyn Beach and connecting with the Great Sea to the south. Official representatives, selected from both Clericsfold and the other communities throughout Abria, would act as the judges there as well as throughout the rest of the Statuo.

For fairness, the rules stated both parties would have to agree upon the outcome and present the results together. Each official on a time-based event had trained themselves in the art of keeping time, but all judges had to agree on the final outcome for it to be official.

"Mid-morning. We're the second event in Alwyn. Will you be there?" Davien winced. He wanted to, but had a meeting with the Clericsfold Council at the same time. He looked at his son, who was distracted and staring at the ground.

The Council will just have to wait. Or we could move the meeting to Alwyn. "Yes," he replied, making his decision. Kyrie already had made it clear she would be at all four events Enid was participating in. This meant she, too, would be unable to watch their son perform. *The boy deserves to have at least one of his parents there.* "I'll see if I can track down Father, too."

"Great!" Tiernan jumped out of his seat and gave his dad a side hug, excited at the prospect of having both his father and grandfather present.

Davien smiled, putting his right hand on Tiernan's arm. His son felt the gesture, and hugged his dad tighter in return. "I'll see you later, Dad. I'm going to meet up with Wayland before he leaves town." Davien held his son's arm for a moment longer, giving it one final squeeze before letting go. With a head gesture, he motioned for the boy to leave. Tiernan ran out of the hall as Davien turned back to the window. Far in the distance, the sun was just beginning to make its appearance. The faintest hint of morning daybreak meant only one thing.

By the end of the evening, the future of the Kingdom would be decided.

Statuo.

Chapter 14

Let the Games Begin

Kyrie sat down. She was the first to arrive in the stands overlooking the field where Enid would compete. The morning sun had just risen over the Valley Mountains, which signaled the start of the Statuo.

Held throughout the day, the various running events were going to be the most watched and highest attended. In particular, the final race had stands in key spots throughout the course. She wanted one near the end, which also acted as the beginning. Kyrie couldn't believe it was finally happening. With the arrival of the Statuo, the culmination of years' worth of planning had finally come to fruition. Whatever happened today would decide the fate of Abria.

Kyrie had run into Enid as she was leaving the Castle. The latter sat calmly in one of the dining halls, eating a bowl of fruit. She waved hi to her mom, so Kyrie walked into the room to give her daughter a few words of encouragement.

"You know no matter what happens today..." Enid raised her hand.

"Mom. Stop. I'm fine. I'm excited." A minor glow began to envelop Enid's hand, which embarrassed her. She put it under the table.

Kyrie noticed as she sat down. "Is this the first it's happened in a while?" Enid shook her head. "Have you been doing the meditation we found in that old book?"

Enid shook her head again. "I've been too busy with training."

"Enid…"

"Mom, I will start. I promise. Right after the Statuo." Dissatisfied, but realizing she wouldn't get anywhere today, Kyrie stood up. She kissed her daughter on the head before walking toward the door. She turned back, gave Enid an approving wink, and left.

Enid pulled her hand back out from under the table. She opened her palm to reveal a small, glowing orb. The sphere gave off the appearance of a burning ember of fire, yet it retained its shape as a perfectly round object.

Enid hated lying to her mom, but decided this wasn't a lie. She just chose to *omit* some information. It was true she hadn't been doing any of the *meditation* exercises her parents ran across in one of the dusty old books from the Archives. Someone from one of the faraway towns on the other side of the Kingdom had worked hard to move them to Alwyn. Enid couldn't ever remember his name, but decided it didn't matter.

What did matter is a vast treasure trove of information was now stored safely nearby in the Alwyn Böchord, as everyone kept calling it. Her parents commissioned a team to scour those old records for any mention of a red dragon.

The sages had found long buried records with evidence Graelans, too, once possessed the power of magic. Those who wielded it were reputable mages, often controlling vast swaths of territory.

Correction: they controlled vast swaths of what would eventually become the Kingdom. Based on the earliest available records, magic was believed to have disappeared right around the founding of the New Era. No one knew what this connection was, though discovered references indicated mages often spent time deep in meditation.

In an attempt to help, Davien and Kyrie put together a daily routine for Enid. Once she began preparing for the Statuo, however, it fell by the wayside. During her training she realized heightened emotions — not subdued ones — allowed her powers to manifest. She had spent many of her solo runs finding ways to stimulate her emotions. Enid claimed to her family that her privacy helped her get faster.

Which was true. The isolation also allowed her to learn more about this newfound power. Once, she decided to run abnormally close to a cliff. She closed her eyes, putting herself in genuine danger. As her foot hit the edge, a wave of fear and adrenaline rushed over her.

As if on cue, her hand lit up like the forge of a blacksmith's shop. She stopped and admired the glowing orb in her palm, and relished in its presence as the rest of her forearm ignited. Nearby, she noticed a rock. She didn't know what would happen, so she instinctively threw her hand in its direction.

To her surprise, a blast of energy left her body and enveloped the rock. In an instant, the rock emitted a dull, red glow. Once it subsided, she leaned down to touch it. It had a semi-glassy feel, though the effect faded with each passing second. Eventually, the rock returned to normal.

Enid found different emotions created different effects. Fear led to a glass-like result. With anxiety, she could evaporate water using heat.

With infatuation, she could quite literally create fire. Today, Enid was excited, which was a new emotion in connection with this power. She closed her palm and walked over to a nearby axe hanging on a wall. She picked it up, and watched something new transpire. Almost as if the axe itself was one with her body, its head transformed from metal to a fire-like blade. She reached out with her other hand and touched it.

Glass. Burning glass. This was new. *It's as if I can transfer my power to the weapon itself.* To test her theory, Enid released the handle and watched as the axe returned to normal. The orb was also gone from her hand. She turned around to make sure no one was looking through the open door. It was clear, so she grabbed the axe and ran it up to her room before heading out to start her day.

Folas hated the amount of energy the cloak of invisibility took out of him. Today was the longest he had ever held it, using his powers to activate the magic from the moment Kane departed for the northern Alwyn shoreline with the rest of the Council. Kane's hatred of the Royal Family meant he had chosen to stay outside of Farna, housing himself within a tent near the eastern edge of the Abrian Plateau.

Kane was in a bad mood after a messenger informed him the meeting with Davien had been moved. Folas had shared a tent with Kane, as the arrangement was in line with their mutual goals. Keeping his distance from anyone from Abria allowed Folas to be here without anyone knowing, while Kane kept his distance from those he despised.

As long as he could, anyway. There was no way to avoid the meeting, as the entire Clericsfold Council had to meet with the Abrian delegation per the terms of the Statuo agreement.

An hour later, Folas stood outside the gates of the mighty Farna. If he could perform his next move correctly, it meant everything was going according to plan. In preparation, Folas had practiced this maneuver several times in recent months.

His teleportation magic required he know where he was going. To move from the Rosewood Forest to Clericsfold was easy. He knew both locations and had seen them with his own eyes. All he had to do was visualize his destination and, with a snap of his fingers, he appeared where he wanted to go.

Unfortunately, he had never been inside of Farna before, let alone Castle Abria itself. His goal was to transport himself just inside of the gates while maintaining his invisibility. Months of testing, though, couldn't prepare him for the final act. One wrong move and he could end up inside of a city wall, visible to those inside of the city walls, or a lethal combination of the two.

He took a breath, raised his invisible hand, and snapped his invisible fingers. No matter what happened, there was no turning back from this moment.

Folas materialized inside of an armor shop, standing in the center of the room. It wasn't the field he wanted, but he was inside. *One small step.*

"Who are you?" a voice from behind asked. "And how did you get in here?" Folas whipped around to see the shop owner standing behind the counter. Instinctively, Folas tried to engage his cloak of invisibility.

No luck. The double magic maneuver of invisibility plus teleportation had utterly drained the Tall Elf. He was now visible, which could derail all the plans they had. The shop owner grabbed a sword off of the wall and began to rush toward Folas.

Using what bit of energy he had left, the Tall Elf raised his left hand. This act froze the shop owner in place. Folas moved his hand again, bringing the shop owner high into the air.

"Who…what do…you…wan…" Folas raised his right hand and brought his fingers together into a fist. The shop owner's throat started to close off. Fear gripped him as it became more and more difficult to breathe.

Folas didn't know how long he could hold the shop owner like this. He couldn't let the man alert others to his presence, but he also couldn't stand here forever.

As the shop owner closed his eyes, no longer able to breathe and beginning to pass out, Folas released his right hand, leaving it open momentarily. The man gasped, opened his eyes, and looked at the face of his torturer.

A mix of coldness and determination stared back at him. Before he could yell for help, the shop owner's eyes widened with dread as he watched Folas' next move.

In his right hand, a yellow sphere of energy formed in his open palm. Folas smiled as he looked the shop owner square in the eyes.

The Tall Elf raised his hand, aiming its open palm directly at the man's heart.

With a swift motion, Folas released a torrent of Wind Magic his way. Sadistically, Folas' magic began tearing the man apart from the inside. The shop owner was powerless to defend himself. Now immobilized and unable to talk or scream, the most painful sensation he had ever experienced ripped through his body.

Next to the man, a glass case holding various wares and bits of armor shattered. Folas increased the intensity of the attack, and watched as the man's eyes rolled back into his head. Dead.

Folas dropped his broken body on the fractured glass case, face down. *With any luck, it'll look as if he had a heart attack and fell into the display.* Before anyone else nearby could respond to the commotion, Folas pulled an ether out of his satchel and absorbed it. Next, he reactivated his cloak of invisibility mere seconds before the neighboring shop owner rushed in.

This allowed Folas to walk out of the door as another group rushed in to see the fallen shop owner. Folas stopped to look around. With a quick glance, he took in every visible aspect of the surrounding city.

Farna. Soon, this place will be a flattened wasteland. Folas smiled to himself at the thought as he headed toward the obvious entrance to Castle Abria.

Davien paced with nervousness. The Clericsfold Council had graciously agreed to move their meeting. Graciously, that is, except for one of them. A person he hadn't seen in decades, and a person he desperately hoped to reconcile with.

Kane. There he is. The Council walked into the large tent acting as a makeshift meeting hall. Behind Davien stood four other men: Fenwick, Tibor, Boswell, and Midir. Borun, the source of Kane's initial ire, did not attend this meeting. The others on the Abrian side decided his presence might prove to be too much for this tempestuous alliance. One problem at a time.

Eskil, Vadim, and Adair took their seats first. All three were dressed in clothes similar to what Davien himself wore, outfits a layperson might wear during a family excursion to the beach. Teska was missing; Davien later learned she chose to attend one of the other events where a close family member was competing.

Kane wore his preferred clothing, which Davien thought might have been a bit of overkill. Then again, his former friend was known for his dramatic flair. He stood, surveying the room for a moment, before taking a seat.

On the Abrian side, Midir, Fenwick, Tibor, and Boswell joined Davien. All but Davien were already sitting when the Clericsfold Council arrived. All that was left was for Davien to start the meeting. He smiled, stretched out his hands in a welcoming gesture, and finally sat down.

Davien took a deep breath. "Friends." He chose his opening words carefully. Truth be told, he didn't know if anything he said could mend the gap between him and Kane. *But perhaps with the others.* "Whatever the outcome today, this is historic. The Statuo may go either way, but at the end of the day it's our collaboration that will lead toward a peaceful coexistence." *Not my best speech.*

Eskil sat forward. "We have a new condition. One that, upon reflection, this Council feels will best serve our...*interests*." Davien expected this. For as smooth as things had been in planning these games, something had to go wrong. Davien extended an open hand, inviting Eskil to continue. "If Clericsfold is victorious, we want access to the Rosewood Forest. There aren't enough trees in the Valley Woods. We will need supplies for our economic expansions."

Tibor spoke up, capturing the attention of everyone on the Abrian side. Normally a quiet individual, Davien realized Tibor was worried about something if he was butting into the conversation before anyone else. "That's not an *unfair* request," he said with a troubled expression, "But why wouldn't you trust us to supply you with sufficient lumber to begin with? And let's be clear: are you asking for access or joint ownership?" The Abrian Council looked back to Eskil.

"What you're worried about is Alwyn's access to the ocean currents, am I right?" interjected Vadim. "But to answer your question, we propose the area around the Elven settlement become a part of our sovereignty. And Abria will not interfere with the transportation of our property between our two regions."

Boswell vocalized what the rest of the Abrian Council had been thinking. "The terms of the games are the culmination of a unified agreement. Penrod is not here, and this would affect Oakshadow most of all. Nor are the rest of the members present. We would need to get their agreements first."

Midir used the opportunity to showcase the mounting frustration on the Abrian side. "Eskil, you and I spent almost a year hammering out these types of details. It's likely we would have agreed to this condition, but why now? And what if we say no? Practically speaking, without the other members of the Council, your Teska included, would the addition of such an addendum even be valid?"

Davien realized Kane was staring directly at him. Almost smirking. *This was part of his plan. No matter what the outcome of the Statuo, the agreement will be in contention. If Clericsfold wins, the other towns — Oakshadow specifically — could reject it. And the result would be civil war. If Abria wins, Clericsfold could claim we didn't act in good faith.*

Civil war.

Determined, Davien sat forward. "Would you agree to a provisional agreement on these terms while we work to get everyone to sign off on this change?" The four present on the Clericsfold Council looked at each other, each nodding. Except for Kane, of course.

"Yes, that would be acceptable. Provisionally, as you said," answered Eskil.

Davien gave Midir a look that said more than words. *Find the others.* He addressed the room with authority. "Then let the games begin!"

By the time the rowing competition had begun, Midir had tracked down several other members of the Abrian Council. Borun was an easy find, sitting in the viewing stands at Alwyn to watch Tiernan compete. Likewise, Ulrich and Kettil were both watching horse-based events in the open fields west of Farna.

Penrod was nowhere to be seen. His absence worried Midir, considering the importance of his buy-in.

Davien took his seat in the stands to watch Tiernan compete. As there was a full crowd around him, Davien hoped he might be able to blend in. He chose his 'dumb vacation outfit,' as Kyrie called it, for two reasons.

One, it was much hotter here than he was used to in Farna. There was no need for royal regalia here, unless one wanted to return to the throne drenched in sweat and smelling like a training excursion.

Two, he wanted to blend in. Almost a return to his pre-royalty life. He sat next to Borun, and for the first time in years, the weight of leadership lifted from Davien's shoulders.

"I know what you're thinking, son. Feels good, doesn't it?" Davien laughed and Borun responded with a loud chuckle. "And this is one of many reasons why I wanted nothing to do with the royalty."

"Yes, I know. You left that to me. Thanks, Father." Davien laughed.

"Son, look around you."

Davien did as instructed. Everyone was enjoying themselves, happily talking, excitedly engaging with each other. While few of the general Abrian populace outside of the Council knew of the importance of the games, everyone — including those in leadership — was enjoying themselves immensely.

"You taught me to embrace life in Clericsfold way back when. You also taught me to accept life as it is, not as we want it to be. Why'd you leave it to me? I've always wanted to ask, and since you brought it up…"

Borun redirected his attention away from the games and toward his son. His eyes softened while, at the same time, showed a bit of sadness. "Do you remember that day, you were probably seven, maybe eight at the most? You watched as another person I won't name…"

Davien raised his hand. "Yes. I know who."

"Right. He knocked over that boy. The short one, the one who always loved looking up at the stars."

"Beauregard."

"Right. Beauregard. That *person* bullied him. And you walked over, put your hand out, and helped Beau stand back up. Then, you gave him your lunch. In the midst of our food shortage, you gave of yourself. I knew then you were special." As Borun finished speaking, they heard a commotion. The emcee of the event was signaling for everyone to be quiet. Next to him sat four judges: two from Abria and two from Clericsfold.

"As we grew closer over the years, and I began to see you as my son, I realized Abria needed someone with your heart. Your compassion. Your propensity to do good in the world despite whatever problems it sends our way. Look, there he is." Borun's heart, already filled with pride for his family, saw his grandson through held-back — and rare — tears.

Near the shoreline, four sets of rowers stood proud, ready to take their seats in their crafts. Davien caught the attention of Tiernan, who had been looking back and forth among the crowd to find his father. Davien made a fist and raised it above his shoulder. Tiernan returned the gesture, smiling.

After a few moments, the crowd hushed themselves into a quiet humming of conversation. Most were listening, but as always, there were those who couldn't help themselves. The emcee finally spoke.

"Welcome to the big event here in Alwyn: the rowing competition. We have four sets of teams. On Team One from Abria, we have five prime athletes: Boaz from Oakshadow, Aasim also from Oakshadow, Ryman from Idlewind, Tiernan from Farna, and Tormond from Lakedon." Davien didn't hear much after that, instead doing all he could to hold back the boastful fatherly pride coursing through his veins. Each youth raised their hand as their name was announced, and the crowd responded in kind.

The emcee announced the next Abrian team with five equally talented athletes. Next were the two teams from Clericsfold. Those ten athletes received the same level of support from the crowd. The competitors all took their seats in their respective boats.

"Just as a reminder, the scoring system will award five points for a first-place victory, three points for second place, and one point for third. No points are awarded for a fourth-place finish. The course will take them from this point, heading westward, following the waterway into the Great Sea. There, they will loop around Alwyn Point and return here."

He turned to the rowers. "Are you ready?" All four teams cheered. "Alright! Eskil, the esteemed mayor from Clericsfold, will do the honors." He bowed to Eskil, who walked up to the place where the emcee had been standing.

Eskil cleared his throat. "On your mark. Get set. Row!" He laughed and cheered as they all started rowing their hardest.

Borun leaned over to Davien. "Right there, son. You never desired power. You always deferred to others out of respect for them as a person, not to mention their ego. This is the only event Tiernan is in, and you let your…let's just say competitor, start it. That's the humble nature befitting of a leader."

Davien smiled. His father's words encouraged the King. Likewise, he had a positive feeling about this race.

✣ ✣ ✣ ✣ ✣ ✣ ✣ ✣ ✣

Folas carefully walked through the halls of the castle. It took a lot of effort to maintain his cloak of invisibility, though he had not mastered the art of silencing his footsteps while being invisible. He had to be careful, and of course, not run into anyone physically. It was an invisibility cloak, not a pass-through-their-body cloak.

Unfortunately, he didn't necessarily know where he was going. If Kane was right, the Soul Sword would be somewhere here.

Would Davien have kept it in a guarded room?

A locked keep?

A weapons room?

No one had seen the Soul Sword in recent history. This meant it could be anywhere, if even here at all. He encountered several guards, eavesdropping in on their conversations. Whenever he approached one, he would stop and listen for clues, indications of unusual routes or confusing assignments.

Sometime later, Folas needed a recharge. The hours of wandering had drained him. *I need another ether*. But, to absorb one, he would have to remove the cloak in an open room, absorb the concoction, and reengage the cloak.

Finally, he found an unoccupied dining hall with a hidden recess. There, he let his guard down and became visible once again. He pulled an ether out of his satchel and quickly absorbed it. As the concoction flowed through his body, Folas relaxed as his energy returned.

However, he paused, realizing something was not right. During most of his time in Farna today, Folas had worn his cloak of invisibility. This was the first chance he'd had to see his own body.

Back at the shop owner's, he had immediately re-cloaked after killing the man. He hadn't had a chance to pause to notice anything off about himself.

"What in Lyra…?" he said, noticing his hand. The tips of his fingers on his right hand, the one he used to send the Wind Magic attack, were as black as coal.

No, darker. Folas had only seen a lack of color like this once before.

"Ultimus…" he whispered. Folas used the fingers of his other hand to tap them. To be sure, he used the fingernail of his index finger, pressing it hard into his now obsidian fingertip.

Ouch. He still had feeling in them. His fingers weren't dead. They were just…changing color. His normally pale complexion was a particularly strong contrast against this change, a fact he noticed as he laid his blackened fingertips onto the top of his other hand.

Folas had used magic for his entire life, but today was different. The Tall Elf's eyes widened as he realized why.

The shop owner was the first person I've ever killed. Kane took care of the boys from the Forest all those years ago. Folas thought for a moment and realized he had killed nothing prior to today.

He didn't know if this was the reason for the change or not, and barely had time to ponder the consequences as he heard footsteps and a voice behind him.

"Halt! Who are you, and why are you here?" Folas whipped around to see a guard. In his carelessness at inspecting his fingertips, he had left himself exposed.

"It's going to be that kind of day, isn't it?" he said as he raised his hand toward the guard, just as he had a few hours earlier when he killed the shop owner.

Tiernan was never more grateful for his push-ups and strength training routine than he was at this moment. His team, nicknamed the Falcons by his fellow competitors, was in perfect rhythm. Currently, they were neck and neck with the other Abrian team, with the two from Clericsfold a few dozen yards behind them.

Tiernan wanted to win. More than anything, he wanted this moment. They approached the upcoming bend in the waterway, an almost 180-degree turn that would loop around the outer regions of Alwyn. He was seated fourth behind Ryman, who was a medium height athlete he barely knew.

Out of the corner of his eye, he noticed the rower in the boat next to him — the rower in the fourth seat he had been pacing with — was beginning to pull ahead. Worse yet, they were in the inner lane, which meant they had a slightly shorter distance than Tiernan's crew, who was in the outermost lane.

"Let's go, Falcons!" Tiernan yelled. "We can do this! Let's pick up the pace! And push!" The front rower, Boaz, began a chant to keep his team in rhythm. *Why weren't we already doing this?*

"Strength. Victory. Strength. Victory. Strength. Victory. You got this, Falcons!" With each utterance of strength, they raised their oars. With each victory, they lowered them and pushed against the water's might. The cadence began to pick up as they approached the curve ahead.

Meanwhile, the Clericsfold group was slowing down. There was an Elf in each boat, positioned in the third seat in both. Whether this was affecting their pace wasn't obviously clear; what was clear was that, if the race held as expected, Abria would claim eight points total in this event.

The second Abrian boat slowed, though still at a respectable pace ahead of the Clericsfold rowers. Boaz continued. "Strength. Victory. Strength. Victory. Stre…" And stopped mid-sentence as he watched the unthinkable happen.

Tiernan didn't have time to turn his head as he matched Boaz's stunned gaze. He simply heard the commotion. The other Abrian boat had flipped over, sending all five rowers flying through the air. A previously unknown outcropping of rocks was later discovered underwater in their lane. It tore into the base of the boat, sending half of it flying one way and the other half the other way.

The distance between Clericsfold's group and Abria's group meant there was enough time for some reaction, though no right decisions. The first boat turned hard to avoid the incoming wreckage. This also meant they turned right into the path of the second boat. The nose of the first jutted deep into the side of the second, which caused the latter to flip as well. Though there wasn't any damage to the boat, the five Clericsfold rowers were likewise thrown from their craft.

However, the first boat was still functional. It took them a few moments — far enough time to seal an Abrian victory, provided there were no more mishaps — to right themselves, navigate through the field of debris, and resume the competition.

A nameless, random Elf sat without saying a word. A look of gleeful satisfaction spread across his face.

Tiernan continued rowing. With each motion, a wave of sickness built inside him. The emotion was complex. Of course, the concern for his fellow athletes, both Abrian and Clericsfold alike, worried him.

But also, gloom hung over his head now too, because his victory would now be marred by what had just happened.

To no one's surprise, Abria won the rowing event. In the ensuing chaos, two Abrian athletes received major injuries; one with a broken arm, the other a concussion. The Elf from the crashed Clericsfold boat almost drowned. Sitting on the Alwyn shoreline, she was visibly shaken.

Tiernan met up with his teammates for a moment after the awards ceremony, congratulating and embracing with them with high fives and other gestures. He walked over to the Clericsfold competitors. High in the stands, Davien watched with trepidation. To his relief, both Clericsfold groups treated Tiernan with kindness and respect — including the Elven competitors.

"You raised him right," Borun said, watching the interactions unfold. Davien crossed his arms and sat back in his chair, a sense of pride overwhelming him. "I had hoped we, well, you, could have had the same influence on our mutual friend back then."

Davien swallowed hard, remembering his time at the orphanage and his friendship with Kane. The wedge driven between them was, ultimately, the cause of all of this.

"I just wish I could have done more to help him," Davien finally said as he watched his son run.

Tiernan sprinted eastbound toward the makeshift stables Alwyn had constructed to support the games. In many ways, it resembled a giant parking area for horses. Tiernan hopped on the first one a stable hand gave him and took off. As the wind blew through his hair, he believed — despite what had just happened — the rest of today was going to be a pleasant day. He just needed to get to his destination in time.

"Hee-ya! Let's go girl!" he said as he gently pressed his heels into the mare's sides. The horse picked up the pace as the two of them raced toward the open fields where his best friend was just getting started.

Tiernan arrived just as Wayland was beginning his second event: show jumping. Wayland placed last in jousting, a fact that irritated the young man beyond any reasonable measure. Abria had also won this event, with the two Clericsfold competitors coming in second and third. Wayland had scored no points and was determined to rectify his personal failure.

Tiernan dismounted from his horse, a steed he affectionately named Chocolate because of its deep, rich, cocoa-tinted fur. Tiernan handed him off to the stable hand at the makeshift stables. He made eye contact, mouthed the word "mine" and pointed to his chest. The stable hand scratched something on his pad and nodded. Tiernan waved and ran in the direction of the show jumping observation stands.

Wayland was the third competitor behind an Abrian and Clericsfold athlete. The horse jumping arena consisted of nine jumps. A purely time-based event, each competitor would run the course three times, with their best counting as their official time.

Wayland hopped on his horse, gave it a slight pat on its side, and motioned to the judges. The emcee turned to Wayland, who returned the look with a thumbs up.

"Competitor, get ready!" He turned to the crowd. "Ladies and gentlemen, up next is Wayland, son of Talcot and Hoydan from Farna." The crowd cheered, and the emcee looked back to Wayland. The athlete raised his arm, making a fist in the air.

"Strength is victory!" he yelled, while grabbing the reins. The emcee took a step back, standing closer to the judges' corner.

"On your mark. Get set. Go!" Wayland shifted in his seat and tapped his heels. In response, the horse took off. The jump, an easy one-pole barricade, was only a few meters from the starting point. Wayland squeezed the horse's side a bit more, causing it to gallop faster. Instinctively, the horse vaulted over the first jump with ease. Tiernan cheered loudly from the sidelines, continuing to walk toward the stands as Wayland approached the second jump.

Tiernan passed by the judge's stand, eavesdropping to hear the official timekeeper's count. As Wayland made the second jump, Tiernan heard the keeper say, "Plus 1.1."

Wayland is ahead of the other two competitors during his first round! Tiernan considered staying here, but decided he wanted a vantage point from the stands to see the event without obstruction.

By the time he sat down, Wayland was on the fourth jump, a difficult two-pole stand requiring the horse to gallop at the perfect speed. Tiernan watched as his friend's horse increased speed — clearly a result of Wayland's expert horsemanship skills — and jumped with incredible ease.

Wayland repeated this for jumps five, six, and seven. Each was strategically positioned around the arena, with the rider, using skill and finesse, having to turn their horse after every second jump. Wayland saw jump number eight straight ahead, a long path that concluded with an astonishing — and almost unheard of — three-pole challenge.

"Let's go! Come on! You're doing great! Keep this up and you'll be in first!" The surrounding sounds drowned out Tiernan's yells of encouragement, as everyone was saying similar — or, in the case of Clericsfold attendees, heckling — phrases. Wayland lowered his head, shifted in his seat, and gave his horse two quick squeezes with his heels. The horse accelerated, and Wayland repeated this motion again.

As the horse blazed down the route, the excitement throughout the stands grew. Tiernan noticed the Clericsfold fans began pointing, a hush falling over the previous cries of heckling. One started clapping. Another couple higher in the stands started cheering. One by one, the rest of the stands followed suit, collectively enraptured by Wayland's speed.

For a single moment, there was no Side A or Side B. There was a single, unified Kingdom. And Wayland was there, bringing them all together: Graelan and Elf alike.

Tiernan stood, taking charge as a future king should. No matter who they were rooting for, in this moment, he wanted everyone in the crowd cheering for his friend. He turned and began raising his hands to get the crowd up on their feet. As if a mighty rush of water overcame them, they all stood virtually simultaneously, a wave that spread from one side of the stands to the next.

"Let's go!" Tiernan let the last word trail long in the air, trying to encourage others to continue with the chant. Wayland's horse approached the eighth jump. One final tap with his heels encouraged the horse, and almost like magic, its feet left the ground and cleared the obstacle as if it was merely out for a midday stroll.

Next came the hard part. Wayland had to slow his horse to make the curve without running into the fencing. To do so would add a five second penalty to his time. Wayland sat back on his seat bones, sitting up tall with his hands on the reins as a last-ditch effort to slow the horse's momentum.

No need. The steed slowed as intended, as if it and Wayland were one and the same. They made the curve with at least half a meter to spare, and Wayland once again began tapping the horse's sides with his heels.

"Come on. One more jump!" he said to her, shifting in his saddle one more time. The horse picked up the pace as it approached the final jump.

And just like that, his first trial was done. The horse cleared the jump with an appearance of majestic brilliance, and Wayland crossed the finish line immediately thereafter.

The crowd erupted in cheers, Clericsfold and Abria spectators alike. Tiernan himself began jumping and fist pumping into the air. He turned around and gave the random person behind him a massive hug. He didn't care that it was a girl; he would have hugged a bear had it been there.

Realizing his lapse in judgment, he apologized. "Sorry!" She smiled and shook her head, saying something back to him. He thought she said 'It's okay,' but wasn't sure exactly. As Tiernan turned around, the girl's friend next to her nudged her and whispered into her ear.

"That's the Prince," she said. Eislyn nodded her head.

"I know," she said.

Meanwhile, Tiernan had begun to make his way through the crowd toward the judging stand. The emcee was trying to quiet the crowd to no avail: everyone was enthralled by Wayland's performance. Tiernan got close enough to where he thought he could read their lips.

"One minute, thirty-two seconds," the timekeeper said to them. Each judge looked at the paper in front of them where they had kept their own tally. One by one, they agreed with the time. The timekeeper spoke again. "He's ahead by a full seven seconds. Do we agree?" Again, they reviewed their charts. All four judges — two from Abria, two from Clericsfold — nodded.

Tiernan jumped, punching his fist through the air. Wayland was in the lead. He had to repeat this two more times, though his time had beaten any record Tiernan had ever heard of for this style of event.

This may be an Abrian record, he thought as he returned to his seat. He caught the eye of the young woman he had hugged earlier.

"Wayland won!" he said to her with excitement. Eislyn mouthed what Tiernan thought meant 'Alright' though he wasn't 100% sure. Upon returning to his seat, He reached out his hand for a high-five.

She smiled and instead leaned in for another hug. Tiernan was taken aback, but realized he didn't care. He couldn't be happier than he was in this moment.

Chapter 15

A Friend's Legacy

Enid took a deep breath. Her first event was before her, a manageable 400-meter sprint. Unlike many of the other events today, there were far more than four contestants in the running events. Each Abrian community sent their best runner, leading to a total of 10; even Whispersong, the Kingdom's unincorporated collection of homes, sent athletes.

Per the terms of the Statuo, Clericsfold would select ten runners as well. However, just like the other events, only the top three finishers would earn points. Theoretically, this meant both Kingdoms could walk away receiving no score from any running event, assuming runners from the other side finished in the top three slots.

I've got one shot to get this right. Enid was the eleventh runner, though she wasn't sure if she preferred to be first, last, or in the middle like she was. If she was first, the other competitors would know the time to beat. If she was last, her nerves might get the best of her. Here in the middle, there was still a chance for someone to best her, not to mention the wait.

In the stands, Kyrie sat without saying a word. On both sides of her sat people she didn't know, which was somehow comforting. She was nervous for her daughter, which helped her forget about the larger implication of today's games.

"She'll do fine," a voice next to her said. Kyrie was taken off guard, pulled back to reality from her thoughts. It was the woman to her right. Kyrie didn't know who she was, but appreciated the comment and smiled in response.

"Thanks. She's trained for this day and night. What's your name?" Kyrie asked as she extended her hand.

The woman grabbed it. "I'm Teska. You may have heard of me, I'm from the..."

"Ah yes, the Clericsfold Council. My husband..."

"King Davien."

Kyrie realized Teska knew more about her than she was letting on. *Was this a setup?* "Yes, Davien, he's mentioned your name a few times during the planning of these games. He always spoke fondly of your input." Teska nodded, looking toward the field.

"You know, I'm not the bad guy."

She's direct. Usually if you have to say you're not the bad guy, it means you are.

"I think these games are a great idea. A way of unifying everyone, regardless of what happens."

Kyrie regarded Teska for a moment before returning her gaze to the field. *Time to be a queen.* "So, if I may be so bold..."

"What's our problem?" Kyrie was taken aback. She wasn't used to being cut off mid-sentence as Teska kept doing. She wondered if she would ever get to complete a full sentence during this conversation.

"That's one way of putting it. I was going to ask why Clericsfold wanted to break away, but since you put it that way, yes, what's your problem? It's been over a decade, and I've never heard anyone really say why things are so uncomfortable between our two...*regions*."

Teska smiled. *She can't call us a Kingdom. Fair enough.* "I think you know the answer." Kyrie lowered her head. No one had admitted it until this moment, but the division between her husband and his former friend was ultimately the cause.

"Why does he hate Davien so much?" It was Kyrie's time to be direct. "We don't want to lose Clericsfold. These games," she put her hand out toward the competitor's field and paused. "These games are meant to bring us together. The end result? We hope it can create unity regardless of the outcome. Why do I feel that isn't going to be possible, no matter what happens?"

Teska clasped her hands together. "I've known Kane for years. I knew your husband when we were younger, before Borun moved away with him. He was always so kind.

"Kane longs for connection. That's always been his thing. He lost it when he and Davien drifted apart. It brought out the worst in him."

Anger welled up within Kyrie. *Push it away, watch what you say here.* "So, you're telling me our Kingdom faces potential civil war because Kane was lonely? There has to be more to it." Teska yelled someone's name, and Kyrie turned her attention to the field to watch the competitor along with her. Teska didn't say anything to Kyrie until the competitor finished their attempt.

"Who was that?"

"My niece. You were saying?"

"Kane. He was lonely? That's why we're all here today?"

Teska smiled. "I think he felt betrayed and abandoned. His obsession with studying in the Archives just amplified the problem."

Kyrie wanted to enjoy Enid's run without this distraction. At the same time, she recognized the need for her to be the Queen here. "So, do you agree with Kane? You believe Clericsfold should break away and form its own Kingdom?"

Teska smiled and, in a moment of vulnerability, answered the question plainly. "No. I don't. I also know better than to question him. If I stood up to Kane, it might lead to problems at the orphanage where I teach."

"And if Abria wins today?"

Teska looked at the field where Enid was lining up. She tapped Kyrie on the shoulder. "Let's forget about that. Your daughter is up."

Folas hovered over the slain body of the guard he had just killed. He hadn't reactivated his cloak of invisibility yet. Instead, he was staring in the direction of the dead body.

His eyes, however, were not focused on the guard. He held his hand out, noticing how much more pitch black there was than just a few moments earlier. With each life he took, this new inky tone moved further down his hand.

After killing the guard, it now encompassed most of the fingers on his right hand. He decided it was time to conduct a few tests.

Folas inherently possessed Wind Magic. This change had never happened before, such as when using his powers to knock down a tree. Since the Tall Elf wasn't totally sure what was causing this change, he decided to try another type of magic.

From his satchel, he pulled out a ring with a green stone on it. *Let's see if this has the same effect.*

As he put on the Poison Ring, a surge of magic moved throughout his body, beginning in his right hand before spreading to each appendage. He opened his hand and watched as a flickering ball of green appeared. *Now, who to test this on?*

He noticed movement in the corner of the room as a rat scurried by. He opened his hand as he did when he typically threw Wind Magic. Instead of yellow, a green blast of Poison Magic emerged and enveloped the rat.

It began coughing. Its color changed from a typical gray-brown to a darker hue. Folas walked over and picked it up. The rat's eyes were a sickly green. With callous disregard for the creature's life, he tossed it to the ground. The poor critter scurried as it tried to escape the presence of its captor.

Folas looked at his hand. No change. He made a fist, satisfied. He looked back at the rat as it slowed down. Its smaller size meant it would succumb faster to the poison than a Graelan would.

The rat made it as far as the door before it came to a complete stop. It fell to its side, unable to move forward any longer. After another cough, it took one final breath, stretched out its feet, and never moved again.

At the same time, an odd sensation vibrated in his hand. He opened his fist and noticed the ink-like shade had now moved to include all of his fingers. It was a small, barely noticeable change. But a change nonetheless.

Folas realized with each life he took, he transformed. He heard about this once, when he was in exile with his brethren. An Elf back home had used her magic for deeds such as this, and slowly became what the other Elves dubbed the Dark Elf. It took the combined efforts of all the Elven elders to bring her down.

She was also the last person he had ever known who could cast Ultimus. It made him wonder if killing others — death — was the key to unlocking this dark power.

"So. I'm the new Dark Elf. No matter." He decided there was no coming back from the course ahead of him and instead chose to embrace it.

Folas closed his eyes to reengage his cloak of invisibility. He moved out of the hall and into the open areas of the castle. *Where is the mythical Soul Sword?*

Kane knew his plan today could fail. If Clericsfold won, the sense of unity permeating throughout the Statuo meant there was a strong possibility the Council would end up falling back in step with Abria anyway.

Furthermore, if Folas didn't find the Soul Sword, there was an even stronger possibility their shaky partnership might fall apart. He was pacing back and forth near an archery event. He was supposed to judge the competition, one of two Clericsfold citizens selected to act as impartial observer.

"Nervous about the score?" his companion asked. Kane didn't know this man, as he was a volunteer from the community who was of no practical consequence. Kane ignored the question, while also irritated it even had to be asked.

Halfway through the day's competition, the unofficial count had Clericsfold trailing Abria by a full ten points. *As long as Folas finds the Soul Sword, it won't matter who wins.* He stopped and decided to play nice with this man.

"I'm nervous for the athletes. I want all of them to do well. Even those from Abria." Three back-to-back lies, obviously. Kane wanted Abria to suffer horribly and for Clericsfold to show superiority. He decided to change the tone of the conversation. "Do you have anyone competing today?"

The man smiled. "My son. He's on the rowing team. Have you heard how they did this morning? I had obligations back home and only arrived an hour ago."

Kane feigned compassion. "I'm so sorry. You didn't hear about the accident? One of the Abrian boats hit a group of rocks. Their boat was destroyed, and some of the debris caused one of ours to wreck as well. One was flipped over." Kane watched as all of color drained from the man's face. He decided to drive the knife in deeper. "The Elf rower almost drowned. I don't know if there were any other injuries on our side."

A look of pure fright overtook the man's face. "Excuse me. I may not be able to judge this. I need to check on my son. Do you know if there is a plan for backup judges?" Kane shook his head.

The man looked to the field and back toward Alwyn. "Excuse me." As any good father would, he began running in that direction.

Kane smiled. *Serves him right for asking such a stupid question about points.* He began eyeing the stands for a familiar face. Someone from the Council, a shop owner, perhaps one of the educators.

He was in luck: sitting near the top of the stands was Dolan, one of the instructors he had come to despise. Most called Dolan a good man; to Kane, he was a weakling. But more importantly, he was a man that could be intimidated.

Someone who, if he played his cards right, could potentially sway the results of this event and give Clericsfold a few more points.

Cloaked, Folas stood in silence within one of the central gathering rooms. Several guards were running toward the hall where he had killed one just a few moments ago. After testing the Poison Ring on the rat, he left that room and waited for someone to notice the fallen guard's body. Once another sentry discovered his passing, more began gathering. He stood far enough away that no one would bump into him accidentally, yet close enough to hear their conversation.

With any luck, one of them would say something to point him in the right direction.

"He's dead. There's no doubt about it."

"But how? He was fine when I saw him earlier today."

"He looks like he was in pain when he died."

"Hey, I know this is odd, but on my way here today I heard about a shop owner who had also died like this."

"Yeah, I heard the same thing. But he was pretty old."

"Speak for yourself. 227 years is *not* old."

Mindless, random chatter. Folas was beginning to get annoyed. He might need to kill someone else soon, just out of spite if these idiots didn't begin to say something helpful.

"This is bad. He was supposed to swap with Edek downstairs later this afternoon." This caught Folas' attention.

Could this be it?

"Edek will just have to stay there longer, or one of us will need to take his place. King Davien made it explicitly clear: no one was allowed near that room while he was gone today, and we were to rotate frequently." Folas's invisible lips curved upward.

Now to find where Edek is.

"I'll do it," said a stocky, well-built guard. "Someone needs to contact his family. You two," he said, pointing to two of the guards, "secure the body. You two, find his wife. I think she owns a sewing shop across the field." Those two guards nodded and left. "The rest of you, spread out. We can mourn later. If you're here, it means you're leaving someplace else unguarded here in the castle. You have a duty. Go."

All the other guards responded, in unison, with "Yes sir." Wilbret kneeled down over the body of the deceased. "I'll make sure your family is cared for, Blaziel. Rest easy, my friend." He stood, nodded to the two guards preparing to move the body, and began walking. Folas followed him through the maze of hallways, stairwells, and tight corridors.

After a twisting journey through the catacombs, the guard arrived at the end of a passage far below the surface. There, two men guarded a large wooden door. They snapped to attention, though they weren't necessarily slacking off, and the act seemed more of a formality than anything.

"Wilbret, sir!" He raised his hand, removing his helmet.

"At ease, guys." He coughed to clear his throat. "I'll get to the point. We found Blaziel dead in one of the halls. He apparently succumbed to an unknown condition or illness. It looks like a heart condition based on the way he appeared to be in pain." Both of the other men exchanged a look of concern. The one on the left spoke first.

"No. No, that can't be. His wife is expecting their second child in Nove. She'll be *devastated*." Wilbret shook his head in agreement.

"I know, it's tragic. He seemed so healthy during our lunch today, too." He considered mentioning the shop owner's death as well. It was an odd coincidence, but stranger things had happened.

"I'm here to relieve you, Edek. In Blaziel's place." He put his hand on Edek's shoulder. "We'll all mourn our friend later. Right now, we have a job to do. King Davien made it clear no one was allowed down here besides the Abrian Royal Guards. Have you seen anyone?"

Both men shook their heads.

The other guard, named Gromil, spoke. "Do you know why this door is so important? It doesn't lead anywhere as far as anyone around here knows." Wilbret shook his head.

"It doesn't matter. Our King has given us an order. We'll follow it. Edek, go rest, and patrol the halls for your next watch. If you see anything out of the ordinary, let me know immediately." Edek nodded his head in acceptance of the order. He bolted up the hallway toward the staircase on the opposite end. He barely missed Folas, who had to lean as close to the wall as he could to avoid discovery via impact. The wind of the guard's speed caused the Dark Elf's invisible clothing to reverberate in the breeze.

The motion also caused an almost imperceptible disturbance in his cloak. Gromil narrowed his eyes, unsure if he had seen anything. He motioned to Wilbret. "Sir, look."

Wilbret turned around. He didn't see anything, but put his helmet on and took his place on the other side of the door. "Your eyes playing tricks on you?"

"Possibly. I'm probably just nervous. I just thought I saw...I don't know, a shadow for a split second." Folas took this information in stride. He realized he was probably low on magic.

This meant he would need to climb the stairwell, uncloak, absorb another ether, reengage the cloak, and somehow deal with these two.

He climbed at least half a flight of stairs just to be sure he was out of sight, taking each necessary step that would give him the advantage in the upcoming battle.

While uncloaked, he took one last look at the usual complexion of his right palm. He was sure, after dealing with these two, this would be the last time he would ever see it this color. He also took off the Poison Ring and replaced it with a dark purple one. Except this time, he put it on his other hand. Folas was right-handed and had limited success using magic with his non-dominant one.

A sweeping realization washed over his face. By using both hands for some kind of attack magic, the change that had been limited to just one of his hands would now spread to both.

No matter. A surge of magic flowed through Folas as he slid the Gravity Ring on his left index finger. He considered absorbing another ether as an extra boost, but only had two left. He might need those to get out of here.

With that thought, he reactivated the invisibility cloak. He silently made his way down the stairwell and momentarily stood facing his soon-to-be victims.

He decided he would cast Gravity on the large guard who was standing on the left. With any luck, the effect of the magic would pull the man to his knees. If he cast it hard enough, he might even get the man to fall to the ground, possibly hitting his head and knocking him out, maybe even killing him quickly.

For the smaller guard on the right, he was going to blast him into the back wall with Wind Magic. *Here goes nothing.*

He made a fist with one hand and snapped his invisible fingers on the other. Instantly, he appeared before both men.

Folas grinned before he spoke. "I'm no shadow." He opened both palms. From his left hand, purple Gravity Magic emerged and flew toward the large guard. It surrounded him, freezing him into place.

From his right hand, yellow Wind Magic followed suit and hit the smaller guard straight in the chest. It threw him backward, with his head hitting the wall hard. Not quite enough to render him immobile, but definitely enough to stun him into submission momentarily.

Meanwhile, the Gravity Ring didn't have quite the effect he had hoped for with the large guard. Whether because of the man's size, his strength, or being on Folas' non-dominant hand, Wilbret resisted the attack. The Tall Elf intensified his efforts, sending the guard to his knees.

"Arrragghh!" Wilbret let out a moan and through the pain, tried to speak again. "Gromil, are you…" Folas sent a continuous blast of gravity toward the large guard, pulses of energy hitting like sacks full of sand into the man's body.

Out of nowhere, Folas heard a large crack. His eyes widened as he looked up and down, trying to figure out what made the sound.

The guard, in his defiance, had been gripping his sword and shield with all his might, attempting to raise them to attack. Now in indescribable pain, he dropped both. He let out a guttural cry as Folas realized what had happened.

The power of the Gravity Ring, combined with the man's attempt at forceful resistance, had shattered both of the man's shoulders.

Meanwhile, Gromil stirred. He began using his hands to try to get his balance. Folas responded by raising the hand holding Wilbret immobile high in the air. He snapped it down hard, sending the larger guard to the ground. Wilbret collapsed in a heap, his backside hunched in the air with his face and shoulders flat against the ground.

Folas stopped the Gravity blast and used his right hand to raise Gromil up into the air. He opened his left hand again and sent a single blast of Gravity magic straight at the other man's head.

It had the intended result. The combined effect of raising him high in the air while equally sending a strong blast of Gravity snapped the smaller man's neck.

Now dead, Folas dropped him and returned his attention to Wilbret. He walked over to his victim, who was trying to move anything not broken.

"Who...ughh...who...a...are...you?" Wilbret could barely ask. Folas kneeled down beside him, glancing at his right hand. Now, it was totally tar black down to his wrist, changing tone from having killed the guard referred to as Gromil.

He grabbed the hair of his soon-to-be-victim, raising the man's face upward to make eye contact. Wilbret groaned in pain.

"I...am the Dark Elf Master." He added Master to his title, realizing for the first time that the depth of his powers would allow him to control the other Elves as well. He dropped Wilbret's hair somewhat forcefully, letting the man's face smack the ground one final time with a bit of spiteful intensity.

Folas stood up and pulled out another ring from his satchel, a red one he placed on his right index finger. He used his left hand to levitate Wilbret up off the ground. This act was quickly becoming his favorite, almost a signature finishing move.

"Time to die, Graelan scum." He watched as Wilbret's broken limbs flailed aimlessly in the air. With almost every major bone in the guard's body broken, there wasn't much he could do.

That is, besides watching in terror as Folas opened the palm of his right hand. There, a small, burning ball of energy took shape. The Dark Elf Master sent a horrifically painful blast from the Fire

Ring straight into Wilbret's body. The guard's eyes widened as his body began burning from the inside out.

After a minute of unbelievable torture, all was silent. Folas experienced another odd and unexpected sensation. This time however he liked the emotions that came with it.

Accomplishment. Pride.

Satisfaction.

His time in Castle Abria taught him more about his abilities than he had learned throughout all the previous years of his life. Folas, like Graelan mages of years gone by, possessed one form of inherent attack magic. His was Wind Magic.

Folas also possessed other abilities including levitation, teleportation, and invisibility. He had only used his wind-based attack for "tasks" such as knocking down trees for his fellow Elves to harvest. Today, that changed with the shop owner.

In one of the old books, Kane discovered a reference to Magic Rings. When Graelans could wield magic, they had similar limitations: one type of inherent magic, and the rest available through various rings. All Magic Rings in the land had been forged by studying the Power Ring, one of three Abrian ancient artifacts. However, this was a relic of an era long gone. From time to time, Magic Rings would show up at the various markets, though their lack of functionality made them more appropriate as decorative items than weapons.

The last recorded instance of a Graelan mage was around this same time: the beginning of the New Era. Kane scoured the Archives until he found a passage vaguely describing how to forge Magic Rings once again. This happened in Clericsfold, under close guard, with few knowing about the process happening right under their noses.

Now, rather than travel from town to town and hope a vendor might be selling a ring, they could be forged as needed for the Elves.

His victory aside, Folas realized he had made a grave error. With both men dead, and the cause of their deaths clearly more than a heart attack compared to his previous two victims, he would be discovered soon. To avoid detection, Folas needed to dispose of the bodies somehow, making it appear as if both had deserted their posts. At least, the ruse needed to last enough for him to make his escape.

Folas looked at the door before him. He knew the risks of teleporting without knowing exactly where he was going. He kneeled down, looking through the keyhole for anything that might help him at least see where he was going.

Nothing. Pitch black. *I could end up inside of a wall if I'm not careful.* He looked around for something flammable. He walked over to one of the fallen guards. *His tunic!* Folas kneeled down and tore off a small piece of it. He rolled it tight, small enough to fit into the keyhole. Next, Folas used the power of the Fire Ring to ignite the tip and quickly slid it through the keyhole.

He didn't need much. Just a glimpse. As the torn fabric slipped through the keyhole and landed on the ground, it gave just the slightest hint of light so he could see the open room for a split second before it burnt itself out.

Now Folas knew where he was going. He closed his eyes, snapped his fingers, and reopened them. Much to his delight, Folas was standing inside of the locked room.

"It worked!" he exclaimed to the empty space, his voice echoing off of the walls. Folas opened his hand, letting the light of the Fire Ring burn in his palm. This acted as a light source, and he waved his hand around until he saw a torch on the wall.

Once the torch was burning brightly, he teleported back to the hallway. He grabbed the body of the first guard and returned to the locked room with it. He repeated this with the body of the burned guard and placed both in one of the corners. They would be found one day, though by the time they were, it would be too late.

"Now, where are you?" Folas looked around the room. It was a relatively nondescript space. The walls were made of the same golden material as the rest of Farna. It was large, roughly ten meters square. On the walls were various Abrian imagery: drapes, flags, a painting.

"Who are you?" Folas said, inspecting it. A regal man, possibly a king? He had dark brown, wavy shoulder-length hair. His tunic was a vibrant red, with an unremarkable crown on his head. He had a goatee instead of a beard, with a scar running down the side of one cheek.

The inscription on the placard said nothing more than 'Farris.' From Kane's studies, Folas knew this was the king before Telford.

Satisfied, he moved on, exploring the room. There were a few generic swords and shields strewn about, with no particular weapon looking any more or less special than the others. He picked up one, inspecting it and flipping it around. He wouldn't know if this was the Soul Sword from the sword that once slayed a mythical dragon or the one that committed a random murder.

On a far wall, there was a closed armoire. He noticed it and dropped the sword on the ground. It clanged to the ground, its echo bouncing back and forth on the stone walls. Folas walked over to the armoire and opened the double doors. His face morphed into a menacing grin.

On the right, hanging on the back of the armoire, was a solid gold-colored shield with a single bright fuchsia orb in the middle. Surrounding the orb was a navy band.

On the left, a gold-hued ring with a navy band sat on a shelf. In the middle was a large circular protrusion with a fringe-like pattern on its edge. In the middle of each, mimicking the north-south-east-west positioning of a compass, were four smaller fuchsia orbs. Connecting them was a navy band encompassing another protruding gold section and possessing a star-tipped pattern laid on top of a fuchsia background. Finally, in the middle of the ring were three teal jewels.

The Mind Shield. The Power Ring.

Last, but not least, hanging in the middle, fastened by its navy handle, was a sword with a gold hilt. This color continued in the form of overlays running alongside both edges of the blade, ending in a fuchsia tip. Between the gold edging was a teal background that continued down the blade until it intersected with a section just before the hilt where a navy jewel sat. Finally, six white, glowing orbs decorated the blade on each side.

"The Soul Sword." Folas had not only found the primary object he came looking for, but *all three* of the ancient — and until this moment, believed mythical — Abrian artifacts. He reached to grab the ring first. If the Archives were right, this would double his power.

An invisible barrier repelled his hand. It was painful, causing him to retreat backward a few steps.

"What in Lyra?" He walked back to the discarded sword and grabbed it. He returned to the armoire and used it to trace the border of the barrier.

Each of the three items was encased in a similar invisible field. How this was here was beyond his comprehension. This was some kind of Barrier defensive magic, and no Graelan could cast such a spell.

No Graelan.

"No Graelan. Tolith. Tolith, you traitor!" Folas threw the sword across the room, where it made a loud clang against the other armor and weapons nearby. Tolith had died years ago, mysteriously to most but obvious to Folas.

All it took was the promise of a few gold din to convince a down on their luck Graelan to poison his meal. Tolith had died in his sleep later that evening, though Folas later learned Borun had rechristened the market near the traitor's home in honor of the deceased. Apparently, before his passing, Tolith had encased the three artifacts in an impenetrable Barrier. The spell could only be broken by the one who cast it or those who the caster empowered to penetrate it.

"Had I known you did this, I would have killed you myself. At least you're already dead, you worthless piece of glarg. May your legacy among our people be remembered as that of a traitor." Folas didn't necessarily believe in curses, but hoped this one might stick.

He fruitlessly tried one more time to penetrate the Barrier, summoning all the magic he could pull from deep within his body.

Tolith's Barrier pushed back on the Dark Elf's hand with every attempt. Nothing could get through, and the spell repelled his futile attempt to use his other forms of magic. The effect was absolute, as if he wasn't even trying.

Folas would have to find another way to get the Soul Sword.

By the late afternoon, all but the big event had finished. Clericsfold had made some progress, scoring unexpected points in the archery games where they pulled out a few surprise victories. Overall, Abria led by six points. However, the score was too close. If both Clericsfold runners could come in first and second place, it would give them a total of eight points. The third place Abrian runner would give them one, yes, but the total would favor Clericsfold by one.

The problem for Clericsfold? Enid. She had placed first in *all* of her events and was favored to win this event as well. An hour before the start, Enid was sitting in an open field with her brother,

her parents, and her brother's stupid, if impressively strong, friend.

"You just need to place second. Don't let the pressure get to you, Sis." Enid's return stare made Tiernan realize, while attempting to be helpful, his words were falling on deaf ears. She rolled her eyes and turned away from her brother. Enid had one goal and one goal alone: first place. Anything less would be a failure to her.

"Tiernan..." Kyrie chastised her son in a single word, though the intent was clear. *Leave your sister be.* "Enid, this is your moment. You don't have anything to worry about."

Wayland chimed in. "I think what my friend is trying to say is you're the best runner our Kingdom has. There's nothing to be nervous or worried about. You've got this." He smiled as he said this, a gesture Enid returned.

Tiernan caught the exchange, and for the first time, began to suspect his friend had more than a cousin-like friendship in mind. *Oh gross. There's no way...*He pushed the thought from his mind.

Enid finally spoke. "Thanks, Way. T, I know you mean well too."

Davien spoke next. "No matter what happens, I'm proud of you. All of you," he said, looking at Tiernan, Wayland, and Enid. "This has been a great day. Have you heard the excitement, the emerging unity as everyone got caught up in the fun of the day? Today, Abria was one. United with Clericsfold. Strong." He laughed to himself and looked at each of the teens. "After all, Strength is Victory."

Enid closed her eyes and smiled as her father said the phrase for the first time. She stood up. "I can't just sit around and wait. We have, what, an hour before things kick off? Come on, T. Let's go for a jog. Way, if you wanna tag along you can too. I just need to do *something*."

Wayland's eyes lit up as Enid invited him along, and Tiernan groaned inside once again. *He does. How could I not see it all this time? That's why Wayland worked so hard to get in shape.*

"Stop," said Kyrie. "Come here." Enid walked over to her mom, who gave her a tight hug. "We'll see you at the starting line. I love you, Enid." Enid closed her eyes and pulled her mother in closer to her through the embrace.

"I love you too, mom," she said, releasing her. She ran over and gave Davien a kiss on the cheek. "Come on, boys. See if you can keep up." And with that, she darted off, Tiernan and Wayland not far behind.

Voron was the last Elf competitor of the day. This was also his first event, and one he had trained for rigorously. As an Elf runner, his short stature was both an advantage and a disadvantage. It would take more for his shorter stride to keep up, especially with the highly rated Enid expected to win. But it also meant he would face less wind drag, which, if he paced himself right, could let him save some energy.

"You're the fastest Elf in the Forest. You beat out runners from all across Clericsfold for this. Stop worrying. Stop freaking out. It's…"

"It's been said only lunatics and madmen talk to themselves so much," a voice said behind Voron. He turned to see who it was, embarrassed another person had heard his verbal monologue.

No one was there. Voron closed his eyes and extended his hands out to his side. His gift of Second Sight would allow him to see what was hidden. Usually, it let him see someone's intentions. It was also helpful when he was younger, playing a game of tag with his friends. It also allowed him to see those who were invisible.

With his eyes closed, he saw the Tall Elf standing before him. Second Sight gave everything a dark red hue, with a cloaked Elf taking on an inverted tone compared to their usual colors.

In this case, Folas appeared as normal. "Your Second Sight not working as intended? What's your name?" Voron didn't know what was happening or why his Second Sight was off like this, but even more frightening were the hands of the Tall Elf.

One was almost completely black. The other was beginning to show a similar discoloration.

"What do you want? And how are you doing this?" Folas, still invisible, walked over to Voron. He put his hand on Voron's head.

"Enough of this. Open your eyes." Immediately, Voron's eyes popped open, though they lacked their usual green coloration. Instead, they were glazed over, a milky white with no discernible iris or other characteristics.

"What…are…you…doing?" Voron struggled as his will faded.

Folas realized had something changed inside him too, as if a piece of Voron was now a part of the Dark Elf. *This is new, and I like it*, he thought as he embraced his new role along with a new power: Absorption.

"Listen to me, and listen well. You're going to do exactly as I say. And if you don't, the pain you're feeling now will be the least of your concerns."

Chapter 16

Forty-Five Kilometers

At the starting line stood twenty runners lined up in groups of four. In the second row were Enid, Voron, an Abrian runner from Idlewind named Dair, and a Clericsfold runner named Grosvenor.

The emcee paced with a frustrated look on his face, unable to start the event since the crowd was cheering too much to control. He looked at the four judges, who just shrugged their shoulders and laughed at his plight.

High in the stands, Davien and Borun sat side by side. Borun let out a loud, boisterous laugh as well. "This is going to be great!" Davien agreed, and leaned over to his wife, who was sitting on his left, to ask her a question.

"What do you think, hon? Should I try to get control of the crowd? Exert my 'kingly persona' for once today?"

Kyrie smiled as she welcomed the surrounding joy. "Nah. Let them enjoy it. Abria is one. Let's keep it that way."

Elsewhere in the stands, Tiernan and Wayland sat side by side. Wayland was smiling, his eyes fixated on Enid. Tiernan noticed and elbowed him.

"Ow! Hey, remember what I told you? This section," he said, pointing to his mid-section once again. "No more punches. Elbows count in that too." Tiernan did it again and punched Wayland's arm for good measure.

"Better?"

Wayland returned the jab, physically saying no without verbalizing it. Wayland's stronger hit made Tiernan wince. "Okay, man, I got it. No more punching. I'll stop."

"Liar," Wayland retorted, knowing his friend would do it again soon.

"For today, anyway."

"Thought so."

After a bit, the emcee noticed the crowd was beginning to settle down. He stood within eyesight of most of those in attendance and raised his hands. He began waving, signaling for the people to quiet themselves.

"Ladies and gentlemen. Laaadies and gentlemen! Please. Thank you. Welcome to the big event! A *forty-five-kilometer* run through the Abrian and Clericsfold country sides. The same rules apply here: we'll award five points for first place, three for second, and one for third. Let's introduce our athletes." He rambled off the names of each of the twenty runners, mentioning the names of their parents and the city they were from. In the case of Enid, no mention was made of her parents' status. Instead, he referred to Davien as a carpentry tradesman along with his beloved wife Kyrie, a stay-at-home mom.

Everyone knew, of course, but respected the King and Queen for their modesty.

After introducing those in the final row, the emcee moved back to a central position. "Runners, are you ready?" Each athlete responded in their own way, some with cheers, others with raised hands.

Enid placed her hands on her hips.

"Excellent! Judges, are you ready?" Each signaled they were with a thumbs up. "Okay, then let's get started. Runners, on your mark, get set, and…GO!"

BONG! The big race was the only event with a special starting bell, an enormous gong made by Borun himself to commemorate the event. The runners in the first row sped off, side by side for the first few dozen meters. It took a moment for the subsequent rows to cross the starting line, and the crowd of bodies made it difficult for anyone in the back to push themselves forward right away.

As they passed the stands where Davien, Kyrie, and Borun sat, the three stood in support of Enid.

"Let's go, kid!" Borun said.

"It's all yours, honey. You've got this!" cheered Kyrie.

"Yeah! That's my girl!" screamed Davien, overwhelmed by emotion and pride for his daughter.

The four runners in Enid's row remained neck and neck as they passed the set of stands where Tiernan and Wayland sat.

"Let's go, Enid!" Tiernan was jumping and fist pumping in support of his sister, and she cast him a quick glance and the side smile of a sibling bond.

Wayland clapped and raised one hand, fist clenched. He mouthed 'Strength is Victory' to her, and she nodded.

I have to do what the Dark Elf told me to do. I don't want to. But I have to. He came to a realization. *If I do this, I might have a shot of winning.*

The allure of a victory cemented his decision. He smirked and winked. The ground in Enid's lane vibrated and, imperceptible to most, *grew* a stone.

Imperceptible to most, that was, except for Tiernan. From the stands, he watched in slow motion as Enid's left foot caught the newly formed stone. Powerless to help, his sister fell flat on her face.

The other three runners continued their journey, with Dair casting her a quick glance before continuing his run. The remaining rows behind her navigated around her fallen body, meaning she had to wait until everyone else had passed to stand back up.

Finally, Enid got to her feet and began to run again. As she did, Tiernan began yelling.

"The Elf cheated! Didn't anyone else see that? Oh, come on! Seriously! This is such a load of…" and before he could finish, Enid stopped dead in her tracks.

She turned.

She looked back at him. Her eyes said it all.

Shut up.

Sheepishly, he sat down and mumbled to Wayland next to him. "But he did cheat. You saw it, right?"

"I didn't see anything, T. Look, there she goes. She'll recover. Enid's got this." It was a lie because Wayland did see *something* — just not what Tiernan saw.

Wayland's eyes watched Enid's clenched fist and the slight ripple of red enveloping it. Almost undetectable, of course, but visible.

As soon as Enid relaxed her hand, the effect dissipated. The guys watched as their champion runner turned a corner and continued her race, now several crucial seconds behind the rest of the runners.

At the end of the race, Abria and Clericsfold were once again a united Kingdom. Abria came out ahead, with Dair winning the overall race and Enid coming in a close second. She made up the lost time from falling during the back half, passing both Voron and Grosvenor along with everyone else near the bend between the western and southern Abrian paths.

However, Dair maintained a respectable lead, and even with a final sprint, she wasn't able to close the gap. She crossed the finish line less than six seconds after Dair. The next closest runner crossed the finish line a full two minutes later.

Voron leaned against the trunk of a tree in solitude, contemplating the day's events. He wasn't far from where he encountered the Tall Elf — *no, the Dark Elf.* Whatever Folas had become was something different, something sinister.

Earlier, Voron had felt his brain shake as Folas tortured him, bending him to his will. Now, especially after a competitive race, the combined effect gave him a splitting headache. Somehow, it made it easier to think as he realized the guy in the stands was right.

He did try to cheat.

Voron sighed. Folas' actions caused the smaller Elf to compromise his integrity. He could feel his people being torn apart through this process. Years ago, there was a small group who had caused some problems near Milston. Voron didn't know who among his brethren had done so, obviously, though he had a few suspicions.

The perpetrators would have inherent Frost Magic, and there were only a handful who possessed such a gift. He had also heard they used Stop powers, which narrowed down the list of names even more. Voron hoped those perpetrators weren't trying to stir up any more dissension within the Forest, but also knew better.

He opened his hand and watched as a purple ball formed in his palm. Above him, high in the tree, hung an Abrian Sweet Apple. He fired a tiny blast from his hand, using his Gravity Magic to make it fall to the ground.

"Nice trick," a voice said to his left. Voron jumped to his feet. As before, the voice was cloaked. Voron sat back down and picked up the fallen apple. He took a bite before replying.

"I'm done playing your games, Folas. You can come out of hiding. Clericsfold lost. *Enid lost,* no thanks to you." Folas revealed himself, and Voron noticed the inky black portions of his skin had grown even more pronounced.

Now, both hands were as dark as midnight. *No, darker even.*

They were almost as void as the core of Ultimus magic, an incredibly rare magic said to come from another world or dimension.

It was a spell only a handful had ever possessed, and Voron knew little of its origins.

No one did. That's what made Ultimus such a foreboding power. It was unnatural, and Voron wondered if somehow Folas had tapped into its source.

Ultimus would make him the most powerful person alive...

Noting the smaller Elf's gaze, Folas opened and closed his hands, showing them to Voron.

"Do you like? Reminds you of Ultimus, doesn't it? I haven't seen that since our time in Exile." He lowered his hand and looked coldly at Voron. "You may *think* you're done. You've only just begun."

Folas walked in front of Voron, standing close enough the smaller Elf couldn't help but stare at him. Voron took another bite of the apple before launching it at Folas' chest.

The apple paused mid-air, hovering. Folas' lips curled into a sardonic grin as he brought the apple to his face. Without holding it, he took a bite. He chewed it with an open mouth, letting pieces fall to the ground and splattering against his tunic.

"You're disgusting. *I'm* disgusting." Voron stood to his feet and charged at Folas, fist raised. Folas smirked, blinked, and froze the smaller Elf in place.

"How quaint," he said, mouth still full of bits of apple. He turned his head, spit them out, and stared deep into Voron's eyes. "You want to see another trick? Watch." He backed up, still holding Voron in place, while concentrating his gaze on the apple. With a flick, he snapped his free hand.

The apple withered. Slowly, it shrunk in size. All the water remaining within it evaporated until the apple was as hard as a rock. Bit by bit, it began to crumble to dust. The particles were still levitating in the air until Folas, in an act of presumed superior spite, blew them away into the breeze with his breath.

"I learned this little trick today. I didn't know I could do this until I bumped into a guard accidentally. What do you think?" He walked closer to Voron. Using his powers, Folas raised the smaller Elf into the air until he was face to face with the Tall Ef. "This will happen to you too unless you do exactly as I say. You think your headache is painful *now?* You don't know pain. Do I make myself clear?" Voron struggled to move. He couldn't talk.

In his mind, he cried out in agony.

"You should have won. For your failure, you have one last chance to make me happy. Failure means…ah, what do we have here?" A squirrel had climbed down another nearby tree. Folas dropped Voron, who fell to his knees in pain.

Folas extended his hand toward the squirrel, freezing it in place and bringing it toward the smaller Elf who had only risen to his knees. "Perfect timing. Here is what will happen to you. Watch its pain, and remember it carefully." Folas leaned down, raising Voron's head with his blackened right hand. "Because if you do not complete what I'm about to require of you, if you fail in any way, this will be the result."

Voron tried to recoil away. "Nah ah ah. You would miss the fun," said Folas. He used his other hand to hold Voron still once again. He brought the squirrel face to face with Voron. The smaller Elf could see into the poor creature's eyes, could sense its fear, and empathized with its plight. As Folas continued his assault on the squirrel, Voron lost the contents of his stomach. He cried in anguish as the poor creature tried to emit a howl of pain before falling silent and withering away to dust.

Folas released Voron, who promptly punched the ground. Kneeling on all fours, unadulterated rage toward Folas consumed him.

I hate him. Voron wanted to hurt the Tall Elf, but knew he was powerless to do so. Resigned to his fate, tears streamed down both cheeks as he finally spoke.

"What do you need me to do?"

Across the field, Enid went over the race in her mind again. And again. And again.

She replayed each step, analyzing where she should have pushed harder and where she should have backed off. *Did staring at T cost me?* She tried to recount the time she stood there, but it felt like only a few seconds. Dair beat her by twice that amount.

Was there a downhill where I didn't run faster? A place where I held back? The Abrian Plateau had a series of natural rock steps leading up from the grasslands to the top. She hadn't done much speed work with stairs. *Is that why I came in second?*

Kyrie, now wearing the regal gown of a queen, found her daughter after a great deal of searching. The Queen had to switch from her recreational clothing to her royal outfit for the final ceremony in Farna. Enid's clothes were still soaked in sweat, a stark comparison to her mother's proper persona. Standing behind Enid, Kyrie cleared her throat.

Enid turned around and ran to her mom. She started to hug her, but paused.

Kyrie laughed. "The treaty signing is over. Your father is busy with the other city leaders. I'm done for the day, other than enjoying the closing ceremony with my family. Hugs *are* permitted." Enid ran toward her and embraced her, burying her face deep into her mom's arms. A single tear ran down her exposed cheek.

"I tried. I wanted to make you and Daddy proud." Kyrie rubbed her daughter's back, laying her head on Enid's.

"You don't think we are? You came in second. Unbelievable, considering what happened." Enid released the hug, turning her back from her mom to stare at the open field toward Farna.

"Did you hear Tiernan?" she asked.

Kyrie walked up next to Enid and put her arm around her daughter's shoulders.

"Whether I did or did not is a matter of…irrelevance. Things are still precarious, despite the treaty. We have to watch what we say."

Enid leaned on her mom. "In other words, you saw it happen, too. We know Clericsfold tried to cheat, but can't say it." She sighed. "Abria won. Do you and Daddy think things are going to be okay?"

Kyrie did not think so, but didn't want to acknowledge her fears. Instead, she shifted the conversation. "Your father met with Eskil not long after the race. There is talk of a second Statuo next year.

"Next time, it will be different. It won't be an 'us versus them' competition. It will be as a united Kingdom. The rules will change. There is talk about each city competing for medals, sending their best athletes for every event."

Kyrie laughed, realizing the absurdity of what she was just about to say, considering the uncertainty earlier in the day. "Eskil enjoyed himself so much today he suggested we make it a week-long event. This would give time for more competitions, more athletes, and more fun."

Enid let her mom's arm fall off and faced her. "So why didn't you answer my question?"

Kyrie looked lovingly at her daughter. "You're too smart for your own good. There *was* another event where a sudden outgrowth of rocks appeared. Like in your's, it derailed things. Actually, it was the rowing event where your brother's team won.

There's also..." She paused. *People die all the time.* Yet two people mysteriously passed away in Farna today, both in an eerily similar manner.

And several guards were missing, including the chief of the royal army. "Nothing. We can't predict what will happen today, let alone next year. Today, Abria is a united Kingdom. Come on, let's go get you changed so we can celebrate."

Together, they walked in the direction of the Castle where a special celebration would start soon.

"I mean, yeah, Enid did great. But she would have *won* this race if..." Tiernan and Wayland walked away from the starting line. After the event had completed, both of them had sat in the stands long after everyone else had left.

"Yes, yes, I *know*, T. If the Elf didn't cheat. You made your point *abundantly* clear. You know your sister will not see it that way." Wayland smiled. He was picturing her at the finish line, giving it her all.

Strong. Fast. Determined. Tiernan noticed his friend's smile and finally accepted what he didn't want to admit.

"Oh man, stop it, please. I can see it on your face. Give her some space. Enid is going to have training on her mind from here on out. She's only going to want to get better, especially if there's another big event like this."

Wayland's face changed from a look of puppy love to concern. "Training. As in her special powers." Tiernan started to reply, but hesitated. He didn't know how to respond. "It's okay. Man, whatever happened when the two of you were born must have been special."

Tiernan's annoyance welled up. "Are you kidding me, Way? The King of Abria literally died as I was born. Literally.

That's why my parents had to name me what they did. 'This boy is a special one, yes he is.'"

Tiernan kicked a nearby piece of debris as they walked side by side. "Stupid clerics. Making us abide by some ancient tradition. My mom didn't get to give me the name she wanted to. Edward. You know, a strong name. Do you know what it means, Way?

"No, T, I don't."

"Rich Guard. Rich! Maybe I was supposed to be famous or something."

He kicked another piece of debris in frustration. "All I can think is why? Why me, Way? Why did I have to get pulled into this?

"Besides, what special powers are you referring to? I meant another race. You know she's not going to stop here. Whatever comes next, if it's a race, she'll be there."

The route they walked brought them closer to the open field near the entrance to Castle Abria. Wayland kicked some of the trash out of the way from the celebrations as Tiernan continued ranting.

"You know what happened next. Instead of having time to spend with both of us, they rushed Dad here," he said, pointing at the castle. "Dad found out he was somehow related to the dead guy, and he had to become King of Abria since our grandfather wouldn't step up. We all know the story. It's not like my parents don't remind me of it. Every. Single. Chance. They get."

He sighed as they walked by a few shops in Farna. He turned back around. Far in the distance, through the city gates, he could see his mom and sister also heading in the same direction. "It's Enid that..." Tiernan let his voice trail off. He couldn't finish the next thought. Wayland put his hand on Tiernan's shoulder.

"I've been with your family enough to know they don't bring it up every single day. Listen, Tiernan, we *all* know. You guys got a raw deal. Your parents didn't know they were having twins. That, in and of itself, is pretty special.

"But then they almost lost her, had to change your name, and become King and Queen all within a few hours. It was a lot." Wayland looked up toward the sky. "Has anyone ever explained the Dragon?"

Tiernan stopped in his tracks and shot his friend a look. He opened his mouth, preparing to answer as he looked back once again in the direction of Enid and Kyrie. "They were mythical until the day I was born."

"The Day of Tiernan."

"Let's not call it that." A sigh. "But yes, that was the day everyone learned dragons were still out there, far beyond the wilderness. Who knows? Maybe they rule the rest of Grael."

"Hey, maybe one day we'll be able to travel beyond Abria to find out. Wouldn't that be fun, a guy's trip across the world to find them? 'Way and T against all odds!' They'll sing songs about it for years."

"Yeah man, it sounds fun. And yes, the dragon saved her. But that's all I know about what happened back then." Tiernan didn't like lying to his best friend. From time to time, he *had* noticed the same thing Wayland saw at the race.

A spark of light. A red glow. Even a quiver of fire. Each coming from his sister in differing levels, at various times, and based on different situations. He didn't know what the dragon did to her, other than it made her special.

And that was something he was determined to protect with everything in him.

Builders completed the first Drunken Alligator in Lorelei over five hundred years ago. Each one was different, though they shared similar design elements.

The owners of the Alligator in Farna realized today, for the first time, they should *not* have followed the standard blueprints. Instead, they should have built a much larger establishment.

Squeezed into the four walls, and spilling into the streets, were delegations, athletes, community leadership, and lay people from all across Abria. Ulrich of Milston was seated at a table with two athletes from his city. At the adjacent table were Fenwick of Lakedon and Kettil of Northwick. The geographic proximity of these three cities had led to a bond forming between the men.

Crowded between their tables and the bar stood Eskil and four the Clericsfold athletes. Among their number was Voron, who, despite the surrounding excitement, looked disconnected and distant. He put his hand in his pocket, relieved. *I haven't lost what Folas gave me.*

Tibor of Alwyn was across the room, sitting at a table with King Davien and Manus Midir. All three men were excitedly discussing plans for the second Statuo. Standing next to them were Penrod, Mayor of Oakshadow, along with Council members Vadim and Adair from Clericsfold. Adair was laughing, having placed his hand on Penrod's shoulder and mocking something the latter had just said. Midir stood up with a burst of energy and motioned for Vadim to follow him. They made their way to the bar as Tibor leaned in to speak to Davien.

"You've done it, you know, that right? Look around. Everyone in this room is happy. No one is at each other's throats. You brought us together, and now Abria is one."

Adair nodded in agreement. "Strength is Victory. Isn't that what your side kept saying during this?" He raised his hands high in the air, spilling some Lorelian Mead from the pint glass he was holding. "And now, we're an even stronger Kingdom." He lowered his hands and extended his right one to the King. Davien gave him a firm handshake as Adair spoke again. "So I say again, Strength is Victory!" Midir squeezed his way back to the table with a glass of mead and a Dorian Ale, putting the latter in front of the King.

Davien released Adair's hand and grabbed the glass. He raised it high to the men surrounding him. "To Abria!" They all echoed the toast and took a drink together.

Borun, sitting nearby, took in this scene with glee. Today justified his decision to adopt his son. There was no doubt about it: Davien was the right leader for Abria.

Before he continued celebrating, a twinge of guilt hit his chest. Would none of this have happened if he hadn't turned his back on Kane all those years ago? He shook the feeling off and decided to get another pint of Lorelian Mead from the bar.

Being a larger man, it was more difficult for Borun to make his way up to the bar. Finally, he caught the attention of the barkeep from a distance and raised his hand with an extended finger in the air.

One. *One more glass*. He'd finish it here, then find his grandson and granddaughter. They were elsewhere, too young to partake in these kinds of festivities, yet preparing for the celebration just the same. Davien had arranged for a parade of sorts for all the athletes, Abrian and Clericsfold alike. They would be starting within the hour, most of the crowd making their way to the sidelines to watch.

Borun sat back down, and a few moments later an Elf brought him his drink. He smiled. Borun thought he remembered his face, but had already had one too many pints to think with a clear head.

"Here you go, sir. I was just heading out. The lady at the bar asked me to give this to you." Borun took the glass, and raised it in a sign of gratitude to the Elf, who used his shorter size to squeeze through the crowd easier than Borun could.

Borun took a drink and sat back, content.

Today was a good day.

As Voron left the Drunken Alligator, tears welled up in his eyes. He couldn't decide which emotion he felt more.

Was it guilt, now at a level even worse than when he caused Enid to trip over the rock?

Or was it hate, as he wanted nothing more than to tear Folas apart from head to toe?

The parade started at the entrance to the city with all first-place teams or individual participants at the forefront. Second, third, and fourth place finishers followed next, though in no specific order. It was decided this formation would be best, an attempt to not make anyone feel bad about how they placed. One change for the second Statuo was the closing ceremonies would consist of a city-by-city grouping instead of a finisher's lineup.

The adults enjoying themselves within the Alligator eventually made their way to the start. The emcees of the closing ceremonies, King Davien and Mayor Eskil, stood side by side. Davien had deferred much of today's events to Eskil, allowing him to take control of the proceedings so as not to give the appearance of a 'conquering' side.

Eskil was gracious, and after saying a few words, motioned for Davien to speak.

The King rose from his chair and turned to face the crowd first. "Welcome, citizens of our *united Kingdom*!

"To those who participated in today's events, whether as a participant or an observer, I welcome you to Farna. Let this, the

15th day of Fawnmist not be known as a date when one side won *over* the other.

"Instead, let it be remembered as the Day of Unity, when the Kingdom came together as one." The crowd responded kindly to this, with the various council members from Clericsfold in the crowd reacting in kind and showing their approval.

Kane was nowhere to be seen.

Voron viewed all of this from a distance, high above the walls surrounding Farna. He had already decided he would not be marching in the closing ceremonies.

Instead, he found a set of stairs leading to the top of one of the city walls. There were other observers up there as well, so he knew he wasn't breaking any rules.

Deep in his heart, Voron knew he had no business being a part of the closing celebrations. What he had done today would seal his fate, and while one day he would try to atone for his misdeeds, nothing could relieve him of his overwhelming sense of guilt.

Next to him, an invisible voice spoke.

"Kane is pleased. We will call upon you again. Until then, enjoy the show." Voron leaned over the edge of the nearby wall in despair. His anger welled up in him, and he quickly snapped into his Second Sight gift. If he saw Folas, he knew he would do everything he could to end the Dark Elf's life.

Folas was gone. He must have teleported after torturing the smaller Elf one last time today.

Voron returned to his normal sight, opening his eyes as the parade began moving. He watched as the first-place finishers raised their hands, waving, fist pumping, and high-fiving those near the open field. The rest followed behind, just as happy as those in front.

He made out Enid, who was one of the few not in a celebratory mood. She was in the rear of the first-place group, having won all running events.

Except, of course, the big race. Voron realized his other crime was about to come to fruition as well. While he continued to watch, the first-place athletes approached the box where Eskil and Davien were standing. Behind them were two other mayors, one with a tanned complexion which made Voron think he probably came from Idlewind.

And another kind, burly man. A larger-than-life man known throughout Lily of the Valley as their leader, their caretaker, and their loudest champion.

A tear once again ran down Voron's cheek. He swallowed hard as he watched the man shake his head.

"First, he'll think he had too much to drink. Then, he'll start to lose his footing. As the poison makes its way throughout his system, it'll eventually cause his heart to stop. Do you understand what you must do?" Voron recalled the words of the Dark Elf as he watched each of these actions play out in succession. Watching them in real-time, the smaller Elf wanted to vomit.

First, Borun wondered if the last drink at the Drunken Alligator had been one too many. Next, he wobbled on his feet. He stumbled, trying to catch himself. The man beside him tried to steady him. Borun first waved him off, but just as fast leaned into his arms. Midir said something, and the King turned around.

Borun grabbed his chest in panic and found it hard to breathe. In the parade, Enid tapped her brother's shoulder. Tiernan looked up to the box where his father and grandfather were and watched Borun fall out of sight. Davien rushed to his side, and from the twin's vantage point, they could no longer see what was happening.

Far above, along the city walls, Voron could. He watched as Borun gasped for breath and put his hand out to grab his son. From a doorway out of sight, Queen Kyrie rushed in and knelt next to her father-in-law. Davien held his hand and began yelling for a doctor.

Midir turned to the crowd, doing the same. "We need a doctor up here. NOW!" But it was too late. Voron pulled the small purple vial out of his pocket. He kept it concealed in his hand where no one could see it. He squeezed it hard, shattering the container as anger boiled up inside of him.

Voron turned back to watch the scene unfold, his eyes full of remorseful tears. The parade stopped. A hush fell over the crowd.

"Dad. Father. Please. Hold on. The doctor will be here soon," Davien pleaded, trying to keep his father from fading. Borun blinked and looked at his son through glazed-over eyes. He smiled one last time.

"I love you, son." Those were the last words Borun ever spoke.

Chapter 17

Family is Strength

Lily of the Valley was normally an active, busy place. Every day, from sunup to sundown and beyond, there was no shortage of activity, fun, and excitement. Whether high noon or the dead of night, something was always happening.

In the years since the Tolith Market opened, the Valley been completely transformed. True, it still possessed the sense of serenity many of the residents preferred from years gone by.

Nevertheless, something was always going on which gave the town an impressive vibrancy, attracting many tourists from across Abria. At any given time, the nearby Inn was full, with visitors sometimes even staying within the homes of hospitable residents.

Today, everything was shut down. All the shops and vendors in the Tolith Market had their doors locked and windows closed. There would be no buying or selling of goods today. Most visitors had returned home, save for a select few.

Even the Drunken Alligator, which was open 26/7/338 days per year, was closed, with the owner recruiting volunteers from across the Valley to prepare a large funeral dinner.

Only the Royal Family had taken up refuge within its walls. Davien rested by the fire in Borun's chair, staring blankly into the flames. Kyrie and Enid reclined on a couch near the bar, the latter leaning on her mother's side as she napped.

Tiernan sat at a single-seated, unoccupied table in the corner along the western wall. The table was relatively new, a recent purchase from a carpentry vendor in the Tolith Market. As a fruitless way to pass the time, Tiernan ran his hands along its veneered surface. It was fresh, clean, virtually untouched.

Deep in his heart, sadness overwhelmed Tiernan. He had never built a connection with his adoptive grandfather. Even at the Statuo, he expressed resentment toward the older gentleman, blaming him for his family's responsibility of ruling the Kingdom.

For the past two days, his resentment had been replaced with guilt and remorse. With Borun now gone, Tiernan realized there was a missed opportunity he could never recapture. Borun was of advanced years, over four hundred years old, true. But his behaviors, lifestyle, and personality exuded youth and vibrance. No one expected him to pass away this soon.

Tiernan leaned against the wall next to his table. He noticed it felt sticky, so he touched it with his hand. *Somebody needs to clean these walls, give them a different coat of paint. When I'm King, I'll make sure places like this take better care of their patrons. No public drunkenness, no sticky walls, no…*

His sister interrupted his teenage angst across the room. Enid had stirred and opened her eyes. She looked up at Kyrie. "What time is it?"

"Last we checked, the sun was just past the second hour of the afternoon," Kyrie responded. Tiernan watched without saying a word. His sister had been asleep for a while, not long after they had arrived at the Alligator earlier that morning. Curiously, his sister closed her eyes again. "Not enough sleep?" their mother asked.

Enid yawned before she answered. "I'm fine. I just…I was with Grandpa in my dream. I want to go back to it." Her words stung Tiernan. In response, he pulled out a small knife from a hidden sheath tied to his pant leg, strategically placed within the upper edge of his boot. He began flipping it as Enid continued. "He was at the end of the parade, waiting for me and T to cross. He was standing there next to, what's his name? The guy from Idlewind?"

"Midir," Kyrie answered.

"Yeah, him. Except he wasn't Midir exactly. He was, I guess, different. Taller, maybe.

"Anyway, as the parade ended, Grandpa reached out to give me a hug. Told me he was proud of me. That my strength came from my family -- you, Dad, and T." Kyrie gave Enid a kiss on the head. She trailed her fingers through her daughter's hair.

"You should get up soon. The memorial service will start in a few hours." Tiernan flipped the knife one more time, this time catching it by the handle, and quickly stabbed it into the top of the table.

Whoops. Cautiously, he looked around. Davien was still meditating. Kyrie had her eyes closed, resting her cheek on the top of Enid's head. Enid had yet to reopen her eyes, and the owner of the place wasn't anywhere to be seen. No one had heard the noise, loud as it had been, or acknowledged they did.

He pulled it out, noticing the small indentation the knife had left on the previously perfectly smooth surface. Tiernan leaned back and looked at the table's rounded edge. *If I do this quickly…*

Using the knife, he began etching three letters into the edge. A large capital F. Then a smaller, lowercase I. Followed by a larger capital S. He mumbled under his breath as he carved each letter.

"Family…is…strength. There." He looked around again. No one in the room had caught his act of vandalism. *Just one more thing to do: rotate the table so the carving is up against the wall, hidden out of sight.*

Interrupting his thoughts, Davien rose from the chair. Tiernan leaned over the table, using his body to hide the damage. The teenage vandal put his hand over the indention on the top too, just as a precaution.

The knife! As Davien grabbed his cloak from the nearby chair, Tiernan carefully slid the blade into his shirt sleeve, keeping just the edge of the handle at the base of his palm. The cold metal of the blade pressed against his forearm, and he made a mental note to keep his arm as straight as possible so he didn't accidentally stab or cut himself.

"Come on. We should go," Davien said to his family. "The service will start at sundown, and we need to be there early."

On the couch, Kyrie and Enid began moving.
Enid sat up off of her mother, sitting with her arms dropped between her legs for a moment, and yawned. Kyrie began adjusting her hair, but realized the futility of such a thing without a mirror.

"Davien, I'm going to freshen up. I think there's a washroom in the back. Come on, Enid, I'll fix your hair too." Davien raised his eyebrows at the comment.

"And you think a place like this is going to have facilities to your liking?" Kyrie shot him a cold stare.

"Have you forgotten where we came from *before* this?" she asked, motioning to their royal clothing. "Trust me, my dear, I'll make do."

Davien gave his wife a tender smile and shrugged. "Right. Okay. Tiernan, let's go." The king moved toward his son, who tried to act as if he, too, had just awoken.

"Hey Dad, I'm going to do the same thing. I'll wait for them to be done first, then I'll catch up." Davien began to protest, though Tiernan cut him off. "I'll be quick. I promise. Just a minute or two behind them."

Davien shook his head. "You can always use your grandfather's estate. He had a much nicer…"

"Dad. I'd rather not. It doesn't feel right, okay? I'll hurry, I promise."

Frustrated, Davien granted him his request. "Fine. I guess I'll go alone." He looked back at the ladies. "I'll meet everyone at the well in the middle of town. *Soon*." He emphasized the last word, making his expectations clear. Everyone nodded.

Satisfied, Davien walked toward the door. He turned back one last time. "I know this is hard. Thank you for being here today." With that, he left. Enid and Kyrie made their exit as well, heading to a small room in the back of the Alligator.

This is my chance!

Tiernan first pulled the knife out of his sleeve and stuffed it back into its sheath. He jumped to his feet and began rotating the table. It was far heavier than its appearance would have a person believe.

"What in the name of Aila? Why…is…this…so…heavy?" Each word coincided with a turn of the table. Thankfully, his exercise routine for the Statuo was paying off here, otherwise he wouldn't have had the strength to turn it at all. He kneeled down close to the edge, inspecting to see if any of the letters were visible from any angle. Only the upper edge of the S was unobscured, but one would have to be looking for it to see it.

Lastly, he looked around. On a table across the room, a small candle within a metal stand sat by itself. He bolted over to it and grabbed the object. Returning to his seat, he placed it on top of the damaged spot.

The small stand hid the indention well enough, and the owners might even believe the base caused the damage. He thought about carving his initials into the top, but decided that would be going too far.

Believing he was in the clear, Tiernan turned to the exit of the Alligator before his sister and mother were done.

Davien was a patient man in most cases. Today, his nerves were on edge. Midir and his family chose to stay at one of the two Valley Inns, in this case the one on the eastern outskirt of the Tolith Market. Sitting on the edge of the well, Davien could see his friend's family walking through the aisle ways between the different shops and storefronts.

Davien crossed his arms, hoping his family would show up here *before* Midir made his way through the closed market.

Tiernan carefully opened the door to the Alligator, and to his relief, Davien was facing the opposite direction. Tiernan looked around and saw his escape. The door of the Drunken Alligator faced south, so his plan was to move west toward the mill. He would walk through the various buildings making up the town, weaving between them carefully before meeting up with his father from the south.

The plan almost worked as intended. As he walked, Tiernan rounded a corner and saw Wayland, along with his father, Talcot. Apparently, they had visited Borun Mill. Wayland raised his hand and began to yell.

Tiernan waved him off, put his finger up to his mouth, and gave his friend an 'I'll kill you' gesture, running his finger along his neck with widened eyes. He motioned for Wayland to follow him, who said goodbye to his father as he caught up with his friend.

As they looped behind a nearby building, Wayland whispered. "Hey, T. Slow down. Hey. What's going on?" Tiernan shook his head, then put his finger up to his lips again.

"Just play along," he whispered. "Agree with whatever I say. I need to go meet up with Dad." Wayland gave Tiernan a look that said 'Whatever' and followed behind. They looped behind a few more buildings until Tiernan believed it had been enough, and they returned to the main path through Lily of the Valley. He spoke again. "Let's go. See, Dad is there at the well."

Davien saw Tiernan walking in the distance, but didn't show any kind of reaction. Kyrie and Enid were still missing, so this was curious. "There's Wayland too." He waited until the pair were close enough to begin asking questions.

"Hey, Dad."

Tiernan looks flustered. Something is up.

"Tiernan. Wayland." Davien nodded at both before he began interrogating his son. "T, how did you end up out *there*?" He pointed as he put the emphasis on the last word. "Your mother and sister aren't here yet, so you should still be in the Alligator. Waiting on them."

Tiernan mustered up all the courage he had. His lie had to be perfect. *Here goes.* "I decided to go over to the place where Wayland was staying. I got ready over there instead. I figured that would be faster than waiting on Mom and Sis."

Davien eyed his son. His hair did not look any different from when he last saw him. His tunic looked disheveled. If Tiernan had gotten ready, he'd done a terrible job at it. Davien turned his head to talk to Wayland.

"Is this true?" Wayland nodded his head. Davien looked back at Tiernan. "And your grandfather's place wasn't good enough?" Davien sighed.

"Forget it. Tiernan, you *don't* look presentable. May I remind you of your responsibility not only to this family, but to the Kingdom as well? You're the Prince of this land and you need to look like it."

Tiernan swallowed. In his rush, he hadn't thought to actually freshen up. "I'll, uh, go back and get ready. Better this time. Okay?"

Davien had never been fond of reminding Tiernan of his place in the Royal Family. Today was different. Here, in this moment, he needed his son to recognize the gravity of what was before him. He decided to send the two away. "Go. I expect to see you in the garden shortly. When your mother and sister show up, you'd better already be there.

"And presentable, son. Do I make myself clear?"

Tiernan nodded. "Yes, sir." He grabbed Wayland's arm, who was still confused by the entire exchange. "Do you have the key with you?" Wayland nodded. Together, they quickly walked back to the home Wayland's family had stayed in.

Once they were out of earshot of the King, Wayland finally started asking questions. "T, what just happened? Because I don't like the idea of lying to the King, even if he is your father."

"Don't worry about it. Dad will forget all about this by tomorrow."

"He'd better. But seriously, what is going on?" Tiernan decided he didn't want to confess his 'crime', and changed the subject as they were walking.

"Enid will be there. You look more formal than normal. I didn't know you even owned clothes like that. Are you trying to impress her still?" Wayland stopped and punched his friend on the arm. It was a sizable jab, and one that caused Tiernan to recoil in pain. "Ow, man. Hey, I could have you arrested!"

"You wouldn't dare. Besides, *now* you're going to play the royal card? Just like that, years of friendship forgotten? After whatever I just did to save your sorry self?" He dropped to his knees. "Oh please forgive me, dear 'Prince of the land'." Wayland grabbed Tiernan's hand, feigning regret while he mockingly repeated some of Davien's words. Tiernan yanked his arm away.

"Shut up."

The memorial service for Borun was held in the northern gardens. Kyrie had never seen such a beautiful place for an internment. Its beauty even impressed her father who gave Davien a rare compliment on the design.

A waist-high brick wall surrounded the gardens on all sides, save for a small entrance to the south. Within the garden, the fields on all sides of the seating area were full of the magnificent Valley Rose. Exclusive to this part of Abria, it grew in several shades: red, blue, purple, yellow, and a soft pink. Each rose color smelled subtly different, which gave the garden a stimulating, aromatic atmosphere.

Borun's body was buried in a resplendent royal casket adorned with detailed, ornate carvings on all sides. It was colored a deep mahogany with gold hardware.

The artisans worked so fast, Kyrie thought to herself. Though Borun had died just a few days ago, a skilled craftsman from the Valley offered to customize it to bear her late father-in-law's likeness. When it was presented to the Royal Family today, they were all impressed by the detailed carving of Borun's face at the head of the casket.

At the service itself, several from the community spoke of his kindness, his joyful persona, his friendship with Tolith, and the way he was a champion for everyone in the valley. The manager of the mill spoke too, since it had been open for most of the past decade and employed many Valley residents. Several shop owners from the market spoke before Midir shared the story of the white dragon. After, Davien concluded the service with a short eulogy for his father.

Once it was over, and the other attendees had left, all that remained were Davien, Kyrie, the twins, Wayland, and Midir. Tiernan stood at a distance with Wayland, while the others were gathered around the casket.

Outside of the gardens, patient volunteers waited for the Royal Family to conclude their moment of mourning before beginning the arduous task of lowering Borun's casket into the ground.

In front of the family was a roped off area. Davien had commissioned a statue of his father from craftsmen in Milston, and it was expected to be completed by Origlow. Once delivered, it would stand forever in this spot, looking out over the beloved Valley he had helped build.

Still feeling his guilt, Tiernan finally approached. Davien was standing near the carving of Borun's face as his son walked up. The King turned to look at him and smiled. Tiernan kneeled down and pulled out his knife once again. He waved his father away from the casket's head, a gesture Davien didn't quite understand but obliged for his son.

Below Borun's face, Tiernan carved three letters: F.I.S.

He looked back at Wayland and motioned for him to come up. Tiernan put his arm around his friend's neck, embracing him as a brother. Davien observed this as a couple of tears ran down his son's face. Wayland hugged Tiernan tighter as the Prince began crying.

Enid walked over too, wrapping her arms around her brother from behind. Kyrie and Davien exchanged a tearful look, yet smiled at the tender moment between the three.

Finally, Tiernan let go and placed his hands on the casket to brace himself. Enid stepped back as her brother explained. "It means 'Family is Strength.'"

Enid put her hand on top of her brother's, giving it a light squeeze as she realized the message from Borun in her dream inspired her brother's carving. She smiled at Wayland with a slight, almost imperceptible hint of flame behind her eyes. Tiernan was the only one who saw the exchange and rolled his eyes upon seeing it, but decided he should learn to be at peace with the things he couldn't control.

Davien looked around at each person standing around the casket. He knew it would have made Borun happy to see them here.

Midir, a loyal ally not only of the Royal Family but also Borun's late brother, Tiernan the First.

Wayland, his grandson's best friend and all-but-by-blood brother.

Tiernan and Enid, the twins who had overcome impossible odds from day one.

Kyrie, his beloved daughter-in-law who had stood by Davien through the bad times and the good.

And Davien himself, Borun's adopted son who had, through no fault of his own, became a beloved King of the land.

Family.

"Family is Strength," Davien echoed.

Chapter 18

Intermissio 3rd

Tiernan picked up and held the last page he had written. The inscription he had carved felt even more relevant than before, especially in light of all that had transpired since then. He stacked up his papers, putting them neatly in a pile. He then ran his hand along the top of the table's surface.

It was worn with use and age, but still retained much of the same rich color from when the owners of the Valley Drunken Alligator had first purchased the fixture. *How long ago has it been?* He cleared everything off of the table, putting his writings on the chair opposite his.

Tiernan began looking for the telltale mark. There were other scratches, indents, and chips in the tabletop, but it didn't take long to find what he was looking for.

A deep indention on the surface. One a flipping knife of a seventeen-year-old younger version of himself had made so many years ago. The small gash made him smile, recalling the memory. Next, he pushed his seat back, bent over, and began running his hand along the hidden edge of the table.

The years of repeated use had taken their toll. Now, a gritty, sticky, and slimy texture dominated the once smooth surface. Just as before, he could see the upper edge of the letter S, hidden out of sight for all these years.

Using every bit of strength in his arms, he began moving the table back into its original spot from all those years ago. It was harder this time; Tiernan wasn't a fit teenager anymore, having neglected his push-up routine in the intervening years.

From across the room, Tammith yelled at him. "What are you doing? Who do you think you are? This is my bar!" She walked over as he continued rotating the table.

"There…you…are," he declared with a final, satisfied turn. Etched into the side of its rounded surface were three letters. Tiernan ran his fingers over them just as Tammith walked up.

"F.I.S. Family is Strength. I know the phrase well. Did you do that?"

Tiernan nodded. "Many, many years ago. Before you bought this place from its first owners. I carved it the day we buried Borun. I even etched it into his casket."

Tammith eyed Tiernan up and down. She wet her lips and sighed, having made a decision she hoped she wouldn't regret. Her usual stoic expression softened — barely, yet it was noticeable.

"You can stay a *bit* longer. Hungry? I was about to make some Abrian Gourd Stew. And I suppose you can have some more water if you'd like."

Tiernan smiled and nodded his head. She left for the bar, preparing to start her next culinary masterpiece. Tiernan picked up the last bite of bread on his plate, tossed it into his mouth, and sat down to continue writing.

Chapter 19

The Protectors of Abria

Statuo had many meanings. In the case of the games, it referred to the conscious act to 'decide' the outcome of the tensions between Abria and Clericsfold. For others, the Statuo had grown to mean the willingness to 'choose a path', such as a preferred career path or asking for your beloved's hand in marriage.

For King Davien, today's Statuo was all about coming to terms with his role as King despite the unpleasantries that would follow. He knew he was about to make his hardest leadership decision to date.

"We need to tell them," he implored to his wife. "This is too significant to keep just between you and me. I've already had the bodies moved, but I have a feeling this is going to affect everyone else, too." Kyrie braced herself on the open window, head lowered. She knew the result of the games was almost too good to be true. She had been preparing for some kind of disaster, and had hoped Borun's untimely passing would be it.

Davien fidgeted with the key in his hand, retrieved from his father's tunic not long after he had passed. As he spun it between his fingers, he waited for her response.

Finally, Kyrie answered, her voice shaking with trepidation. "Are we *sure* their deaths are related?" Without turning around, she reflected on all her men had discovered.

First, upon their return to Farna, she ordered a complete investigation surrounding the disappearance of the two who were supposed to have been protecting the door leading to the Soul Sword. Shortly thereafter, the Royal Guard learned a sentry patrolling an open field to the south had also disappeared.

The list of coincidences continued to pile up. A dead shop owner; a guard within the castle who died in a similar way; the missing Wilbret and Gromil; the unaccounted sentry to the south; and a husband and wife lying side by side, somehow dead from what appeared to be a random fire in the middle of an open field.

On a hunch, Davien opened the door guarding the three relics, only to discover the burned and broken bodies of Wilbret and Gromil leaning haphazardly in the corner.

"There is no way any Graelan could have gotten in there. None. My father…" His voice broke at the mention of Borun. "He had the only key. You would need to teleport inside, and only Elves have this ability. You know that. I know that."

Davien started pacing. "Remember what my father said when those Elves froze the Lorelei River? Out of nowhere, the Tall Elf appeared. That's teleportation, Kyrie.

"Tolith mentioned his name: Folas. He aligned with Kane years ago. Somehow, he's connected to these strange deaths. I know it."

Davien paused. Kyrie knew what her husband was thinking. She waited for him to say it.

"His death might even be connected somehow."

"Davien, my poor love." She walked up and put her arms around his waist from behind. "One of the guards is still *technically* just missing. He could be alive…"

Davien put his hands on hers. "What about the husband and wife in the field out by the cemetery? Even if the other guard is just missing, that's still unusual. Nothing else around them showed any sign of fire. Their bodies were just burned, as if they had fallen into a fire and never walked out.

"This is all too much to be a coincidence." Davien broke the embrace, turned around, and considered his next words carefully.

"I know that look. Davien, what are you thinking?" The King looked away. He knew Kyrie would not approve of his idea.

He answered, still unable to look her in the eye. "Abria may be unified, but there is still division out there. Folas, whoever he is, was active during the Statuo. No one saw him, but he was here. We can't deny that, and whatever magic he used is beyond our comprehension.

"I could ask the others on the Council for their opinion too, but I believe this needs to be a family action." He motioned for his wife to follow as he left the room, still unable to meet her gaze face to face.

"Davien, wait. Davien!" Kyrie's hunch as to what her husband was thinking grew stronger. She followed behind and caught up to him near the primary stairwell within Castle Abria.

Neither said another word until they made their way through the halls, down another flight of stairs that led to a passageway far below the surface. They approached the locked door where the three magic items rested.

Kyrie dismissed the guards at the door with a commanding look. Once she could no longer hear their footfalls in the distant stairwell, she finally spoke.

"The three items. They're safe, right?" Davien nodded. She continued, unconvinced. "You know what I mean, Davien. Are they *truly* safe?"

"You know they are, my love. Tolith's Barrier spell is still active, may he rest easy. Only his hand and one other can pass through its protective blockade."

"Your hand, yes, I know. That was what your father thought was best."

"But listen to me, Kyrie. If Tolith could cast a basic Barrier, what could the *other guy* do? He teleported in here, sight unseen. He killed people all throughout the land without anyone seeing him or catching a glimpse of his face." He pulled the key out, speaking as he stared at it. "How long do you think Tolith's Barrier will last?"

"I don't like where this is going."

Davien spoke while looking cautiously at the key. "I knew you wouldn't. I'm not sure the Council will approve either," he said as they waited, whether afraid to open the door or afraid of what opening it meant.

"On the other hand, I am the King of this land. It's my job to protect it. Something is brewing, Kyrie. I know it. Kane isn't going to be satisfied with the terms of the Statuo. He's going to make another move soon." He looked his wife directly in the eyes. "Tell me I'm wrong and I'll walk away."

Davien hoped he was wrong, and Kyrie wasn't thinking the same things. She began staring at the key, too. Finally, she held out her hand.

Maybe I am wrong. Here goes nothing. He put the key in her open palm and started to take a deep breath as a sign of relief.

Before Davien could finish his exhale, Kyrie inserted the key into the lock, turned it, and pushed the door open. She fastened her hand around her husband's with determination.

"We're in this together. You and I. It's been that way since the beginning, from the moment you asked me to marry you until now. Whatever the future brings, Davien, I'll be by your side. Always." He smiled at her words, and they walked in together, unified.

While neither carried a torch, they didn't need it. They knew it by heart. The path before them might as well have been fully lit up as they walked in darkness toward their intended destination.

Davien spoke again. "Midir said he saw some book in the Archives that talked about Zoran. A Dark Emperor or something one of my father's ancestors sealed away." Neither the King nor the Queen said anything else until they reached the back of the room.

Kyrie swallowed hard as Davien opened the closed doors of the armoire.

Together, they stared at the three items. The subtle glow of the orbs within the Soul Sword cast an ethereal glow on the other two. After a moment of quiet reflection, Davien finally reached his hand toward the Soul Sword. "Telford sealed Zoran away with this," he said, as he put his hand through Tolith's Barrier.

Davien pulled the Soul Sword through and held the item close to his body. "Whether you or I want to admit it, we both know Enid has powers," he said, pointing to the Power Ring.

"And Tiernan. The Shield?" Kyrie asked. Davien nodded.

"The bearer of the Mind Shield has to be at peace with their past. You saw Tiernan at the funeral with his carving."

"I guess I'm the odd one out," she said, smiling. Davien handed the Soul Sword toward her, to which she pushed back onto his chest. "I was kidding. I still don't like this. *Any of it,* Davien. You understand, right?" She sighed, but leaned over to kiss her husband. The loving gesture reassured the King.

"But, as much as I *hate* to admit it, I *agree* with your logic. What about the Council?"

Davien looked carefully at the Soul Sword. *First things first.* It was time to give his children an advantage in whatever battle awaited them.

Enid and Tiernan sat side by side in the dining hall where their parents had summoned them. Enid's hand was clenched, glowing red, as she leaned back against the chair. Tiernan showed no reaction to his parent's revelation.

"Aren't you going to say something?" Davien asked. On the table before them laid two of the three magic items. The Soul Sword, he decided, needed to stay behind Tolith's Barrier until needed.

Enid eyed the Power Ring. It looked larger than any of her fingers, almost large enough to be a bracelet if she could somehow slide it over her hand and onto her wrist. She finally sat forward and ran her finger along the top of its surface.

"Dad, when you told me I was the 'Prince of the Land' or whatever over in the Valley, I..." Tiernan began to speak, but couldn't quite articulate his words.

"You didn't think it would mean also being its protector," Kyrie finished for him. Both parents stood in front of their children as a sign of unity. "It seems as if we're no ordinary family. I know you didn't sign up for this, Tiernan. You too, Enid. From the moment you two were born, things haven't been how your father and I expected either."

"Family is Strength, Mom," Enid responded, finally speaking for the first time since seeing the relics. She turned around and eyed an axe on the wall. After taking it to her room the morning of the Statuo, she had returned it here a few days later.

Enid stood up, walked over to the wall where it hung, and removed it with her glowing hand. Immediately, the head of the axe exploded into a glass-like state with a flame both surrounding and emanating off of it.

Tiernan winced as the fire was intense. The axe head itself glowed a bright yellow, almost as vibrant as the Graelian sun. Enid brought it over to the table, and with her free hand picked up the larger-than-expected Power Ring. She extended her right ring finger — the same one holding the axe handle. As she slid the ring on, it shrunk perfectly to fit on her finger.

Almost imperceptibly, she heard something in her mind. An echo of a single word.

Dragonborn.

At the same time, the intensity of the light, as well as the flame itself surrounding the axe, dimmed, almost as if Enid had more control over it now.

"Looks like the ring helps you manage your powers, Sis." He acquiesced to his fate and pulled the Mind Shield closer. It was larger than a normal shield and unwieldy to hold. He read the inscription, written in ancient Abrian, out loud.

"Animo clipeo uti soli qui in pace sunt. Nice, but what's it mean?" Unlike when Enid grabbed the Power Ring, the Mind Shield did not shrink to Tiernan's size.

His father answered, "Only those who are at peace with their past can use the Mind Shield." Tiernan tossed the shield onto the table. It made a clanging noise against the wood, an audible sign of his frustration.

"So much for that," he mumbled as he sat back in his seat.

It was Enid's turn next. "What does the Mind Shield do? T was right. I feel in control of…whatever the dragon did to me. So the Power Ring helps me keep these powers in check…"

Davien cut her off. "Not just that, Enid. It's believed the Power Ring amplifies your abilities. Significantly, if what my father said is true. As for the Mind Shield, his interpretation was the wearer would be invisible to evil."

Kyrie spoke up, "So in theory, you could approach whoever went on their killing spree last week and they wouldn't see you. At least that's what we think would happen."

"So what about the other one, the…" Enid began to ask.

"Soul Sword," Davien finished. "Well, that one is a little more complex. In the ancient language, 'psychē' is the word for Soul, and it translates to seat."

"The Seat Sword." Tiernan laughed as he said it.

Davien shook his head. "Not as in a chair, but as in the actual center of your being. The thing that controls your desires, your feelings, your aspirations. The 'seat' of you and of all you are."

"That's why the Soul Sword was able to seal away Zoran. His quest for power drove him over the edge. It took all he was and isolated him away from it," Kyrie said. "Whatever lies ahead will require the same."

"You mean Kane." Enid didn't say it as a question but as a recognition of the next evil to be sealed away. Davien lowered his head and paused. He hadn't wanted to say it yet, but knew it was true.

"Yes," answered Kyrie for her husband. Davien looked over at her, appreciative of the cover.

"But Kane wasn't capable of doing the things you described to us earlier. He can't teleport. Enid is the first Graelan in over a thousand years to be able to wield magic," Tiernan said as he looked at his sister. "You're not just a Dragonborn. You're a Dragonborn *Heroine*. I remember hearing rumors about them in history class."

Enid shot him a look, but also knew it was true. "So the Elf who killed everyone is working with your former best friend to do what?" she asked.

"Midir said Kane studied the history of Zoran. When we moved the Archives to Alwyn, all volumes on Zoran were missing. Kane himself disappeared after judging the archery event. I wouldn't be surprised if he's nowhere to be found in Clericsfold, but out there with whatever Elf committed all of these atrocities." Davien rubbed his temples. All of this talking was giving him a headache. He noticed his son pick up the Mind Shield one more time.

Tiernan slid his arms through the straps. The Mind Shield did not shrink. This frustrated Tiernan. He shook his head and reached with his other arm to take it off.

"Son. It's no secret you have regrets. That this..." He pointed to their royal clothing. "...is not the lot you wanted in life. The artwork you carved in the Drunken Alligator..." With those words, Tiernan's eyes almost doubled in size. "Yes, I know what you did. I went back later because I just didn't buy your story with Wayland. No matter. You have a good friend."

Enid shifted in her seat as her father said those words. Tiernan couldn't tell if his sister was feeling the same toward Wayland as he felt for her.

"As I was saying, your artwork is hidden. I put it back up against the wall exactly as you left it. Hopefully, the owners don't see it. But I also know you carved the same letters into my father's casket. It tells me you're beginning to accept things." He leaned in. "The Mind Shield won't accept you until you fully embrace all of this. Your name. My father's choices. And you and your sister's role as the protectors of this Kingdom."

Within the largest dining hall in Castle Abria sat each member of the reformed Abrian Council. Davien had decided there were too many dining areas for the Royal Family. They did not need fourteen places to eat. One was more than sufficient.

He designed this space as the permanent Council Hall, complete with a table large enough to accommodate a representative from each city within the Kingdom. They would act as a proxy for their community. There were eleven seats around the table, each reserved for a member of the Council. All were occupied except for one.

Lily of the Valley was still recoiling from the loss of Borun and had not selected a representative from their community. The rest, including Clericsfold, were all present.

Davien did not know the names of anyone here yet, save for two: Midir and Eskil. The presence of Midir was comforting, and acted as a sense of continuity between the old Council setup and the new one. While unusual for a mayor — Manus, in Midir's case — to be here, the gravity of today's meeting, along with having two allies present, would be helpful.

After the normal pleasantries, Davien finally spoke. "Thank you for coming here on such short notice. I did not expect to summon a Council meeting until the end of Flametide. Midir, and the representatives from the other eastern cities, thank you for your expedited arrival. I promise I will not waste your time today."

A person across the room raised his hand. Davien gestured for him to speak. "Thank you, sir. I'm Sayger from Lorelei. We have heard rumblings of a few disturbances during the games. Your call for a meeting would seem to be a confirmation of this."

"You're not wrong, and your directness would make me think you knew my father. That was something he was well known for.

"To answer, yes. There were *oddities* during the Statuo. In light of the precarious nature of the treaty, I've taken the liberty of informing Mayor Eskil of those situations before anyone else."

Eskil nodded. "During the various events, there were multiple deaths throughout the area. Guards here in Farna. A family in one of the nearby fields. I recently learned of an untimely death of a stable hand by Alwyn. Each of them died mysteriously and, in some cases, in similar ways.

"I've come to the conclusion, as has King Davien, the disturbances you referred to could have only happened if they were committed by someone who can wield magic."

"In other words, an Elf aligned with Clericsfold," said one of the other Council Members. "I'm Jarrod from Lakedon. Forgive my bluntness, but you can appreciate my nervousness considering my town's proximity to Clericsfold and the fact we were almost *torn away* from Abria." It was apparent to all present that Jarrod did not think highly of Eskil.

Eskil frowned. "I understand your concern, and I do not take offense at the accusation. Please understand Kane was the driving force behind the so-called 'cold war'..."

"Doesn't that make you an ineffective mayor if your leadership fell to the whims of a madman?" Jarrod wasn't backing down.

Davien interrupted. "To your point, yes. It's highly likely an Elf aligned with Kane — not Clericsfold — did all of this."

Eskil turned to Davien. "The thing you did not tell me, though, is what necessitated a meeting so quickly after the signing of the treaty. Have you finished the investigation into their deaths?"

Davien stood motionless. *Time for the big reveal.*

At the same time, Midir shifted his head, recognizing Davien's uncomfortableness. He could tell something was off, but wasn't sure what exactly.

"One of the hard parts about being King, and I hope none of you ever have to face this, is you sometimes have to make decisions in the moment. In most cases, I would have run something of this magnitude before this Council.

"I consider you to be my advisors, but for better or worse, the final decision falls to me. Earlier this week, I made a choice that may threaten the fragile unity of this Council," he said, casting Jarrod a look. The man looked away, whether in shame or defiance. "However, just like many of your mayors, sometimes a leader must make a decision using whatever information they have at that time, and hope it's the right one.

"That's what I did, and this meeting is to *inform* you of what I believed had to happen, not to ask for permission."

Midir stiffened in his chair. *I don't like where this is going.*

Davien turned around and motioned to the attendant. He bowed, then walked out of the room. "I don't know how many of you are familiar with my children, Tiernan and Enid. They are twins, both born on the day my predecessor — my adoptive uncle — passed away. My son carries his name because of a royal edict. Enid..." He hesitated, pursing his lips as he chose his words carefully. "Enid died at birth. You may know the story of the giant red dragon in Farna?"

A few nods around the table confirmed to Davien most knew of the red dragon, even if they didn't know its effect on her.

"I've rarely favored my children. That being said, there is something more going on here than a few random fatalities. Two of my guards died *horrific* deaths. The couple out in the field died in an unexplainable way, burned from the inside out." He paused, letting the image of the deceased rest in everyone's minds for a moment. "Meanwhile, the room my guards were found in was locked from the *outside*, yet somehow their bodies made it *inside*."

He took a deep breath and exhaled it with timed reflection. *This is it.* As if on cue, Tiernan and Enid walked in from the attendant's summoning.

Tiernan held an oversized shield and a traditional sword. Enid held her axe, its head ablaze, with a ring on her right hand. Davien turned to greet them with a smile before turning back to address the Council.

"I need to be clear here. Their bodies were in a *locked* room deep below the surface of the castle and they died in such an unexplainable way. They were posted outside of the locked room, a place where inside rested…" Davien emphasized each word that followed. "Three. Magical. Items. Secured behind a protective magical Barrier."

He looked to Midir, whose face displayed a look of both betrayal and hurt. "I limited the official knowledge of the mere *existence* of these items to a handful of people prior to today. Members of the Council, I present to you my children: The Protectors of Abria," he said as he stood, motioning toward each as he said their name. "My son Tiernan, bearer of the Mind Shield, has begun formal swordsmanship training.

"And the Dragonborn Heroine, my daughter," he said, beaming, "Enid. The *first* Graelan magic wielder — a mage — in *over* a thousand years. She wears what is known as the Power Ring."

He turned back to the Council and leaned on the table. "These are two of the three items. The third, still locked away, is known as the Soul Sword." Midir lowered his head. "With it, I will join my children and together, we vow to defeat this evil. Whatever darkness is plaguing Abria, we will seal it away."

He paused, gauging their reactions. Some looked concerned. Others indifferent. He knew he and Midir were going to have words soon.

"And once we've completed this solemn promise, we're going to destroy these accursed items."

Few from the Council had opposed Davien's decision. The lone voice of dissent was, as expected, Midir. To him, such a dramatic revelation was both unnecessary and inappropriate, considering the tumultuous decision Davien had made on his own. It was the first time the two friends had disagreed to this extent. Only the intervention of Eskil prevented them from coming to blows.

Eventually, Midir talked Davien out of destroying the items once the task was completed. Instead, the two men — together — would seek out a loyal Elf that had moved to Oakshadow, who could modify Tolith's Barrier so another person could retrieve the items at a later date if needed.

Both men committed to working together, but the damage had been done, and the relationship strained. During one especially heated debate, Midir asked a pointblank question.

"Out with it, Davien! What does the Soul Sword do?" Davien admitted he truly didn't know, barely knowing of its existence and rumored prior actions. The decision not to bring Midir into the inner circle put a damper on their relationship, and Davien often expressed regret to his wife, sometimes almost daily, for months afterward.

"You know Kane did that too," Kyrie would respond. "He purposefully planted a seed of doubt in Midir's mind by hinting there were magical items here in Farna in the first place. That's how you learned they existed, but still did not know what they even were. You don't even know that now."

This helped sometimes. Finally, Kyrie approached her husband during a random, remorseful day. "Davien, stop. You knew they existed, but not what they were. You did what you thought was best for the Kingdom."

Davien knew she was right, of course. After, his wife would continually remind him his decision wasn't made out of secrecy or duplicity but instead a single goal: to protect Abria. Though right, Davien acknowledged it didn't make the decision any easier.

Such was the life of a king.

Chapter 20

Shifting Relationships

Three full years passed without incident. Davien kept the Soul Sword hidden away, honing his sword fighting abilities by using a generic sword from the armory. Tiernan continued trying to reconcile his past so the Mind Shield would accept him.

Enid, on the other hand, became a fierce fighter. Day by day, she learned how to refine her magic, its focus, and its intensity. Every time she sparred with someone, she used the same axe. It became her personal favorite.

On this day of training, she was once again using her preferred weapon — and she knew she possessed the upper hand. Using all of her might, she went in for what should have been a killing blow against any other opponent.

"Wimp," she said. Her axe came down in full force, a swift motion few could have defended against. It clashed with a sword, a valiant and notable effort of defense. In retaliation, Enid kicked her opponent in the chest, pushing them back a full meter. She shrugged, a motion her attacker noticed.

"You afraid of something, Sis?" Tiernan removed his helmet and smiled. "Oh, what was that? I didn't hear you." He put his hand up to his ear. "Oh right, you're frustrated because I defended against your weak attack."

Enid's shoulder was a bit sore, but she wouldn't let him know it. "It's nothing, Tiernan. I thought I felt something, like a firefly on my back. Turns out it was just the wind. Let's go."

"Liar," he said as she rushed him. He quickly lowered his helmet back onto his face. Blow by blow, swing by swing, Tiernan and Enid sparred back and forth. To his credit, Tiernan looked as if he was having the time of his life.

Despite the oversized shield he was carrying on his other arm.

"Are you ever going to accept..." she said, swinging her axe downward. Tiernan defended the move by swiping it away with his sword once again, which caused her to retaliate and push down harder, "I said accept…"

She drove the axe down more. "…your…"

Enid pushed with even greater force.

"…*past*!" she roared, with an emphasis on the last part of the word betraying her frustration. The axe head ignited in a fierce display of energy.

The Mind Shield was still far too large for Tiernan. However, in the time he had spent with it, he had learned to draw on its size to hone his physical strength even more. Much to Enid's frustration, the ancient item had made him a formidable foe.

Tiernan answered her by pushing upward against the burning weapon. To his surprise, it flew out of her hand, and returned to its normal state as it landed on the ground. "Are you ever going to accept Wayland's offer for a date?"

Oh no, wrong thing to say. Tiernan barely had time to think those words before Enid flipped around and lunged toward her brother, her right hand aglow with the power of the dragon. Tiernan raised the Mind Shield upward, letting it absorb the blast.

And for the first time, watched as it shrunk in size. Not a significant amount, but a little. Just enough to cause both combatants to stop their sparring session.

"You saw that, right?" Tiernan said.

Enid nodded her head. "So, apparently accepting your past means you have to accept your loser friend may one day be your brother-in-law."

"Ah ha!" Tiernan dropped all of his weapons and pulled off his helmet. "So, you are going to say yes? I knew it!" This time, without the protection of the Mind Shield, Tiernan was powerless against his sister's attack. She lunged at him again, palm open. Her hand landed on Tiernan's chest, knocking her twin to the ground. With his sister's hand firmly planted, Tiernan's torso began to glow.

"Hey, ow…oh." His response surprised them both as the area grew brighter. She stood up and offered him a hand to help him up. Tiernan stretched his arms out to each side as the effect subsided. He rolled his shoulders and twisted at his waist from side to side.

"Huh. Thanks. You know, I worked my upper body really hard yesterday. I was feeling a little sore, but now…well, now it's gone. As if you healed the sore muscles." He smiled. "Appreciate it, Sis. Though I have to wonder what you were planning to do."

Enid threw her head back as she took a drink of water from a nearby bench. "I went in for the kill. Wasn't that obvious?" *Let him think that, anyway.*

"Right," Tiernan responded, though he wasn't entirely convinced. Together, the twins picked up their gear. Tiernan put his arm around Enid for a moment, and she leaned in to give him a side hug.

"Same time tomorrow?"

"You know it," he answered.

Eislyn combed her hair, looking at its length in the mirror. "Do you think I should get this cut?" In the three years since the first Statuo, Eislyn had been trying to catch the attention of a certain someone. A person whom everyone now knew as one half of the famed 'Protectors of Abria'.

A man she met via an errant hug during the first games.

Now, three years later, he was the emcee of the event. Each time she ran into him, Eislyn had hoped for a glimmer of remembrance or interest. And each time, Tiernan was nothing but a perfect gentleman. He seemed determined, focused, responsible, and – much to her disappointment – disinterested.

Not to mention strong, handsome, kind, caring, and a born leader. Tiernan had developed a reputation as a talented fighter during his training sessions. While his sister continued to compete each year in the running events, Tiernan seemed content to sit out the Statuo. He had a friend though who had won first place at least once in each of the past several years. *Way-something?*

Tiernan had not competed since the rowing event in Alwyn three years ago. He also hadn't seemed interested in courting her either, despite his general friendliness.

Eislyn hoped to fix that today.

"I told you, no." Her sister, Aoife, was two years younger than her. Aoife was also participating in the games this week against Enid in one of the running events. "Did it ever occur to you Tiernan might have other things to do than talk to a girl like you?" Eislyn pushed her sister away with a gentle shove, not wanting to hurt her with the big event tomorrow.

"Maybe you're right, he is the Prince after all. I guess I don't see him that way. He's just…a nice guy."

Aoife jumped on the bed next to Eislyn, landing on her stomach with her head next to the seat where her sister sat. "Just a nice guy, huh? He gave you an accidental hug. Tiernan is the town's most eligible bachelor. And you are?"

Eislyn smiled. "The daughter of a bar owner. I know." She continued combing her hair, then used two of her fingers like a pair of scissors. "I think right here would be perfect. Thanks for your feedback, Aoife." She kissed her sister on the forehead. "I'm going to go get a haircut."

Wayland paced back and forth in his room. Over the past three years, he had been patient. Or rather, he had acted patient. Deep down, he was hoping things might change soon.

For as long as he could remember, Enid had held his heart. This feeling became even stronger the day of Borun's funeral when Tiernan — the person he already thought of as a brother — motioned for him to stand next to the casket with the Royal Family.

Wayland often thought Enid had shown small signs of interest over the years since then. And every time he was with her, he tried little things to catch her attention. A kind smile, a polite clap, an encouraging word — all to gauge her reaction and see if the feeling was somehow mutual. He didn't want to appear desperate nor jeopardize their friendship. But, he also didn't want to let time pass him by.

That's why, just yesterday, he finally asked her if they could meet at one of the restaurants in the market for a lunch date. He almost didn't call it a date, for fear of sounding too aggressive. Wayland wanted it to feel casual and non-threatening. At the same time, Tiernan had finally given Wayland his blessing to ask, which meant it was now or never.

The moment came after an intense training workout with his best friend. The two men had been sparring with Tiernan having bested Wayland in hand-to-hand combat.

"Good workout," the Prince had said. Wayland sat back against the bench to rest and elbowed his friend.

"T, look." Tiernan turned his head in the direction Wayland pointed. Enid was fighting another soldier from the Royal Guard. Their weapons were intertwined and neither moving.

In a swift motion, Enid used her left leg to swipe the man's foot out from under him. He dropped his sword, and without hesitation she lowered her axe to his throat.

"I yield." She brought the axe back to her side and helped the man to his feet. On the bench, Wayland and Tiernan started clapping.

"When are you going to ask her out?" the Prince asked. The question took Wayland back a bit, leaving him speechless. Tiernan chuckled slightly and began stuffing his gear into a carry bag.

"It's now or never, Way," he said as he stood up. "Don't wait too long." Tiernan started to walk away, but turned back to his friend one more time. "Just don't be weird about it, okay? It's already weird enough." Wayland threw his hand up at Tiernan. He turned his attention to Enid. She began packing up her supplies, which prompted Wayland to walk over.

"Way. Hey. How was your training with Tiernan today?"

"Good. He's got a strong arm. Hey, would you like to meet for lunch soon? A date, I guess. Just to talk." She stopped packing and looked at him.

Oh no. This isn't going to end well, he thought.

To his surprise, she smiled and replied, "I'll let you know in a few days." She resumed putting her things away. Wayland swallowed and turned around to grab his stuff as well.

"Hey, Wayland." He had only made it a few steps before turning back to hear what Enid was about to say.

"Tiernan favors his right side. If you plan it correctly, you can use it against him. Especially if he's wearing his dumb shield." She smiled again. "See you tomorrow, Way."

It had been five days since their exchange. The five longest, most excruciating days of his life. The Statuo would kick off tomorrow, and Wayland didn't know if Enid was waiting until after to let him know.

He hoped not.

Finally, he decided he had to leave his room. He opened the door, passing through the halls of his parents' home. His family was elsewhere, so he didn't waste any time. He walked through the dining area and into the open fields of Farna.

Time to get an answer.

The mid-day sun rose high above Farna. Since before it began peeking its head above the Valley Mountains, Tiernan had been busy. He was on a time crunch, and unfortunately, would have to skip sparring with his sister today.

Or fortunately. Tiernan wasn't sure how he felt about missing his routine. A few days earlier, Wayland had caught him off guard and landed a decisive blow during their last sparring session. Tiernan didn't show it, but he was hurting. Wayland's strength had landed just the right way, and his muscles had been aching ever since.

Also, as emcee of the fourth Statuo, Tiernan often complained he needed more hours in the day. He looked over the schedule sitting on the table before him. Since the first competition, it had expanded from a single day's event to a full week to, now this year, a full ten days. One of the Abrian Council's ideas was to host more of the games within several of the nearby towns of Clericsfold, Alwyn, and Oakshadow. This made for less congestion within Farna, but required more planning, including transportation.

Midir suggested the Council appoint someone to act as the manager of the Statuo each year. Instead, Tiernan volunteered to take it over indefinitely. This meant he wouldn't compete again, though it also he could support his family and friends as an observer.

Leaning against a nearby wall was the Mind Shield. In the years since he had been entrusted with it, it had only shrunk once.

"There. Now everything is ready. Runner!" From the outside hall, an attendant walked in. Tiernan rolled up the large canvas and handed it to them. "This needs to be delivered to the Abrian Council as fast as possible. Once approved, see that the archivist creates five copies of it."

Tiernan stood up as he continued talking. "Then, once it's been duplicated, get copies to the emcees in Oakshadow, Clericsfold, and Alwyn. Make sure the town manager of Farna has a copy as well. Finally, choose the fastest from your team and run it across the Kingdom to Lily of the Valley for the closing ceremonies."

Tiernan paused for a moment, thinking. He followed up, "On second thought, you may want to get a horse. It's a long way there."

The attendant nodded, bowed, and ran out of the room. It was Tiernan's idea to hold the closing ceremony in the Valley this time instead of Farna.

For one, it only seemed fair to let each city and village throughout the Kingdom host the ceremonies. Next year, he was already planning to host most of the Statuo in Lorelei, giving Milston, Northwick, and Lakedon an opportunity to showcase their respective communities to the rest of Abria.

The opening ceremony would be held in Lily of the Valley, acting as a transition. Wherever the closing celebrations were held, that town would also host the opening events of the next year. He hadn't decided which town it would host the closing yet, though he was leaning toward Idlewind. Their relative isolation might make for a creative fifth Statuo.

In the corner, the central jewel of the Mind Shield lit up. Tiernan didn't notice at first, minding his own business while taking care of a few other odds and ends. Finally, the brightness caught his attention.

"Hello, you." Before today, he had never personalized the Mind Shield. As an inanimate object, no one understood its power — though no one understood the other two items either. He walked over to it and picked it up.

Instinctively, he slid it on his arm. To his surprise, it shrunk some more. It wasn't quite the size it needed to be yet, but getting there.

At the same time, he heard a voice inside of him. A message he didn't understand. Almost as if the Mind Shield was trying to tell him something.

You're almost there.

Far across the land, deep in the north at the top of the unexplored Northern Plateau, Folas recoiled in pain. He placed both of his darkened hands on his temples, leaning down and eventually falling to his knees. He let out a tortured cry, drawing the attention of several Elves who were busy building a wall.

Folas realized he could now only partially see the Royal Family. He pushed through the pain and opened his eyes.

"Take me to Kane," he said. Two of the Elves dropped their tools and rushed to him. They helped him to his feet and steadied him, guiding the Tall Elf step by step until he eventually reached the makeshift cabin where Kane now lived. He nodded to each Elf to dismiss them, and they scurried away. He snapped his fingers, blowing the door open to Kane's residence.

"I told you to stop doing that," Kane said from the far end of the cabin. He had his back turned to the door, but instinctively knew who had interrupted him.

Folas walked in. "You're not going to like this." Kane continued preparing his lunch, a stew of some kind that Folas had watched him eat often. On the east wall, there was a small fire burning in the nearby fireplace. A half wall separated the kitchen area and the seating space, which had a handful of wooden chairs scattered about. Kane dropped his knife and turned around to face the Dark Elf.

Such an appropriate name, Kane often thought. The majority of Folas' exposed skin had transformed. Only portions of his neck, along with his face and head, retained their previously pale complexion.

With each life he took, Graelan, Elf, or otherwise, Folas' skin had grown more ominous. Nothing seemed to be able to reverse the transformation, and instead of fighting it, Folas embraced it. Reveled in it.

Grew to like it.

"Have you figured out if you can tap into Ultimus Magic yet?" Folas didn't respond, so Kane let the issue drop. "Sit," Kane offered as he motioned to a chair.

Folas remained standing, to which Kane was indifferent. "Suit yourself. You're in a mood today. What is this news you wish to tell me?" Folas walked over to Kane's desk and pulled out one of the latter's favorites.

Zoran, 432NE.

The Dark Elf flipped through the pages and found the passage he wanted. He read it out loud.

"Only those who are at peace with their past can use the Mind Shield." Kane had just taken a sip of his stew when he realized what Folas was saying.

He walked away from his kitchen area and closer to Folas. Kane sat on a nearby stool as Folas asked, "Shall I read the next passage?"

Kane didn't answer, so Folas continued. "It's said those who control the Mind Shield can block the patrolling eye of ultimate evil." He closed the book. "As of now, I do not know where the boy is. I can only *generally* feel the location of the rest of the Royal Family.

"The Dragonborn is somewhere in a field. I think. The woman is in Farna, though I do not know where. The one you hate is in Alwyn, and I can see him as plain as day."

Folas slammed the book on Kane's desk. His face echoed a sea of desperation. Of frustration toward powers no longer working as expected.

"A bit dramatic," Kane smirked. The Dark Elf's temper was hotter than Kane had ever seen, though it did not faze him much.

"You've waited too long. Do you understand me? If one of them has the Mind Shield, it also means there's a good chance the other two relics are in their possession. Maybe even…" He stopped as he realized the most likely outcome. "The girl. She will have the Power Ring. Her Dragonborn abilities are a perfect match, and no other Graelan in all the world can wield magic."

Kane stood up from the chair. "Not yet anyway. Stop. This is good for us."

"Good?"

"Yes, good. We now know the general range and effectiveness of the Mind Shield. If the King is in Alwyn and you can still see him, it means the Shield's power is not absolute.

"Besides, all we need is the Soul Sword. The other two items are useful in battle. I'll grant you that. But the Sword is what can break the seal to release Zoran. Once that happens, it won't matter what the twins try to do. With the power of Zoran and the Soul Sword in hand, we'll be unstoppable."

Folas didn't say anything. Both man and Elf stared at each other for a moment. Finally, Folas turned and walked out, using his powers to shut the door behind him.

Kane walked over to a shelf on his wall and pulled out one of his favorite books: *The Song of the Poet.* He flipped through the pages, leaning back against the half wall separating the kitchen from his living area.

He skimmed through the passages of the novella. A small smile emerged on his face as he remembered certain scenes and story lines. Kane flipped to the front cover and found a note from the person who had given it to him.

Kane,

No matter what lies ahead, remember how the story began: a group of friends, inseparable until the end. Davien and I will always be there for you.

Teska

In a burst of anger, Kane tore the page from the book. *Where are you now, Teska?* He ripped it in two, walked over to his fireplace and tossed the torn page into the fire.

"Yes."

Wayland could hardly believe his ears. Before him, Enid was readying her axe. Across from her was a giant target. She had requested the silhouette on it be painted in all purple. Most of those passing by knew who she was thinking of, though no one dared ask her to confirm. She closed her eyes, igniting the axe head with Fire Magic. With one giant, powerful wind-up, she threw the axe.

It flew across the field, penetrating the image on the target in the dead center.

Immediately, the wooden target burst into flames. Satisfied, she turned to Wayland. "What's wrong, Way? Elf got your tongue?" She smiled as she ran across the field to retrieve the axe. After she pulled it out, she laid her hand on the target. In response, the fire extinguished and the burned areas began to regenerate.

"I, uh, well, uh yes. I wasn't sure if you would still see me as T's overweight friend."

She threw her head back and laughed. "Should I be insulted? What if you were? You think looks alone are all that matter to me? Maybe now I should say no," she teased with a smile.

"No, no, that's not what I meant. I just…"

"Relax, Way. I'm just giving you a hard time. What'd you have in mind? Something about dinner or lunch? Lame. That's the best you can come up with?"

He opened his mouth to speak, but realized he actually didn't have a better idea. When he had asked Enid out, he naturally suggested lunch since that's what he saw most people do. He had never thought to come up with another idea.

"We could, um. Well, the games are this week, so maybe after they're over we could…" Enid walked over to him, putting her open hand on his chest.

"Just stop. Let me handle it." She gave him a kiss on the cheek and began to wind the axe up once again.

Though he often tried to deny it, Tiernan found himself distracted whenever he ate at the Drunken Alligator. But it wasn't the weight of planning the games consuming his thoughts here.

Nor was it the unimaginable responsibility of the Mind Shield. It wasn't even the fear of what awaited him in the future, knowing one day he would succeed his dad as ruler of Abria.

None of that mattered when he came here. Instead, it was the beauty of the woman behind the bar that captivated his attention. Every visit, he had noticed small things about her. A dress she would wear. The way she pulled her hair back into a ponytail when she got busy. The kindness she demonstrated to everyone she served.

Her perpetual smile. The softness she showed whenever she greeted him. They all acted as a distraction, making it difficult to keep his mind focused on his work whenever he bought his lunch here.

Today, he arrived at the Drunken Alligator later than usual. He took his usual seat, similar in proximity to the one he had vandalized in the Valley.

She saw him, smiling and nodding while raising a single finger as if to say, 'I'll be with you in a minute.' Tiernan nodded, and she said a few things to the patrons at the bar.

Meanwhile, Tiernan continued to stare. Yesterday, her hair was long and flowing, almost all the way down her back to her waist. Today, it was mid-shoulder length, which drew attention to her sculpted cheekbones, glittering cerulean eyes, and petite frame even more than usual.

Finally, she walked over to ask him for his order. "The usual, sir?" Tiernan started to answer, and for once, found himself unable to speak.

All because of a haircut? Pull it together, Tiernan. He breathed deep, an action she was sure to have noticed, but was too courteous to comment on.

"Uh, yes. Yes, the usual. Thank you." She smiled and walked away.

Take that, Aoife. I was right. Behind the bar, she began talking to the other workers to let them know what to prepare for the Prince's meal. After a few minutes, they had everything ready to go.

"Here, Eislyn. I'll take it over to him," one of them said as they reached for the dish.

Eislyn served as the manager here, since her parents owned the place. Her employees, some of the best workers in Farna, were always trying to help and would frequently volunteer to do whatever was needed to make her job easier.

Though in this case, Eislyn wanted to handle it for herself.

"It's okay, Nigel. I've got it," she responded.

Tiernan had been watching her the entire time, and smiled as he realized Eislyn would be the one to bring him his food and drink. *Don't be an idiot, don't say something stupid.*

"Here you go, sir. Just the way you like it." She put the order on the table in front of Tiernan. "Let me know if you need anything else."

Be bold. "Hey, would you care to sit down with me for a moment?" *What are you doing? She's not interested in you. You're just captivated by her haircut. You have too much planning for the Statuo to....*

"Oh, how kind of you. Thank you," she smiled as she sat. *Checkmate, I've got him.*

Tiernan tore off a piece of bread and passed it to her. "It's a tradition I want to start. Sharing bread. Here."

"You don't already do something like this in Castle Abria?" Eislyn asked before taking a bite.

Tiernan shook his head, mouth still chewing on his small piece. "I mean, we do little things here and there. But, I've always liked bread. It's warm, inviting. And when you want to get to know someone, you should share bread with them."

Whoops. Tiernan realized he shared too much. Eislyn capitalized on the comment.

"So, am I someone you want to get to know?" She said it with a playful grin, though a slight blush moved up her cheeks.

"That's, uh, I mean…" Tiernan tried to cover his slip up, but failed.

"It's okay," she said while reaching out to touch his hand. "I'll share with you." Eislyn tore another piece off, taking a second bite of the warm baked good. She didn't typically eat during her shift, but she could sense today was different.

"Tell me about the Prince of Abria. What does he do with his free time? What does he like?"

Tiernan smiled. *Is it okay if I say 'you'?*

Chapter 21
Courtship

As expected, the fourth Statuo games were a roaring success. In the end, Oakshadow walked away with the most first place victories, with Lorelei at a close second. Idlewind consistently placed third almost every time.

"You were great," Wayland said to Enid. "Another forty-five-kilometer victory. How many years in a row is it now?" He knew the answer, of course, but was looking for small talk.

"Thanks, Way. You did pretty well yourself." The two sat side by side on the edge of the Lily of the Valley central well. Overhead, the stars shone brightly. The Ailan Huntress was visible far in the distance, the tip of her broadsword just barely touching the edge of the faraway Kingscrown Bay.

Wayland was looking for something to say. He thought perhaps too much time had passed, and was beginning to get frantic.

Before he could say anything, a hand touched his. Wayland looked down, shocked to see it belonged to Enid. He looked at her and smiled with a sheepish expression.

Enid noticed his awkwardness and decided to have fun with it. "You're such a bunny," she said as she squeezed his hand from the top.

"A bunny?" Wayland jumped off of the edge of the well and turned to face Enid. "Did you just say *bunny*?"

"Yeah. Like a timid, soft thing. Remember?" She tussled her fingers through his hair and laughed as Wayland remembered.

"Oh. Right. The first Statuo. You called me that during training. Am I right?"

"You haven't changed a bit, Way! So here's the plan. Tomorrow, I want you to meet me here when the sun is just coming over the top of the Valley Mountains. Bring comfortable clothes," she smirked as she leaned in to kiss him on the cheek once again. "Actually, you might want to bring a change of clothes too, just to be safe." Wayland wasn't sure what she meant, but at that point, he didn't care.

Enid's kiss was the only thing he could focus on.

"I'll see you tomorrow, my little bunny." With that, she stood and headed toward the eastern Valley Inn.

Over by Borun Mill, another couple walked through the fields hand in hand. "So, this is the mill?" Eislyn asked. Tiernan nodded.

"Yeah, it's the weirdest thing. So much of the Statuo's origin has its basis right here." He pointed toward the door as he said it, and slowly motioned for her to follow. In the air, the smell of the Valley Rose was overwhelmingly intense, with a strong breeze out of the north dispersing the scent throughout the community.

"How so?" she asked as Tiernan pushed on the door. To his surprise, it opened without question — apparently unlocked. He realized this was the first time he had ever been inside.

The entrance to the mill consisted of a large lobby. At the back of the hall, a desk stood where an attendant sat. The mill was shut down today because of the Statuo's closing celebrations; at the same time, the attendant recognized who Tiernan was. Seeing Eislyn with the Prince, they simply smiled and returned to whatever they had been doing previously.

"You know, I'm not entirely sure. All I know is The Big Bad Guy…"

"Kane or something, right?"

Tiernan nodded again as they rounded the corner from the lobby and into the mill's main area. The smell of freshly cut wood was strong, almost intoxicating. *Maybe carpentry runs in my veins too?*

"Yeah. Kane hated Dad and Grandpa for some reason. Anyway, when he opened the mill…"

"Your grandpa?"

"Right. When Borun opened it, Kane did whatever he could to shut it down. At the same time, he was, I don't know, trying to set everyone in Clericsfold against us. Dad's idea was to unify everyone through the Statuo. Abria's victory healed the division, and Kane disappeared.

"Which is why we're here today." Just a few hours earlier, Tiernan had announced the games would be held in the Valley as well as the rest of the eastern Abrian cities next year.

"Because…?"

"Because I wanted the closing ceremonies here to be symbolic of moving past division. Proof we can heal. That whatever…," he paused, thinking of the inscription on the Mind Shield, "Whatever happened before doesn't have to hold us back. That only those who are at peace with their past can truly heal." He smiled, wondering if the Mind Shield was going to shrink again next time he put it on.

Eislyn wasn't sure what he meant, but decided to change the topic. "You're awfully fond of speeches, aren't you, Mr. Prince? Your sister told me you like to talk a lot." Tiernan turned to look at Eislyn.

"You've been talking to my sister?"

Eislyn nodded. "She's a regular at the Alligator. Just comes in at different times than you do. So what now, Mr. Prince…"

"It's Tiernan."

"Right, right. Okay then, Mr. Tiernan, so what? You brought me here to do what, exactly? Show me how you are finally coming to terms with your past?" She moved in closer to Tiernan as she said it, putting her arms around him.

"Hey, who told you that?" he asked, smiling.

"I told you, Enid has told me all about you."

The truth was, Tiernan himself had told Eislyn about his fears and concerns. They somehow ended up on the topic during their first deep conversation at the Drunken Alligator. There, he told her he wanted to start going by the name of Edward. That he wasn't sure he wanted to be the next King.

And most of all, he expressed regret for having never connected with his grandfather.

"But it wasn't her this time. I admit it," she said, moving in even closer, "No, I think the person who told me also said something about wanting to get to know me better."

"It was the bread, wasn't it? Bread always works," he responded with a teasing grin. "Well. Maybe. Did it work on you?"

Eislyn half-laughed. "You think you're charming, Mr. Tiernan." She looked him square in the eyes. "Truth is, I think I might be falling for you. Have been falling for you since that hug."

"The hug? Way back at the first Statuo?"

"Uh huh," she said, leaning in for a kiss.

"Is that so?" He, too, leaned in for a kiss. For the first time since that unexpected moment in the first games, joy consumed Tiernan. As they embraced, the Prince was filled with more happiness than he could ever remember.

Kingscrown Rock. Wayland wouldn't have picked *this* place for a first date, but he liked it. Enid had been waiting at the central well with two horses, and Wayland at first thought they were going for a country side ride.

He would have been more than happy with that too and was surprised as they neared the south bridge over the Lorelei River. They crossed it and raced for a bit. Wayland had become a master at horseback riding. His core strength and natural talent meant he had won a horseback event in some capacity at every Statuo since the first.

He just didn't know Enid was as skillful on the horse as he.

They arrived around mid-afternoon. They dismounted at the base of Kingscrown Rock itself and tied both horses to a nearby tree.

"Ready for an adventure?" Enid asked. "Kingscrown Rock is the perfect place if so."

"I guess. I thought this place was unexplored."

"Some, though many who've entered never come out. Does that scare you, my little bunny?" Enid laughed again, delighted she had found a way to tease him. Wayland's skin turned red, embarrassed but also intrigued.

It was at this moment he realized Enid had brought her axe along with a sword, both strapped together to one side of her horse. She unwrapped both and tossed the sword to Wayland.

"You do know how to use this, right?" she teased. "Oh, here's something to help keep you safe." Her right hand — the one with the Power Ring — began to glow, and she squeezed it tight. It shone brighter than it ever had before. The Dragonborn Heroine closed her eyes. Wayland stood speechless as Enid raised both hands high in the air. She brought her hands down in front of her and opened her eyes.

Eyes now alive with a vibrant red flame in their depths. "Watch this," she said, though her voice now had a slight, echoing wobble to it. She picked up the sword and it, too, glowed as bright as the sun. She reached out to put her other hand on Wayland's shoulder.

With her touch, something foreign rushed through his veins. *Is this…magic? Or love?* Either way, he didn't mind. Enid handed him the sword, alive with her power. When Wayland took it from her, he expected the magic to dissipate.

Instead, Wayland found himself aglow with the same Dragonborn magic that flowed through Enid.

"Is this…is this how you feel all the time?" he asked, his voice carrying the same — if less obvious — wobble as Enid's.

She didn't answer his question. Instead, Enid just laughed, enjoying the moment.

"Let's go! Race you to it!"

Enid and Wayland cautiously passed through the entrance to Kingscrown Rock. Perhaps, more accurately, Wayland was cautious.

Enid seemed to have no fear as they took the first steps inside. The eternal glow of the rock's facade was just as luminous inside as it was outside.

Wayland hadn't moved beyond the entrance. Something about the place made him uneasy, more so than the heat and light of the rock face.

His companion noticed, feeling his trepidation. "Scared, Way? You're such a cute bunny," she said it with a semi-mocking tone, enjoying her date's nervousness more than she would ever admit.

He shook his head.

He's such a liar, trying to impress me by hiding his fear.

Wayland curiously placed his hand on a nearby wall. It was cool to the touch, betraying its fire-like appearance. "Hey Enid, check this out." She turned around to see what he was referring to. Enid had hiked ahead of him by almost ten meters. Eager to explore, she begrudgingly turned around and walked back to the entrance.

"Touch it," he said. She shrugged, but did as he suggested. "Notice how it's cool?" She nodded.

"So why is it so hot in here?"

"You got me. Where to next?"

They continued their trek, with Wayland finally venturing deeper inside. Enid stayed closer to him this time. After all, this was their first date. She decided she shouldn't wander off too much.

So far, besides the light and the immense heat, it didn't seem dissimilar to any of the other various caves spread out across Abria. They approached a split in the path.

"Left or right?" she asked. Wayland squinted to see. Both paths, illuminated by the rocks themselves, seemed to go on forever. There didn't appear to be a right or wrong answer to her question.

"They seem to be the same, so…" He paused to think. "I'm left-handed. That's as good of a reason as any." He motioned to her. "After you, Dragonborn."

Enid pushed him in retaliation for the comment. Though this shove was unlike the ones between her and Tiernan.

This one was more playful. Wayland caught the difference and smiled.

"Is that the best you've got in you? I thought you were a fierce war…" She flipped around, and this time pushed him harder — so hard he stumbled back into the wall.

"Better?" Wayland swallowed, realizing their faces were far closer than they had ever been. Enid recognized it too, and in a rare moment of embarrassment, her face blushed. Wayland's eyes grew wide as he saw it.

Through a playful smile, he responded. "I'm okay. Lead the way." Enid released him, and they continued walking down the rocky path.

Unbeknownst to either of them, a winged shadow observed this interaction from a distance.

The deeper they walked into the cavern, the hotter the air became. Wayland wiped sweat from his brow. Thankfully, he had worn light clothes. Enid said to dress comfortably, so all he had on was a sleeveless tunic and a cut off pair of trousers. Wayland wished he had worn a pair of his training shorts instead, as the fabric would have been more breathable and easier to walk in.

Enid was dressed similarly, though she — knowing where they were going — wore a pair of thin shorts she often ran in. She wiped her neck and realized for the first time she was sweating more in here than during even the hottest training day.

"You feel it too?" he asked, beginning to sweat more profusely.

"Yeah, I knew it was hot in here, but not like this."

"Might explain why no one has ever explored the caves before?"

"The Fire Caves are more like it. Some people have tried to study them. I heard this is right about when most bow out."

"Enid, look." Wayland pointed down the path where an abandoned satchel, backpack, and sword laid on the ground. The couple ran up and picked up the items. "You said something about people bowing out. Guess you were right."

"Who do you think this belongs to?" Wayland shook his head in response. Enid flipped the sword around, looking for a marking or crest that might point to the identity of the owner. She noticed burn marks along one side of it. "Wayland, check this out."

"It definitely was put in a fire of some kind."

"Yeah, but from where? These walls are…" Enid touched the one closest to her. "That's what I thought. They're still cool to the touch. I don't see anything that would cause…"

Mid-sentence, Enid had her answer. Just a meter ahead of them, a towering wall of fire ignited, completely blocking the path forward. It sent both of them stumbling backward. Wayland raised his hand to his face, recoiling from the immense heat.

"There's your answer, I think. Here." He reached out and took the sword from her. He put the tip of the blade into the flame, and instantly the metal started to turn red hot. He pulled it back and brought it closer to inspect.

"That was quick. It would take a blacksmith in Lorelei far longer to get a blade this hot." She looked around, spotting a handful of gold and silver dinage laying near a fallen piece of rock debris. "Let's take these with us and try the other path."

"You lead the way," he replied.

After a few minutes of walking, they came to the split, this time looping around to take the right path. It didn't take long before they encountered another discarded satchel, along with a shield and dagger.

"Enid, this doesn't feel right." She was rummaging through the bag. Inside it was a ring with a blue jewel on top. She pulled it out and looked it over.

"Ever see something like this?" Wayland had been standing guard, and upon hearing her question, looked down.

"Hey, I've heard about this from your brother." Enid looked surprised.

"From T? I'd ask why, but I feel like the answer would only raise more questions. Or bore me. What is it?"

"He told me, after reading something from the Alwyn Böchord, there used to be rings just like this all over Abria. Back when Graelans could use magic. Different stones enabled the wearer to cast different kinds of magic. Red for fire, green for poison. You're holding a Frost Ring."

Enid held it up to her face and inspected it. Most of her powers seemed to be fire-based, especially from an offensive standpoint. She had restorative and transitive powers too, though she barely understood the latter. Thinking on the last one, she smiled.

"Hey, Way. You know how you felt, well, magic flowing through you earlier?" He nodded.

"Yeah, though I think it's sorta faded the longer we've been in here. That, or the heat, has made it harder to feel."

"That's probably more likely because I feel weakened, too. But, just for fun…" She stood up and reached for his hand.

"What are you doing?"

"Oh come on Wayland, you know you've always wanted to exchange rings." She laughed, proud of her joke. "Bet you never thought it would be a *magic ring* of some kind, did you?"

Wayland's face flushed, which was saying something considering the way the air temperature already made him feel. "No. This *isn't* exactly what I had in mind. Also, your father might have something to say about this."

"Oh, just put it on already." She grabbed his finger and slid the relic on. Immediately, Wayland stumbled backward. He bent over as if in pain, leaning his lower back against the wall. "Way! I'm so sorry. Are you okay?"

Enid began to grab the ring, but Wayland pulled his hand back and clenched his fist. He stood up, took a deep breath, and opened his eyes.

Eyes that, unlike Enid's, were glowing a vibrant shade of blue.

"Give me your hand," he said. Enid grabbed it. It was ice cold.

"Wayland, your hand. It's almost frozen."

He pulled it close to his face. "That's the thing, Enid. It doesn't feel that way to me." He looked around. "Also, the caves don't feel hot anymore. I wonder if I could put out the fire…"

Enid put both of her hands on his face. "Stop it. We're not going to test that." A beat. "Well, today anyway. Besides, I don't know how much longer you'll even have magic. I've never tested this on a Graelan before."

"Tested!? I thought I was a bunny to you. Soft and cuddly. Instead, I'm a test subject?"

"Sorry, that's *not* what this was." She let her hands fall from his face and turned away. "Okay. The truth." She turned away. "For a long time, yes, I've wanted to spend time with you. It's probably all those years you spent hanging out with my dumb brother. And also, I've always wanted to explore these and with you I…" She closed her eyes. *Oh boy, here goes.* She opened her eyes and continued speaking.

"With you, I feel safe." She turned back around. "I've known I was different from a young age. You were always just there. You were nice, unassuming. I knew I could be myself around you, even if you were my brother's dumb friend.

"And yes, I've tested transferring my powers to others. The first time was an accident. I was holding a dog. I was six, Wayland. Six. I hid it from my family, but it began creeping out here and there.

"The dog ran around for a bit, catching the grass on fire." She smiled, remembering. "He really was having a good time. The effect didn't last long, but enough I knew my life was going to be different.

"So every so often, I'd see if I could control it while out running. A small squirrel. A deer. Once…" She paused for dramatic effect. "A bunny."

Wayland threw his head back and laughed. "What *is it* with you and bunnies, anyway?" He moved closer to Enid and put his arms around her.

She ignored the comment, though she did notice how cooling to the touch his hands felt on her sides. The icy effect of his Frost Ring somehow made the heat of Kingscrown Rock more manageable.

She laid her hand on his chest. "Everything I touched always seemed to inherit some kind of magic. So I thought maybe, just as a precaution, I would see if it worked on you, too." She moved away from him and motioned around. "This place is unexplored for a reason, and I didn't want anything to happen to *you*."

Wayland smiled. "I'm honored. Truly," he said as he bowed ever so slightly in a sign of respect. "Why do you think I spent so much time getting in shape? Your brother is more than a friend to me, Enid. He *is* my brother, as close to one as I'll ever have. As I grew closer to him, I began noticing you. At first, it was weird, but eventually it just felt…"

"Natural."

Wayland nodded in agreement. At the same time, Enid noticed the blue glow in Wayland's eyes was beginning to fade. "Hey, Way. Try this quick." She ran back over to him. "Your magic is fading, but let's see if you can control it. Open your hand." She grabbed his wrist.

"And do what?" he asked. "I don't have any experience with this, you know."

"Just trust me."

"I do."

"Then concentrate. Feel it in here," she said, touching her heart. "And visualize it here." She pointed to his open palm.

Wayland didn't expect anything to happen, but didn't want to disappoint Enid, either. So he closed his eyes. Tried to clear his mind.

And opened his eyes with the blue glow even brighter than before. "Hey, what's…" He realized Enid may be transferring her powers to him again. "Enid, is that you?"

"Hmm? Me? No. This is you. Focus. Picture it." For the first time, Enid wondered if she wasn't alone in the land. *If Wayland can control magic like this, all I need to do is figure out how to make this permanent. Then I won't be the only mage in Abria.*

Wayland closed his eyes again, and a small, flickering ball appeared. It wasn't consistent, fading in and out. He opened his eyes again as it appeared. "Now what?"

Enid looked around. There was a small rock behind him. "There. I don't know how to tell you to do it, Way. Other than you need to *push it* out of you and onto the rock. Push it like you're giving it your all in training. Like you're holding a plank."

"You've watched me holding planks?" he asked with a teasing smile.

"Focus, bunny!" Wayland turned. Enid let go of his wrist as he did. Holding his hand open, Wayland did as he was instructed and focused all of his thoughts and energy onto the rock.

And at almost the same time, his eyes grew wide as he saw a small shift in the orb in his hand. It transformed from a perfect sphere to a blast of energy. It left his hand and almost made it to the rock.

To his disappointment, it dissipated before reaching it. Wayland's eyes also returned to their normal color, and his tolerance for the cave's temperature decreased. He breathed deep, a gasping reaction as the effect of Enid's magic transfer wore off. Once again, the air around him felt hot, humid, and uncomfortable. He looked down at the sword she had given him.

It looked normal. No more magical glow. He turned around to her.

"Looks like you're back to normal." She smiled. "Boring, annoying old Wayland. My soft, fluffy bunny." She grabbed his hand. "Wanna get out of here?"

The observing shadow moved along the side of the wall as they walked out, hand-in-hand. Once out of sight, the form coalesced into a vaguely Graelanoid shape.

Not a Graelan. Nor an Elf. Not even a creature of the fields.

Instead, it had a beak-like protrusion on its face. A golden and purple outfit where claw-like appendages extended longer down its torso than a Graelan's would.

It possessed a quiet yet threatening presence no one had seen since 432NE.

It spoke, though not in a language an Elf or Graelan would be able to understand. Instead, it 'talked' in a series of ticks and clicks evocative of an insect. From a distance, the creature continued to study them while murmuring to itself in a language known only to this ancient species.

"A powerful mage. And a Dragonborn at that. Along with another mage. At last. Zoran's return is at hand. Soon, the Divider will free you from below, my fellow Shapeshifters."

The creature changed forms again, this time into a raven-like avian. It turned and flew deeper into the caves.

The rest of Wayland and Enid's date devolved even further from the young man's expectations. After exiting Kingscrown Rock, the sweat-drenched couple quickly secured their belongings on the sides of their horses, including the spoils they had found within the caves.

Wayland kept the Frost Ring on his finger, hoping its power might reactivate again.

Together, they rode southbound to Kingscrown Bay. Once there, they tied up their horses again, though this time to a nearby signpost.

Still dressed in their sweat-soaked exploration outfits, Enid ran straight into the ocean and dove in. A wave pushed her back toward the beach, so she took a breath and began kicking and swimming further out.

Wayland wasn't much of a swimmer, but he wanted to get cooled off. So he reluctantly followed her into the Great Sea, enough for a makeshift bath, enough to wash the stench of the caves from his skin and clothes. At the least, he hoped.

After a few moments, Enid's head emerged a few dozen meters out in the bay.

"Is that all the further you're going to come out?" Wayland gave her a thumbs up. "Oh, come on, Way. Stop being a bunny. Once you get past the first break, it's actually really calm."

"Enid, look out!" Behind her, a giant wave approached. It picked her up and tossed her into the wake. Her head disappeared below the water. It did not resurface.

"Enid? Enid!" He began diving and looking through the water, frantic she would be floating along somewhere hurt, or worse. No matter where he looked, he found nothing.

Enid was gone.

Wayland began contemplating what to do. The date had turned from a fun excursion to his worst nightmare in the blink of an eye.

"No. No, no, no. I'll find you, I have to..." he said as something pulled on his leg. He looked down and saw Enid, and her head quickly emerged from under the water.

"Hey there. Were you saying something?"

Wayland put his hand on his chest, visibly shaken. "I thought I lost you underwater."

She threw her head back as she laughed. "From that? You should know me better than that, Way. That wave was nothing." She stood in the sand next to him, waves lapping around them.

"You thought you lost me, *or* were you afraid of my father? Of what the King might do to the man who let the Princess die." She thought she was teasing him with her words. To her surprise, Wayland reciprocated the verbal ribbing.

"*Both*," he teased. "I was oh *so worried*, yes. But in those few seconds, I had already begun making plans for my ultimate escape. I thought I might book passage to another land where I could share all of Abria's secrets."

Enid eyed him for a moment. "Sure, Way. Whatever you say." She laughed again. "You're not good at this, are you? Am I the first girl you've ever asked out on a date?"

He didn't answer. Instead, for the next several hours, they swam and enjoyed each other's company. Later, they sat on the beach and talked. Enid surprised Wayland, bringing a disc they threw back and forth.

Wayland talked about his dreams of becoming a performer at Mystic Mornings. Enid talked about her doubts that she could ever protect the land, even with the Power Ring. Wayland spoke of his grandfather, a man who had taught him many skills and life lessons. Enid mocked her brother.

Finally, the sun began to set far away on the distant horizon near Alwyn. They used a nearby dilapidated structure to change out of their wet clothes, switching into the dry outfits they brought. Enid changed first, with Wayland using the excuse that he would stand guard as her protector. When she was done, she walked out and tossed her soiled outfit at Wayland, who barely caught it.

"Seriously. That's the best you've got?" she said, throwing his earlier words from Kingscrown Rock back at him. "You couldn't catch a bundle of clothes. So much for being my protector.

"And now, who's going to protect me while you're in there?" she teased. Wayland kept his mouth shut.

Truth be told, she could probably kick my butt along with a dozen others at the same time.

Chapter 22

The Shapeshifter

The Shapeshifter — in raven form — flew all evening. First, it crossed Central Abria and the town of Clericsfold. It passed over the Cave of Tera, a large structure leading to an underground set of caverns and mining tunnels. Next up was the northern path, the section of road connecting Oakshadow with the rest of the Kingdom.

Below, a family from Northwick was just finishing their travels. The Shapeshifter decided to follow. They eventually arrived at Fabled Wonders, a curious construction that hadn't existed the last time the Shapeshifter was in this part of the land. Since the Imprisoning, it hadn't left Kingscrown Rock.

The family was greeted warmly by an attendant who helped carry their belongings to their room along the rear section of the lodging area. Quietly, the creature began its descent and landed in a tree. It made sounds just like a raven, flapping its wings as it landed.

A small chipmunk approached it. The creature turned and angrily cawed, scaring the small critter away. The Shapeshifter resumed its activity of carefully watching the family. This group consisted of a father, three children, and a mother.

The Shapeshifter began looking around for another form to take. Finally, in a nearby field, it saw its victim: a man carrying supplies from a distant shed up to the main facility.

The raven took off and cautiously flew behind the Graelan. Once it was in the clear, it landed and transformed back into its native Graelanoid form.

This Shapeshifter prided itself on its ability to stay quiet. However, a gust of wind at just the wrong time caught it off guard. It lost its footing as its foot materialized, and muttered to itself in its native language of ticks and clicks.

It was only a few sounds, but enough for the Graelan to hear. He spun around and was terrified at what stood before him.

"Who…no, what are you?" The Shapeshifter didn't respond. Instead, it reached out with its claw-like left appendage and grabbed the man's shoulder, digging its talons deep to hold him stationary.

He cried out in pain. "Stop, please! What are you…" The Graelan continued to protest as the Shapeshifter grabbed his other shoulder with its right claw, drawing blood as it pressed its claws deeper into the man's skin.

Now, completely immobilized, the man began begging. "Please. Why are you…"

Before he could finish the sentence, dark orbs of energy began glowing throughout the Shapeshifter's body as the creature pulled the Graelan closer.

"Noooo…" was the last thing he said as the Shapeshifter drew the man against its torso. The orbs surrounded his body as well, pulling him inside of the Shapeshifter.

Within a few seconds, the creature had consumed the man. Whoever he had been was now permanently gone, with portions of his essence temporarily a part of the creature. The Shapeshifter recalled the memories, the skills, and the emotions of the person it had just absorbed. An overwhelming juxtaposition of Graelan and creature flooded consciousness.

Those sensations would stay there until it absorbed another entity, whether Graelan, Elf, or animal. Whatever skills it had from the raven were now gone.

Those same dark orbs began transforming it into the form of the man. It continued walking toward its destination: the top of the Northern Plateau.

"Going to be a long walk," it said. The Shapeshifter realized it had been almost five centuries since it had last spoken in Abrian. It hated the way Graelan mouths moved and the unnatural sounds of their language.

Still, it was a necessary trade off if it wished to free Zoran and its brethren.

From one of the windows in his guest room at Fabled Wonders, a former guard named Jothan watched these curious events unfold.

By daybreak, it had climbed the treacherous, rocky outcropping surrounding the Northern Plateau. Few Graelans had ever tried to do this, since there was no direct path and the rocks themselves were prone to dislodging. And of those who had, none had lived to tell the tale. This is what made the Northern Plateau so mysterious to the rest of the Kingdom. It was one of the few unexplored regions left within the land.

The Shapeshifter realized it may have been faster to have flown here as the raven and absorb a random Elf upon landing.

However, it didn't know how its soon-to-be accomplice would take to that. Besides, the climb itself was no problem for it. While mostly retaining a Graelan form, the Shapeshifter transformed its 'hands' back into its normal claw configuration. These made it easy to grab onto the right areas, to penetrate the rock face in a way Graelan fingers could not, and to scale the mountains with ease.

It was a slower process than it would have liked. Once the creature reached the top, it transformed its claws back into a Graelan appearance, and finished walking toward a giant structure nearing completion.

Once it arrived, it noticed how the Elves seemed to scurry around, unaware of its presence. None of them seemed to notice the 'Graelan' walking. It passed by several, within a meter of each.

"It is as if they are oblivious to my presence."

"It's because they are. I wouldn't be the Dark Elf Master if I couldn't blind them," said a voice. The Shapeshifter looked toward it and saw a Tall Elf walking toward him.

One that looked as if he had just taken a bath in every bit of Ultimus Magic in existence. From head to toe, the Tall Elf's skin was darker than an ink well.

"My name is Folas. What is yours?" Confused, the Shapeshifter walked closer to Folas. "You don't need to act confused. I saw you coming the moment you left Kingscrown. Nice trick there. You'll have to teach me that one. Kane is this way."

The Shapeshifter followed Folas through the construction of what would, the creature assumed, become a large fortress-like structure. In the back, where a wall had already been built, was a home. Folas snapped his fingers, and the doors flew open.

"Folas, come in." The Shapeshifter heard the voice coming from deep within the building. Folas gestured for it to walk in, and it quickly did so. The owner of the voice, Kane, looked up as it entered with the Dark Elf.

"Another Graelan. Perhaps an ally? Folas, you always bring me the best gifts." Kane said each word with sarcasm. In reality, it was a test for the creature to reveal its hand first. "Please sit."

Kane took a seat at a table, and the Shapeshifter did the same. Folas sat across the room on a bench at the bar in Kane's home. "What is your name?" it asked, its voice sounding like that of a normal Graelan.

"Kane. And yours?"

It did not answer. As far as it knew, it did not have a name. The Graelan it absorbed had been known as Trevick, but that was *his* name.

"I come with a warning for the Divider. The Dragonborn grows in power." Kane gave a quick glance to Folas.

The Dark Elf shrugged. "Continue. Who is the Divider?"

The Shapeshifter pointed at Kane. "It was foretold long ago the return of Zoran would follow the arrival of the Divider and the rise of the Dragonborn." This was new information, as Kane had never heard of either prophecy.

"I did not know Graelan fortune tellers were real, at least in Abria." Kane said it as a half-truth. He looked at Folas, who echoed the statement with a nod.

From Kane's studies in the Archives many years ago, he had read some Graelans had the ability of *foresight*. This was usually nothing more than a premonition, almost a 'pre-flex'-like ability to see what was coming split seconds before it did. They could never predict events.

But, as with all Graelan-based magical powers in Abria, the ability disappeared almost 1,000 years ago.

"The prophecies came from Zoran himself. He said once the Power Ring was freed from its prison, the Soul Sword would be next."

The Shapeshifter's voice changed, transforming into a deep baritone with a reverberating-like echo. "'The Divider will build his empire upon my tomb. But, the Dragonborn must grow in power first.'" The Shapeshifter hated speaking in Abrian. More than anything, it wanted to revert to its natural form. But to do so would mean neither Kane nor Folas could understand it.

"How did you come to know of the Soul Sword? That's what sealed Zoran away. I have the *only* books on Zoran here with me. They're not in the Alwyn Böchord."

Though Kane did not see what happened next, Folas did from across the room. The Shapeshifter's dangling left hand slowly transformed into a claw-like appendage, a subtle dark glow, similar to Ultimus, surrounding the appendage as it appeared and returned to a Graelan shape.

It's struggling. Now, if I can just steal its power...

The Shapeshifter's voice returned to its previous pitch and tone. "There are other records of what happened. I know you seek the Soul Sword. I want to help."

Kane feigned a look of surprise. "That would be great. Our forces are mostly limited to disgruntled Elves and a few from Clericsfold who joined me. The more Graelan help we get, the faster we can retrieve the Soul Sword from Farna."

The Shapeshifter shook its head slowly from side to side. "The Soul Sword is in the Valley." Kane could not hide his shock. *Davien was actually dumb enough to take it with him?*

"Well, that is news. Folas, it might be time to expedite our plans."

Folas stood up from the bench. "With pleasure." He sent a blast of Wind Magic toward the Shapeshifter. The impact threw it against the wall and caused it to revert to its natural shape. Folas ran over to it as Kane tossed a sword to him.

The Shapeshifter was normally quite strong, but it did not expect this attack which threw it off balance. Also, Folas' power had physically hurt it, a sensation it hadn't experienced since the Dark War a long time ago. It stood up, prepared to assault Folas in return.

It had no chance to do so. Almost as soon as it stood, the Dark Elf Master drove the blade through the Shapeshifter's torso.

Pain racked its body as it coughed, a stream of dark purplish-black blood running down the corner of its mouth.

To finish the job, Folas pushed the sword all the way through, impaling the creature against the far wall. It let out a shriek, followed by ticks and clicks.

"Such an awful language. Ugly. Disgusting," Folas said as he put his free hand on the creature's head. "Just like you." Folas closed his eyes. "Give me your...ah...yes. There it is." The Shapeshifter's eyes rolled back into its head. Its tongue fell out of the side of its beak. Until this moment, it had both claws poised for a rebuttal attack. They both fell to its side, lifeless.

A fuchsia orb of energy moved from the Shapeshifter's body up through its head and into Folas' hand. The power moved from his hand to his arm, to his chest, and spread throughout the rest of the Dark Elf's body.

Folas raised both hands in victory, releasing the handle of the sword. Even Kane was impressed, which was rare. "How does it feel?"

The Dark Elf Master turned to Kane. "You were right. Zoran put a tiny bit of his own magic into each of his minions. There wasn't much, but enough."

"Can you transform like it did?"

Folas shook his head. "Its ability to absorb and mimic another life form is unique to its species, wherever they come from in Grael. However..." He snapped his finger. In his other palm, a glowing pink orb appeared. "This will help me see *through* the eyes of anyone I cast it on. As a side effect, it will eventually kill the person.

"But until it does, whatever they see, I will see too. This can be advantageous as we track Davien's movements."

"And in those moments, the Mind Shield will be worthless." Kane thought about the implications of this for a moment. He spoke once he realized their next step.

"Folas, you've been to the Valley."

"Yes. Is that a statement or a question?"

Kane ignored his response. "If you could teleport there, cast this on a handful of Davien's entourage…"

"…then we would be able to know exactly where they are. Ambush them. And take the Soul Sword for ourselves." Both men smiled.

"So, Divider, when do we get started?"

Kane's plan worked almost as intended. Folas absorbed three ethers. Then, using the boost of power, he teleported himself from the Northern Plateau to the field behind Borun Mill. The residents of the Valley, along with volunteers from the Statuo, were busy cleaning the streets from the closing ceremonies. Many vendors were open, feeding those individuals and preparing for whatever lie ahead.

Folas engaged his cloak of invisibility and began to wander around. He knew casting his magic might be precarious, but if he timed it right, it would give them the advantage they needed.

He was also confident he could infect any of the Royal Guards without uncloaking. The person might feel an odd sensation, but with any luck, they might just ignore it.

Based on how I feel, I should be able to infect five of these worthless Graelans. It didn't take him long to find his first victim: a guard standing near the edge of the Mill's entrance.

Folas approached the guard from behind, careful not to make a sound while invisible. He closed his eyes and summoned the Zoran Magic from his innermost being. Folas extended both arms to his side, pushed his chest out, and reveled in the small burst of energy as it left his body. It hit the guard from behind, who stumbled over at first, but righted himself once the effect wore off.

The guard turned around. But, since Folas was invisible, he assumed his loss of balance was from the wind. *Time for the test.* Folas turned his back to the guard and closed his eyes once again.

Sure enough, similar to the gift of Second Sight, Folas could see through this guard's eyes. The Dark Elf stood in place as his victim paced back and forth. At first, the sensation gave him motion sickness. *Can I handle this?* Folas almost teleported back to the Northern Plateau, but after taking time to clear his thoughts, he adapted to the feeling.

Okay. Next. He surveyed the land and saw another guard by himself. Not dissimilar to the first, he was able to infect this one even easier than before.

He found a third by a garden in the north. A fourth was nearby. The fifth took the longest to find, as no other guards were patrolling on their own. Folas almost settled for four victims when he saw a face he didn't expect to encounter.

Eskil, you traitor.

Folas had heard rumors the mayor of Clericsfold was serving on some kind of Abrian Council. This would give Kane direct access to those meetings.

Eskil walked away from a nearby group and headed to the central well. He leaned on the edge, looking deep into the well's depths for a moment. Folas cautiously approached him and, as Eskil stood back up straight, repeated the same steps he had taken with the other victims.

Eskil immediately started coughing. The man had put on some weight since the first games, and Folas wondered if this was a sign of a health-related issue that would complicate this new type of magic.

Nevertheless, the job was complete. Five spies. Five assets. And none of them had any idea what was going on.

Satisfied, Folas headed back to the field. He didn't want to risk teleporting in front of anyone for fear of becoming visible, even if for a moment. Once he reached his destination, he uncloaked.

"Soon," he said as he snapped his fingers and disappeared in a quick blast of light.

Chapter 23
The Tokei

Celebrations were one thing Tiernan believed he did right. Today was a special day to celebrate. He turned to the group of friends he had gathered with: Eislyn, his sister Enid, and his best friend Wayland.

"920NE. Can you believe it? We'll turn twenty-one in less than a month, Sis!" Tiernan's shock — and perhaps a bit of awe — at his forthcoming age was almost an afterthought to Enid. While he cared about such matters, to her, they were of no consequence. She was merely happy to be with the man she loved and her family.

Tonight, they were gathered together in the original Drunken Alligator in Lorelei, a place none of them had oddly been to until today.

"T, I'm telling you, sometimes the weirdest things seem so…excitable to you." It was Wayland who echoed Enid's thoughts as he wrapped his arm around Tiernan's neck. "But I love you anyway, Brother." With his other hand, he took a gulp of his Lorelian Mead.

While the ladies were sitting at a table near the bar, Wayland was standing next to Tiernan, each with one of the city's famous drinks in their hand.

The two men clinked their pint glasses together, taking another drink after. Eislyn and Enid exchanged a look as if to say, 'Here they go again.'

Each of the ladies had a large ring on their left ring finger.

"Yeah, you'd think he'd be thinking more about our upcoming wedding than turning twenty-one, Way. But, what do I know?" Eislyn had quickly blended in with the group, and even adopted some of the teasing habits toward her betrothed that Wayland and Enid were fond of. Tiernan shot her a look and leaned down to give her a kiss.

"You know I can't wait for that day." She returned the offer and grabbed his cheeks with her hands to showcase her love for her fiancé.

"Is that so, T?" Now it was Enid's turn for some playful banter. Her question made the two break the kiss, which if Enid was being honest, went on for a hair longer than she cared to see. "Last I heard, you hadn't even booked the hall for the wedding, yet had booked this place for a birthday celebration." Enid gave Eislyn another look as if to say, 'Here it comes!'

"Hey, I'm the *Prince of Abria*. One of the two famous Protectors of the Land! I have no doubt the owners of the Gléineach Hall will be more than glad to accomoda..."

"Oh, shut up, Brother. I've never heard someone like to hear the sound of their own voice more than you."

Eislyn tapped the seat next to her. "Now come, my dear. Sit. You've been pacing ever since we got here." Tiernan sheepishly listened to her instructions. "Good. Now stay. Hey," she said, turning back to the others, "Does anyone know how much time is left until midnight?"

"I heard someone say a little bit ago the moon was almost directly overhead. That's good enough for me," responded Wayland. "Do you guys wanna go outside or stay in here?"

Enid responded first. "I'm fine here."

"Well, I just sat down..."

"Oh, come on, Tiernan. Let's go outside for a bit," suggested Eislyn. "I mean, if that's okay?" The others shrugged their shoulders as if to say, 'Let's go.' All except for Enid, though her expression of protest fell on blind eyes.

"Moon Rise is so slow. It's going to be like watching water boil." Wayland reached out to grab her hand.

"Do it for me." Enid rolled her eyes, smiled amicably, and stood. Together, the four walked outside. There was a noticeable difference between the atmosphere in and out of the Alligator. Inside, it was relatively low-key despite being a well-known tavern. Patrons had mostly been drinking in silence, couples having a reflective moment together to close out the year, and a few men sitting alone contemplating whether the new year would be better for them than this past one had been.

Outside, it was nothing short of a party. People were celebrating, dancing, laughing, and sharing unforgettable moments together. Lorelei was as much alive as the closing ceremonies of a Statuo.

Tiernan looked around and noticed a person sitting alone by the central well. He appeared to be mouthing while messing with a contraption in his hand. Tiernan grabbed Eislyn's hand and pulled her with him.

"Where are we going? Enid and Wayland aren't following, T. Hey, what's that man doing?"

"Precisely." Together, they stopped walking and watched him from a respectable distance.

"Forty-five, forty-six…" The man appeared to be counting and mumbling something while holding a small contraption in his hand.

"That's so unusual," she said. Tiernan nodded his head in agreement.

"Let's go." The distance between the Alligator and the well was far enough removed so the din of the celebrations was quieter, giving them a moment of solitude. They took advantage of the privacy as they exchanged a quick kiss before moving on.

"Look, T." The thing in the man's hand was making a ticking sound and his words seemed to align with the noises.

"Hey, mister," she said, "Aren't you going to come enjoy yourself? There's so much going on out here. You're going to miss the moon's peak."

The man looked at the couple, then stood while still counting.

"Thirty-three, thirty-four." He handed the device to Eislyn. "Count. Thirty-six, thirty-seven, thirty-eight." He started nodding as Eislyn got in rhythm.

"Thirty-eight, thirty-nine, forty."

"Good. Keep that up. When you reach sixty, start again at one." He reached out to grab Tiernan's hand for a shake. "Hi. I'm Saito. I'm, uh, not from around here." With those words, Tiernan noticed for the first time the man wasn't dressed in traditional Abrian clothing.

"Yeah, I can see that. Where are you from?"

"Watodo. Hey, don't stop," he said to Eislyn. "Anyway, this is something I've been working on since I arrived here."

"Through one of the ports?" The man nodded.

"The one north of here. I've been staying here for a while, trying to understand some things."

"Understand…some things?" He nodded again before explaining. He pointed to the device.

"This land is different. I can't explain why, but it stopped working the moment I stepped foot on your soil. Back home, it helps us keep time. Here," he looked around. "Here, it's as if something disrupts its natural rhythm. I've been tweaking it, and tonight… Hey, keep counting!"

"Sorry," Eislyn replied, "Ten. Eleven. Twelve."

"Anyway, I'm using Moon Rise to see if my changes have helped the stupid thing start to work again. If I'm right, your lady friend here will complete the counting cycle eight more times and then the moon will be directly overhead." He smiled. "And that's when Moon Rise will be here."

Tiernan reached out for it. "Keep counting, love." He flipped it over, inspecting it. It made a ticking sound aligned with each of Eislyn's words.

The contraption seemed simple enough, and as if it could be easily mass-produced. The face of the device contained a language he didn't recognize. *This could make timekeeping at the games* so *much easier.* "My name is Tiernan. I'm actually…"

"Yes, you're the Prince. Everyone knows you around here, it seems like. I've heard dozens of people comment about you and your group being inside the Doken Alligator."

Tiernan laughed. "The *Drunken* Alligator."

"Ah. Forgive me."

Tiernan thought for a moment as Eislyn kept counting in time with the device. "Listen, we'll be returning to Farna in a week. Come and see me then. I might have a job for you." The man smiled and nodded.

"I'll see you seven days from now. Here," he said as he reached out for the timekeeping device. "Keep counting." He looked at Eislyn. "Six more minutes. Better go find your friends before Moon Rise rolls over. It was nice to meet you, Prince Tiernan."

The man resumed counting in sync with Eislyn. "Twenty-seven, twenty-eight, twenty-nine…" He waved her off and continued as Eislyn and Tiernan turned back around to find Enid and Wayland.

"A way to keep time?" she asked.

"We wouldn't need four judges counting during events. They could just use four of those things and actually enjoy the competitions they're judging."

After returning to the Alligator's makeshift side patio, Tiernan and Eislyn found their companions buried in a crowd, close enough Tiernan could still see the man from Watodo standing by the well. Wayland's drink was empty, and he looked visibly buzzed. He and Enid held hands as they watched a group of musicians perform.

"Where were you guys?" he asked, slurring his words a bit.

"It's a long story," answered Tiernan. He put his hand on his sister's shoulder. "You know, I really should talk to Dad about ending public drunkenness." Wayland shot him a look.

"Oh, shut up, Tiernan!" she responded, pushing him away. "It's time you got off of your almighty, all-knowing, all-arrogant, ignorant, feeble-minded…"

Tiernan cut her off. "We only have a few minutes to Moon Rise! Tell me what you think of me next year, ok?"

"Almost the new year!" echoed Eislyn. She grabbed her fiancé's hand and grinned. She leaned in to whisper into his ear. "I cannot wait to marry you next year."

He turned to her and gave her a quick kiss. She, of course, reciprocated, but then pushed him away before it lingered too long. "Hey, no cheating. Save it for Moon Rise, Mr. Tiernan."

Tiernan laughed, then turned to look for the timekeeper at the well. *Saito, right?* Tiernan caught his eye, and the man waved back. He raised a hand with two fingers extended.

"Two minutes to Moon Rise," Tiernan said to Eislyn. Then he yelled the same to the crowd. Those who heard began cheering and passing the message along, unaware if they were right or wrong, instead getting caught up in the moment.

"Hey T, how did you know *exactly*?" asked Wayland.

"It's a secret. I'm magic. Like my sister!" Enid did not appreciate the comment and turned around, rolling her eyes. She grinned as a small flame flickered in her pupils. She turned back around with her eyes aglow.

"Like this, Brother?" Tiernan ignored her, instead turning back to the timekeeper. He raised his hand with one finger up.

"One minute to Moon Rise! Fifty-nine, fifty-eight, fifty-seven..." Tiernan raised his voice announcing the countdown. Around him, the crowd joined in. The excitement and energy spread across the city.

Those who were dancing danced harder.

Those drinking raised their glasses in solidarity.

And those holding the hand of their beloved squeezed it just a little bit tighter in anticipation.

Second by second, the citizens of Lorelei counted down. With fifteen to go, Tiernan turned around to confirm they were on count with the timekeeper. However, the man was nowhere to be found.

Tiernan shrugged and continued the countdown. "Ten. Nine. Eight. Seven! Six! Five! Four!" He squeezed the hand of his fiancée tighter. "Three! Two! One! May the Moon's fortune grace you this year and always!"

The crowd echoed the blessing, some saying it with him, others after he finished. Tiernan pulled Eislyn in close and gave her a long kiss. After the moment had passed, Tiernan looked deep into the eyes of his betrothed. "May the Moon's fortune grace you this year and always, my love."

"The same to you, my dear." They kissed again and turned to congratulate Wayland and Enid.

Who were *still* enveloped in the same first kiss of Moon Rise. "Oh man, Way, stop it already. Get a room." Wayland and Enid stopped and looked at Tiernan. Both smiled. Wayland grabbed Tiernan's hand and covered it in a thin layer of ice.

"Hey, how did you..." Tiernan saw the Frost Ring on Wayland's hand. Apparently, he had slid it on at some point once they walked outside. Enid spoke.

"Just think, T. In just a few short months, this bunny of a man is going to be your brother-in-law." Tiernan smiled and pulled Wayland in for a hug with his unfrozen hand.

"Can't think of a better man in all of Abria for my little sister." Wayland smiled as he hugged his best friend. "Family is strength, remember?" Wayland and Tiernan pounded each other on the back before releasing from the embrace. "Do you mind unfreezing my hand, Sis? It's beginning to hurt." Enid laughed and used her Fire Magic to melt the layer of ice covering Tiernan's hand.

Saito slowly walked through the streets of Lorelei, far out of sight of Tiernan and his group. He smiled in eager anticipation of his meeting with the Prince next week.

Deep down, he always hoped he might be able to sell his timekeeping device to the Kingdom. At its basic level, the details were not complex. Each unit included mechanical components, nothing more than a few gears any blacksmith could forge. There was also a small crystal in the center of it.

This unit was the hardest part to integrate, but even at that, all it did was act as a balance. These crystals grew in most of the caves within Watodo, and Saito was sure they could be found here, too.

Until then, though, he was just happy to have finally met the Prince he had heard so much about.

"For the glory of Watodo!" he exclaimed. Unexpectedly, he coughed. If he didn't know better, Saito would have thought a gust of wind had blown behind him. The force of the sensation took his breath away unlike anything he had ever experienced.

The people around him did not react accordingly to this gust of air.

"Strange," he said as he headed toward the inn where he was staying.

An invisible Folas smiled as the final pieces of their plan began falling into place.

"Last night, I infected another spy." Kane didn't respond, but continued chewing on his bite of food. "This one will give us a direct line of sight to see what the bearer of the Mind Shield is up to. My victim has a meeting with him next week." Kane still didn't respond and instead took another bite. "Say something. Anything. I thought you'd be happy."

Kane finished chewing and put down his sandwich. "Last year, you infected five people. Since then, how many more have you cast your spell on, Folas? A dozen? Twenty? I've lost count. There are spies everywhere. What's one more?"

"Did you not hear what I said? He has a meeting with the Prince. The abomination who holds the Mind Shield. You don't think that's significant?"

"Eskil sat on the Abrian Council until your magic eventually took his life. That gave me a direct line to Davien himself. He's the one who has the Soul Sword. You should have infected his replacement instead."

Folas started to speak, but bit his tongue. There were moments like these that made him question his partnership with Kane. For all his strength and planning, Kane could be short-sighted at times. Folas decided now wasn't the time to push the issue.

"This person came from a distant land. Watodo, I believe? Have you heard of it?" Kane nodded.

"We've had visitors from there from time to time. Mostly traders. Some of Clericsfold's foliage came from seeds someone brought decades ago. They're supposed to grow some kind of berry, but no one there could ever make it happen.

"Have you had any luck infecting anyone else on the Council?" Kane moved on from discussing his hometown back to his plan of revenge with dispassionate ease.

"No. Since you brought it up, once Eskil died, and in a similar way to the other four victims, security has tightened around each member of the Council. I almost got Midir a couple of weeks ago, but his guards were too close."

Kane took another bite, chewing as he talked. "How can the guards be 'too close' when you're invisible?" Kane didn't give Folas time to answer. "Your spy idea isn't working. We need a way to draw Davien out with the Soul Sword in hand. Any ideas?"

Folas rubbed his temples. Kane's obsession was in high gear today, and no matter what the Dark Elf said, it wouldn't make a difference. Folas leaned on a nearby counter for a moment, thinking.

"Well." He sighed. "This is a long shot. But what if we could convince the Royal Family their children were in danger? That would be easier if we had a Shapeshifter. Of course, I killed the only active one in Abria."

"What about one of the fiancés? That would draw them all out. We could kill all four at the same time."

Folas meditated on this new idea for a moment. He slowly nodded. "Let's see how this meeting goes next week with the man from Watodo. Will you at least give me that before doing anything stupid?"

Kane rose and walked over to Folas. He slapped his hand on Folas' shoulder. The Dark Elf wanted to wince since Kane hit his arm with an intensity that had to be intentional. "Okay. We'll do it your way. Just know this: by this time next year, Davien better be dead."

As promised, Tiernan granted a meeting with Saito one week after their initial meeting. And much to Saito's delight, the Prince commissioned him to create a set of the time-keeping devices for this year's Statuo at the rate of two silver din per unit. Tiernan would provide unlimited access to the blacksmith shops within Lorelei, and agreed to reimburse any lost revenue to those trades professionals focusing on this project instead of their usual business endeavors.

"We'll need a name for it. What do you call it in Watodo?"

"A tokei," Saito responded.

"We might need to come up with an Abrian name for it. But for now, let's go with that."

Through the eyes of Saito, Folas watched the exchange. He learned Tiernan's wedding was to be held during Daisymoon. The fifth Statuo would be two months later during Fawnmist, as usual, just a week after the couple returned from their honeymoon. And, one month later, during Flametide, Enid and her fiancé would finally be married.

And better yet, he learned Eislyn worked at the Drunken Alligator and would be making a supply run to Oakshadow on 21 Daisymoon to bring home barrels of Dorian Ale for their wedding.

"And that will be our move. We'll capture Tiernan's soon-to-be wife and lure the Royal Family to a place near the Cave of Tera where the plains are wide and open. We'll send one of the Elves to let them know where to find her. And to come alone."

Kane smiled. "I underestimated your new spy, Folas. He gave us all we needed."

Chapter 24

Supply Run

Most of the staff at the Drunken Alligator, not to mention Tiernan himself, opposed Eislyn's decision to make the supply run alone. Despite repeated protests, she held her ground.

"Listen, the Kingdom has been peaceful for years. Kane hasn't shown his face since the first Statuo." She smiled, running her hand along her fiancé's cheek. "This will give me a chance to connect with a few vendors in that area. Apparently, the Tolith Market in Oakshadow is doing extremely well. There's even this new concept they're calling Food Wagon Alley. Supposedly, it's a bunch of traveling vendors serving their recipes on the go.

"If I'm right, this is a concept I'd like to bring here. It could completely shift the dinner scene here in Farna." Tiernan leaned on the window overlooking the open fields below, replaying her argument in his mind over and over. Eislyn had been gone for a few days, which was normal.

He couldn't shake the feeling something was horribly wrong. Once again, leaning against one of the walls in his study was the Mind Shield. Tiernan turned his head to look at the ancient artifact. In the years since his training began, he hadn't built the same level of connection with it his sister had with the Power Ring.

He had, thankfully, started to become at peace with his past. He let go of the idea of changing his name. He accepted his role within the Kingdom.

He wasn't sure he wanted to be King, despite the outward expression of such. Surprisingly, he had come into his element as the permanent manager of the annual Statuo. Tiernan was considering the veritable possibility he may step aside from the throne and instead embrace a career in city planning.

Still, there was the Mind Shield to consider — not to mention the looming threat of Kane, despite his relative absence. There were rumors from hikers in the Milston Mountains. They caught glimpses of some kind of structure at the top of the Northern Plateau. However, scaling the rocky outcroppings surrounding the Plateau was impossible, so no one could confirm this activity.

It would be easy to hop on a dragon, take a flight, and survey the Northern Plateau. However, since the day of his birth, no dragons had conveniently decided to show up. The only two Abrian denizens who had the luxury of seeing Abria from the sky had been Midir and his late grandfather, Borun.

"The Mind Shield is supposed to block evil's sight. Could it somehow enable sight too?" Tiernan asked this question time and time again. "Why must it be a one-way thing? Perhaps it could work both to hide and to reveal!"

Archivists scoured the Alwyn Böchord inside and out, looking for notes that might shed some light on the artifact's power and how to use it in such a manner.

So far, they had come up empty-handed. Kane kept many books for himself, a fact Davien and the Clericsfold leadership were unaware of until it was too late. Whether those records contained details on the Mind Shield's power was irrelevant without the ability to study them.

Tiernan pushed himself up off of the window's ledge and walked over to the spot where it sat. With trepidation, he picked it up. In the four years since he had been given it, the Mind Shield had slowly shrunk down to a more manageable size. It was still bigger compared to a normal shield, which means he still had one or two more things to work out.

He flipped it around and slid it on his arm. Tiernan knew he didn't have magic ability. That was something unique to Enid. After all, she was the first Graelan mage in over a thousand years. Wayland once told him a story of how Enid would temporarily transfer some of her power to him, which explained how his friend had frozen Tiernan's hand during Moon Rise. The effect never lasted long, but allowed his best friend to wield a Frost Ring he apparently always kept on him. *Maybe Way is a mage too?*

Tiernan brought the Mind Shield up to his chest, as if he was defending himself from an errant arrow. He closed his eyes.

"Please show me Eislyn." He waited. And waited some more. *Come on, you worthless relic. Help me.*

Time seemed to slow to a crawl as he waited. Finally, Tiernan opened his eyes. Nothing. The Mind Shield hadn't shown him a single thing, and it made him angry. In his frustration, he slid the artifact off of his arm and tossed it onto his desk, where it made a loud crashing sound.

Eislyn hadn't been to Oakshadow in several years. Yesterday, she arrived after a couple days of travel and booked a room at one of the local inns.

Today, she was busy exploring the city. Unlike Farna and Castle Abria, the structures here were made almost entirely of wood. Every building — whether a storefront, home, or restaurant — was made of deeply colored, dark planks. The doors were almost universally a lighter color of brown, similar to natural tones, which made Eislyn wonder if the rest of the structures were artificially dyed or stained.

There were only two structures here made of anything but wood: the bricks surrounding the central well and a statue in the middle of the Tolith Market modeled after its namesake. It was smaller than the one in the Valley, but fulfilled Borun's requirement: to bear the name 'Tolith' meant it must also bear his likeness in some way.

"Can I help you?" Eislyn had been lost in her thoughts, mindlessly walking through the Market while taking it all in. Before her was a Food Wagon vendor.

"Oh, I'm sorry. I accidentally stopped here. I was admiring the beauty of your town and the Market." The man's countenance dropped a little, and she realized she may have offended him. "But I'm always up for a fresh experience. What do you have?"

His face lit up as he walked her through each of the items he was selling. Many of his creations were creative twists on Abrian classic fare. Eventually, she picked one: an Abrian Tallbread sandwich.

"Thanks," he said as he handed it to her. Eislyn walked through the Market until she found a grouping of tables. She sat down and took her first bite. The flavors seemed different from standard restaurant fare, somehow fresher. Whether it was the experience or creativity of the vendor, she did not know.

"This is going to be a hit. I've got to bring this concept to Farna!" While many of her patrons came into the Drunken Alligator for the mead with the food as a secondary — yet still significant — consideration, this could be the thing she needed to set her family's Drunken Alligator apart from the rest of the Kingdom.

"Impressed with the market?" She looked up to see who asked the question.

"Very." The man sat down.

"I heard you mention Farna? Are you from there?" Eislyn didn't want to reveal too much, and realized by talking to herself she let her identity slip. She shook her head while concocting a believable story on the spot.

"I run a small restaurant." Lie number one: the Drunken Alligator was the largest place to eat in Farna. "We mostly serve salads." Lie number two: Lorelian Mead made up a whopping sixty-five percent of her sales. "My husband is here looking for suppliers and I'm just out for a stroll while he conducts business."

Lies number three and four: she was betrothed to Tiernan, but the wedding was still several months away. As of today, she was absolutely unmarried. Furthermore, Eislyn was here to bring home barrels of Dorian Ale for the celebration, using this as a chance to check out the Market. No husband was out looking for supplies.

"Well, you've come to the right place! We've modeled a lot here after the Tolith Market in the Valley, of course. But the Food Wagon culture is totally new. It's taken off within the city.

"Buuuut, if you're looking for something even more outside the box, you should head up to Mystic Mornings before tonight's performance. That's the proper Food Wagon Alley."

"This isn't the alley we've heard so much about in Farna?" she asked. Eislyn looked around. The volume of portable food vendors already seemed impressive. She wondered how they would squeeze even more near Mystic Mornings.

"It's a sight to behold. This is about half of what you'll see there tonight."

The man stood up. "I need to get back to work. Enjoy the Market. I run an apothecary. Stop by if you're looking for a new skin cream." Eislyn blushed. "I'm not saying you need anything right now," he said as he tried to cover his faux pas. He laughed and cleared his throat. "You have a very lucky husband. Just something to think about down the road."

"Thanks. You know, I think I'll check out Food Wagon Alley tonight after all. When do they usually show up?"

"About two hours before the performances." With that, he bowed and turned around to return to his shop.

Unknown to the shop owner or Eislyn, Folas was sitting at the base of the Northern Plateau observing this entire interaction through the man's eyes. Next to him were Kane and several other Elves.

Folas opened his eyes. "Let's move."

The day's show at Mystic Mornings was *Song of Aila*. "A riveting performance detailing the legend of the Ailan Huntress. This should be fun. I wish T was here to see it with me."

Eislyn held the program, mentally reading off the names of the performers. She had decided to attend the show, and bought a pass from a ticket vendor in the Market. It gave her a coupon for a discount for one meal from a vendor in Food Wagon Alley.

The path to the theater began at the edge of Oakshadow itself. Mystic Mornings sat at a northern outcropping edge of the Rosewood Forest. Behind it, an extension of the wilderness mountains rose majestically. A well-marked path lit the way to the theater itself. This light provided a peaceful ambience, with the sounds of people walking toward the theater setting the stage for an exciting evening.

Eislyn passed a group of half a dozen food wagons and was genuinely impressed with their creativity. She didn't know what she would eat before turning in her pass at the theater's entrance, but hoped it would be as impressive as her lunch.

Ahead, there was a small gap in the Food Wagon Alley. The first batch set their wagons up between Oakshadow and the Forest entrance. After, there was a lull. It was the only place along the path without other people.

However, this didn't last long. Just inside of the Forest she saw a friendly vendor who waved her down. It was an Elf. *Possibly one of the families that relocated to Oakshadow before the first Statuo?*

"What would you like, miss?" He had a slight accent that sounded as if he was trying to talk more like a Graelan and less like an Elf.

"Oh, I'm just looking. Right now, I'm just blown away by the number of Food Wagon vendors I've seen already. I honestly don't know what to try first. There's so much to choose from!"

"Yes, Food Wagon Alley is full of diverse options. I think this is some of the best cuisine in all of Abria!"

"Are there more further up the path to the theater?

"There are, but that's why I'm here."

"Oh yeah? Why's that?"

"To catch your attention, of course. See, the bulk of the sellers in Food Wagon Alley are set up near the theater entrance. And the group back by Oakshadow still kind of feels as if you're in the city. Am I right?"

Eislyn had to agree with his question. In her mind, Food Wagon Alley was something you would only get along the path within the Rosewood Forest. "You're right, the vendors back there looked like they had some tasty options, but I chose to wait until I was in the Forest."

"Exactly! And I figured why not be the first thing people see once they enter the Forest!"

She smiled. "A sound decision. I run a restaurant myself elsewhere in Abria. I know the importance of being the first one open."

"So, would you like to try something? Maybe something small, saving room for another vendor further up the way?" She looked at his menu. Organized by appetizers first, followed by main offerings, and a small dessert selection, most of the words were written in Elvish.

"Well, um…"

"Oh right. You can't read that! Here, what if I surprise you? I'll give you my appetizer special. On the house."

"Sure, that is very kind of you." He began putting together a small appetizer, a mix of greens, bread, and some fruit she didn't recognize. After a moment, he handed it to her. "Thank you." He nodded as she took her first bite.

Eislyn opened her eyes. She couldn't see anything, and realized her head was covered and her hands bound behind her back.

"Hello? Where am I?" No one responded. Instinctively, she started struggling in an attempt to break free. She made small grunting sounds which made her *feel* like she was making progress.

Practically speaking, it was all futile. After a few moments, a voice confirmed it. "Those cords are tied and they have a binding spell on them. Doesn't matter how hard you try, miss, you won't be able to break free. Trust me, I tried the same thing when I got here, too."

Eislyn stopped moving and turned her face toward the sound of the voice. "Who are you?"

"Voron. I'm just as bound as you, except our captors didn't feel the need to blind me."

"Where are we?" Eislyn asked. Voron looked around. The fields were open as far as his eyes could see. He cranked his head around to look in the other directions around them.

"Well, fields of grasslands surround us in every direction. In front of us, oh, maybe twenty meters or so are our captors."

"Who?"

"Do you know the name Folas?" Eislyn shook her head. "What about Kane?" At the mention of his name, all the blood left her still-hidden face.

"Yes. My…someone I know has mentioned his name a few times."

"I know who you are. You're referring to your father-in-law, well, soon-to-be, anyway."

"Ye…yes. He and Kane used to be friends together at the orphanage…"

"…in Clericsfold. You're engaged to the one who wields the Mind Shield I believe?"

"How do you know Tiernan?" Eislyn's confirmation of Tiernan's name made Voron's heart sink for more reasons than one. He closed his eyes as he remembered Borun collapsing, as well as his actions during the race.

"Enid will be your sister-in-law." It wasn't a question. It was a statement full of regret.

Eislyn struggled some more, despite Voron's warning. "Who are you? Are you aligned with Kane?"

"No, I'm not. But I owe the Royal Family much. A large debt. One, I'm afraid, I can never repay." He explained the story of the rock that tripped Enid. He didn't hold back as he described the torture he experienced at Folas' hands.

And, in sadness, he revealed his own hand in the death of Borun.

Eislyn didn't know how to respond. She knew in her head Voron was just as much of a victim as anyone else. But, at the same time, in her heart, anger welled up. Once it reached a tipping point, she said as much.

"I don't blame you. I've loathed myself since that day. I hid in the mountains by, what do you Graelans call it? Mill Stone?"

"Milston. As if you combined the words mill and stun."

Voron continued. "I didn't deserve to take part in the games after that. But I also didn't feel right going home to my people. Besides, who would take me in? Would they be a friend or foe? I didn't know which of my brethren were aligned with Kane or Abria. And besides, the guilt I felt…"

"…Was entirely misplaced. That day you did a brave thing, and today you'll earn your reward." This time, it was Folas. Voron hadn't noticed him walk up, nor had he noticed Kane alongside him. "You taught me something about myself."

Folas pointed to Eislyn. A nearby Elf ran over and removed her hood. She blinked as her eyes adjusted to the light. The Elf vendor from the Forest stared back at her, a spiteful look encompassing his face.

"Do you remember when I first met you, Voron? How I put my hand on your head to…ah, *persuade* you to help me?

"It was in that moment I realized I could absorb the power of another creature. Of course, non-magical ones such as a poor, defenseless squirrel just…" He used his hands to mimic dust on the breeze. "…fade away. But with magic-endowed creatures like you, I can take their power as my own. You gave me a little bit of your magic, and I thank you for your service."

Eislyn didn't know whether to protest or cower in fear. She watched as Folas walked over to Voron. Her eyes grew wide as Folas laid his hand on top of the other Elf's head.

"Stop…please…" Voron begged. Bound and unable to move, his eyes rolled back into his head. From his body, a blue, swirling mist of energy emerged from his chest, through his head, and into Folas' hand.

"Well, this is new." The Dark Elf turned to Kane. "I knew he had the ability to control both the ground and the water. But his magic goes so much deeper."

Folas' eyes opened wide. "He has Lightning Magic! No…it's *more* than that." He smiled, showing his darkened teeth and mouth. Eislyn recoiled in disgust. "Elemental! I only knew one other of my brethren who had this type of magic."

"Tolith?" Kane asked.

"That's right. Let's get this over with." The color faded from Voron's skin. Already pale, it turned a sickly gray. His hair transformed from a warm brown to a snow-like white. The blue energy finally stopped transferring, and Voron's skin began to wrinkle. Eislyn tried to slide away as best she could.

After a few more moments, all that was left of Voron were the clothes he had been wearing, laying in a small, discarded clump on the ground. The rest of what remained of his body — nothing more than dust — caught a breeze and dispersed into the air.

"Now, let's summon the Royal Family, shall we?" Folas raised his hands high to the sky. Far above, the sun disappeared behind a wall of clouds. A storm began brewing, pelting Eislyn with sharp drops of rain.

The storm extended beyond the plains and encompassed all the surrounding regions. It began to thunder, with bolts of lightning crackling throughout the sky.

Kane turned to the Elf from Food Wagon Alley. "You know what you have to do next." He nodded, snapped his fingers, and disappeared.

The Elf reappeared in Farna within Castle Abria. Guards surrounded him in an instant, swords and spears drawn.

He raised his hands. "I have a message for the Royal Family. Kill me now, and you'll never get the girl back." The guards exchanged a few looks between them. One of them, a larger guard dressed in different regalia and the apparent leader of the group, nodded to another. He ran off while the others kept their unexpected visitor detained.

Minutes passed until finally, Davien and Kyrie emerged down a flight of stairs. Tiernan ran down another set, the one closest to his study. Enid stood on a nearby balcony, her clenched fist full of her Dragonborn power, ready to strike.

Davien spoke first. "What girl? And who are you?"

"It doesn't matter who I am. I serve the Dark Elf Master." He pointed to Tiernan, though the motion caused the guards to move in even closer with their spears. Several of them had the tip of their blades pushed into the Elf's body.

"My Master has your young lady. If you want her back, the four of you will head to the center of that storm." He smiled. "And bring your fancy items with you. No guards either. This is between you and him." He tried to raise his hand to snap his fingers. However, the surrounding blades prevented him from doing so.

The Elf sighed. "My life is of no consequence. Kill me if you must; it won't save the girl." Kyrie, as the commander of the forces, moved forward.

"Stop. Let him go. Where is the center of the storm?" The guards backed off. Surprised, the Elf walked over to her.

"In the fields north of the Cave of Tera. Really, you shouldn't have let her travel alone. So careless. Makes you wonder if the Prince really loves her after all."

Tiernan's rage — and guilt for letting his fiancée go by herself — got the best of him. He yelled, letting out a guttural sound as he ran at the Elf. He used the face of the Mind Shield to knock him away, and the Elf went flying. He raised his sword to charge him.

Only a swift grab from King Davien prevented Tiernan from following through. "Stop. That's an order, son." The Elf stood up, dark green blood running down the side of his mouth. He smiled at Tiernan.

"I like this one. Be there by tomorrow evening, or the girl dies." He snapped his fingers and disappeared.

Chapter 25

A Family Statuo

Tiernan had never been known for his patience. Today, his body language had this character flaw on full display. "I'm telling you, Dad, there's no time to summon the Council!" Tiernan's frustration was building, though not at his father per se.

Instead, helplessness surrounded each member of the Royal Family. Each had resorted to throwing out random ideas. No one believed it was safe for them to travel by themselves, as the Elf instructed. If they risked taking protection, Eislyn would be killed. It was a no-win scenario and there didn't appear to be any path forward. Tiernan walked over to the wall, prepared to punch it in frustration. Only a comment from his father prevented him.

"Stop. Now, son. Sit down." Tiernan complied, though his anger was still evident. "I didn't say we were going to. *Only* that I wish we had time to." Davien's response to his son, while louder and more commanding, was less kingly and instead full of the same frustration. In truth, all he wished in this instance was that he could get the Council's *approval* for the action he was about to undertake.

"So what happens if we take these relics out in the field?" Enid asked, referring to the Power Ring, Mind Shield, and Soul Sword. All three were laying together on the table in the Council room where the family had gathered.

"I don't understand why we're taking them in the first place," said Kyrie. "Davien, you've been practicing your sword fighting skills with *generic* swords." She sighed. "I have to admit, I miss seeing you with a lathe instead of a blade…"

He stopped her. "This isn't the time for remorse, regret, or wishing things were different, my love. We need to accept how things are now. It's that simple." He picked up the Soul Sword. Davien realized he hadn't held it much, other than when he took it with him during the yearly Statuo. For the first time, holding it with the intention of using it made the King realize it was noticeably lighter than the swords he had been practicing with.

"I'll admit, I don't know what this will do." He looked back at his wife. "But I have to *try*. Kane has made his move. This is different from trying to split the Kingdom. This is not a schoolyard disagreement between two ex-friends." He met his son's gaze. "This is personal. It's an attack on our *family*."

Enid reached over and grabbed her brother's hand. Tiernan looked down, realizing his fist was clenched so tight it was almost white. "She is family, T. To all of us. That's our greatest asset. Family is Strength, remember?"

"So is Wayland," Kyrie echoed. "Family, that is. He should be here, too. We may need his help."

"Help for what, exactly? Do we even have a plan to get her back?" Enid's words reverberated through the room. Each member of the Royal Family sat in silence, waiting for someone else to speak up.

The Mind Shield hadn't shrunk for years. As Tiernan held it on his arm once again, he hoped it might. In his other hand was his favorite sword, a medium-sized blade he used during most of his training.

"She's ready, sir." Tiernan blinked, snapping himself out of his blank gaze. The voice of the stable hand brought him back to reality once again.

"Thanks." Tiernan handed the sword to the man, and the stable hand walked around to the other side of the horse to secure the scabbard to the saddle. He put his foot into the stirrup and mounted the steed. Across the field Enid, was doing the same, holding her preferred axe with the same hand as the Power Ring. The head of the axe was already aflame, poised to strike at a moment's notice.

Next to her was Wayland, his eyes aglow with the power of his Frost Ring. Enid had apparently transferred some of her power to him again. His role here was going to be critical, acting as a scout.

Davien and Kyrie were likewise ready to go. Davien held the Soul Sword in his hand and a large shield from the armory mounted nearby. Kyrie rode next to her husband, a longsword mounted on one side of her horse and a circular shield on the other.

The five riders departed Farna, with Kyrie casting a parting glance at it behind them. The ride would take several hours at top speed.

Tiernan couldn't explain why, but the plan seemed lacking. Davien and Kyrie were going to confront Kane head on. Tiernan and Enid would follow behind, keeping an equal distance between Wayland and their parents.

Wayland's job was to scope out the surrounding fields looking for Eislyn. His frost powers were meant to be used as a last resort, temporarily freezing any errant Elves or Graelan supporters he encountered.

The hope was Wayland would find Eislyn and rescue her while the Royal Family dealt with Kane. If the Mind Shield could stay close enough to everyone, it might block Folas from seeing their activities.

The reality was they didn't know where Eislyn was in relation to Kane, and the entire thing could fall apart easily. Wayland may have to move far out of range. Realistically speaking, no one knew how the Mind Shield worked or how far off a range it had. Tiernan and Enid may need to leave their parents unprotected so Wayland could do his job. Several other unpredictable outcomes could play out.

Worse yet, Tiernan knew there was no backup plan. However, in his mind, there could only be one outcome. He looked at his sister next to him as he remembered what he told her in the armory.

"Today, I will come home with Eislyn or not at all."

Far above the northern Clericsfold grasslands, the sky was dark and foreboding. An errant lightning bolt crackled across it, an omen Kyrie thought contained an almost intentional tone. Far in the distance, she could see their destination: two standing figures, one of whom had developed an immense hatred of her husband years ago and another who had aligned himself with that individual for reasons she didn't understand.

Kane and the Dark Elf Master. Kyrie had hoped things would have resolved themselves after the first Statuo. That maybe even Kane's disappearance after the event meant everything was going to be okay. As she approached them with her husband, all she wanted was for things to go back to normal.

Before she first donned the crown.

To the west, Wayland rode north. He was out of visual sight of the King and Queen — and by extension, Kane and Folas — but close enough to the Mind Shield to stay hidden from the Dark Elf's powers. Wayland stayed within a hundred meters of Tiernan and

Enid at all times as he rode his horse, desperately looking for signs of Eislyn in the grasslands.

"This will work, T," shouted Enid as they galloped side by side. Tiernan looked toward his parents.

"I know. Remember, I told you, I'm not leaving here without her."

Kane and Folas watched the group approach. "Look at them, Folas. Their children are scared. Staying a ways back."

"Yes. Curious, isn't it? I wonder if they're planning something?"

"It doesn't matter. Look. Davien has the Soul Sword."

"Perhaps we should change the game?" Folas suggested.

As the King and Queen got closer to Kane, Wayland continued to stay just out of sight. He knew looping around the outer fields would take time. But if Tiernan continued in the same general direction and stayed close enough to his friend, Folas wouldn't know what Wayland was up to until it was too late.

Once again, another lightning bolt cracked across the sky. It continued its path directly toward Davien and Kyrie. The bolt's path ended above the King and Queen's heads. It grew brighter, enveloping them.

In a flash, they were gone — as were Kane and Folas. The twins brought their horses to a complete stop.

"Where did they go?" Enid exclaimed.

"I don't know. Look Enid, their horses are still there."

"Should we go looking for them?" Tiernan didn't respond, because he truly didn't know what to do at first.

Finally, he made his decision. "We *need* to find Eislyn. Let's meet up with Wayland."

Kyrie and Davien opened their eyes at almost the same time. Both were lying on their backs on a grassy field. Their horses were galloping past them with Enid and Tiernan not far behind.

"Davien, what happened?" He shook his head in confusion. "Look, there go the kids. They're heading north."

"It's as if they don't see us."

"Very astute, my dear *friend*." At the sound of the voice, Davien's hand gripped the Soul Sword tight. He jumped up, pulling Kyrie with him. Standing across the field were Kane and the Dark Elf.

"Kane." Kyrie stood behind her husband as the King uttered their opponent's name. She looked back at the twins riding further away in the distance.

"Oh, they can't see you right now. It'll wear off in time. My friend can't maintain a cloak of invisibility on all four of us forever."

"What do you want?" Davien asked. "Why did you take the Princess?" Davien referred to Eislyn by her future title to make a statement. Eislyn wasn't any normal citizen of the land.

She was a member of the Royal Family of the Kingdom of Abria.

"I thought it would be *fun*." Kane was only partially lying. Torturing the Royal Family with her capture had sounded like fun.

It also brought Kane exactly what he wanted: the Soul Sword, which now glowed in Davien's hand. Kyrie noticed.

Davien also noticed, though he didn't show any kind of acknowledgment. Instead, he heard the relic talking to him in the same way Tiernan often described the Mind Shield communicating with him.

Eislyn will be okay.

"We just want Eislyn back. Then we'll leave." Davien's words were direct and to the point. As the King said them, as if on cue, the Dark Elf recoiled in pain. Kane looked at his companion in confusion.

"The twins must be close to her, because I can no longer see her." Folas' words made Davien realize what he hoped would be true: the range of the Mind Shield continued to hide Wayland during this.

Tiernan must be close enough to her. And the Shield is blocking the Dark Elf's ability to see both of them. Davien nodded at his wife.

"It's fine. She isn't our concern anymore. Only these two." As Kane spoke, Davien thought he heard another impression from the Soul Sword.

Release me.

Following its instructions, Davien raised his hand and brought the ancient relic high into the air. He felt something well up deep within him. Kane observed all of this with morbid curiosity.

"This ends here, Kane." From the Soul Sword, a blast of bright white power emerged. It traveled far into the air, and the Dark Elf collapsed. In the sky, there was a subtle change. Whatever field, or 'cloak of invisibility' had surrounded the four, was now gone.

Its destruction ripped through Folas like a bolt of lightning and brought him to his knees. In agonizing pain, he yelled. "We're visible! We have to act now!"

Wayland swung his sword with one hand, cutting down a random man who charged at him. With his other hand, he emitted a blast of Frost Magic at an oncoming Elf. It froze in place from head to toe.

Another Elf grabbed a Fire Ring out of its pocket. He used its power to send a blast of magic toward Wayland. Wayland defended using a reciprocative blast of Frost Magic. Though successful, he realized the force of his attack was weak, as if he was running out of his temporary powers.

"Enid!" he yelled. "I'm running low, love!"

"I'm a little busy." Her response was an understatement. The flame on her axe was in full display, and she easily took down several of her attackers with a single swipe of her weapon.

Meanwhile, Tiernan had taken the lead and now was surveying the fields while looking for the love of his life. He realized finding her might be like finding a needle in a haystack.

One Elf near Wayland suddenly looked worried. He yelled something in Elvish, and several others began moving away from Wayland and Enid.

"Way!" Enid yelled. Wayland swung his sword and defended against an oncoming attack before responding.

"What?" She pointed at the small group of Elves now moving away from their battle.

"T must be getting close. We gotta finish this." Wayland finished dealing with the current attacker and rushed to his fiancée.

"Can you give me another boost?" She nodded and put both hands on his shoulders. Her eyes lit up as he closed his own. At once, he opened them with a bright blue glow.

"Thanks. Now, enough of this." His voice carried the booming echo of Enid's Dragonborn power as he spread his arms out to his sides. With an impressive blast, Wayland sent every bit of Frost Magic within him across the field. It hit each attacking Graelan and Elf, freezing them in place.

"If we weren't fighting for our lives, I might be impressed, my little bunny." Wayland smiled at her comment.

"Well, don't get too excited," he said, his voice back to normal. "That drained me. I'm out of magic, and I don't know if I have the energy for something like that again. Come on, let's go find Tiernan."

Rain had soaked the field where Kane and Folas had left Eislyn. With each step, Tiernan's horse left deep, muddy imprints on the ground. As he approached his fiancée, Eislyn looked as if she had been here for quite some time. The hours spent in the rain stained her once clean clothes.

Eislyn's hands were still bound behind her back, though she had forced herself up to her knees when she saw Tiernan approaching in the distance.

"Tiernan! Over here!" Tiernan shifted his legs to push his horse harder. The steed picked up the pace, but wasn't fast enough. An Elf teleported in front of her and pointed its open palm at her face.

"Stop, Graelan, or I'll burn her alive." Tiernan slowed his horse to a stop, keeping it at a distance as several more appeared in front of Eislyn.

Wayland and Enid rode up next to him. She dismounted from the horse and raised both of her hands in an offensive posture.

"Enough of this nonsense," she said, firing blasts of magic at the group of Elves. Her attack enclosed some of them in a glass hold while the legs of several others ignited.

"She's good," said Wayland, looking at Tiernan on the horse next to him.

"You're telling me. Always jumps right in, never holds back." The men hopped off of their steeds and ran over to the immobilized group of Elves. Wayland handed Enid the Frost Ring, and she froze each of the burning ones.

Tiernan kneeled down to Eislyn and immediately kissed her before untying her bound hands.

"Tiernan, I'm so sorry."

"Hey," he said, giving her another kiss, followed by an embracing hug. "I'm here. That's all that matters. You're safe."

"Tiernan, look," said Enid, pointing southward from where they had just come. A giant beam of white energy had just emerged from the field.

"That seemed intense. Do you think that's where Mom and Dad are?" asked Tiernan. He gave Eislyn another hug, helping her to her feet.

"We were *just there*. Though it would make sense with the Soul Sword here," responded Enid.

"Wayland, I need you to get her back home." Tiernan handed over the Mind Shield. "Take this too. I hope you don't have any skeletons in your closet you're holding on to, otherwise this might not work."

Wayland slid the shield on. It didn't grow or shrink, which Tiernan hoped was a good thing. The Prince was playing it by ear, and didn't know if only he could wield the Shield or if his best friend could too. With Wayland's ability to wield Frost Magic — albeit with a boost from Enid — Tiernan assumed the Mind Shield would protect his friend.

Tiernan whistled for his horse, which headed toward him.

"Tiernan, what's going on?" asked Eislyn.

"Our parents came too," responded Enid. Tiernan nodded and kissed his fiancée again.

"Go with Way. I'll be in Farna soon enough." He helped her up onto Wayland's horse, turning to his friend next. "Take care of her for me, Brother."

"You know I will." Wayland mounted the steed and turned to face the twins. "I'll take her straight to the castle. Be safe. I'll see you two soon." He blew a kiss toward Enid before galloping away with Eislyn.

Enid tapped her brother on his shoulder. She pointed to the Elves, some still trapped in a glasslike structure, the rest frozen in place and struggling to break free.

"What do we do with these?" Tiernan looked at his parents in the distance and back at the Elves. He swallowed hard, not sure how to respond to his sister's question.

"I told you Central Abria is mine. Your little contest was only a stall tactic. I will rule this land whether you accept it or not." Davien cocked his head to one side. He couldn't remember Kane *ever* saying something like that, a sign of the delusional state his former friend had descended into.

"Abria is a unified Kingdom, my friend."

"Don't call me your friend, *carpenter*!"

Davien continued. "There's no more division. We settled that dispute years ago." Davien's response didn't seem to faze the other man. "We can settle this too."

"No! I am the Divider. You may have thought it was over, but it's only just begun. Remember, we told your father to shut down his mill. Instead, he expanded it. Turned the Valley into some kind of destination town." Kane shook his head. "And that's why he paid the price for his ignorance."

Davien stiffened, the gravity of Kane's words sinking in. Most presumed Borun died of natural causes. Instead, Kane just confirmed Davien's suspicions.

"It was you, Kane? *You* killed him? How?"

Kane smiled, clearly cherishing the memory. "It was easy. My friend here sent one of his little minions to poison Borun's favorite drink: Lorelian Mead. Remember when you were all gathered in the tavern that day? You probably don't, so let me remind you.

"Your father ordered 'one more' drink. One more pint of Lorelian Mead. Our accomplice kindly volunteered to bring it to him, pouring an extra bite into it. One tiny vial of poison and it was goodnight Borun." He smiled. "Well, perhaps I should say goodbye, Borun. Tell me, did you cry at his funeral? I heard it was a lovely gathering."

Kane's moment of joyful remembrance quickly turned to rage: pure, unadulterated hate toward his former friend.

"You're a *mistake*, Davien. You should be tending to the horses or making chairs. *Irrelevant* things. You're a nobody, a fatherless nothing who just happened to fall into royalty.

"You didn't deserve any of this and yet here you are, the King of Abria." Kane cleared his throat. "Leave here, Davien, and I'll let you keep half of the Kingdom. Cross me, and you'll pay."

Kane raised his sword toward Davien. In response, the King raised the Soul Sword in front of Kyrie to protect her.

With a gasp, the Dark Elf spoke. "I can see them." He grabbed Kane's tunic. "I can see the twins. That means they do not have the Mind Shield anymore. They're on their way."

"So where is the Mind Shield?" Kane asked. Folas shrugged.

"I still cannot see *her*. The woman must have it."

Kane nodded. "No matter." He turned his attention back to the King and Queen.

Davien and Kyrie exchanged a look as if to say 'Wayland has her'. The Queen spoke. "Davien, we should go." Davien looked at his wife. His gaze shifted to the two approaching figures on a single horseback in the distance.

"We will, my love." He looked back at Kane. "Kane, I thought of you as a brother once. I know what happened in the past hurt, and you may never forgive me or my father. But I ask, if not for me, then for the Kingdom, please try to understand I'm sorry.

"I know we can work through this somehow now that Wayland has Eislyn." Kane did not know who Wayland was, but the mention of a fifth person enraged him even more.

"I said to bring no one!" He nudged the Dark Elf. Quickly, Folas used one of his hands to send a blast of Elemental Lightning Magic toward the Royal Couple.

Davien swung the Soul Sword at the incoming blast and deflected the beam away from them. The blast illuminated the darkened landscape, traveling high into the air before exploding across the ominous sky.

The Soul Sword began to glow a bright red color. For a moment, it seemed as if Davien had deflected the attack.

One last time, the Soul Sword spoke to Davien.

This is not what was supposed to happen.

Davien didn't know what it meant, but it didn't matter. The Lightning blast caused the Soul Sword grow hotter and hotter.

Within an instant, the Soul Sword was on fire.

In pain, Davien dropped it. Kyrie grabbed her husband's arm as he recoiled from the sensation.

Folas used his powers to draw the Soul Sword toward him. What followed next was just barely visible to the approaching twins.

First, the Dark Elf sent a blast of Wind Magic at the King and Queen. Second, using the Soul Sword, he sent another stream of unknown energy at them.

Together, these two forms of magic enveloped the Royal Couple. Davien and Kyrie barely had any time to react. Once it dissipated, the two of them collapsed.

Davien and Kyrie were dead, locked in an eternal embrace in each other's arms as the life drained from their bodies. No final words. No expressions of emotion. No chance to say goodbye to their children.

Once again, the King of Abria was dead.

Folas handed the Soul Sword to Kane once it cooled off. The latter regarded the ancient relic, flipping it back and forth in his hand.

"Not bad," Kane said. "Let's go." Folas snapped his fingers and teleported the two of them far from the plains where Davien and Kyrie now lay slain.

A few moments later, Tiernan and Enid arrived at the scene. Both jumped off their horses mid-gallop and rushed to the fallen bodies of their parents.

"Mom. Mom!" Enid began shaking Kyrie's body. "Daddy. Daddy, wake up."

Tiernan fell to his knees in tears, blaming himself. *Why me? Why do things keep going wrong?*

He blamed himself for Eislyn's capture, for the lives he took today to rescue her, for not having a more effective plan.

And worst of all, Tiernan now blamed himself for the deaths of his parents, both of whom would still be alive if he hadn't allowed Eislyn to leave the protective guard of the Mind Shield.

The joint funeral for Davien and Kyrie was a spectacle rivaling the closing ceremonies of the Statuo. Many attended from across the Kingdom. Kyrie's parents graciously helped plan most of it, as Tiernan suddenly found himself thrust into a position he didn't even know if he wanted in the first place: leading the Kingdom.

Likewise, Enid would take on an equal position of authority. Neither sibling thought ascending to the position of King or Queen made sense right now. While Tiernan was the eldest, this detail mattered little to the twins. Instead, they agreed to rule jointly as brother and sister, Prince and Princess, until one of them married.

The events of the past several days made both couples feel as if their engagements were irrelevant. Neither set was in a rush to get married and postponed additional planning until Tiernan and Enid could work out what needed to happen next for Abria.

Together, the twins walked through the halls of the castle. On this day, it seemed much emptier than usual. The missing presence of Davien and Kyrie loomed over their home like a drifting phantom, clouding everyone and everything it touched.

Finally, Tiernan spoke. "I talked to Midir earlier."

"What did he say?" Enid wasn't sure she wanted to know the answer, but asked anyway.

"The scouts from Idlewind were chased out of the Rosewood Forest. The entire remaining Elven population living there has now turned on Abria. All of them. They've claimed the Forest as their own and blocked the path to Mystic Mornings. It's entirely cut off from the city," he said as they entered the throne room. Enid sat on a bench by one of the windows, her gaze aimed north toward the Oakshadow region.

"The loss of the theater will destroy their economy." Tiernan walked across the room and placed both of his hands on an opposing window.

"It gets worse. Apparently, there was a group of performers rehearsing on the day of the attack. No one has seen them since. The Elves have begun calling it the Darkwood Forest or something, as if changing the name makes it their own." Tiernan looked out across Farna. Below, activity seemed more subdued. The deaths of the King and Queen had affected both trade and commerce.

Tiernan slammed his palms on the ledge. "Traitors. Telford *invited* them in. Their whole group of refugees, taken in as if they were members of his own family. And now, despite that hospitality, they align with Kane to overthrow the Kingdom?"

"You do know not every Elf is on their side, right? Many of the Elves found themselves refugees once again. Some are in Oakshadow, others in Lakedon. And you know Grandpa even had a friend who…"

"Yes, Sis, I know. And I'll…sorry. Yes, we should grant the Abrian aligned Elves protection here in Farna."

"Do you really think moving them again is a wise choice? They've already fled from their home in the Forest and are trying to get settled in Oakshadow and Lakedon. Maybe we should just wait before doing anything."

Tiernan's anger finally got the best of him. He turned to face the edge of the window where he was standing and punched it with his bare fist.

He didn't recoil in pain as the adrenaline-fueled rage meant he didn't feel *anything*. Instead, the only sign of his activity was a bloodied right hand.

From her viewpoint across the room, Enid couldn't tell if it was broken. She sighed, stood up, and walked over to her brother. "Let me see." She carefully placed his hand in the palm of one of hers, cupping it with the other hand. Instantly, all three glowed. Within a few moments, a bright red and orange sunset-like haze enveloped Tiernan's busted hand. It blinded him for an instant with its intensity.

Slowly, she removed her hands. The blood was gone. No sign of bruising or internal breakage. As far as anyone could tell, Tiernan's hand had never been hurt even once in its life. It looked perfect.

"That one is free. The next one won't be." She leaned in and hugged her brother. "It's going to be okay." Tiernan closed his eyes, trying to keep his emotions in check.

"It's my fault. If only I had gone with Eislyn…" were the only words he could say as he began sobbing uncontrollably. Enid hugged her brother tighter and, in response, he rested his face on her shoulder.

"You know this was a clean tunic, right?" The comment made him slightly chuckle, breaking the intensity of his outburst.

"Are we finally even for that game of tag when we were five or so?" She gave him one more squeeze.

"Never."

Chapter 26

Zoran, 920NE

They traveled forever. At least, that was the way the passage of time felt to Kane. He was a patient man, but this journey was finally getting to him. Looking for something to act as a distraction, he finally asked a question.

"So how does this work, exactly?" Kane's question, for perhaps the first time in his life, was an honest one. His voice echoed with the question, reverberating off of the slick, dark walls of the Cave of Tera. His companion didn't answer. Instead, they walked for a ways longer before finally stopping.

The Dark Elf used his open palm — one containing a ball of fire acting as a makeshift torch — to direct Kane's attention further down the path.

"What am I supposed to be looking at? We've been in here for a long time. It's all beginning to look the same."

"That's the point. King Telford sealed Zoran away deep under the Northern Plateau. We have a long way to go yet."

"And you know this how?"

"I think I absorbed some of the Shapeshifter's memories, too. I have a vague recollection of a fierce battle. Of a plateau that *didn't* exist, but now does."

"You're just now telling me this?"

"I'm just now *remembering* it. This is new to me too, Kane. I don't know if the proximity of the Soul Sword has reawakened those memories or..."

"Or…?"

"I don't know. Come on." Folas moved further ahead into the darkened cavern. Kane followed behind with a small contingent of Elves carrying gear. One of them ran up to Kane and handed him an apple.

"Thanks." Kane rubbed the head of the Elf, who returned to the group trailing behind. "They make great gophers, don't they?"

"They don't know what they're doing. Most of them are acting out of the instinct I put into their minds."

Kane lost track of the time, and it could have been hours or days later. He didn't know.

When they reached a large collapsed passageway, he almost turned back. Boulders blocked the path, making it completely impassable.

"Now what?" Folas said. They had followed the only northbound path and came to a dead end.

With curiosity, Kane reached out to touch the fallen rock. His hand encountered an invisible barrier, causing him to recoil in pain. The tips of his fingers were a deep red — not quite burned, but definitely irritated.

"What in Grael was that sorcery?" exclaimed Kane.

The Soul Sword glowed. Folas noticed it first as Kane was too distracted, looking at his hand, which ached more and more with each passing second.

"Kane." Folas wasn't sure what to say exactly other than his name. This broke Kane's focus on his wound and redirected it to the Soul Sword. Kane raised it up to eye level.

"This must be it. King Telford sealed them behind these rocks and encased it in this Barrier spell."

"I don't think it's a simple Barrier, but you're right about the rest. How is your hand?" Kane looked back at it.

"It's excruciating. I've never experienced pain like this before."

"That's saying something."

"So what do we do?"

Folas thought about it for a moment. "The Sword knows we're here. It's as if it has a consciousness of its own. See if it can penetrate the energy field."

It was a solid idea, and Kane didn't know if it would work. King Telford did not record *how* he locked Zoran and the others away. Nor did anything in the Archives describe how the old King created the barrier.

"Here goes," Kane said as he put both hands on the hilt of the weapon. With a forward motion, he rammed the invisible Barrier with the Soul Sword.

The tip of the ancient relic resisted at first. Little by little, however, it continued to push its way through.

"Help," Kane demanded. Folas stood behind Kane and placed his hands on Kane's arms. The Dark Elf used his strength to continue the motion, supporting Kane as they continued to push through whatever seal was before them.

With their combined efforts, the tip of the Soul Sword broke through. In a blinding flash of light that threw both Kane and Folas backward, the seal exploded. It made a sound so intense it hurt everyone's ears. In response, all occupants of the cave covered the sides of their heads with their hands.

Once the sound subsided, Kane and Folas stood back up, ears still ringing. A moment later, the boulders blocking the path crumbled. Bit by bit they transformed into smaller rocks, then to smaller pebbles, and eventually to dust that faded away.

Looming before Kane and Folas was a colossal cave. The Dark Elf raised his hand to illuminate the area with his Fire Magic. A large blue tail, one that coiled around the room, was the first thing anyone saw.

"What is that?" asked the Dark Elf. He motioned with his hand, following the length of tail as it coiled around the room, eventually finding its blue body and enormous head. Not unlike a serpent, the beast had a wide head extending from one side of the room to the other. Its body, while comparatively smaller, was as thick and round as a castle guard tower, though like a snake's it gradually got more and more narrow closer to the tail.

"The Leviathan," Kane said. "Look." Next to the head of the slumbering beast was another ferocious, if far smaller monstrosity.

"The Gamelyon," Folas stated. The creature's brown and tan hide reminded Kane of the coat of a deer, but with wings resembling a dragon coming out of it. Folas pointed at one of them.

"Below the wing," he said. Kane straddled the tail of the Leviathan that blocked the passageway, sliding over the slippery appendage as he entered the room.

"It's still wet." He walked toward the wing of the Gamelyon. Folas followed, noticing there were other bodies strewn about at the far end of the cave. Bear-like Graelanoid creatures dressed in battle gear and another set of blue, smaller wings obscured other creatures in the cavern. Warriors resembling Graelans, though several feet taller, held various forms of attack gear. There was a pack of other creatures he didn't recognize, though not too dissimilar to a large, fanged lizard. They appeared to walk upright on hind legs with smaller, claw-like hands. Next to them were…

"Shapeshifters." Folas remembered their loathsome appearance and vulgar-sounding language. Further in the cave behind the others were dozens of sets of wings belonging to this species. Their gold and purple coloration was recognizable even in the fire's red flame.

"That's what I thought. There he is." Folas turned around to see what Kane meant. The wing of the Gamelyon hid a man.

Not a man, Kane realized. He had similar features: a face, hands, feet, and a Graelan-sized chest and torso. "Zoran."

Each of these seemed unnatural somehow. He wore some kind of armor, a helmet with two protruding crescents, one facing left and the other right. His hands were as black as the Dark Elf, but had a stone-like appearance to them.

Zoran wore a purple and navy ensemble, one that looked regal and foreboding. His legs appeared as if they were made of granite, and he wore boots with a more squared-off shape than typical footwear. Upon a closer inspection, Kane realized none of this was clothing.

It was his *body*.

Another curiosity: Zoran's face had a Graelan, yet somehow otherworldly, appearance. Folas moved in to inspect it. Bronze with odd indentations within his skin, there was an unnatural metallic reflection even here in the darkened cave.

If Zoran was Graelan, he was the most unusual one the Dark Elf had ever seen. This was saying something, considering the various Graelanoid-like creatures he had encountered in the wilderness during the Elven exile centuries ago.

Zoran was unlike anything he had encountered in his over 580 years of living.

"Are they dead?" Kane asked. Folas leaned in close to one of the nearby bear-like Graelanoids. It wasn't breathing. He grabbed one of its arms and was able to move it with ease.

"This one lacks the usual rigor mortis of a dead body, and considering how long ago Telford sealed them away, it would have set in centuries ago. Not to mention the expected decomposition.

"But none of them are breathing either. It's as if they're frozen in time." Kane, hearing this, kneeled down and grabbed Zoran's arm. Just as Folas said, it could be moved without resistance, though Zoran showed no sign of life. His chest did not move. His muscles did not flinch. Kane even poked Zoran's metallic face and watched as his finger left an indention but quickly returned to its normal shape.

Kane laid the arm back down on Zoran's chest, trying to position it in the way he found it.

In a thoughtless moment, Kane laid the Soul Sword on the ground close to the arm he had just repositioned. Neither Kane nor Folas saw what happened next as they were busy inspecting others in the cavern.

The Soul Sword glowed once again. Meanwhile, Kane ran his hands along the edge of Gamelyon's wings.

"It's soft, yet scaly at the same time. I've only heard about this creature in legend. The Archives mentioned the great Gamelyon beast as it tortured the desert, but that was about it. There's no record of where it came from."

Folas was busy looking at the lizard-like creature he had noticed earlier. "What about this one?" Kane turned to see what the Dark Elf meant. He had to walk across the cave to inspect it. It had claws for hands and giant hind legs. Its face came to a distinct snout-like end.

Folas used his hand and raised the creature's upper lip, revealing the rest of its impressively sharp teeth. Kane felt the skin of the beast, which had a lizard-like feel to it.

Both walked around the cave to explore some more. Folas discovered something new, a group of creatures the 'Great Lizards' had obscured.

"Spiders…" Some were smaller, about the size of a rat. Of that segment, half possessed a pure black exoskeleton, while others seemed to have various levels of red, orange, and yellow throughout their bodies. Both groups nestled themselves against an even larger spider, one almost the size of a Graelan.

Thanks to the effects of gravity and Kane's meddling, Zoran's arm slid inch-by-inch off his chest.

"With this army, we can conquer Abria with ease. The twins won't have a chance!" exclaimed Kane.

A moment later, Zoran's arm finished its journey and landed on top of the blade of the Soul Sword. His eyes shot open as the Soul Sword lit up the room. Immediately, Zoran's body awoke from its slumber.

He took a deep breath and released a guttural, beastly growl. It reverberated throughout the room, echoing far down the pathways of the Cave of Tera. The Elves, still further back in the passageway, cowered in fear.

Folas and Kane reacted to the sound by once again covering their ears. Instinctively, they turned around to Zoran. Kane's eyes went from the awakened 'man' to the Soul Sword and back. The ancient relic glowed brighter than he had ever seen.

Kane ran across the cave and grabbed it before anything else could happen. He didn't know how Zoran would react, only that he wanted to retain possession of the item.

As Zoran moved, he seemed stiff, which slowed him enough for Kane to retrieve the item. Zoran rolled over and pushed himself up from the ground. When he stood, Kane realized he was easily a head and a half taller than either of them, and would eclipse most Graelans in Abria by at least half a meter.

Zoran's first words were full of rage and anger. His voice carried a sinister edge, a deep baritone with a chilling echo. Both men had heard it before: when the Shapeshifter changed its voice. It was a commanding presence, and there was an unnatural 'ting' to each word.

"Where is King Telford?"

It took some time for Folas and Kane to catch Zoran up on what year it was and what had happened since the Imprisoning. Zoran paced as he listened to the story, his body still maintaining its stiff behavior.

When Kane mentioned Telford's grave in the Royal Cemetery, Zoran stiffened up even more, almost appearing saddened. As he heard the summarized version of the first Tiernan, Davien, and now the twins, he seemed disinterested.

It was only when Folas mentioned Enid's powers that Zoran's eyes showed any other sense of emotion.

"How did she obtain these powers?" This was only the second thing Zoran had said since the Soul Sword reawakened him. His reaction told Kane – the Dark Emperor, as the Archives called him — knew something he wasn't sharing.

"The story, as we understand it, is that a large, red dragon…" Zoran turned to face the Dark Elf, "…came to her birth and transformed itself into…"

"A beam of light," Zoran finished. "Dragonborn." Zoran repeated the guttural growl from before, walked over to the nearest wall, and punched his fist through it. This time, Kane and Folas were used to the sound of Zoran's rage, though they were impressed by his physical ability to punch through the stone.

"You know of the term?" Folas asked. Zoran did not answer the question. Instead, he asked one himself.

"Why did you awaken me?" Kane and Folas exchanged a look, with the Dark Elf nodding at his companion to answer instead of him.

Kane took the lead. "We want to destroy Abria. The Royal Family has wronged each of us in ways that can never be forgiven." He moved closer to Zoran, something the latter was not used to seeing. "I want to level Castle Abria. I want to destroy Farna because I am meant to be ruler of Abria."

Zoran did not react to any of these revelations. He simply returned Kane's gaze, coldly staring back.

"My people arrived after you were sealed away. We've been subservient to the Graelan population in Abria ever since." Zoran broke the stare down and looked at Folas.

"Where did you come from?"

"The Lyra region. Far on the other side of the world. I don't know where exactly. Barbarians destroyed our homeland centuries ago, before I was born."

"Lyra..." Zoran said, though Kane didn't know why. It seemed as if Zoran recognized it, but if he did, the Dark Emperor didn't explain why.

"With this," Kane said, holding the Soul Sword, "we can awaken the rest of your army, just as it woke you. Will you help us?" Zoran eyed the relic. Kane noticed the reaction, seeing an almost lustful gaze within Zoran's eyes. In response, he gripped the weapon's hilt tighter.

Zoran answered, "I am weakened by the years of slumber. I need magic.

"But beyond that, there is one more pressing matter: the Dragonborn. My power cannot be realized while she lives." Folas began to feel uneasy with the exchange. Something about the encounter didn't sit right with him, though he couldn't put his blackened finger on what exactly.

Kane smiled. "We can help with that. If you promise to help us."

Zoran regarded him for a moment. Finally, he extended a hand. "If memory serves, I believe this is the customary way for you Graelans to 'seal a deal'."

Ignoring the 'you Graelans' comment, which Kane would need to explore later, he reached out and grabbed Zoran's hand.

"It's a deal."

Chapter 27
Intermissio Fin

A surge of sickness enveloped Tiernan as he finished writing his most recent passage. He learned of the details surrounding Zoran's unsealing from a captured high-ranking Elf. Under duress, an action Tiernan later regretted, the prisoner of war confessed to and described the events from that day.

How much truth there was to the story, or if some of the details were a bit off, Tiernan would never know for sure. The Elf didn't have a reason to lie, and everything he said seemed to flow with the way the next several years unfolded.

Tiernan took another drink. Or rather, he tried to. The cup was empty. Far across the tavern, Tammith was busy with something. He did not know how long he had been here or even what hour of the day it was.

He found himself fidgeting. More accurately, he was feeling the edge of the table where he carved the initials of his favorite saying all those years ago.

How is this closure?

"I do not want to relive these memories," he said. Tammith heard him from across the Alligator. She put down whatever she had been working on and walked over to him.

"May I sit?" Tiernan motioned to the seat across from him. Tammith flipped through the piles of pages he had written. "You've been busy. What are you planning to do with this?"

Tiernan shrugged. Would he document everything, concluding the story today with his arrival in the Valley? Would he stop writing on *that day,* the one he was dreading reliving? Or would it be what came after when he, after much struggling, realized all was lost and threw in the proverbial towel?

"The old man said people need to know what happened." Tammith didn't acknowledge the mention of the man who had somehow disappeared without a trace from her establishment. Instead, she reached out and put her hand on Tiernan's hand.

"Listen. Do you want to know why I never replaced the table, even after Dagnall and I bought it from the old owners?"

So Tammith knew about my artwork, too. "Why?"

"It's because, despite all that happened to your family, I saw strength. My husband still talks about the way your grandfather danced with him. Dagnall was only a couple of years old and it's a *core memory* for him. He attended Borun's funeral, and still speaks highly of all that man did for our town.

"You and your sister assuming the throne after your parent's passing might have been one of the hardest things you ever did. But it reinforced what all of us throughout the land saw from the Royal Family time and time again."

"Family is Strength."

"That's right. So whatever you're going to do with these papers, my King," Tiernan's eyes widened as she acknowledged his old title, "might not matter *today*. I don't think you'll know right away. Instead, do what you need to. The table is yours for as long as you need it. More water?"

Tiernan hadn't realized it, but he had teared up. Tammith's offer for more water broke through his emotions, and he began sobbing. She rubbed the top of his hand as he nodded in response to her offer. With that, Tammith walked away. Tiernan picked up the quill.

Time to record the final journey.

Chapter 28

The Big Day

Midfest was a time for celebration and excitement. Many families took vacations or planned special gatherings to celebrate the midpoint of the year. For the Royal Twins, Midfest 920NE would forever signify something else.

The Big Day.

In the months leading up to Midfest, Tiernan and Enid had come to an informal agreement. Together, they would rule Abria jointly as Prince and Princess, a unified leadership between brother and sister, until the day one of them married.

Whichever twin tied the knot first, the other would abdicate the throne. After, of course, the married twin returned from their honeymoon. The new husband and wife would ascend to it as the new formal King and Queen of the land.

Neither twin considered the implication of what a joint wedding might do to their plans, though the bond between the four of them meant it was the most natural way to move forward.

Who became the next King and Queen would have to be saved for another day.

Outside of Eislyn's window, the ocean breeze blew across the Alwyn shoreline. Her roommate, Enid, had been awake for several hours and had even gone out for a run along the beach.

"On the morning of your wedding? Are you crazy?" Eislyn laughed as Enid walked back into their suite. "I'll never understand you. Tiernan always said you were intense. I guess he wasn't kidding!"

Enid walked behind a divider in the room to where a warm bath was waiting. "Yeah, I know. But you know, my brother was probably out late last night drinking with Way." She stepped into the water, and slid down deep into the tub.

"Ahh…you know, on most days I would prefer a cold water bath after a run like that. Today, this feels right. Nice and relaxing."

Eislyn paused while combing her hair. "Aoife used to do the same: cold water baths after her training. Mom and Dad never understood it either." She closed her eyes. Enid couldn't see Eislyn from behind the divider, but she knew her soon-to-be sister-in-law well enough to know the mention of her sister came with painful memories.

"You okay out there?" Eislyn resumed combing her hair.

"Yeah, I'll be fine. It happened long ago." Eislyn closed her eyes one more time, remembering when her family had received the news. Aoife and the man who had been courting her boarded a ship in Northwick on a fishing expedition.

Unfortunately, an unexpected storm blew in and sunk their boat. After a week-long expedition, they were forced to abandon the search. No one found the bodies.

"Do you think the guys are awake yet?" Eislyn asked, changing the topic.

"Oh, you know they're not!"

"King Midir!" The attendant mockingly called out to the Manus, hoping to elicit some kind of response.

"You know not to call me that here!" Midir responded. The other person, Cosgrove, had just entered the room. This man had served with the Manus for decades. They had developed a friendly relationship in the intervening years, despite Midir's position of authority over the other.

"As you say, *my liege*." A shared chuckle. "In any case, a runner just arrived from Alwyn. Last-minute instructions from the Royal Family. Royal Couple. Couples. Whatever they are. Here." Cosgrove handed Midir a sealed envelope.

"It's going to be interesting, isn't it? I don't know how those two expect to pull off a joint leadership." Midir put the paper down. "And what do we call their spouses? Will Wayland be a prince too? Is Eislyn a princess like Enid? If so, when we say 'the Princess', to whom are we referring?"

"You're echoing what we've all been saying, Manus."

Midir picked the envelope back up. "Thanks, Cosgrove. You're dismissed." With that, the attendant walked out of the room.

Midir walked over to the desk where Tiernan often sat. Though he hated to miss the wedding, Midir recognized the importance of his presence here in Castle Abria.

After all, with the Royal Twins getting married, *someone* had to be here to run the Kingdom. Manus Midir was feeling the effects of old age, but gladly continued to serve Tiernan the First's family even into these advanced years. He was also honored the twins thought enough of him to ask him to be the temporary ruler of the Kingdom. He inspected the delivery.

"Wow, they even used the Royal Seal." Midir grabbed Tiernan's preferred letter opener and slid it through the envelope. Inside was a letter from the twins.

It wasn't instructions. It was a thank you. The upcoming Statuo, along with the uncertainty surrounding Kane and the loss of the Soul Sword, meant they decided they both wanted to get married sooner rather than later. Everyone knew this.

At the same time, each of the newlyweds planned a week-long vacation to celebrate their newfound matrimony. This letter, handwritten by one of them and signed by all four, expressed their gratitude for helping to make their special day possible.

Midir smiled and thought of the elder Tiernan. "Abria is in good hands, my old friend. May you rest easy."

Standing behind Midir, an invisible form thought to himself *Not for much longer*. With a flick of his invisible hands, one of the Dark Elf's minions returned to the Northern Plateau.

Tiernan rolled out of bed with a bit of a headache. Across the room, Wayland was still out cold. The Prince pushed himself up and sat on the edge of the mattress, hands on his head.

"Oh man, Way, why did I let you talk me into that?" Both men had spent far too long at the Drunken Alligator in Alwyn the night before. For the first time, Tiernan believed he understood the meaning behind the Alligator's name. He also remembered his comment earlier this year to his sister about outlawing public drunkenness.

Wayland began stirring. Tiernan picked up a pillow and chucked it across the room at his friend.

"Hey, loitersack," he continued, "Get up." Wayland, still lying face down, used his free hand to flip Tiernan's pillow off of his head. Tiernan shook himself to try to clear his mind. Since Wayland hadn't woken up, Tiernan stood up. He walked over to Wayland and poked his friend's exposed shoulder.

"You! *Loitersack*! This is your fault, you know that, right?" Wayland grumbled as he pushed his friend away.

"You know, loitersack is a word only *old people* use. Besides, I don't know what your problem is, T. You suggested we do something *fun*," he said, rolling his head over. He opened his eyes. "That's all on you. How did Enid put it all those years ago? That's right, your almighty, all-knowing, all-arrogant..."

"Yes, yes, whatever. But I seem to remember *you* being the one who kept ordering rounds of Lorelian Mead."

Wayland sat up and grabbed his mead-stained tunic from the edge of the bed. "Speaking of which," he said as he slid it on, "Did you feel it wasn't as good as what we had in Lorelei during Moon Rise?"

Tiernan nodded his head as he stretched while walking over to look in the mirror. His hair was a mess. He needed a shave, and his eyes looked bloodshot and hung over.

"I look like death rolled over. Eislyn is going to kill me. But yeah, I don't think it was fresh. Makes me wonder if they ship it through Northwick to bring it here by boat instead of across land."

"Going around the Windale Desert would delay it getting here for sure."

"And make it cheaper to transport." Tiernan shrugged. "I need a bath. So do you, Way, you smell like mead. My sister won't be happy if you show up looking like that."

Wayland finally stood up from the bed and walked over to the mirror where Tiernan was standing. Wayland saw his bloodshot eyes in the reflection, along with a visible layer of facial hair.

"I think the person at the check-in desk said something about a washroom in the basement."

"And yet, the girls get tubs *in* their room. That's not right." Wayland laughed.

"And so it begins, ladies first, right?"

"Which means you can use the washroom first," Tiernan teased.

"Whatever. Hey, T, I've been meaning to ask you. What will my title be? You're the Prince, she's the Princess, and that makes Eislyn and I…?"

Tiernan began to open his mouth to say something, but closed it when he realized he had *no clue*. He turned to Wayland with a mischievous grin.

"Well, we've never had a Royal Dunce before!"

Even during the Statuo, the Alwyn air had never contained this much energy. As was the tradition of an Abrian wedding, the reception was scheduled for after the honeymoon.

This meant preparations were well underway for the party that would kick off one week from today. The air was already full of aromatic smells, with the scent of baked goods and other types of treats spread out far and wide across the beaches. No matter where you were in the Alwyn region, it was impossible to avoid the aromas permeating throughout the land.

Families from all across the Kingdom were here too, including leadership from each town — save for Midir who was in charge of the Kingdom until the couples returned.

The local Drunken Alligator was acting as a central hub, storing goods and wares for the next week's party. Storage facilities had been built under the Alligator, using the cooking techniques Draydog's Emporium pioneered in the Valley to keep the perishable goods fresh and ready for the reception.

The seaside breeze, normally sweet and salty, had a distinctive aroma today. That, of course, was the smell of every type of pie, bread, and pastry one could imagine, not to mention a smorgasbord of smoked treats courtesy of Ofund's Roastery.

The guests staying in Alwyn would enjoy many of these delicacies during the honeymoon week. Others were in the process of being preserved, and many, many more would be baked in the latter half of the week leading up to the celebration.

Beyond the food, the essence of joy was thick in the air. Everyone was excited about the weddings, though many were still unsure how this joint leadership would work now that both the Prince and Princess had tied the knot.

Though, as with all things surrounding the Royal Family, there was an innate sense of trust. Whatever Tiernan and Enid decided, it would be for the best. That much was certain.

In front of a large hall, a man stood motionless. Guarding the doors, he held two giant bells in his hands. The sense of anticipation permeated throughout the soul of every person walking around Alwyn, waiting for the grand announcement.

After what seemed like an eternal wait, another man stuck his head out of the doors of the hall. The individual holding the bells snapped to attention and began swinging them.

This sound grabbed the attention of those nearby, and they alerted those deeper within Alwyn that the moment had arrived. Within a few moments, an impressive crowd gathered in front of the hall, leaving a gap in the middle of the stairs.

The doors burst open. Out walked two couples. The women were dressed in beautiful, floor length wedding gowns. Both of the men were dressed in Royal Regalia. A man appeared behind them. From the viewpoint of those in attendance, from left to right, stood Eislyn, Tiernan, Enid, and Wayland.

"Ladies and Gentlemen, it's my pleasure to introduce to you for the first time our newly wedded couples. First, Prince Tiernan and his bride, Eislyn." He motioned to Tiernan and Eislyn, next to Enid and Wayland. "And Princess Enid and her groom, Wayland!"

The crowd erupted in cheers, whoops, yells, clapping, and screaming. Throughout the assembled group, there were additional sounds of bells and attendees whistling.

As the newlyweds walked down the stairs, both of the guys began waving while holding the hands of their respective brides. The ladies reached out and hugged those they recognized while acknowledging the congratulatory wishes of those they did not know.

Tiernan twirled his new bride around and tipped her back as he leaned in for a kiss. Remembering their first back at Borun Mill, he let the moment linger.

If back then was bliss, this was a hundred-fold better.

Each couple took their honeymoon in Alwyn. Tiernan and Eislyn stayed in the home of one of the town leaders, a rich businessman who had a luxurious place along the coastline.

Enid and Wayland spent their honeymoon in one of the inns further east along the water, having rented out the best suite in the place. They reserved the rest of the rooms for the Abrian Royal Guard and various attendants, such as the chefs, bakers, and musicians for the upcoming reception.

Per their respective requests, both couples wanted privacy. In the case of Tiernan and Eislyn, the homeowner had completely blocked off their private beach access to the rest of the community. As an extra layer of protection, Abrian Royal Guards would patrol 26/7, far enough to give the couple privacy but close enough to respond to anything unexpected that might happen.

For Enid and Wayland, it was easier for sentries to protect them since most of the guards slept in the same building as the couple. As best they could, the staff kept their distance and the Royal Guards only interacted in passing.

They met up one night at the home where Tiernan and Eislyn were staying. That night, Tiernan and Wayland spent time reminiscing about their childhood. Eislyn and Enid, meanwhile, connected over their newfound sisterhood.

Kane walked through the familiar passageway he had grown accustomed to visiting. The Cave of Tera remained unexplored, though both Kane and Folas felt they were becoming experts in its winding passageways.

Zoran had retreated to the fortification at the top of the Northern Plateau. His powers were far weaker than Kane had expected, which made him doubt his quest to unseal the Dark Emperor ever had merit to begin with.

Folas was already in the cave where the rest of Zoran's army was still lying dormant.

"Why are *you* in here?" Kane asked. Folas flipped around, surprised to see Kane as well.

"Zoran said he requires sustenance. When I offered him food, he said I didn't understand. So I'm bringing him one of the dormant Shapeshifters. I think he needs their energy, their magic, or something.

"At least, I think so. I don't *think* he's going to eat it." Folas, while embracing his darker tendencies, appeared revolted by the mere concept of devouring flesh. Kane enjoyed watching his companion suffer, even if only for a moment. It reminded him of the way he would torture helpless critters during the days of his youth in Clericsfold.

At the same time, Kane shuddered. He now had a visual picture in his mind he didn't want of Zoran eating. The Dark Emperor's Graelanoid appearance betrayed his origins, and more than once had Kane questioned their decision to wake him.

"Anyway, why are *you* here?" Folas asked.

Kane pointed to one of the lizard-like creatures. "I came for one of them. I thought about using the Soul Sword to awaken it. Maybe releasing it into the fields near Idlewind." He shrugged. "Sounded like fun. They look vicious, and I'm sure it would eliminate one or two of our enemies once it roamed the desert long enough."

"Interesting idea. But…" Folas looked around the room.

"I know that look far too well. What are you thinking?" Kane followed Folas' gaze as the Dark Elf began eyeing the two giant beasts, the Leviathan and Gamelyon.

"Why don't we give the Royal Couples a belated wedding gift?" suggested Folas.

In the center of Alwyn, a giant table sat under a large open tent. It was ornate and classically decorated, using some of the best glassware and place settings in all of Abria.

Sitting at the table from left to right were Tiernan, Eislyn, Enid, and Wayland. They were once again dressed in their wedding attire, with perhaps less formality than a week earlier.

Throughout the Alwyn streets, market, and deep into the beach areas were tables and chairs, all strategically positioned under tents to protect the people from the hot sun. Many of these had been here all week, with a few exceptions such as wedding guests who were unable to stay all week waiting for the reception and instead had to return home for various responsibilities.

Tiernan used his fork to tap his glass. Those within earshot stopped talking to listen to him. As the hush fell over the front tables, the silence continued spreading.

Tiernan used his loudest possible voice to address the crowd. "Friends, Eislyn and myself, my sister, and yes, even my lame friend Wayland," he said, which elicited some nearby laughter, "want to thank you for helping us celebrate this wondrous occasion. Most of you know what happened to our parents earlier this year." Enid's face turned sad at the mention of Davien and Kyrie.

"The days that followed were lonely for both of us, sometimes on different days, and sometimes even at the same time.

"But, even in the midst of our sadness, we felt the love of everyone in this Kingdom. We feel it here again today." He sat, and Enid stood up next.

"Well, I'm not as good with words as my brother. He loves to hear his own voice. I tend to prefer fighting over talking. Or running." More laughter as those in attendance recalled her many first-place finishes.

"But everything he said is true. For all we've gone through, there are three words Tiernan likes to remind us of time and time again." She looked at the others at the table. "Get up," she whispered. Grabbing the hands of Wayland and Eislyn next to her, who grabbed her husband's hand too, Enid spoke one more time.

"Family is strength."

The four of them repeated it in unison. Tiernan leaned over and kissed his bride. Wayland first hugged Enid, afterward kissing her — though as with all things between them, the kiss lasted far longer than usual.

"Hey man, cut that out. Get a room," joked Tiernan. Wayland opened his eyes and stepped away from Enid for a moment.

"Prince to Prince, T? Mind your own business." The comment made Tiernan laugh as he wrapped his arm around Wayland's shoulder in a half-hug.

Meanwhile, those in attendance had gotten caught up in the moment, with echoes of the sentiment carrying across the Alwyn air. "Family is strength!" Some close to the head table took a cue from Wayland and kissed their spouses, professing their continuing love for each other. Others took drinks from their glasses, whether Dorian Ale, Lorelian Mead, or water.

Eventually, the ruckus died down. The two couples sat back down as the feast began.

"You ready to go home?" Eislyn asked Enid.

"No, not at all. This has been nice. First downtime I've had in a long time."

"Maybe we should rotate schedules?" butted in Tiernan. "You know, you take a week away. Eislyn and I will be in charge. You and Way can be in charge when we take a week off. What do you think, Sis?"

"Maybe. I dunno, I'm sure Midir would gladly 'ascend to the throne' for us again too, if we wanted time off at the same time." She leaned her head on Eislyn's shoulder. "I've become kind of fond of my sister here." Eislyn closed her eyes as she leaned her head on top of Enid's. With Aoife gone, Enid had softened the sting of loss.

After the meal was well underway, each couple spent time in conversation with their new spouse. After a humorous chat with Tiernan, Eislyn looked back out across the assembled crowd.

"You know, T, I don't think it sunk in to me what it meant to marry the Prince. I'm not sure I'm ready for this."

"Neither was my mother, and she did a fine job. You'll do great, Eislyn." He leaned back in his chair to ask Wayland if his parents would move into Castle Abria. Eislyn's had declined, choosing to stay closer in Farna to their beloved Alligator.

While the two chatted, Eislyn began noticing a dark cloud on the distant horizon. It was far out in the ocean, well beyond the coastline. She took a drink from her glass, looked at the men as they talked, and back at the cloud.

It was growing exponentially and appeared to be moving closer to the coast. She nudged her husband.

"Are we going to have to cancel this? Look."

"Hmm?" Tiernan hadn't noticed until Eislyn said something, but once he did, it sent a chill through his body. *That's no cloud. Where's the Mind Shield?* He looked around and saw it behind him on the ground, just behind the table.

"Enid." His voice carried with it a sense of fear and concern.

"What, Brother? Can't you let me enjoy a…" Tiernan pointed to the coastline. "Oh. Oh, no." The same concern, a pit-in-your-stomach understanding of an omen, hit the Dragonborn, too. By the time Enid saw it, the cloud had grown larger and was almost impossible to ignore.

"Guys, the wind is picking up," said Wayland. Others in the crowd were noticing the change in the weather, with many pointing to the incoming storm.

"The temperature is dropping. Fast. I think we need to get the people inside," said Enid. Wayland was proud of his wife and the way she went from her newlywed bliss to her status as Protector in just the blink of an eye.

Tiernan stood up. He motioned to the Abrian Royal Guards nearby. "Get these people to safety. The hall, the Archives, anywhere. Get them off of the…"

"Tiernan!" Eislyn yelled, cutting him off before he could say 'beaches'. Tiernan turned back to his wife, whose gaze was fixated on the shoreline.

Now, the cloud cover had extended well beyond the waters and had encroached not only on the shoreline, but well into the city of Alwyn itself. And as if the bad omen revealing itself, a giant whirlpool circling just past the coastline shelf was growing.

Without warning, a hard rain pelted people with painful, sharp blasts of water. A few hit Eislyn's skin, and it reminded her of what she experienced in the fields north of Clericsfold.

Lightning flashed across the sky. Thunder rumbled. The wind howled.

Tiernan looked back at the guards, all of whom had already begun moving people to safety. He snapped into Protector mode himself.

"I said move! Let's go, people. Get everyone inside. Take them to the Alwyn Böchord or Gléineach Hall. Now!" Enid and

Wayland jumped up from the table and began directing people. Tiernan looked back at his wife.

"I want you to take the Mind Shield. Get to the Böchord." She shook her head in defiance.

"I stay with you. You may be half of the so-called Protectors, but you're also my husband. Let me help." He kissed her as the ground rumbled.

"T!" This time it was Wayland who stared at the coastline. First, a massive blue tail rose out of the water. It flipped back and forth, stirring up more water as its monstrous head emerged.

Leviathan, the Scourge of the Ocean, had returned.

Far above, in the skies over the town of Idlewind, a monstrous shadow appeared over the city. Residents noticed it one by one until its form began to block out the sun as others pointed at the emerging shape.

Few had heard of, let alone seen, a creature of this size. The last time something similar was anywhere near Idlewind was when the white dragon appeared. This was smaller, yet far more sinister and foreboding than those beasts.

As it came into focus, residents noticed it had the face of a beast no one knew, the legs and body of a bear, and the tail and wings of a dragon.

A frail, old woman in the crowd realized what she was seeing. It was the Scourge of the Desert she had heard about from her great grandmother. A beast no one truly believed was real until this exact moment. In her fear, she yelled its name.

"Gamelyon!" No one knew what a Gamelyon was or what it meant. Gradually, the beast continued to descend. Its wings stirred up the desert, causing blinding storms to overtake those outside of the protection of the Idlewind walls, burying and suffocating many in thick sand.

As it made its approach, it hovered over the southern half of the city. Finally, Gamelyon landed on the house of Manus Midir, a symbolic gesture from the Divider and his Elven accomplice. The beast's feet flattened the home while its wings knocked down other nearby residences.

The beast let out a loud growl. It lowered its wings to knock down multiple nearby structures. Some people were caught up in the wind, tossed around as if they were nothing more than rag dolls. A few hit the walls of the city, cracking their heads on the stone enclosures. Most of those who did never woke up again.

Idlewind's southern region was now completely under siege from the beast. City guards began directing people northbound toward what was normally the market region. If they could evacuate enough of the citizens, they could use the gates between the two sections to shut themselves in.

But how long would such a defense last?

Leviathan was the largest — and ugliest — thing Wayland had ever seen. Its body coiled around like a snake with occasional spikes near the tip of its narrow tail. Its body possessed a deep blue color with scattered white sections. There were portions of Leviathan's torso — if it could be called that — with a ribbed texture. It looked almost damaged, and these areas were rougher than the rest of its smooth body.

Its head extended left to right, well past the size of its body. It had a ridge that ran around the top of its head with a chin — or perhaps face area, no one could tell. This came to a v-like peak. Both sides of its head had large tips.

Leviathan's mouth was a single hole where a deep red recess seemed to form. On what could only be described as its chest, there was a single red pulsating orb in the middle of its ribbed torso.

Once the beast emerged from the water, its size created an imposing shadow on the entire town of Alwyn. With one swipe of its tail, it crushed the nearby docks and a few boats waiting to be unloaded.

Wayland continued to direct people toward the Böchord when the beast released its first major attack. A forceful stream of water emerged from the points on both sides of its head.

"Water? Where is that coming from?" he asked Enid.

"I don't think it's natural, Way. It has to be Kane *somehow.*" The blasts of water crushed structures along the coastline. With its speed, a few errant people who couldn't move fast enough got caught in the blast. The impact of the water buried their bodies deep into the sand.

It was impossible to know if they survived, nor was there time to mount a rescue attempt with so many more people trying to make it to safety.

"We have to stop it," Enid said.

"Yeah, but how?" Wayland asked. Enid realized her favorite axe was back at the inn. The only thing she had on her was the Power Ring, which she never took off.

"I can use this," she said impulsively. Enid ran off toward the beast.

"Enid, no!" Wayland motioned for a guard. "Keep these people moving. Give me your sword and shield." The guard nodded and handed them both to Wayland.

"I'm coming, my love." Wayland ran after Enid, who had just taken up an offensive spot on the beach. She closed her eyes, summoning her fire-based dragon attack.

The magic of the Power Ring surged through Enid's body, taking charge as she opened her eyes. They were full of flame and poised to strike. Wayland thought he could see a vague, ghostly outline of wings made of fire emerging from her back.

Whatever she was doing, it was drawing out the power of the dragon within her. Enid raised her hands to attack.

Leviathan saw her and raised its tail to strike down its opponent. From the shoreline, Tiernan saw the attack coming. Too distant to do anything, his world crumbled in slow motion as he watched the unthinkable happen.

"Enid, no!" Tiernan yelled. He grabbed the Mind Shield and rushed toward his sister. Eislyn continued to direct the evacuation effort in lieu of her husband.

However, despite his speed, Tiernan was too far away to do anything. The tail of Leviathan came down swift and ready to crush its attacker. At the same time, a large ball of Fire Magic began to emerge from Enid's body.

Whether it would strike first or she, no one was sure. Before anyone could find out, a voice cried out: "Enid!"

It came from Wayland. He pushed Enid out of the way of the beast's tail just as it came crashing down. He landed hard, though far enough away that Leviathan's attack missed both of them.

This enraged the beast as it began searching for the person who ruined its mission. Enid's Fire Magic disappeared as she turned around to look for the person who saved her life.

In her heart, she knew who it was. She had hoped she was wrong. Enid stood and turned, making eye contact with her beloved just as he rose to his feet. After landing flat on his chest, he had a layer of sand caked on his freckled face and throughout his curly blonde hair. The shirt he wore for their wedding, a custom-made gift from her, tore when he fell.

Enid and Wayland exchanged a look. It said all that needed to be said.

I love you. Always.

Get out of here! Run!

The focus of Leviathan now shifted toward a different victim: Wayland. His push had put Enid out of harm's way, but there was no one to do the same for him. Leviathan bellowed and raised its tail, poised to strike. Wayland tried to turn and run, but to no avail.

Leviathan raised its tail and swung it at the helpless warrior. It caught him squarely in the chest, causing Wayland to drop his weapons in the ensuing impact. As Leviathan's tail continued its momentum, Wayland went with it.

Helpless, Enid watched as Leviathan tossed Wayland far out into the ocean. Time stood still for everyone watching as they witnessed his body hit the water's surface with a hard 'thump' and immediately sink.

A moment passed. Then another. Then two more.

He never resurfaced.

In an instant, Wayland — husband to Enid, friend of Tiernan, repeat victor of the Statuo, and respected warrior of Abria — was gone.

"Noooooo!" cried Enid. Her despair turned to unadulterated rage as she turned to face the giant beast once again. In a show of power unlike anything Tiernan had ever witnessed from anyone, Enid's entire body lit up like a flame. Her eyes glazed over in a white-hot fire. Blazing red energy swirled around her, including her hands where two searing white-hot balls of energy began forming. She clasped them together. Like before, a dragon-like, ghostly persona appeared around her body, with fiery wings spreading out as wide as Leviathan's head.

The Dragonborn charged her magic.

Everyone still on the shoreline watched in awe as the ancient power deep within Enid manifested itself. Her eyes flared with a powerful glow, fully white-hot and glazed over with energy. Her body soared high in the air, coming face-to-face with Leviathan.

In one final swift moment, Enid opened both of her hands and released the full fury of her firepower directly onto the head of the Leviathan. The stream of energy was consistent and intense, burning the top of the creature's head from end to end. She continued her attack, bringing the streams of her magic further down its body and scorching its chest. This caused Leviathan immense pain, with its bellowing cries echoing throughout Alwyn.

It thrashed back and forth for a few moments, taking out the seaside house where Tiernan and Eislyn had stayed. Unable to contain the blaze and feeling portions of its body beginning to crisp, Leviathan retreated into the depths of the water to extinguish the flame.

Immediately, the rain stopped. The clouds cleared and the sun broke through. The waters calmed down and the sounds of seagulls returned.

The smell of charred fish filtered through the air, a remnant of the Dragonborn's attack. Peace returned to those in Alwyn.

Except for Enid, whose grief overwhelmed her. She fell to her knees sobbing, mourning the lost love of her life. Still glowing with her power, she looked up at the sky and screamed. Her outstretched palms glowed with Dragonborn energy, which she emitted high into the sky as an unintentional — yet fitting — tribute to her beloved Wayland.

Chapter 29
The Only Option

The search for Wayland lasted for well over a week, though the surviving ships from the Alwyn docks were limited in their capacity. Leviathan had destroyed many of them in its attack, which hampered rescue efforts. After ten days of searching, Enid called it.

Wayland was gone.

Tiernan cautiously walked into the open dining hall, now acting as the Abrian War Room, where his sister had been for the past few hours.

The day was 21 Fawnmist. Earlier in the morning, they had held a memorial service for Wayland, though with no body there was nothing to bury. Instead, they would need another way to honor him. Enid selected a spot to be set aside in the Royal Cemetery for her departed beloved. And, much like the statue for Borun in the Valley, Tiernan commissioned a similar one for his best friend and all-too-short lived brother-in-law.

After the service, Enid had retreated here: the room where she first found her treasured axe. Tiernan wasn't exactly sure of the significance of this particular room or if it had any meaning to his sister. Her repeated visits here naturally turned the room into a planning space for the battles ahead.

Tiernan stepped through the doorway. Enid leaned against the table facing the southern wall with her arms crossed, staring blankly at the spot where her axe used to hang.

"If I've told you once, Tiernan, I've told you a hundred times: you walk like a horse. I heard you coming from down the hall. What do you want, Brother?" She turned to him and pulled out a chair to sit, crossing her feet on the table as Tiernan finished walking the rest of the way into the room.

"You know why I'm here, Sis." She made a dismissive sound, leaning her head back against the chair with her eyes closed. Tiernan lowered his head, sadness filling the air. Enid realized how her reaction came across.

"I'm sorry, T. That wasn't directed at you. It's just…Grandpa. Mom and Dad. Now, Way." She opened her eyes, looking at her brother sideways. "Who *else* is going to die before this is over?"

"I know. I've had the same thought. I don't think…" Whatever Tiernan was going to say no longer mattered. Into the room walked Midir, his face drained of all color. He pulled out a chair and slumped into it while staring at the table, a blank expression on his face.

"Manus Midir," Tiernan said. "Are…are you okay?" Midir shook his head.

"A messenger just arrived from the desert. Leviathan wasn't the only attack in Abria on 7 Fawnmist. A beast known as Gamelyon leveled many sections of Idlewind in my absence. It later retreated, perhaps somehow in response to Enid's attack on the water beast.

"Why it chose Idlewind, no one knows. It took the Council over a week to find an uninjured runner capable of making the trip across the Kingdom. I just informed them of the attack on Alwyn. They're heading back home now.

"But, in any case, Idlewind suffered many casualties, and the damage is extensive. Apparently, most of the residential area was utterly destroyed."

Enid removed her feet from the table and sat forward. "It has to be Kane." Tiernan assumed this as well, but remained silent.

"Do the two of you remember hearing, maybe from your father, about my encounter with Kane? It was several years ago, in Clericsfold, when we were trying to negotiate the terms of the first Statuo. I know you were small when it happened, so maybe you haven't."

"No, we have. Dad mentioned something about a person named Zoran," Tiernan answered.

"Right. And Kane wanted to unseal Zoran, who was hidden away somewhere in the land. The passage I read also mentioned two beasts: Leviathan and Gamelyon. I think it's safe to assume Leviathan was the one who attacked Alwyn, especially if a creature known as Gamelyon just leveled portions of Idlewind."

"If both of those beasts are active again..." began Enid.

"...it probably means Zoran is as well," finished Tiernan. He stood up from the table and shoved his chair into it. He rubbed his forehead, thinking. "Who is Zoran? What is Kane's obsession with this person from so many years ago?" Tiernan looked at the other two and received equally confused looks from both.

Standing in the hallway, a nervous guard knocked on the door. All three looked his way.

"I'm sorry. I don't mean to intrude." The guard removed his helmet. "My name is Lucerne. I've served in the Abrian Guard since..." He shook his head, barely able to contain his tears.

He regrouped and continued, "...since Kane made me and six other orphans from Clericsfold put on a makeshift demonstration in the Rosewood Forest." The use of the old name for the Forest piqued Tiernan's curiosity. He motioned for Lucerne to sit.

"Thank you, sir. One day, Kane came to the orphanage, enraged."

"The one in Clericsfold?" asked Midir.

Lucerne nodded. "That's right, before Abria opened the two smaller ones. It was during the Clericsfold dispute and well before the planning of the first Statuo.

"Kane conscripted seven of us, along with a man named Lennart, to stage a fake attack on wild bears in the Forest."

"That…doesn't sound like it would accomplish anything besides make the bears angry at your group," stated Enid.

"You're right. The plan felt rushed, incomplete. I'll explain more in a moment. But you should first know: I was the *only* survivor. During the assault, a bear threw me against a tree. It knocked the wind out of me, and I slumped to the ground while another bear trampled a friend of mine.

"Everyone thought I was dead from the impact, including Kane and even the bears. I did everything I could to keep the charade going.

"Until?" asked Enid.

"Well, see, the commotion attracted the attention of Folas, the Elf we all now refer to as the Dark Elf."

"The one who killed Mom and Dad," Tiernan stated coldly. Lucerne closed his eyes, reflecting on the loss of the King and Queen. He threw his arms up in the air in frustration.

"Kane's plan was *ridiculous*. He thought he could convince the Elves that a group of rogue guards came to the Forest to cause problems or something. And somehow our actions would cause the bear population, in their rage, to turn and attack the Elves.

"The Elves would blame Graelans, specifically the Abrian Royal Guard, and naturally align with Kane."

"Not a great plan. There are gaps in his logic." Enid's voice carried nothing but disdain for the man who took her beloved from her.

"Folas called him out on it. And Kane admitted it was a weak plan, but that his anger got the best of him."

"This could be an important detail. It gives insight into Kane's strategic thinking, or lack thereof. So how did you escape?" asked Midir.

"Like I said, I took a hard blow. I laid there as still and as quiet as I could, and…" Lucerne closed his eyes, reliving the heartbreaking memories he had tried to bury. Enid reached out across the table to touch his hand.

"It's okay," she said.

Lucerne smiled as he opened his eyes. "Let's just say I did my best to act as if I was dead. I guess it worked. I overheard all of their plans."

Tiernan stiffened. "*All* of them?"

"Well, not all. Enough to realize if I ever revealed myself anywhere in Clericsfold, I would be a dead man walking. That's why, when I came here, I lied and changed my story about who I was and where I was from. I joined the Abrian Royal Guard as a trainee as soon as I arrived."

"What are you now?" asked Midir.

"Nothing special. I had to stay out of sight as much as I could. I volunteered to take every odd posting I could to stay away from Castle Abria during each Statuo. After, when you moved the games, I would volunteer for duty here."

Tiernan's face softened. *This poor guy was nothing more than a scared kid when he came to Farna. An orphan, like Dad.* "So, like you said, you overheard their plan?"

"Yes, my liege."

"Just call me Tiernan. You've been through enough. No formalities." Midir smiled, recalling the time Davien said something similar during the initial Statuo planning at Borun Mill.

"That's a little weird, but I'll try. While I was laying there, Folas talked about where he came from, the Elves' journey of exile from their homeland, how many died on their way here, and how King Tel-something invited them in.

"He also blamed the Royal Family for keeping the Elves locked away in the Rosewood Forest for all these years."

"That's unfair," said Enid. "The Elves who moved to Oakshadow had been nothing but grateful until Kane started causing problems."

"Is it possible this was a view only Folas himself held? And, with his unique height and power, he swayed others," Midir suggested.

"I don't know. What I do know is Kane also talked about Zoran and what he had learned about him from the Archives."

"Tell us!" exclaimed Tiernan. Enid shot her brother a look to say 'slow down', though deep down she was also ready for the reveal.

Tiernan cleared his throat and explained his eagerness. "No one else has seen those volumes in any extensive detail, so what you know is more than any of us here."

"Well, my friend Jothan would be better to tell you about some of those details. He serves here too, defecting to Abria during the tensions with Clericsfold."

Midir's head tilted at the mention of the name Jothan. "That's a name I think I remember. Tell me, did Jothan serve as a city guard for Clericsfold?"

"He did. I think he's out on patrol outside of the walls of Farna."

"Bring him here," Enid said, turning to a guard standing watch by the doorway. The guard turned to retrieve Jothan. "Continue, Lucerne. What else do you know?"

"Zoran is not a normal person like you or I. He doesn't come from Abria, but the Archives didn't say much beyond that. As far as Kane could find, anyway.

"It was also said in those books Zoran controlled a vast army of creatures: the two great beasts that, from what I overheard just now, sound like they just attacked Abria. Plus, there was talk of a group, something called Shapeshifters, among others. That Tel-guy sealed them all away under the Northern Plateau. And they were supposed to stay there as long as the Soul Sword remained in Abria's possession."

Enid and Tiernan traded a sick expression as all the blood drained from their faces. They had kept the loss of the Soul Sword between themselves, at least until this moment. Midir saw the exchange and lowered his head, disheartened.

"You've got to be kidding me. You two are terrible liars. Don't even try to cover it. I can see it on your faces." Both of the twins looked at Midir. "Let me guess: you've lost it, haven't you? That's..." His voice softened and drifted off as he made the connection. "I'm sorry, you guys. That's when your parents died. Davien had the Soul Sword with him, didn't he?"

Both Tiernan and Enid nodded, and Lucerne's eyes widened at the revelation.

"You have to get it back. With the sword, he can unleash Zoran upon Abria again."

"I think that's what has happened already, young man. Think about it. If Zoran and the beasts were sealed away *together*, and two of them have shown up, it must mean the others aren't far behind," explained Midir.

Tiernan nodded. "I wouldn't be surprised if we start seeing more of Zoran's forces throughout Abria. Midir, you need to know what happened."

"I'm all ears, Tiernan."

"They captured Eislyn. We tried to stage a rescue, and Dad took the Soul Sword with him to try to defeat Kane and the Dark Elf once and for all while Enid, Wayland, and myself rescued her."

Tiernan swallowed hard. "Like Kane's plan in the Forest, ours backfired too. Mom and Dad didn't come home, and Kane stole the Soul Sword."

Midir sighed. "Well, I can definitely see why things played out the way they did. Davien wanted to destroy the relics once this was all over."

He paused, regrouping. "Alright, so this is what we know so far. A 'vaguely Graelanoid-like evil entity', let's call Zoran that for now, is out there, now unleashed in a way we don't understand.

"Meanwhile, two of his main minions? Henchmen? Monsters? Whatever you want to call them, I guess. They just attacked Abria at the same time in two different regions.

"We also know Kane and Folas have aligned, but we haven't seen them since they killed the King and Queen. I feel like there is a piece missing still."

Tiernan and Enid looked back and forth between themselves and Midir. Finally, Tiernan looked at Lucerne again. "Is there anything else they said that maybe you forgot?"

Lucerne focused hard, trying to remember. "I was in pain, trying to stay quiet. They talked for so long." He put his elbows on the table and rested his face on both of his palms. "They mentioned the Soul Sword and…" Lucerne raised his head in fear.

"What?" Tiernan asked, feeling the sickening pit grow in his stomach.

"Kane said something about the magic that keeps Farna a paradise."

Enid, despite still stewing in her grief, managed a small laugh. "That's just a rumor."

"Is it?" asked Midir. "Think about it, Enid. Thirty years ago, I might have said the same thing. But now? We have magic swords, shields, and rings — including the one you're wearing. No offense, your highness, but Dragonborn powers aren't *exactly* common around here. I don't know of any other mage in all the land."

"There was another," she said, clenching her fist and slamming it on the table. "Wayland. He couldn't maintain his powers without my help, but he had them deep within."

"I'm sorry, I did not mean to bring up…" Enid raised her hand at Midir's apology as if to say it was unneeded.

"Midir is right," interjected Tiernan. "No one knows why Farna is a paradise, even in the middle of the season of Frost. I mean, let's face it, outside of the Abrian Plateau it can be deathly hot during the season of Flame, but absolutely perfect weather in here."

"Fine, I'll buy that, T. There's magic somewhere below Farna. But so what? What is this magic? How do we find it? And why do they need it?" Enid's verbal questions were what everyone else was thinking as well. Finally, Lucerne spoke up.

"Before Kane and the Dark Elf left, he said something about needing both the Soul Sword and the rumored magic underground to unseal Zoran. He's already done that, but correct me if I'm wrong, no one has seen Zoran. Just the beasts."

"That's right. What are you getting at?" asked Tiernan.

"What if the magic of Farna is what *Zoran* needs? Like an energy boost." Those words hit Enid hard, as it was the phrase she and Wayland used to describe the way she would transfer some of her magic to him.

Jothan walked in. Tiernan motioned for him to sit. Midir reached out to shake Jothan's hand.

"Nice to see you again. It's been a long time."

"Likewise, sir. I'm surprised you remember me. Why am I here?"

"Zoran?" asked Midir.

"Ah. Yes. Kane and Folas talked a lot about him in the old Clericsfold Archives, at least before I heard enough and left. I'll tell you everything I know."

"Why did you leave? When you escorted me through Clericsfold, you seemed..." Midir searched for the word. "Content."

"Looks can be deceiving, Manus. It was an unjust war. It only happened because Kane used his political influence to sway the Council his way."

"Can we back up a bit?" Tiernan asked. "Start with the basics. How often did you observe the two of them talking about Zoran?" He asked pointedly.

"Only a handful. A few years before the first Statuo, I left the city and tried to make a living for myself in Alwyn. That was before I came here and joined the Abrian Royal Guard.

"The first time I heard them talking about Zoran was accidental. I overheard from outside of the door to the main study area. The rest I was more cautious, trying to piece together what they would discuss with what I had already heard.

"It didn't always make sense. They talked a lot about Shapeshifters too. I think I saw one myself, actually. A raven landed behind a man, transformed into an awful, ugly creature, and absorbed the man's body *into* him. It turned into the man and began walking northbound."

"Toward the Northern Plateau?" Enid asked.

"That would make sense, yes, but I could only see so far."

"Do you know anything about magic below the surface of Farna?" she followed-up.

"Yes, your highness. One time during a heated conversation, Kane and Folas argued whether there was something magical below Farna."

"We've used the Abrian Royal Guard to explore all the catacombs below Castle Abria ever since Dad learned of the ancient relics in the first place. There's nothing down there but abandoned rooms and blocked passageways," Tiernan interjected.

"The Cave of Tera," mumbled Midir, remembering the dragon flight he and Borun took many years ago. "There are caves throughout the countryside, right?" Tiernan nodded. "But, the Cave of Tera?"

"Oh, that's barely explored," Tiernan said. "Much like Kingscrown Rock, the path inside always seemed to be more confusing and treacherous than any expedition could handle."

Enid closed her eyes at the mention of Kingscrown, reflecting on the time spent with her lost love on their first date. Finally, she spoke up again. "Do we have *anything* to go off of besides all of this speculation? We *think* Zoran needs energy. We *think* we can get there through the Cave of Tera. We're thinking a lot of things here, but what happens if we're wrong?"

It was a valid question. Finally, Midir made a suggestion.

"We don't know until we try. And since the two of you are needed here, there's only one solution."

"Manus…"

"No titles. Remember, Tiernan? Those were your words. Besides," he said, accepting reality. "I'm old. I've been around for a while. After all, I grew up with your uncle when he was a boy. If I'm being perfectly honest, I always preferred to be in the middle of the action. And, if things go wrong, well, it's okay. I've lived a long and happy life as it stands."

"But what about your son?" Enid interjected.

"Rhys understands the importance of sacrifice." Midir's answer didn't sit well with anyone in the room, but nor could they come up with a reasonable objection to his offer.

It was Lucerne who broke the silence in the room. "I'll go with you," he offered. "You'll need a trained guard."

"Count me in too," echoed Jothan.

"We should send more than just Lucerne and Jothan with you, no offense," said Enid to the guards. "Also, what if the three of you encounter trouble?"

"A small squad then. Ten or twelve, perhaps. Lucerne, Jothan, the two of you will be my right-hand men. Tiernan, I'll need a runner too, someone who can return to Castle Abria quickly in the event the worst happens to us."

Midir's group set out for the Cave of Tera the morning of the 22nd day of Fawnmist. Enid sent a total of fifteen with him: one runner, Lucerne, Jothan, and twelve additional members of the Abrian Royal Guard. They expected to arrive by the next evening.

Tiernan looked at the calendar in his journal. "24 Fawnmist. If they encountered trouble, surely the runner would have returned by now?"

A horrible thought crossed his mind. *Unless they're all dead.* He heard someone walking down the hall. Tiernan poked his head out and saw his sister.

"Hey, Sis." Enid refused to meet his gaze. Tiernan didn't know if her grief was still consuming her or if she was nervous. *Probably both.*

On the morning of 26 Fawnmist, Enid rose early for a run. She had to do *something*. Her course took her along the initial portions of the route of the first Statuo race.

We're going to have to cancel it this year, aren't we? Enid's rage boiled up, and she used her magic to ignite a nearby shrub. Just as fast, guilt consumed her. She turned around and walked back to it.

Wayland, my love. With your frost powers…

Enid had tried to contain her emotions. In the nineteen days since she lost him, she had only cried twice in public.

Today was number three. Enid fell to her knees, yelled with all of her might, and slammed her fist into the ground. After granting herself this moment of sadness, she used her restorative powers to return the shrub back to normal.

She cut her run short, returning to the castle from that exact spot. She saw Tiernan walking as she entered the main hall. He nodded, but continued to wherever he was going.

I'm sorry, Brother. I can't talk…

4 Flametide began like any other day, except Eislyn was already awake when her husband got out of bed. She watched him grab his robe and head to their washroom. He didn't say a word. She could feel his apprehension.

Not only his. Enid's fear, combined with Tiernan's has consumed the castle. Midir, please come back soon…

By the afternoon, they would have their answer. An anxious guard burst into the throne room. Enid was alone; she had no idea where her brother was.

"Yes?" was all she could ask. The guard, out of breath, answered in a dismayed tone.

"Midir's runner has returned."

Tiernan was tired of meetings. He was ready for action. Still, he needed to learn what had happened, and the runner was waiting for the twins in the War Room.

Tiernan walked in to see his sister sitting with the runner, who wasn't saying anything. Several guards were in the room, as well as a small group in the hallway, as heightened emotions following Midir's absence had everyone on edge.

Tiernan sat. "I'm not sure I'm ready to hear what you have to say," he said to the runner.

"Midir explored the Cave of Tera, just like you asked. He first went north. They traveled this way for a long time. There, he found the ancient cave where King Telford sealed away Zoran.

"Subsequently, his...*legion* returned south and found a passage that brought them to a cavern directly under Castle Abria."

Enid and Tiernan sat side by side, listening to the runner's story. Both twins had the same unsettled look on their faces. Tiernan turned his head at the mention of the word 'legion,' especially with the way the runner oddly emphasized it.

To Enid, something told her to be on guard, though she couldn't quite put her finger on what exactly.

"So, what happened?" Tiernan asked.

Enid spoke up. "Wait, T." She cleared her throat. Her brother shot her a confused look. "You said Midir traveled *north*? Why?"

"Under Castle Abria is the sum of all Graelan magic."

"That's not what I asked you, and your answer sounds more like a riddle than anything. What do you mean, exactly?" Enid asked. "'The sum of all Graelan magic.' Why did Midir go north? Explain."

"It's what Midir said. I don't know what he meant. I'm just a messenger. I only know that below Farna is a magic beyond what *any* of us can understand."

Enid removed her hand from the table and clenched her fist, summoning some of her magic out of sight. *Something doesn't feel right.*

"So, where is Midir?" asked Tiernan.

"Dead. The other knights who were with him fought valiantly, but Zoran was too strong. He killed them all. I barely escaped." Enid tried not to react, but under the table she opened her palm, ready to strike.

"What were the names of the 'knights'?" Tiernan looked at his sister as it dawned on him, too.

Abria doesn't have knights. That term fell out of use around the fifth century.

"I don't remember, it all happ…" Enid couldn't wait any longer. In an instant, she stood to her feet and threw her Glass Magic powers at the runner. It encompassed their chest, freezing them in place.

"Liar. Who are you?" The runner's face twisted and distorted. A beak-like protrusion formed where a Graelan mouth once existed. Its hands, while immobilized at its side from the attack, grew long, talon-like claws in place of the fingers that were there only a few seconds earlier.

Immediately, it stopped uttering Graelan words. Instead, it vocalized an unintelligible series of ticks and clicks.

"Is this a Shapeshifter?" Tiernan asked as he rose to his feet. "Guards!" The group in the room already had their swords drawn. Another rushed into the room, poised to attack. The creature began twisting and turning, trying to break free of Enid's attack.

It was fruitless, of course, and within a moment, swords surrounded it at every angle. It made an unintelligible cry before it resigned itself to its fate. The Shapeshifter transformed its face — and only its face — back into a Graelan form to communicate again.

"They. Are. Our. Captives." Each word was split between a tick or a click, as the Shapeshifter fought between its natural form and its Graelan disguise. "Below. The. Power. Of. Abria. We. Claim. As. Ours."

"Prince Tiernan, look out!" The Shapeshifter's claw began to move, primed full of magic. Finally, it broke free of Enid's glass casing, shattering it in a final defiant act. It raised its hand in Tiernan's direction as it fired a blast of some kind of pink magic toward the Prince.

The guard who yelled jumped in the way, taking the full brunt of the blow. The other guards immediately thrust their swords into the creature, which let out a violent and ear-piecing sound before reverting to its natural shape and dying.

The guard who absorbed the blast landed on the table. Tiernan stretched out his hand to the man, helping him stand to his feet.

"Are you okay?" Tiernan asked. The man bent over and coughed several times. Tiernan reached out to grab him, but the guard just pushed him away.

"I think I'll be fine. What was that? It looked pink. Did anyone else see what happened?"

Enid nodded, moving closer to the dead Shapeshifter's body. "We're just learning about magic, so I don't know what that was. It wasn't any of the usual forms of attack magic." The man righted himself and stood at attention before them.

"Well, whatever it was, it didn't seem to do any kind of harm. I feel fine."

Chapter 30

A Personal Statuo

Folas opened his eyes and turned to Kane. The Dark Elf smiled. "For once, your plan worked. The Shapeshifter gave me a direct view of the twins, even with the Mind Shield right next to them. And before it died, it infected one of their guards."

"Did they take the bait?" Kane asked. Before Folas could answer, one of the guards grunted. Kane turned to the prisoners, each bound at their ankles along with their wrists behind their individual backs. In addition, none of them could talk because Kane gagged them upon capture.

"Something you want to say?" Kane asked. Midir tried to elbow the guard, who was growing restless. The man began trying to break free.

"I tire of this. Kane, deal with him," Folas demanded. Kane grabbed the Soul Sword and walked over to the prisoners. He grabbed the guard by the hair.

"You know, I've been thinking and I'm pretty sure I remember your face. You used to serve in Clericsfold, didn't you?

"I despise traitors." Kane spitefully pushed the guard's head against the rock wall behind the group. The man winced and barely had time to shift his body before Kane made his next move. He grabbed the hilt of the Soul Sword and thrust its blade through the man's heart. Midir winced as the guard reacted painfully, slowed down, and eventually slumped onto Midir's legs.

Kane pointed to a nearby Elf. "You. Dispose of this trash." The Elf grabbed the man's ankles and drug him through the passageway. It pushed the man's lifeless body off the side of a ledge, never to be seen again.

Kane turned to the rest of the prisoners. "Three to go." Midir looked at what remained of his contingent. Lucerne was to his right with Jothan next to him. Jothan's eyes were huge, as he didn't know whether the deceased guard had served in Clericsfold or not.

However, Kane somehow hadn't recognized him. Maybe Kane confused the other guard with Jothan. Or maybe Kane did recognize Jothan and killed the other guard as a warning of what was to come.

Either way, he was frightened. Kane turned away. He paused and turned his head halfway back. He made eye contact with Jothan for a moment and turned his attention back to other matters. Midir closed his eyes, remembering the way each of the other soldiers had fallen.

Meanwhile, the runner from their group had been absorbed by a creature assumed to be a Shapeshifter. Midir based this on Jothan's description of one from two weeks earlier, as well as the visual evidence as the creature took the man's form after absorbing his body.

Besides the three of them and the guard who had just been executed, all the other guards had perished in an ambush.

After their capture, Kane and his forces had drug them here: deep within the caverns and passageways that branched off from the Cave of Tera. Now, sitting at the base of a blocked path along a vast chasm, Midir assumed whatever was behind the fallen boulders held immense value. It might even be the supposed magic repository.

Whatever it was, Kane's group hadn't left this area for several days, with Elves coming and going.

Folas had spoken little and instead focused his attention on the boulders blocking the way. Kane had brought several packs full of food — though he refused to share with the prisoners. Midir was starving, but tried to focus on other, more important matters.

Such as how they were going to escape, if at all.

"I think the fake runner confirms there is some kind of magic deep below the surface." Enid's comment partially fell on deaf ears as Tiernan was busy sorting through various papers on his desk. "Did you hear me, Tiernan?"

"I heard you, I'm busy."

"With what?" Tiernan slammed his hands on his desk.

"Give me a moment, Sister, please." Enid threw up both of her hands and walked over toward an open window. She began to talk again, but decided to give her brother the silence he requested.

"There. Here it is." He pulled out a paper and read it. "King Farris founded the Kingdom of Abria at the beginning of the New Era. Around that time, dragons went extinct and Graelans lost their magical powers."

"That sounds familiar, but what is it?"

"A report I wrote in school. Mom helped me put it together for my Abrian History class. Back when we were ten years old or so."

"And you kept it all this time because?" Tiernan shrugged. "Okay, fine. So what's the point, T?"

"Think about what the creature said. 'Below Farna is a magic beyond what any of us can understand.' And something about Farna holding the sum of all Graelan magic, right?" He pointed to the paper. "Where did this magic go from the mages?"

"You think it's below us? That something *took* all Graelan magic away and put it below Farna? Why? What's the purpose?"

"I can't say why, but I'm convinced more than ever it's what Kane and the Dark Elf are after. Think about it, Sis. There are no records before the New Era. None. The Archives *start* with the New Era. What came before?

"We know from occasional mentions in the history books the time before the New Era had mages and dragons. Who knows what else? The magic had to go somewhere.

"Hasn't it ever bothered you that Abria is completely cut off from the rest of the world? We have minimal trade with the other Kingdoms throughout the rest of Grael. Why? Something *happened* back then, and our enemy is trying to undo it."

"Okay, so let's say you're right. You've cracked the puzzle. Congrats, Tiernan. You won." She leaned in. "What do we *do* next?" Enid's reaction was uncharacteristic of her, and for good reason.

Tiernan didn't know it, but Enid was terrified for the first time in her life. What he did know was, ever since she watched Wayland die, his once invincible sister hadn't acted like her normal, confident self.

"I think we use these," he pointed to the Mind Shield and the Power Ring on her finger. "We take back the Soul Sword." He walked over and picked up the shield. Sliding it on his arm, both of them reacted as the Mind Shield shrunk for the final time.

Now, it was the perfect size for his body. Peace flowed over Tiernan. In his mind, he heard a single word reverberate.

Acceptance.

Enid raised her eyebrows as he continued. "Enid, time and time again we react. They captured Eislyn, so we staged a rescue. They attacked Alwyn and Idlewind, so we sent scouts to investigate. Today, they sent a spy into our midst. Do we sit around and wait for the next incursion, or do we take the battle to them?"

Enid picked up her battle axe laying against the nearby wall. "Isn't this another reaction? Maybe that's what they want us to do."

"You could be right, but I don't think we should just sit around and wait."

"Okay. Fine. You're right. But we shouldn't go alone. I think we should take as many of the Abrian Royal Guard as we can justify. Leave the rest here to protect Castle Abria, of course."

"Of course." Tiernan walked over to his sister and put his hand on her shoulder.

"So, who do we leave in charge?" Enid thought for a moment before a soft but certain smile spread across her face.

"*Queen* Eislyn."

"No. You're *not* going." Eislyn's reaction was to be expected. Kane and Folas seemed to always be one step ahead of them. Eislyn was convinced there was something else waiting for the twins deep underground as well. "Tiernan, I can't lose anyone else to this stupid war."

Tiernan sympathized with his wife's feelings.

But now was not the time for feelings.

He had his back to her, gazing out the window. The sun had set a while ago, and the Abrian sky cast a hazy purple and pink tone over the land.

"I don't know how else to say this, my dear. Enid abdicated her position." The words didn't sink in at first, so Tiernan let them linger. The longer he didn't say anything, and the more Eislyn thought on his words, their meaning set in.

"No. No, no, no..."

"That means there is no more Prince and Princess ruling the Kingdom of Abria. There is a King." He turned to her. "And his beloved Queen." Eislyn fell into a nearby seat.

"Tiernan, I always knew this was *possible*. I don't know if I thought it was likely. But definitely possible.

"A joint brother-sister rule was so nontraditional that everyone assumed one sibling would naturally take charge." She closed her eyes, remembering the Alwyn attack. "I had just always hoped it would be Enid and Wayland instead of us."

Tiernan winced at the mention of his friend's name. "Way was a good man, and I miss him more than..." His voice trailed off as it began to crack. Tiernan wiped a couple of tears from his face.

"Wayland never wanted to be in charge, my love. I don't think he would have become King even if I tried to force him." Tiernan tried to focus on the good memories of their brotherhood instead of his loss.

"You could have told me that when we began our courtship, you know," she said with a smile. Tiernan turned around to see her face, at first worried she regretted the marriage. Her face put his mind at ease.

She was trying to soften the mood. "I already see where this is going, too. You're now the King, which means your decision is final. Am I right?"

"It is the law of the land, *technically*. Eislyn, I need you to be on board with this."

"Of course you do." She stood and added a playful tone to her next words. "As long as we're dropping news and making demands of each other, I have one for you, Mr. Tiernan. If you want me to be on board, you have to agree to something for me first."

"What's that?" He walked to her and wrapped his arms around her waist.

"It's simple, really. I need you to promise me something. After all, I'm not raising this child on my own. If you're going, you have to *promise me* you're going to come back." Tiernan wasn't sure how to respond at first. It took him a few moments for the news to truly settle in.

"Wait. Child?" She nodded. "You're telling me you're pregnant?"

Eislyn smiled. "I didn't like not telling you, Tiernan. I wasn't sure, but it's clear. And, I've been up early, sick every morning for the past week. With all that's been going on, there just hasn't been a good time to bring it up.

"So yes, I am pregnant."

"When did this happen?" Eislyn's playful attitude came out in full force as she softly punched her husband on the shoulder. *Just like Way used to,* Tiernan thought.

"When do you *think,* Mr. Tiernan? Do the math." Tiernan thought for a moment and laughed out loud.

"A souvenir from Alwyn?" She nodded with a smile. Tiernan kissed her and pulled her into a long, drawn-out hug.

"Wow! 4 Flametide: the day I found out I'm going to be a father!" As fast as the celebratory joy hit him, sadness followed. Tiernan realized that, while he and Eislyn came home *with* an unexpected surprise, his sister came home *without* the love of her life.

"Well, okay," he said, his intensity softening. "I can't let he or she grow up without their daddy." He pulled Eislyn in closer. "No matter what, I will come home."

"You promise?"

"With all that I am." With those words, Tiernan embraced his wife even tighter before giving her another long, drawn-out celebratory kiss.

Preparations for the Battle at Tera, as the guards began calling it, took several days. A group of twenty-five would accompany the twins. Queen Eislyn, stepping up much as her mother-in-law did decades ago, commanded the soldiers staying behind. Four would follow her around at all times — the only demand Tiernan made of his wife while deferring the rest to her leadership.

Per her instructions, the remainder of the Royal Guards staying behind would be positioned throughout Castle Abria and Farna itself. They would rotate every four hours, resting while another group took their places. To some, it looked like martial law, though this wasn't the case.

Rather, the volume of active Royal Guards was out of a sense of precaution to keep the city safe.

Those going with Tiernan and Enid brought with them a mix of shields, swords, and spears, as well as sets of bows and arrows.

On the morning of their departure, Eislyn and Tiernan shared one final loving embrace before a farewell kiss. Enid kept her distance, unwilling and unable to focus on such a painful concept as love with the memory of losing Wayland hovering over her head.

Once the group departed, Eislyn's presence as the Queen seemed to fit like a well-worn pair of gloves. She embraced the role, and earned the respect of those who served under her command with her swift and decisive leadership.

"There it is, Sis. The Cave of Tera." Tiernan pointed at their destination. The mouth to the cave jutted out of the ground before blending back in at a gradual slope into the Clericsfold fields. Other than this outcropping, no one would know it was even here.

"Guards! Prepare." The twins said nothing as the commanding officer with them issued orders to his subordinates. Several took up defensive positions in front of Tiernan and Enid. Others surrounded them, with a group behind. The lead guard pointed to two of his men.

"You two. Take the lead." These men entered first before allowing the twins anywhere inside. They raised torches, illuminating the path and looking for enemies, before motioning for the group to enter. Upon entering, the next two guards in the battalion drew their swords.

Enid looked at her brother. "You ready?"

"Do we have a choice?"

Everyone physically stuck as close together as they could. Shoulder to shoulder, they explored the caverns and passageways.

The walls of the Cave of Tera were lined with moss and trickles of running water that seemed to go nowhere. Occasional larger drips echoed throughout the various paths. The four guards bringing up the rear walked backward, back-to-back, with those in front of them. Once the entrance to the Cave of Tera disappeared from view and the Graelian sun could no longer provide light, Enid summoned her Fire Magic to further illuminate the caves.

The twins walked in the middle of the pack. This was on Queen Eislyn's orders, and Tiernan decided to defer to her leadership rather than protest. He needed the guards to see her as their commander, and to oppose her instructions could potentially set up a negative precedent in their minds or raise questions as to who actually was in charge of the Abrian Royal Guard. The law said it fell to the Queen, and only the King in her absence. Tiernan was committed to keeping it this way.

Upon reaching the first split in the path, the commanding guard turned to his King. "Which way?"

Tiernan looked back and forth at each. "The left-most option. Logically, we need to end up *under* Castle Abria. We should head westward as much as possible."

This continued for what felt like hours, if not days. The journey would be repetitive, as they had to travel all the way to Central Abria, enter the Cave of Tera, and backtrack underground following an unknown path — all the while hoping they chose correctly.

They rested when necessary. No one slept, which meant everyone was feeling exhausted after their travels. However, in the case of most of them, adrenaline and fear fueled their bodies.

Eventually, the guard in the front heard a commotion. "What was that?" he whispered. "Listen." He raised his hand to the group behind them, and everyone stopped.

Tiernan pushed his way to the front and tapped on the guard's shoulder. Whispering, he asked a question he already knew the answer to. "What did you hear?"

"Voices." Tiernan patted him on the shoulder, taking a deep breath as he walked back to Enid.

"I think we're close," he whispered.

"So it's time. Let's end this."

Chapter 31

Dragonborn

Battlefield might not have been the operable word for where the Abrian contingent found themselves fighting. After following the sounds of the voices, they finally discovered a relatively open area in the caverns.

There, Elven forces were waiting for them. Two Royal Guards had fallen right away, though the rest were holding their own.

There was no sign of Kane or Folas.

Tiernan used the Mind Shield against an attacking Elf, employing it as a battering ram against his opponent's face. The Elf landed hard against a nearby wall and slumped to the ground, unconscious.

How many more are there going to be? This feels like a never-ending river of Elves. Another Elf rushed him, and he drove his sword through his attacker's body. Next to the King, another guard fell to his death down a deep chasm in the middle of the battlefield.

"No!" Tiernan cried as he tried to grab the man's hand. Tiernan once again used the Mind Shield in an offensive manner, swiping at the Elf and sending him down the same crevice.

Enid looked around. The torrent of oncoming Elves flowing through the passageway ahead didn't seem right to her either. "I thought there were only 500 Elves in all of Abria. I feel like…" She stopped talking as she swung at another and sent him flying. "I feel like we've already faced that many and then some."

A guard agreed with her after pulling his sword out of the body of another. "I have friends in Oakshadow. Well over a hundred Elves moved before the first Statuo. Many more since. There shouldn't be this many."

Tiernan stabbed his sword through an oncoming Elf. He kicked him off of the blade. "Why aren't they using magic? I thought Elves possessed magic even if Graelans didn't?"

"You're right. Something is off. Look at the ones who have…" Another rushed her, and she sent it flying backward with a swift kick. "As I was saying, T. Look. The ones we've stabbed or cut down. There's no blood."

Enid grabbed the handle of her axe and firmly planted it into the ground with its head chest-high. Tiernan raised an eyebrow, watching her. *If only Way could see her like this.*

She looked imposing, determined, and in control. With purpose, she opened her palms. She closed her eyes and summoned her powers. Next, Enid released an attack that permeated throughout the area. Every Elf froze in place before they disappeared.

Except for one, who collapsed, now secured in a glass casing.

"I knew it! They were all illusions. Guards, deal with him," ordered Tiernan. Three Royal Guards ran over to the fallen Elf. But before they could finish him, an oncoming blast of Frost Magic attacked them.

It froze the men in place. The cold chilled their bodies to the bone. One man gasped for air, unaccustomed to this level of cold. Around the corner came Folas.

"It's the Dark Elf!" exclaimed a frozen guard.

"No, I'm more than that. I am the Dark Elf *Master*," Folas said as he placed his hand on the man's head. As Folas had done many times before, the man began shaking. His skin changed color and began to shrivel. His face turned sickly, as if he was aging rapidly.

"Stop!" Tiernan shouted, as he threw a nearby discarded spear at Folas. The Dark Elf froze it in place with his free hand, flipped it around and stabbed it through the chest of the still-breathing guard. The third continued to gasp for air. The first guard had turned gray and, a moment later, was gone — nothing more than dust in the breeze.

His clothing fell to the ground, now lacking an owner.

"Tiernan, let me handle this," said Enid. She turned to the Dark Elf. "This ends now, you worthless excuse for a mage."

From a bed within the fortress sitting atop the Northern Plateau, Zoran's eyes shot open. Her presence was undeniable. Zoran realized, no matter how hard he tried, he couldn't see her. This meant she was in proximity to the Mind Shield.

But he could *feel* her and the Power Ring she possessed. That was enough for him. Soon, if Kane and Folas fulfilled their prophesied purpose, this would be over.

"Dragonborn..."

The ferocity coming from his sister made Tiernan proud. First, she melted the ice holding the third guard in place. The man was on his hands and knees recovering, with Enid and Folas sparring just beyond him.

Every attack from the Dark Elf she easily deflected. Magic blasts, whether Wind, Fire, Frost, Poison, Gravity, and even the same unknown pink magic from the attack in the Castle were nothing to her.

Enid swung her battle axe at them all, absorbing them into its head and sending them back at Folas.

Eventually, the Dark Elf found himself on the defensive side of the battle instead of offensive. Reabsorbing his magic was easy at first, but after a bit Enid began sending her own attacks his way on top of his deflected ones.

It overwhelmed him. In desperation, he raised his right hand to freeze her. Enid saw the attack coming and raised her own hand to counter. She sent out a reciprocal blast of magic that transformed his hand into solid glass.

"Aaaarghhhh. You witch!" Enid charged the Dark Elf, ignoring his comment. Leading with her axe, she drove it deep into his chest.

Folas fell backward, and Enid continued pushing. Eventually, the decorative tip of the axe came out of his upper back. Words couldn't describe how much it hurt as Folas experienced something unexpected for the first time since the Elven Exile.

Fear. Using whatever energy he could find, he snapped his fingers and disappeared. Enid swung her blade as she turned to find her brother.

"Where'd he go?" Tiernan asked, rushing over to his sister. Before Enid could say anything, they saw another enemy running their way.

"Ready for round two?"

"After you, Sis."

The new attacker was Kane, wielding the Soul Sword that took the lives of their parents. Around the corner of the cavern, Tiernan caught a glimpse of Midir and others laying bound against a wall.

"T, go. Get them. I've got this." Tiernan motioned for the other guards to follow him, though they would have to take an opposite path around the cave to avoid the rushing Kane as he charged at Enid.

"Enid, here, take this." Before leaving, Tiernan tossed her the Mind Shield. She slid it onto her left arm and rushed at Kane while Tiernan joined the guards, one handing him a spare shield from a fallen comrade.

Kane's attack was stronger than Enid expected. He used both hands to swipe at her with the Soul Sword, a maneuver she defended using the Mind Shield, but took more strength than she expected.

She kicked at his chest, pushing him backward. Tiernan watched the battle from across the chasm as they made their way around the cavern. Tiernan admired her ferocity, but at the same time, was worried for her safety. After a short run, his group made their way around the treacherous path and to the three prisoners.

Midir was unconscious. Jothan was out as well. In the middle of the two was Lucerne, who appeared to be barely hanging on. Tiernan began untying his hands first.

"What happened?" the King asked him.

"They wanted you here."

"Is Midir alive?" Lucerne nodded. *Why did they want us here?* Tiernan looked across the cavern at his sister. Kane's swings seemed to have some kind of intention.

Redirecting Enid.

At first, Tiernan thought it was to push her off of a ledge. Instead, he realized, each of Kane's blows rotated Enid toward a collapsed passageway. He looked at a guard, the one who had struggled to breathe in the frost attack from earlier.

"Get these men out of here. You three, help him. The rest of you, with me." They ran back toward the battle between Kane and Enid. By now, Enid's back was nearly against the wall. Kane rushed at her with the Soul Sword, and Enid deflected it using the Mind Shield.

Kane surprised her with an unconventional move. With one of his hands, he pushed her right hand with the Power Ring against the rock face while thrusting the Soul Sword not at Enid, but into the rock face. The momentum of Enid's left hand caused the Mind Shield to make contact with the boulders.

For a few seconds, all three ancient relics touched the wall at the same time.

"Kane, duck!" While still running, Tiernan followed the sound of the voice.

It came from Folas. He was bandaged and weak. *Why isn't he dead?* He had been bleeding, and his wrapped wound appeared stained with dangerous amounts of green blood.

"Enid!" yelled Tiernan. Kane did as instructed and ducked as Folas threw a magic blast at Enid's body. It enveloped her as all three relics lit up like the daytime sky.

One by one, the boulders transformed, devolving into dust that quickly disappeared. Enid fell backward, landing soundly on her back. Kane and Folas rushed into the open room, ignoring her and leaving the other two relics with Enid.

It took a moment for Tiernan's team to make their way around the path to Enid. Tiernan motioned toward the cavern where Kane and Folas had just entered. Several guards followed, while others stayed near the twins. Tiernan kneeled down to his sister.

"Are you okay?" She stood up, using his arms as a brace.

"I'm fine. Look, T." Kane and Folas were standing before a gargantuan sphere of concentrated energy.

The object flowed, twisted, turned, and spun around itself. It continually emitted a bright palette of colors such as orange, blue, white, red, green, purple, pink, gold, and more, rotating between them in no discernible pattern. The sound of whatever this mass of energy was rivaled the mighty rushing Lorelei River. It echoed throughout the cavern where the battle had just been fought.

"We must be directly below Farna," Tiernan said as he helped Enid to her feet. "The rest of you, go. Stop them." Tiernan helped his sister steady herself. "You ok?"

"Yeah. I think so."

"We played right into their hands again. You were right, Enid. We reacted to what they wanted us to do." Tiernan's words of self-loathing fell on deaf ears as something inside of Enid reacted to the sphere.

The Dragonborn shook her head, attempting to dismiss the voice trying to emerge. "Come on, Brother. Let's finish what we started."

Inside of the cave, two of the guards tried to tackle the wounded Folas. They knocked him to the ground, though he pushed them off, albeit with somewhat of a struggle.

Kane turned and quickly stabbed two other guards with the Soul Sword. The two who had tackled the now subdued Folas turned their attention to Kane and jumped on his back. He retaliated by running backward into a nearby wall, crushing both and knocking them to the ground. Once they landed, he quickly plunged the Soul Sword into their chests.

One by one, each remaining member of the Abrian Royal Guard fell. By the time the twins reached Kane and Folas, only one guard was left standing — the same one who had taken the blast of magic for Tiernan. Kane grabbed him by the hair and taunted him.

"Thank you for being a loyal spy. You allowed us to see this attack before it even happened." Tiernan and Enid stopped in their tracks as he said these words, exchanging a look of recognition.

"The pink magic…" Tiernan began.

"It's some kind of possession spell," Enid finished.

"That's how they knew we were coming." Tiernan yelled in frustration as he and his sister ran toward Kane.

"Strength is Victory!" The guard shouted as he twisted free. He kicked Kane hard in the kneecap and grabbed the handle of his sword. With a swift motion, he thrust it into Kane's abdomen.

Kane reacted by grabbing the blade with his free hand, pulling it out of both his lower stomach and the man's hand, and callously tossed it aside. He raised the Soul Sword high and rammed it into the man's chest. The ancient relic came through the man's back. The man's eyes grew wide in shock, unable to react to both the pain and the realization of Kane's next move.

The Divider raised the Soul Sword and flicked it to his right, sending the man's body across the cavern. He turned to face the twins but recoiled in pain as Enid retaliated with a blast of magic into Kane's bleeding wound.

"Arrghh. Deal with her," Kane said to Folas. Tiernan ran in front of his sister and rushed Folas, who had just stood back up. Tiernan hoped the lack of magic on display from the Dark Elf meant Folas was drained of his power.

Tiernan's hopes came true as he easily engaged Folas, though the Dark Elf did grab a sword from a fallen guard nearby. The two sparred while Kane turned to Enid.

"Back for more?" he said, taunting her.

"This ends here," she said as she swung her axe at the Soul Sword.

Behind the group, closer to the cavern entrance, another figure materialized. It was a dark, foreboding shadow with a bronze face. From a safe distance, he observed the battle unfold.

Tiernan kicked Folas in the chest, close to the wound from earlier. It made the Dark Elf cry out in pain, doubling over as he recoiled from the attack. Drawing back, Tiernan raised his sword to end Folas' life.

Suddenly, his sword was gone. He looked around and saw the new combatant standing.

"Enid! Look!" She performed a similar move to Kane, kicking Kane's injury and ramming his face with all her might using the Mind Shield. Kane fell over, stunned, unconscious, and bleeding from the nose.

Enid turned to see what her brother was talking about.

"Dragonborn." This was enough to let the twins know who they were facing.

"Zoran…" said Tiernan. The Dark Emperor looked at Tiernan and raised his hand. The motion twisted the King almost a full ninety degrees as he hit the far wall hard. The wind left Tiernan's lungs with such force that all he could do was lie on the ground motionless.

The only obstacle between Zoran and his goal was Enid.

The guards carrying Midir, Lucerne, and Jothan stopped to take a break. One of them carefully laid Midir against a wall.

"We should try to give him something. Water, a potion. Otherwise, he might not make it out of here."

"I'm out of water. I think I have a potion somewhere," one of them responded as he dug through his satchel. Finally, he found it and poured it down Midir's throat. The older man coughed and opened his eyes.

He looked around, observing where he was and who he was with. "Help me up," he ordered. The guards obeyed the Manus without question. He looked at Lucerne and Jothan, still on the backs of the other Abrian soldiers. Midir thought about his next course of action for a moment and made a final, fateful decision.

"Give me your sword."

"Manus, King Tiernan gave us orders."

"*King* Tiernan?" Midir wondered what had happened in his absence. "No matter. You guys don't understand. Zoran wanted Enid to come here. He needs her gone to start the next part of his plan."

"What is that?" one of them asked.

"The end of Abria. And if he wins, he'll conquer the rest of Grael once and for all."

Despite her power, Enid had never encountered someone as strong as Zoran. With a mere flick of his wrist, he made it hard for her to walk. It was almost as if he understood her powers more than she did.

Tiernan opened his eyes, shaking his head as he stood up. From across the edge of the room, he saw his sister walking toward Zoran. He also noticed Kane appeared to be unconscious, with the Soul Sword discarded on the ground next to his hand.

Zoran had made no attempt to retrieve the ancient relic.

If I could only get it to her somehow. He looked around for a vantage point, a path he could hide behind.

Nothing. There was literally no way he could get the Soul Sword to her without revealing his intentions.

But maybe I can distract Zoran long enough for Enid to do something. Tiernan committed to his decision, knowing it meant certain defeat — if not death. He stood up to run toward Kane. *I'm sorry, Eislyn. I guess I'll have to break my promise.*

However, before he could do anything, he heard Zoran let out a blood-curdling cry.

Behind the Dark Emperor stood Midir. In the Manus' hand was a sword. Midir had run it through Zoran's body with the blade penetrating through the Dark Emperor's chest. A trickle of bronze blood ran down his chest, a sensation Zoran was not used to experiencing.

Zoran flipped around to face Midir, his unnatural voice echoing throughout the cave. "That hurt, Graelan." Zoran's eyes lit up as he put his hands on Midir's shoulders. Instantly, a mix of gold-toned and red Fire Magic enveloped the Manus.

Midir never had a chance to scream. Almost immediately, his body turned from its normal desert-tanned skin tone to a dark gray. And faster than Tiernan or Enid could process what they were seeing, Midir's body transformed into a granite-like statue, only barely resembling the man's features.

Cracks began to form on what used to be Midir's skin. These spread like spider webs all over his former body. In an instant, the form that used to be Manus Midir crumbled into a pile of stones. These continued to break into smaller and smaller pieces until they were no bigger than pea gravel.

Tiernan's mouth fell open in shock as his father's ally – and their family friend – was no more. *Midir died a hero. It cannot be for nothing.*

For the first time, both of the twins realized the depths of Zoran's power. "Enid, the sword!" Tiernan yelled, seeing an opportunity.

His sister looked over to see what Tiernan meant. Her brother was pointing at Kane. With Zoran distracted as he pushed the sword backward out of his chest, they had an opening.

The Soul Sword. Enid rushed to Kane's fallen body and grabbed the ancient relic.

"No!" bellowed Zoran, realizing his lapse in attention cost him the advantage. With bronze blood still running down his chest, he flipped his hand at Tiernan once again. The King found himself crashing against the rear wall as he had a few moments ago. Tiernan's body slumped to the ground as he powerlessly watched what happened next.

Zoran rushed at Enid. However, this time, his sister was more than prepared. With the combined power of all three relics, she sent a blast of power that flew across the chamber and hit him square in the chest, aggravating and drawing more bronze-toned blood from his seeping wound.

Zoran fell to the floor, overwhelmed by pain from the attack. He could barely breathe, and for a brief moment, it looked as if the battle was almost won.

"Now, Folas!" Tiernan, still immobile on the ground, was helpless in trying to protect his sister from Zoran's order to the Dark Elf. Folas dug up what little bit of magic he could find within himself and released it at Enid. She quickly used the Mind Shield to block it, but found herself in an awkward position.

She couldn't defend against Folas and attack Zoran while standing like this.

Zoran stood up, prepared to strike. Enid heard the same energy she ignored earlier. They spoke to her from deep inside.

Release the magic.

Return it to Grael.

Fulfill your destiny.

As the essence of each ancient relic filled her mind, she felt a fourth, unknown voice.

You are the Dragonborn Heroine, the Protector of Abria.

Enid used the Mind Shield to repel Folas one last time, sending his own energy back into his body. It knocked him flat on his back.

Using the combined power of the three items one more time, Enid sent another blast at Zoran with the intent to threw him across the cavern. The attack worked as intended, sending him several meters backward. Zoran landed hard. He tried to stand back up but realized her Dragonborn powers immobilized his limbs.

Kane stirred, but it was too late for him as well. Enid turned to face the sphere of energy. She spread her arms wide to her side.

Her red magic began swirling in and around her body. Tiernan couldn't tell for sure within his injured haze, but it looked as if, similar to that fateful day in Alwyn, she had wings of flame emerging from her body.

"Dragonborn...no..." mumbled Zoran as the power within Enid emerged from every part of her body. Amplified by the Power Ring, protected by the Mind Shield, and seated by the Soul Sword, Enid used her power to send a forceful blast of magic toward the twisting ball of energy their enemies had tried so hard to obtain for themselves.

While doing so, Enid turned to look at her brother. Like the attack on Leviathan, her eyes glazed over with a white-hot fire. She smiled, not knowing what would happen next but at peace that it was meant to be.

Enid vocalized what Tiernan was thinking. Her voice contained the same reverberation she once demonstrated to Wayland during their date at Kingscrown Rock. This time, however, it carried the effect on a much deeper and grander scale.

"I love you, Brother."

"Sister, no..."

Enid looked back to the sphere and, as instructed by the voices deep within her, fulfilled a previously unknown, but long-awaited destiny as the Dragonborn Heroine. Her dragon-like persona filled the cavern from top to bottom and edge to edge. The fiery dragon wings spread wide and Enid herself levitated once again.

She rose far above the ground. In a brilliant flash of light and an immense demonstration of her power, she sent a blinding blast of magic directly into the heart of the energy sphere.

Kane and Folas started to stir. However, neither could do anything other than to join Zoran and Tiernan in shielding their eyes from the intensity of the sphere. It grew as bright and intense as the Graelian sun.

Time stood still. Enid saw the face of her husband. "Wayland, my love…"

With that, the sphere exploded in a dazzling display of magic, erupting through the ground and traveling high into the air.

It broke through the ceiling of the cavern and continued burrowing through the ground. Abrian Royal Guards began moving people to a safe distance as soon as the ground started shaking and portions of the soil crumbled inward. A few moments later, the field exploded as the energy erupted through the surface within a large field in the northern section of Farna.

From there, the energy spread throughout the sky and began dispersing throughout the Kingdom of Abria and beyond.

Once the light subsided in the cavern, all three magic relics laid on the ground in a quasi-circle. In the middle was a large, red jewel about the width of a book. Glasslike in appearance and with energy flowing through it, Kane pushed himself up off of the ground and walked over to the pile of items.

Tiernan stood too and began looking left and right for his sister. However, Enid was nowhere to be found.

"Enid? Enid!" He rushed toward Kane, who was leaning down to pick up the jewel. Tiernan led with his shoulder, knocking his nemesis to the ground. Already exhausted from the battle, the King landed chest-first on top of the Mind Shield. He reached for the other two items.

Zoran's eyes flared in anger at the fallen Kane. He turned to the Dark Elf. "Get that boy out of here!" Folas snapped his fingers, using the last remnant of his stored magic. In a flash, it teleported Tiernan far from the cavern.

Epilogus

The Tale of Tiernan

Tiernan put down the quill once again. He re-read the last page, thinking about what happened between that battle and today. So much of the story — his story — had been pieced together from his memories and things he had been told.

Closure. That's what I wanted. How is this closure? Tiernan turned sideways, resting his head and body against the wall. Closing his eyes, he reflected on the events he recorded and what still remained to be told. He had never taken the time to connect all the dots until today, and wondered if that was part of what Zachary had wanted him to do through his writing.

The Second Dark War spread from one end of the realm to the next. Life in Abria transformed almost overnight, though it also resumed as best it could in many ways. Trade across the land continued. Alwyn rebuilt the docks. Whispersong tamed horses. Idlewind restored portions of the destroyed residential district. Kyrie's parents, committed to helping those around Lakedon and opened a series of lodges to house the displaced. Some places tried to maintain a sense of normalcy, despite the ongoing war.

Tiernan smiled, recalling one of those 'normal' memories. On 8 Windbloom 922NE, Queen Eislyn gave birth to a son. Tiernan named him Edward in honor of the original name Davien and Kyrie picked out for the King. Edward's birth was a glimmer of hope in an increasingly frustrating existence for the Royal Family.

In the intervening years, all of Abria experienced the growing threat of Zoran. Some things had to change. For the sake of safety, the fifth Statuo was cancelled, postponed indefinitely until the war ended. After all, various regions of the Kingdom had come under siege from Zoran-controlled creatures.

That all came to an abrupt end in 922NE. After a fierce and especially painful to recall battle, Tiernan formally stepped down as King, passing the leadership on to a man from Idlewind named Rhys — son of Midir. *Ironic,* Tiernan often thought, *since Midir was once my namesake's choice to ascend to the throne.*

Edward's age would prevent him from becoming King. The land needed someone who could lead it, and a toddler was not the right choice.

These events brought Tiernan to today. Two years into the rule of King Rhys, Tiernan had walked into the Drunken Alligator in the Valley for the first time since Borun's funeral. He had spent much of the time since then, wandering from place to place and trying to stay out of the way of the current leadership.

"Who was that old man anyway?" he said to himself. Realizing he wasn't going to get an answer, Tiernan picked up his large stack of papers and grabbed his discarded shield from the ground.

As Tiernan stood, he waved goodbye to Tammith. She nodded to the departing former King as he walked out of the door. He wondered if this might be the last time he ever came here.

Tiernan travelled through the streets of Lily of the Valley toward Borun's former home. His family had kept it, choosing to use it as a sort of vacation home if need be. During the sale of Borun Mill, he and Eislyn briefly discussed the possibility of selling the home along with the business. In the end, Tiernan convinced his wife it was best to hold on to it, though he didn't know why if he was being honest with himself.

After all, no one had opened the doors to the place since the day of Borun's funeral. They could have sold it when they sold the mill.

Tiernan put the key into the Borun-designed keyhole. As he broke the seal to this sacred home, he noticed the metalwork of the door pull.

Hello again, Grandpa. Tiernan wondered if this was the original knob or one Borun had made later in life. Either way, it was an intricate, exquisite design.

Tiernan shut the door and placed the stack of papers on a nearby table. He closed the door behind him and surveyed the area.

Compared to the mead-stained scent of the Alligator, here the air smelled and tasted stale. Dust lined the furniture, sitting undisturbed and untouched. The floor creaked with each step he took. Large cobwebs adorned the corners of the foyer.

On the wall near the entrance to the living room hung a set of paintings. The first was of a much younger Borun. Set inside a mahogany frame, the artwork captured the essence of his grandfather's joy and vibrance.

A young man stood next to Borun, his arm resting on the older gentleman's shoulder. Tiernan recognized the face without needing to see the placard. It was the same face he saw in the mirror every day.

His father, no more than seventeen or eighteen years of age. Tiernan placed his hands on the frame next to Davien. He didn't want to stain the canvas with the oils and ink on his fingers.

He also wanted nothing more than to touch his father one more time.

Next to this painting hung a similar one, though with the roles reversed. King Davien sat on his throne with the older Borun's hand resting in a similar fashion.

Through the windows in the door, light from activity in the Valley cast a subtle glow on both men's faces.

Tiernan continued walking, rounding the corner into Borun's living room. Here, cobwebs and dust covered everything in it as well. An abandoned bookshelf stood on the northern wall. Tiernan walked over to it, wondering what book his grandfather had last read.

A journal laid open. Tiernan picked it up to read the last entry.

"Tomorrow, I'll ride to Farna. Davien has worked hard to pull together the Statuo. No matter what happens, I'm proud of him.

"I'm proud of my grandkids, too. Enid, the mighty warrior. She'll go far in life. I'm confident she'll win each race.

"And my grandson, Tiernan. What can I say about him? I see so much of Davien in him. His compassion. His heart. The boy loves his sister stronger than anyone I've ever met.

"Beyond that, he's a leader. A selfless, brave leader. Davien instilled in him everything I saw in my son at the orphanage. He will make a…"

Tiernan's eyes welled up with tears. He struggled to complete the rest of the sentence. His voice broke as he read it.

"…make a wonderful King someday." Tiernan closed the book, a puff of dust flying upward. He placed the journal back on the bookshelf and turned around.

Sitting on one of the seats was the old man from the Alligator. It surprised Tiernan to see someone sitting in here, especially since this was a locked home. Tiernan wiped his eyes, cleared his throat, and placed the shield on a wall before speaking.

"Zachary, isn't it?" he asked. The old man motioned for Tiernan to sit in another nearby seat.

"Okay." Tiernan sat, rubbing his temples with his eyes closed. When he opened them, Zachary had the sword Tiernan drove into the ground earlier within his hand. The old man tossed it in the air. He caught it by the blade and pushed the handle toward Tiernan.

The former King took it but laid it on the ground next to him as he shook his head. "Thanks? I think. Are you going to tell me what this was all about?"

Zachary smiled. "Maybe. Are you done with your story?" Tiernan shrugged.

"I wrote until I felt this story was complete."

"Where did you end it?"

Tiernan frowned, picturing Enid's sacrifice.

"Ah, so that's where you stopped."

It's as if Zachary is reading my mind.

"I am," he said.

"Stop it. *Who are you*? Enough of these games." Tiernan finally let his frustration get the best of him. "Listen, old man. If you can read my mind, if you can make a magic quill and a large stack of papers appear out of thin air, and if you can retrieve a sword I left in a field all the way across town, at some point you just need to tell me what's going on."

"What did you learn about yourself? Did you find closure?"

"Ha! I thought this was for others in the Kingdom. So they wouldn't forget or something. Was I wrong?"

"Family is Strength. Do you still believe that?"

"Of course I do."

"And yet, almost everyone you know is gone."

"Not everyone. Eislyn and Edward are safe. Or so I hope anyway." Tiernan swallowed, worriedly thinking about his wife and son and hoping they were okay in their new home.

"Yes, they are safe. Your plan worked. Both of them are far from here, elsewhere in Grael until this is all over." Zachary leaned forward. "It's *far* from over. Come here."

Tiernan reluctantly stood to his feet and walked over to Zachary.

"Now, give me your hands." Tiernan sighed and reached out. Zachary grabbed him, and the world around the two of them shifted.

In rapid succession, Tiernan saw events flying through his mind. Some had already happened, such as the birth of his son. He saw a face he didn't recognize: a new warrior with the curious name Firefly followed by a talented mage named Airvede. Next to both of them was a solemn-looking paladin named Shig.

Zachary smiled and did something else to Tiernan's hands. The former King couldn't tell what, but a sudden rush of power flowed through his mind even stronger than before.

Finally, Tiernan saw faces that made him cry out in sadness: Wayland and Enid.

"Enid. Way…no. Please, old man, stop." Tiernan realized these were strange glimpses of their faces that made no sense, because they were of memories he did not and should not have.

And perhaps most curious of all, he saw flowing images of a great battle followed by the crumbling of the western mountains.

"Grael…Eislyn…my son…" All Tiernan knew was that he saw their smiles looking back at him, happy and ready to embrace him.

Zachary let go, causing Tiernan to fall to his knees. "Come, there is *much* to do." The old man stood and walked past Tiernan. Streams of tears were running down Tiernan's face as Zachary spoke again.

"One more thing, my liege. You're going to need this." He leaned down and handed Tiernan the quill.

Tiernan flipped his head back to the other room. "Wait, that was in there, how did…Oh never mind." But, before he could say anything else, Zachary was gone once again. This time, however, in the man's place was his robe. Neatly folded, with no sign of its owner.

Tiernan heard Zachary's voice in his head. *You're going to need that too.*

Tiernan sighed and picked it up as he stood to his feet. He didn't know what lay ahead, but decided he had no choice but to go on.

Now go. Tiernan didn't know how long this mental intrusion would last either, but hoped eventually Zachary would stop talking.

I will.

"Stop it, old man." Silence. Tiernan looked around the room, at the house his grandfather built and the memories he never truly experienced here but now wished he had.

Tiernan decided to take a nap, for tomorrow he would head north to Lorelei.

Time to take King Rhys up on the offer. Tiernan walked back to the table and picked up his stack of writings. He carried it with him to Borun's old bedroom. Once there, he sat on the edge of the dusty bed and flipped back to the first page he wrote.

The Tale of Tiernan

This was his tale, though for the first time since arriving in the valley, he realized what Zachary wanted him to learn, uttering his thoughts to the empty room.

"The tale of Abria isn't over. I didn't need closure after all, because the story is just beginning…"

Afterword

For years, I've loved to work out. This included trips to the gym for weight training, home-based lifting, running, and most recently mountain biking and road cycling. Whenever I had a rough day or a stressful project hanging over my head, exercise was the way I would clear my head.

This ended in mid-2022 after a viral infection left me with lingering, and often unexplainable, conditions. One of those was exercise-induced chronic fatigue syndrome. In short, I would recover, resume my workout routine, and crash again — often bed-bound for weeks at a time.

Once we made the exercise connection, my world came crashing down further than it had already been. My most-loved hobby was detrimental to my health. I needed something that could help me recharge.

My family loves board games. I also love video games and have often gravitated toward RPGs. One evening, the idea came to me to combine the two. I began sketching a world, building the overworld map from what I saw in my head. I began putting together a series of questions for my family — the would-be "Adventurers" — to use for their character creation.

From the ground up, I created a complete game system, plot, backstory, and side quest outline that would become portions of the story you just read. I showed my family the base concept for *The Tale of Tiernan,* and right away, they were on board. I handed them the rule book to study while I began a long process of 3D-printing the set pieces for a large physical map. My primary inspiration for this piece came from a classic video game franchise. The three of them would play on the game board, but as soon as they entered a city, we would switch maps to a smaller 28mm scale setting specific to that location.

Over time, we began piecing together mini-figures that would fit the theme of my world. Drawing again from other video games, I assembled a list of bad guys they would encounter while learning the story behind *The Tale of Tiernan*. We opted for a narrative-driven game instead of combat-heavy, though the latter factored in at key points (not to mention overworld encounters to help them level up their characters).

If this sounds complex, it's because it was. I found a new outlet that, while it wouldn't replace my love of exercise, could at least succeed it as a method of stress relief.

The lore grew beyond anything I had originally envisioned. Throughout the game, their characters discovered "Memory Fragments" that began to paint the backstory of what came before their arrival in the realm. After the first session or two, my wife encouraged me to put those in book form. I wrote the prologue for this novel first, using the concept of a tired hero drafting his memoirs.

The thing about the Memory Fragments is just that: they were *fragments* of the overall larger narrative. Fragment One was split between Kyrie's distress before the birth of the twins and an attendant announcing King Tiernan the First was dying. This led my family to believe the titular "tale" was about the guy who passed away.

I didn't reveal Tiernan the child until Fragment Two during our second gaming session. At this point, they realized he had a twin sister during the game of tag, though Enid remained unnamed until Fragment Three.

This piece might be especially interesting to the reader because Fragment Three took place during the big race of the first Statuo. If you're keeping track, that's Chapter 15.

To sum it up, a considerable amount of exposition and expansion comprised the first fifteen chapters compared to the narrative within the game. And, in case you're wondering, this book only made it through Fragment Nine. This leaves three more for the sequel novel already in the works.

When building Abria, I had to make some conscious decisions. Fantasy tales can be set in alternate realities, on different planets, and beyond. One thing I decided early on was the Kingdom of Abria would not be set on Earth, but rather in another world known as Grael. While there are similarities I intentionally included, there are many differences with more to be revealed in future books as well as side-story novellas.

Grael is a big place, though that's all I'll say for now. And yes, we are considering a retail version of the game — stay tuned!

Characters & Pronunciations

Tiernan (Teer-nin)
Enid (Ee-nid)
Eislyn (Ash-lynn)
Wayland (Way-lind)
Davien (Day-vee-inn)
Kyrie (Keer-ee-A)
Borun (Bow-run)
Midir (Meh-deer)
Tolith (Toll-ith)
Kane (Cain)
Folas (Foal-lus)
Zoran (Zore-on)
Voron (Vore-on)
Tammith (Tamm-ith)
Lucerne (Lou-cerne)
Jothan (Jah-thin)
Aoife (Ee-fa)
Zachary (Za-kaa-ree)

Cities, Towns, and Other Regions

Abria (Uh-bree-uh)
Farna (Far-nuh)
Alwyn (All-win)
Clericsfold
Idlewind
Whispersong
Lily of the Valley
Lorelei (Lore-uh-lie)
Northwick
Milston (Mill-stin)
Lakedon (Lake-dun)
Oakshadow
Rosewood Forest
Mystic Mornings
Fabled Wonders
Northern Plateau
Milston Mountains
Lake Conchobar (Cruh-hoor)
Valley Mountains
Valley Woods
Windale Desert
Kingscrown Rock
Kingscrown Bay
Abrian Plateau

The Isles: A faraway land in the southern hemisphere
Lonlin: An island country of farmers
Lyra: A region on the same continent as Abria
Watodo: An empire proficient in mechanical tools

The Abrian Calendar

338 days long | 26 hours per day | 7 days per week |
4 weeks per month | 12 months per year
2 festival days that fall outside of any specific week or month

Day 1: Moon Rise

Season of Frost
Begynde
Florin
Frostend

Season of Bloom
Windbloom
Daisymoon
Lysere

Day 170: Midfest

Season of Flame
Fawnmist
Flametide
Nove

Season of Ember
Origlow
Moonshadow
Darkember

About the Author

James Colson is a husband, father, and pastor-in-waiting. He has worked as a digital marketer/content producer since 2012 and a freelance preacher since 2014. In 2024, he expanded into the world of self-publishing with *The Tale of Tiernan,* fulfilling a lifelong dream of becoming a published author.

In his free time, James enjoys spending time with his family, mountain biking, strength training, playing video games, and traveling.

Milton Keynes UK
Ingram Content Group UK Ltd.
UKHW020755200524
442968UK00006B/822